Peter Clines

CROWN PUBLISHERS
NEW YORK

Published in the United States by Crown Publishers, an imprint of the Crown Publishing Group, a division of Penguin Random House LLC, New York.
www.crownpublishing.com

Library of Congress Cataloging-in-Publication Data
Clines, Peter, 1969–
    The fold / by Peter Clines. — First edition.
      pages   cm
    I. Title.
    PS3603.L563F65 2015
    813'.6—dc23

                        2014045599

ISBN 978-0-553-41829-3
eBook ISBN 978-0-553-41830-9

PRINTED IN THE UNITED STATES OF AMERICA

Book design: Anna Thompson
Frontispiece photograph: Gary Weathers/Getty Images
Jacket design: Tal Goretsky
Jacket photograph: (stars, sky) Gary Weathers/Getty Images; (mountains) Ropelato Photography, EarthScapes/Getty Images; (clouds) Björn Kindler/Getty Images

10 9 8 7 6 5 4 3 2 1

First Edition

Today's scientists have substituted mathematics for experiments, and they wander off through equation after equation, and eventually build a structure which has no relation to reality.

—NIKOLA TESLA

THE
ALBUQUERQUE
DOOR

ONE

"I just don't think it's that good," said Denise. "It doesn't do anything for me."

Becky bit back a smile, even though Denise couldn't see it over the phone. They'd had this conversation every other week for two months now. It still made for a good distraction, though, and helped fill up the time until Ben got home.

It always worried her a bit when Ben was away. Ben was in charge of high-security projects. Mostly weapons. Often in high-risk areas.

Granted, this had been one of the lowest-risk work trips he'd ever taken. Just four days in San Diego. And on a non-weapons project.

"I mean, Marty really likes it," Denise continued, "but it just seems like nothing but boobs and snow and blood. And the frozen zombie things. I just don't get them. It feels like not a lot ever actually happens, y'know? Five years and they're still talking about winter."

Becky gathered up some socks, underwear, two T-shirts, a skirt, and a bra that had been scattered across the bedroom floor. She was a horrible slob whenever she had the house to herself. Worse than she'd been in college, for some reason she couldn't figure out. "So why do you keep watching it?"

"Ehh. Marty really likes it. He won't admit it, but I just think he likes all the boobs. Are you guys still watching?"

She walked to the bathroom, and shoved the armload of clothes into the hamper. The bathroom was a mess, too. Her yoga clothes and more underwear. How had she gone through so much underwear in four days? "We're a couple episodes behind, but yeah," she said. "I think he likes the boobs, too. And the dragons."

Becky put her foot in the trash can and mashed down the small pile of bathroom trash, just enough so it didn't look like it was overflowing. "We were talking about doing a DVR marathon this weekend. Something to relax a bit after his trip."

"When's he get back?"

"His plane landed a little while ago," she said. "He sent me a text saying he had to stop at the office and give a quick report to his boss. Probably be home any minute now."

"Cleaning up your mess?"

She laughed. "You know me too well."

"I should let you go, then."

"Yeah, probably."

"Give me a call next week," Denise said. "Maybe we can all do dinner at that new Japanese place."

"Okay."

She hung up and tossed the phone on the bed. She looked around and tried to spot anything else he could tease her for leaving out. There was a wineglass on her nightstand, and a plate with a few cheesecake crumbs. And another wineglass on her dresser. God, she was a slob. And a lush.

It crossed her mind now and then that she should try to be one of the good wives. The ones who kept the house clean, and had dinner waiting for her husband when he came home. When they'd met, she'd actually been dressed as a 1950s housewife at a Halloween party, complete with martini glass, apron, and a copy of an old *Good Housekeeping* list of duties she was supposed to perform. He'd laughed, said she didn't look like the kind of woman who sat around waiting on a husband, and bought her a drink. They'd ended Halloween night with a few things that were not covered in the *Good Housekeeping* article. Fourteen months later they were married.

She gathered up the glasses and the plate. She could swing by her art studio in the back and grab the dishes there. There was definitely a plate next to her computer from today's lunch, possibly a wineglass from last night. She could rinse them in the sink, maybe.

As she reached the studio door, a faint rasp of sliding metal echoed from the front of the house. A key in a lock. There was a click, and then the hinge squeaked. They'd been trying to fix that damned thing for years.

The front door.

"Hey, babe," she called out, setting all the dishes down on the desk. "How was your flight?" Ah, well. He wouldn't notice them right away in the studio. And it wasn't like he didn't know her by now. She took a few steps toward the hall, then decided to take the back staircase. It was closer, and she'd probably meet him in the kitchen.

Something tickled her brain as her foot hit the first step. The lack of something. The usual chain of sounds she heard when Ben got home had been broken. She hadn't heard the hinge squeak again, or the door close. Or his keys hitting the table in the front hall.

"Babe?"

She lifted her foot from the step and walked back down the hall. From the top of the staircase she could see their front door. It sat open by almost a foot. She could smell the lawn outside and hear the traffic heading for the beltway.

Ben wasn't there. She didn't see his keys on the table. His briefcase wasn't shoved under the table where he always tossed it.

Becky took a few steps down the stairs. She peered over the banister to see if he was lurking in the hall. It wouldn't be the first time he'd leaped out to scare her.

The hallway was empty.

She walked downstairs to the front door. It hung open in a relaxed, casual way. The same way it did when she was heading out to grab the mail or to growl at Pat from down the street for letting her dog crap on their lawn.

Had she left the door open when she went out for the mail earlier? Maybe just enough for the wind to push it open? Had she imagined the sound of the key? Ben was due home any minute. She might've just heard the hinge squeak and added everything else.

She leaned out the door. It was cool. This late in the afternoon, the front of the house was in the shade.

Ben's car was in the driveway. It was right where it always landed, in front of the nearer garage door. She could see a faint shimmer of heat above the hood.

Becky pushed the door shut. The hinges squeaked. The latch clicked. "Are you in here, babe?"

Floorboards settled. The air in the house shifted. Someone was in the kitchen. She recognized the creak of the tiles near the dishwasher.

"Ben?" His name echoed in the house. She took a few strides toward the back of the house. "Where are you?"

The silence slowed her down, then brought her to a stop.

"If this is supposed to be funny, it's not."

Nothing.

She weighed her options. There was still a chance this was a trick. A joke gone bad. Ben would leap out and make her shriek and she'd hit him and then welcome him home.

It didn't feel like a trick. The house felt wrong. Ben's car might be in the driveway, but there was a stranger moving through their home.

They owned a gun. A Glock 17 or 19 or something. She'd taken four classes and gone shooting at the range three times. It was a badass, secret agent–level gun. That's what Ben had said. They'd probably never need it, but better to have it and not need it than need it and not . . .

The Glock was upstairs. In their bedroom. In the nightstand. She could take six long steps back and be at the main staircase.

Or take three steps forward and get a view into the kitchen.

She took two steps forward.

Ben's briefcase and travel bag sat in the hallway. It was a beat-up, gym bag sort of thing he'd had for years. He still used it because it held three or four days' worth of clothes, but it fit in an overhead compartment. Cut half an hour off his travel time to not be waiting on luggage.

"Babe, I swear to God, I'm calling the fucking cops in two minutes." Her voice echoed in the house. "This isn't funny."

A long groan sounded above her. The noise of stressed wood. The spot by her studio, close to the door. Neither of them had stepped on it in over a year because it was so damned loud.

Whoever was upstairs had stepped on it.

They were *upstairs*!

She looked up at the ceiling. Three seconds passed, and another board squeaked. She could almost see the footsteps through the plaster. Someone was circling around the house. Straight through to the kitchen, up the back staircase she'd had her foot on just five minutes ago, and into the upstairs hallway. They were near the bedroom.

Near the gun.

Jesus, why hadn't she grabbed the gun as soon as things got weird?

But why was Ben's luggage in the house? Why was his car in the driveway? Had someone grabbed him at the airport? Did he get car-jacked?

There was a panic number she was supposed to call. In case something happened to him, if someone tried to get to him through her. He'd given it to her, and she'd never even put it in her phone.

It was in the desk in her studio. Of course.

Becky stepped into the kitchen and grabbed her cell phone from the counter. Then she grabbed a knife from the big block. A wedding present from one of Ben's old college friends. It was a great set. The blade of the butcher knife was almost fourteen inches long and sharp as hell. And the handle sat well in her hand.

They'd all laughed at the idea that knives were a bad-luck wedding gift.

She slid her fingers over the phone's screen and tapped in 911. She held off pressing CALL. There was still a chance this was a bad joke. Some stupid plan to get a scream or a laugh or excitement sex or something, but he sure as hell wasn't getting any off this.

And it wasn't his sort of thing.

She circled through the living room. It had a thick carpet, almost silent to walk across. Just make it through the house, give Ben one last time to admit he was an idiot, and then out the door. She'd call 911 from the front yard.

She was halfway across the living room when she heard the sound of metal sliding across metal. It was a fast, back-and-forth with a hard snap at the end. She'd heard it a lot at the range. She'd been the one making it.

She swallowed.

Becky looked down at her phone. Could she raise her voice enough to talk? Did the person upstairs know where she was in the house? What did 911 do when they got a silent call? Did they trace it and send a car? Did they hang up?

She had to get out of the house now.

The front door was closer, but it was a clear shot—bad choice of words—a clear *line of sight* for anyone in the upstairs hall. Almost straight from their bedroom door to the front door.

The back door was farther away, but there was more weaving and someone would have to get much closer to aim—to *see* her. She'd have a chance to make the call. But the backyard was a wall of fences around a pool they hadn't filled for the summer yet. She'd have to run back around to the side gate. And no one would be able to see her. Maybe not even hear her, with all the noise from that new house they were putting up one block over.

Plenty of time and opportunity for someone to grab her and drag her back into the house. It had to be the front door.

Becky gripped the knife, made sure her finger was still near the CALL button, and took three long strides across the living room. The carpet absorbed her footsteps, but she heard the fabric of her jeans and felt the air move around her.

Her foot hit the hall and she heard the creak of the second step from the top of the staircase. She froze. They were on the stairs. They'd see her going for the front door.

She should've gone out the back. She still could. But she'd have to be fast. They'd hear her for sure.

She ran for the door. Feet thumped on the stairs behind her. She reached for the knob.

"Stop!"

She turned and raised her knife. "You fuckhead," she gasped.

Ben stood on the staircase, four steps from the bottom. One foot was still on the fifth. He was wearing the charcoal suit with the cranberry shirt that looked so good on him. The Glock was in his hand, its barrel pointed in her direction. He clutched his own phone in his other hand.

"Put the knife down."

Becky's shoulders slumped and she tossed the knife on the table. It slid to a stop right where his keys usually landed. "You scared the piss out of me, you jerk. I thought someone was in the house."

He lowered himself to the next step. The pistol rose up. She could see enough of the muzzle to tell it was aimed at her.

"I've called the police," he hissed. "They're on the line right now."

She glanced past him up the staircase, then her eyes went back to the gun. Had they *both* been playing tag with an intruder? "Okay," she said. "Calm down and point that somewhere else."

Ben stared at her and came down two more steps. The pistol didn't waver. His wide eyes flitted to the knife, then past her to the front door, and over into the living room. "Where is she?"

"Babe," she said, her eyes on the pistol, "you're freaking me out with the—"

"Where is she?" he shouted. His voice echoed in the hall. The glass in the door trembled behind her.

She shrieked and her mind stumbled for a moment. "She? She who?"

Ben stepped off the staircase and glared at her. He raised the pistol. The barrel was just a black square with a hole in it. He was aiming it right between her eyes. "What have you done with her? What do you want with us?" He took a step toward her, and then another.

Becky couldn't tell if he was angry or sad. The black hole kept pulling her eyes away from his face. It was just a few feet away. She could see the little trembles and shifts as he squeezed the grip. "Babe," she pleaded, "what are you talking abou—"

"Who are you?" he yelled. *"Where the hell is my wife?"*

"Come on, everyone," said Leland "Mike" Erikson. His gaze wandered around the classroom, landing on each face and catching every set of eyes for just a moment. "Pretend you're in control of your hormones for just five more minutes. You've got all summer to be teenagers."

There were lots of ways to get their attention, not as many to hold it with vacation looming. He gave them the Look. One of the tricks of being a good teacher, he'd learned, was not to overuse the Look. Once every other week, tops.

Granted, he had a good face for the Look. Dark hair, dark eyes, and a thin face with a sharp chin, all on top of a body that could be described as wiry at best, usually just bony. In his first year as a high school teacher, a student told him he looked like Severus Snape, the College Years.

The Look settled most of them down. Tyler kept whispering to Emily, the green-eyed honors student he'd been pursuing in his awkward way since Easter. Mike let them talk. The kid had three and a half minutes left in the school year to score.

"One thing you learned this year." He glanced across the young faces. "Olivia."

She drummed her thin fingers on her textbook. " 'The Fall of the House of Usher' is about a guy going insane because his twin sister died."

"Died?"

"Well, he thinks she died, but he really buried her alive."

"Good," he said. "In the general sense. Not that you should all bury your siblings."

Half the class chuckled. One boy cleared his throat. "Mr. Erikson, can we go now?"

"We're trying something different for the last day, Zack. They're going to ring a big bell at the end of the period. What'd you learn?"

"I hate English class."

"Great, I'll tell Mrs. DeNay to expect you in French next year. Ethan?"

Ethan was a tall kid. Even taller than Mike, who stood at six feet. He'd been one of the computer geeks until he beat three of the school's track and field records as a freshman. Now there was talk in the teacher's lounge of tempting him to the basketball team next year. "Thoreau wasn't alone out in the woods."

"More specific," said Mike. "Are you talking about his dog?"

"No, I mean he wasn't out in the middle of nowhere. He was, like, a mile from town."

"Good. Time for two more. Hannah?"

The brunette cheerleader looked up from her text messages. "Ummmm . . . 'The House of Usher' is about a guy who—"

"You just learned that a minute ago. Tell me something else you learned."

"Uhhhmmm . . ." She glanced at the other students around her and down at her desktop. "Oh, wait, getting tarred and feathered is really painful, and it can kill you."

He nodded. "Where'd you get that?"

"The Hawthorne story. Major Molly-something."

" 'My Kinsman, Major Molineux.' " He tipped his head to her. "Very good, Hannah. I didn't think you were paying attention that day. One left. Justin?"

Justin swept back his shaggy hair. "Mr. Erikson really does have a photographic memory."

"Nice. Did you learn anything related to early American literature?"

At the edge of his sight, the door swung open, letting a bald figure in a gray suit slip into the room. Mike let his eyes dart left long enough to see Reggie Magnus. Reggie smiled and leaned against the wall next to the side blackboard. Mike focused his attention back on his student.

"I . . . uhhhh . . ."

"No pressure, Justin," said Mike, "but no one can leave this room until you answer."

A groan echoed through the room as the boy grabbed a double handful of hair.

Mike pulled a pen from behind his ear. He reached behind himself without looking and dropped it nine inches into an oversized Nerd Herd coffee cup that sat on the edge of the desk. It clattered against the sides. "Come on," he said. "Thirty seconds and we can all go home for the summer. One thing. Just tell me one thing you learned this year."

Justin looked up. "Ichabod Crane isn't really the hero of 'The Legend of Sleepy Hollow.'"

"Explain."

"He's, like, the British. You told us that when you said we couldn't just watch the TV show to learn the story. You said that sometimes the bad guy is right there in front of us."

Mike smiled, the bell clanged, and the students lunged up with their all-but-empty messenger bags and backpacks. "Have a good summer, everyone," he said. "I'll see you all in three months. Some of you in just two weeks for summer school." He pointed a finger. "Justin, two points for you."

The teenager's face tried to find a middle ground between a blush and a smirk. "Thank you, Mr. Erikson."

"Thank you, Justin. It was a pleasure teaching you. Now get the hell out of here."

The last bodies washed out of the classroom, and Mike turned his attention to his friend. Reggie had drifted to the back of the room. He was in the downward swing of his latest diet attempt, wearing an older belt and a loose shirt to hide the pounds he'd put on over the past months. He was wearing a dark blazer over the shirt, which meant this visit was somehow business related. Reggie couldn't talk business without wearing a coat of some kind.

Mike cleared his throat. "How are you?"

"Not bad, not bad at all." Sunlight from the window gleamed on Reggie's black scalp. He'd been shaving it since his hair started thinning in college, long before bald was fashionable. "How are you doing?"

"I'm good."

"Not too much pressure here?"

"Nothing I can't handle."

"Good."

"You know it's trespassing to come on school grounds, right?"

"So you keep telling me." Reggie ran his finger along a stack of Norton Anthologies. "After donating two computer labs, I think I get to count as staff."

"Faculty. And it doesn't work that way."

"Really?"

"They've got a firm 'three computer lab' rule in our district," Mike said, closing his laptop. "Plus, I'm pretty sure it was DARPA that donated the labs, not you."

"As far as most of these folks know, I *am* DARPA."

"You sound so cool when you say it like that."

Reggie shook his head, then stepped forward and wrapped his arms around Mike. "Jerk.

Mike squeezed back. "Loser."

"What's up with you?"

Mike scooped up an eraser and brushed it back and forth across the chalkboard. LAST POP QUIZ OF THE YEAR faded to streaks, then to dust. "Well," he said, "I think I've convinced three kids to give high school one more year before they drop out. Talked another five into taking the AP tests. And I'm in the lead to direct the drama club's fall musical."

"What are you doing?"

"I was hoping for *The King and I* but it's probably going to be *Little Mary Sunshine*."

"The one about the girl on the road trip with her family?"

"Completely different."

Reggie sighed and shook his head. "God, what a waste."

"Hey, it was all we could afford."

"I wasn't talking about the play."

Mike tossed the eraser back in the trough. "What then?"

"You know what."

He slid his laptop into his briefcase. "If it makes you feel good, we can pretend we haven't had this discussion a dozen times and you can tell me again." Two teacher's edition textbooks he hadn't opened in eight years followed the laptop into the briefcase.

"Do you know what three of the smartest people in America are doing right now?"

"Right at this very moment?"

"One of them started working with NASA when he was sixteen," said Reggie. "One's an autodidact who spends his spare time working on P versus NP. And the last one's hiding from his potential by teaching high school English in a little bumfuck town in Maine." He picked up the bright red Swingline stapler from the desk and tossed it back and forth between his hands. "We both know this isn't who you are. You're better than this. You could be doing so much more."

"There are," Mike said, "three basic problems with your statement."

"Enlighten me, please."

Mike held up a finger. "There could be lots of smarter people out there who haven't had an IQ test or made their results public. There's also a bunch who've either exaggerated or downplayed their test results. You're making an assumption based on a very limited and somewhat skewed pool of data."

"Fair enough. Next point."

A second finger. "There's a huge range of possible IQ results depending on the test and the subject. You're assuming I have a high IQ because I did well on one test nineteen years ago. I could be the biggest idiot on Earth who just happens to test well."

"I've known you too long."

A third finger. Mike used the hand to gesture at the classroom. "I don't think being a high school teacher is a waste of my time or potential."

Reggie shook his head. "Let's be honest. You're hiding here."

The two fingers on either side dropped away. "Fuck you."

"You're not my type."

"I think college proved you don't have a type past 'female,' and even that's been questioned a few times."

"Fuck you."

"See?"

"Asshole. Want to get some dinner?"

"It's not even four o'clock."

"I haven't eaten since breakfast."

"The last day of school just ended. This is kind of like a holiday. They're having drinks in the teacher's lounge. And then more drinks over in Ogunquit."

"You've got an old friend in town. They'll understand. Especially an old friend who donated two computer labs to the school system. They'll probably insist you come out with me."

"You're being a jerk."

"Yes. It's in my job description. Paragraph six, subsection two."

Mike sighed and brushed a last few things into his desk. It looked clean enough. "Who's buying?"

"Me," said Reggie. "This is a business trip."

"Ah, on the taxpayers," Mike said with a nod. "So, really, I'm buying."

"Shut up."

Mike picked up his briefcase. "Let me go say goodbye to some folks, maybe have a beer, and then I can get out of here."

"Tell me there's somewhere close where we can get a good steak."

"Good's a relative term. All that Department of Defense money's probably spoiled you."

"Did I call you a jackass yet?"

Mike shook his head. "Nope."

"Jackass."

"It's too late to start kissing up."

THREE

The walls of Captain Turner's Steak and Lobster Hut were decorated with plastic lobsters, dusty buoys, old traps, and lengths of rope that had grown brittle with age. Each table was draped with a red and white checkered tablecloth held in place by a collection of condiments and a large candle in a red jar. The placemats had step-by-step instructions for how to eat a lobster.

The hostess greeted Mike by name and gave him a genuine smile. There were only a handful of other people in the restaurant, but Reggie insisted they sit away from the bar and against the wall. They'd given their drink orders to a young waitress who said hello to "Mr. Erikson" as she offered Reggie a menu. She brought their drinks and answered Reggie's questions about the surf and turf special clipped into the menu. She smiled at Mike again before walking away. "Old student?" asked Reggie.

"I think so, yep."

The bald man bit back a laugh. "You think so?"

Mike sipped his rum and Coke. "So, come on," he said. "What's this all about?"

Reggie set his own drink down. "Take the battery out of your phone."

Mike looked around the restaurant. "Seriously?"

"Protocol. You expecting an important call?"

"No."

"So don't be a pain in the ass. Take the battery out and we can talk."

Mike popped his smartphone out of its case and pried off the battery cover. "What about yours?"

"Mine's better. It's got six different security systems."

"I bet I could get into it," said Mike. He stacked his disassembled phone in the middle of the table.

"I bet you could," Reggie said. "That's why I'm here. I've got a job offer for you."

"Another one?"

"Yes. How many is this now?"

Mike picked up his glass. "Thirteen since you joined DARPA, nineteen total since we've known each other."

"Lucky thirteen, then."

"I think it's cool that you keep flying up here so I can reject you in person. Is it another cryptography thing?"

"No." They tapped glasses.

"Robotics? You've got four or five robotics things going on, right?"

"You're sure eager to know what you're turning down." He glanced around. "Do you think we can get some rolls or something until the food arrives?"

"They generally have a bread basket. So is it robotics?"

Reggie shook his head as the waitress appeared with the promised basket of bread and a small bowl of butter balls. He smiled, but kept his mouth shut until she left. He pulled out an end piece and tore off the crust with his teeth.

"You're taking the cloak-and-dagger stuff seriously this time."

"This time it matters." He spread some butter on his second slice of bread. "Here's the deal. You come work for the agency this summer as a freelancer. Three months. I'll start you as a special consultant, but we can bump it up, depending on what happens. Minimum, you'll take home about forty thousand after taxes."

"Are you drafting me?"

"Pretty much, yes, if you think you're up for it."

Mike laughed and tore off a piece of bread.

"I'm serious," Reggie said. "This is the big one. I need you on this."

"That's what you always say."

"This time's different."

"Why?"

"Because this time you're going to say yes."

Mike poked his knife at the butter. The ball spun in the bowl under the blunt blade. "Two hours ago I was one of the smartest guys in America. Now I don't even know what's going on in my own head."

Reggie took a sip of his drink. He looked around the restaurant, then back to the disassembled phone on the table. He leaned forward and lowered his voice.

"There's a project we've been funding in San Diego," he said. "You know who Arthur Cross is?"

"The physicist?" Mike nodded. "You gave me a copy of *The History of What We Know* for Christmas last year, remember? Is he part of this?"

"Yes. How do you think I got you an autographed copy?"

"It's autographed? I never opened it."

"Of course you didn't."

Mike shrugged. "Why would you get a book for someone who's not a big reader?"

"Because it was a *New York Times* bestseller that everyone was reading, and I had a chance to get you an autographed copy."

"Whatever."

"Cross is the head of the Albuquerque Door project," Reggie said. "It's in danger of being canceled, for a couple of reasons. I need you to evaluate it and show it's safe and viable so I can get another year of funding for them."

"The Albuquerque Door?"

"Yes."

"Well, you've piqued my curiosity."

"Good."

"So what kind of project is it?"

"I can't tell you here."

"Oh, come on," said Mike. "I took my phone apart and everything."

"Sorry. Come down to Washington next week."

"I can't."

"Come down and sit in on a panel with me. No stress, no pressure. You can meet Arthur and his team and hear it straight from them."

"Why can't I hear it straight from you?"

"Because they can explain it better."

"I can't just take off. I have a job."

"It's the last day of school."

"I have a summer job. Do you know what teachers make?"

"I do," Reggie said. "I also know what you make fixing amusement park rides over the summer. And I know what I'm offering you is about five times as much for a third the time."

"If I take the job," said Mike.

"You'll take it."

"I wouldn't get down there and find out this is another battlesuit or invisibility cloak?"

"It's called optical camouflage. And no, it isn't. Are you coming to Washington or not?"

Mike's finger tapped against the glass. "Maybe. Why me?"

Reggie opened his mouth and snapped it shut as the waitress stopped by to check their drinks. She assured them their food was minutes away and flitted back to the bar.

"What's her name?" asked Reggie.

"Who?"

"The waitress."

"Siobhan. She introduced herself when she took our drink order."

"And?"

"And what?"

Reggie extended a finger, then swiveled it to point after the waitress. "What else?"

"Why does it matter?"

"I'm answering your question and turning your maybe into a yes. What else do you know about her?"

Mike sighed. The ants were already loose in his mind. They carried memories of sights and sounds in their mandibles like pieces of colorful leaves. "Siobhan Emily Richmond," he said. "Born December twenty-ninth, graduated in two thousand eleven. I had her in my class in two thousand nine to two thousand ten and she got a B+ because she messed up a test on early-twentieth-century authors. Didn't like *Catcher in the Rye* at all. She had three boyfriends in high school, ended up back with the first one senior year. Went to UNH for a year and a half but had to drop out when her father, James, died in a car accident. She likes Katy Perry, the color green, was obsessed with *Supernatural*, and drives a two thousand seven Honda Civic—also green—that she bought from a woman down in Kittery. Her little sister, Saorise, should be in my class in two years. That enough for you?"

"From anyone else that much information would be kind of creepy."

"It's a small town."

Reggie tapped the table twice. "That's why I need you out there."

"Because I live in a small town?"

"Because you do things like that the way other people breathe." He poked the tabletop with his finger. "Seriously, it's like building the world's greatest supercomputer and then using it to play Angry Birds. You're wasted here."

"I'm happy here."

"Great. If you decide to come work for me for the summer, you can make a pile of money and be even happier here."

Mike looked at the parts of his phone. "Just a trip to Washington?"

"Yes. On my dime. I'll pay you a grand out of the consulting fees up front, just for coming down. I'll put you up in a real hotel even though we both know how much you love my couch. It'll be a paid vacation."

"And if I'm not interested, that's it?"

"You're going to be interested."

"But if I'm not, that's it." Mike phrased it as a condition, not a question. "I get to come home with no guilt trips or tax audits or any other downsides."

Reggie's chin went up and down. "If you can look me in the eye after the panel and tell me you're not interested, I'll fly you home first class. I'll even throw in a hundred bucks for drinks in the airport."

Siobhan Emily Richmond appeared with a tray balanced on one hand. Mike swept the parts of his phone to the back of the table and she set down plates. She checked their drinks again, asked if they wanted more bread, and slipped away.

Reggie placed a piece of steak on his tongue. He closed his eyes, chewed four times, and a blissful look passed across his face. He swallowed and looked at Mike. "So," he said, "do I have you at last?"

Mike used the edge of his fork to cut through a scallop. He speared it on the tines and sighed. "Maybe."

Reggie smiled. "When can you leave?"

"I don't know. A couple of days to finish up school stuff. What about the seventeenth?"

"Perfect. We can meet up in Washington and you can sit in on the panel, and then I'll ship you out to San Diego."

"If I decide to do it."

"You will."

"We'll see."

FOUR

Eight days, three security checks, and one plane ride later, Mike was in Washington, D.C., wearing his best suit. It was still the cheapest one in the room. Reggie had loaned him a silk tie after seeing the two polyester ones he'd brought from home. He adjusted the knot against his throat, glad he'd decided on the full-Windsor over his usual half.

The room was almost twice the size of Mike's classroom back in South Berwick. There were no windows. Five people shifted and mumbled and found seats behind a row of tables at the front of the room, avoiding the collection of flags behind them. Ten feet away there was a mirroring row of tables, this one with two dozen chairs lined up behind it in four rows of six. Two other tables ran along the far side, facing the door. The walls were painted in warm colors, but the room felt stark.

It struck Mike that the setup was very similar to a courtroom. Judges up front. Defense and prosecution across from them. Jury off to the side. He was sure it was deliberate.

The five people at the front of the room—three men and two women—settled into their chairs. Mike glanced at each of them. A man in an Air Force uniform with silver eagles on his shoulders and seven rows of color on his chest. A younger man with dark hair and glasses. An older woman with a flag pin on her collar who the ants recognized as a senator. An Asian man with a white line on his finger where he normally wore a ring. A dark-eyed woman with long hair and an athlete's body. Seven people sat back in the body of the room, scratching notes on identical pads with identical pens.

Reggie guided them to the jury tables. Each one had two pristine legal pads with a Department of Defense watermark stretching across the top of each sheet. A matching logo graced a pen placed precisely across the top of the notepad. A blue file folder lay next to each pad.

"What is this?" asked Mike. He adjusted his coat to display more of the borrowed tie.

"Budget review board," murmured Reggie. He popped open his briefcase and pulled out a slim pad. "Standard stuff. It's still DARPA territory, but a lot of departments have invested in the Albuquerque Door. All these folks have some say in what happens next. Some of them are tied to the agency, a few are from the DOD itself. The Air Force colonel over there? He loves this sort of stuff."

Mike glanced across the half-dozen board members to the broad, square-jawed man with bristle-brush hair. "Really?"

"Oh, yeah. Forget anything you read in the papers about the Marines or the Army. The Air Force loves high tech more than any of them."

"So it's all about high tech, but everyone's using notepads and ball-point pens?"

"Remember how you had to turn in your phone at the desk?"

Mike nodded.

"They're not big on laptops and tablets in these meetings. It's a security thing."

"Cool. Can I keep the pen?"

"Yes, you can keep the pen," sighed Reggie. "It only cost the taxpayers seventeen dollars. Here, you can have mine, too."

"What about the notepad?"

"Don't be greedy." He nodded to the front of the room. "Okay, pay attention. These are your new best friends."

Two men and a woman came through the door. The leader, an older black man with a trimmed goatee and a circle of gray hair around his scalp, glanced around the room and up at the board members. He walked with a dark cane in his right hand. It had a silver derby-style handle. He wore silver-rimmed glasses that pulled attention to his eyes. He hadn't changed much since the photo for his book jacket.

"Arthur Cross," said Reggie, following Mike's gaze. "He's probably got the best idea of how this whole thing works, although they'll all tell you it's beyond any one person. That's why you're here."

"I still don't know what 'this' is."

"Patience."

Cross looked across the room at Reggie and nodded politely. The woman with him shot Mike and Reggie a look that was only a few degrees away from a glare. She, Cross, and the other man sat down across from the board.

"The blonde is Jamie Parker," said Reggie. "Head programmer. She's here today because their other physicist has the flu."

Her eyes were hazel, like Mike's, though much narrower than his. Her hair reached past her shoulders, but was bound up in a sensible ponytail. She had on a tight black turtleneck over an equally tight body, somewhat concealed by a gray blazer.

He realized he was staring because she was glaring back at him. Mike rubbed his temple and forced a few ants back behind their wall. "You said it wasn't cryptography."

"It's not."

"Or robots."

"It's the twenty-first century," said Reggie. "I don't think I've got any projects under my umbrella that don't have at least two programmers." He tipped his chin to the woman. "Parker was a black hat at MIT, got in trouble with the feds, but they couldn't prove anything. After she graduated they tried to hire her, and she more or less spit in their faces. Dropped out of sight for two years, and then Arthur found her at a hacker con and recruited her. Major chip on her shoulder."

Mike let his eyes drift to the other man. He had a long, weather-beaten face, and small eyes. His dyed-black hair was slicked back, and his face had a slack look to it that somehow seemed more practiced than genetic. He had lean limbs and perfect posture. It gave the impression of a tall man, even though he was only an inch over Parker. His suit was poorly fitting and almost definitely off-the-rack. It made Mike feel better about his own wardrobe.

Mike nodded at the man. "Olaf Johansson."

"Olaf?"

"Hey, talk to his parents. He's Arthur's partner. Double doctorates in physics and mathematics. Number cruncher. Very little imagination or sense of humor. You two should butt heads nicely."

"Is he related to Scarlett?"

"Not to my knowledge."

"Has anyone told him he looks just like Humphrey Bogart?"

"I tried," said Reggie. "He didn't know who I was talking about."

"How can he not know Bogart?"

"I don't think he's seen *Casablanca*."

"You lie."

"Shut up and play with your pen. They're ready to get started."

The dark-eyed, athletic woman started things. She had a pleasant voice. "So, Dr. Cross, perhaps you could give us a rundown on your project and where it currently stands?"

Arthur nodded. "Well, as our reports explain, the Albuquerque Door began as the SETH Project. It was an attempt to create a viable method of energetic matter transmission, the long-term goal being to create a practical IMT system."

"Doctor?" The Asian man raised his hand. "Could we get that in layman's terms, please?"

Olaf sighed and his brow furrowed for a moment.

"IMT," said Arthur. "Instant matter transfer. We were trying to make a matter-projection system, one that wouldn't be—"

"Teleportation?" interrupted the Asian again. "You were trying to make some sort of teleporter, like on *Star Trek*?"

"They call theirs a transporter, actually," said Jamie Parker.

A faint chuckle rolled across the board's tables.

Mike felt his eyes start to roll. He turned to Reggie. "I thought you brought me down here for something serious," he whispered.

"I did," murmured his friend.

"Physical teleportation's impossible."

The board plowed ahead. "And how much success have you had with your . . . matter-projection system?" asked the Asian man.

"Well," said Arthur, "all things considered, we had a fair degree, sir. There are a number of ways to break something down to the atomic level using existing technology. The challenge, of course, has always been reintegration." He paused to adjust his glasses. "Even a life form as small as a mouse contains billions of cells, each made up of hundreds of millions of molecules, each of which is also made up of possibly millions of atoms. Taking it apart is relatively easy, putting it back together, well . . ."

"I believe your earlier budgets accounted for that, yes?" asked the

Air Force colonel. His precise voice echoed in the room. "Says here you built yourself a supercomputer."

"To build a computer that could identify and track all those particles in real time would pretty much be impossible," Jamie said. "It'd be beyond anything even theorized by modern engineers. The closest thing in existence is the Tianhe-2 in China, and that's only a bare percentage of the calculating power we'd need for a single jump. We were trying to develop a program that worked off an idea similar to quantum entanglement, what Einstein called "spooky action at a distance." We wouldn't need to know where every particle was, so long as we knew where *most* of them were."

The board members glanced at one another and the files. "And that worked?" asked the athletic woman.

Mike leaned in close to Reggie again. "I don't even follow this stuff and I can tell you half a dozen reasons it wouldn't work."

"I'm sure you can."

"I can name at least a dozen physicists who've played with this and moved on to easier things like antigravity or the Grand Unified Theory."

"I told you to be patient already, yes?"

"Mr. Magnus," asked the athletic woman, "did you have a comment?"

"No, ma'am," he said. "Just clarifying a point for my colleague."

Her gaze slid to Mike, then back to Arthur. "Doctor?"

"We had some success," Arthur said, "and a few failures. The first few objects to HD didn't tell us anything, but by the time we—"

"I'm sorry," interrupted another one of the reviewers, the senator. "HD?"

"Oh, it's . . . uhh." Arthur examined the table. "Well, it's an unofficial term we coined for when test objects dispersed rather than reintegrated."

"What does it stand for?" This from the man with glasses.

"Well, it's . . ." He glanced at Jamie.

"Humpty Dumpty," muttered Olaf Johansson.

"What?"

Mike's mind leaped ahead and found a childhood copy of the nursery rhyme. He looked at all six pages of the picture book at once and crossed it with the topic at hand. He winced.

"Humpty Dumpty," the Bogart look-alike repeated. His faintly accented voice sounded wrong coming from that face. "You know, 'All the king's horses and all the king's men . . .'"

"Oh," said the Asian interviewer.

The man with the glasses dipped his chin. "A bit . . . macabre."

"But pretty much dead on," Olaf said. He almost sneered when he spoke.

"So, really," said the Air Force colonel, "how many successes did you have?"

"In the first three years of the project, we managed to teleport two test blocks and a test animal," said Arthur. "Both of the test blocks crumbled to dust a few moments after reintegration. Microscopic analysis revealed fundamental changes in their structure at the molecular level."

The senator swallowed. "And . . . the animal?"

Arthur glanced at Jamie. The blonde examined her blank legal pad.

Olaf straightened up in his chair. "We're pretty sure it was dead the moment we reintegrated it."

"Pretty sure?"

"The autopsy was inconclusive," he shrugged. "If it was alive, it couldn't've been for more than a second or two."

"Are you sure?"

"We're sure," muttered Jamie.

Mike picked up his pen and wrote TOLD YOU! on the pad. He angled it to Reggie. Reggie ignored him.

The Asian man tapped his report. "That was an unauthorized animal experiment, was it not?"

"Yes, sir, it was," said Arthur. "And the reports from that hearing, the ethics committee, and the Humane Society should be included in the packets you have. We are . . . all of us on the Albuquerque Door Project are ashamed of what we let happen. Of what we did then. I can absolutely assure you it will never happen again."

The Asian man nodded. "Please, go on."

"As I was saying," continued Arthur, "our second wave experiments forced us to agree with prevailing theories. Physical teleportation was simply not going to be possible at our current level of technology. Possibly not ever, as many noted quantum theorists have said."

A low grumble started at one end of the board's table and made its way across.

"I can't believe you're funding someone who told you they could build a teleporter," whispered Mike.

"I'm not," said Reggie. "I'm funding Cross because he's done it."

"However," continued Arthur, "during our hiatus, Dr. Johansson and I had the idea that the secret to instant travel might not be trying to manipulate the traveler, but rather to manipulate the distance traveled."

Mike's ants paused in their endless movement, just for a moment.

FIVE

The athletic woman made a show of flipping her report open and referring to something. "And how would you manipulate distances, Dr. Cross?"

"Distance is a relative term," said Arthur. "When you start applying the idea of additional dimensions, it can be manipulated very easily."

Reggie cleared his throat for attention. Mike, the scientists, and the board members all turned to him. "Ummm . . . Just for the record," Reggie said, "and, again, the benefit of our nonscientific members, could you explain that a little more?"

Arthur nodded. "Of course." He ignored the pen in front of him and pulled one from inside his coat. The scientist made two exaggerated dots on opposite corners of the legal pad and stood up—without using his cane, Mike noticed. "For our purposes, let's say these dots exist in a two-dimensional universe, the sheet of paper," he said, adopting the tone of college lecturers across the globe. He displayed the sheet to the room. "Simple enough, yes?"

There were a few nods from the assembled board members.

"Mr. Magnus, since you suggested it, how far apart would you say these two dots are?"

Reggie eyed the paper. "If I remember my geometry," he said, "something like fourteen inches, right?"

"Close enough," Arthur said with a nod. He tore the sheet off the notepad with a flourish, and folded it in half. "Now how far apart are they?"

"Eight inches, maybe."

The physicist folded the paper the other way. "And now?"

"Less than half an inch, if that."

"And yet," said Arthur, "to any creatures in the paper's two-dimensional world, nothing has changed. Their universe is unaltered, and the dots are still fourteen inches apart. But if they had the means to perceive our three-dimensional space, to cross through it, and reenter their own, they could go from point A to point B with just a single step.

"In a similar manner, we manipulate the distance the Albuquerque Door covers by creating a path across another dimension, an alternate quantum state, if you will. One in which our own dimension appears folded back on itself. Where A and B are one step apart."

"The paper bit was your idea?" whispered Mike.

Reggie gave a small nod and lowered his voice. "It's how he explained it to me the first time I asked him. It's a nice visual for us little common folk."

The buzz cut colonel tapped his pen on the end of his file. "So you've found another dimension that allows this?"

"That's the whole crux of our project," Olaf said. Mike found it amazing how much veiled condescension the man could work into his voice. "We don't need to find it. We just tell our equipment we have and everything works accordingly."

"And that works?"

"To date," said Arthur with a cough, "it has worked over four hundred times without any side effects or consequences. One hundred sixty-seven times with human subjects. There has never been a failure in the system."

"Never?"

"Never." The older man sat down as he repeated the word. Olaf and Jamie both crossed their arms.

Mike frowned and glanced at Reggie. Reggie gave him a quick shake of the head. Mike snatched up his pen again and scribbled out IF NEVER—WHY ME? on the pad.

"So, how safe is it?" asked the colonel.

"Utterly safe," said Arthur.

The Asian man tapped his pen on the table. "What about Benjamin Miles?"

A small swarm of ants carried out images and sounds. Mike had visited Washington thirty-two months ago. Reggie had introduced the freshly promoted assistant director as they walked past him in the hall. Short, but with strong shoulders, a square jaw, and sun-blond hair. His tie pin had been a tiny silver-and-red Captain America shield. His office was three doors down from Reggie's, on the left.

A low murmur passed through the room. A few glances flitted over to Reggie. Olaf and Jamie shifted in their seats. The colonel and the senator leaned forward. Arthur met their gazes.

BEN? scribbled Mike. Reggie shook his head again.

"The problems Mr. Miles has had are regrettable, of course," said Arthur. "We all liked him during his brief visit to San Diego. But they have nothing to do with the Albuquerque Door."

"He used it," said the Asian man. It was not at all a question. "Seven weeks ago. And then his first episode happened right afterward."

"His first episode also happened right after he flew back to Washington on Virgin America," said Arthur. "Have you spoken with Richard Branson?"

Mike glanced at Reggie again, but his friend's face was a blank slab.

"That's not an answer," said the Asian man.

"You haven't asked a question," said Arthur. "You've falsely imputed a line of cause and effect between the Door and Mr. Miles's condition. I can tell you with absolute certainty the Door had nothing to do with it."

"How?"

"Because the Door doesn't affect the traveler in any way," said Arthur. "It's still possible to be hurt by misusing the equipment itself, but that would have nothing to do with the actual act of traveling."

"So it's dangerous to some degree," said the colonel.

"It's like asking if a freeway is dangerous," Olaf said. "A freeway's just a long strip of pavement. In and of itself, it's harmless. But it's still possible to get hurt on one if somebody does something stupid."

The colonel considered this and scribbled a note.

The athletic woman who'd begun the meeting flipped through her file again. "Dr. Cross," she said, "there's no actual specifications for your project here."

"No, ma'am," said Arthur.

"Is there another file?"

"No," he said. "Part of our agreement is that we don't share our research, findings, or technology with anyone until the project is ready to go public."

Her eyes widened a bit. "But this is a review board."

There was a moment as the scientists and board members looked at one another. Reggie leaned close to Mike. "This is why you're here," he murmured.

"Doctor," said the man with the glasses. "We're going to need to see your research if we're going to have any discussion about extending your budget for another year."

"As I just explained," Arthur said, "no one sees our work until the Albuquerque Door goes public. Not one equation, not one line of code, not one blueprint. This was the deal we worked out with Mr. Magnus when we switched our research over from SETH."

Several heads turned to look at Reggie. He didn't flinch.

The Air Force colonel slapped his file closed. "Why are we just hearing about this now?"

"Because you don't read your e-mail," said Olaf. "This has been the standing agreement for almost two years now."

"It seems like we're done, then," said the senator, shooting a tired look at Reggie. "If you can't show us any actual results, we can hardly be expected to continue your funding."

"On the contrary," said Arthur. "We can show you the only result that really matters. As I said, the Albuquerque Door works."

"Do you have video?" asked the Asian man.

Arthur shook his head. "On site, but nothing we'll allow out of our labs."

Another sigh of frustration from the board.

Mike picked up the pen, but Reggie set a hand on his wrist and eased it back down.

"I'm sorry," said Arthur, "but it was decided very early on that all information regarding the workings of this project would be on a strict need-to-know basis."

"Well, for the funds we're being asked to contribute," said the man with glasses, "I think we need to know."

"Why?" asked Jamie. "None of you are physicists. You're not engineers. You're not programmers. You wouldn't understand anything we gave you anyway."

"But we have people who would," said the athletic woman.

"And that," said Arthur, "is why we're not sharing information with anyone."

They all focused on him. Jamie and Olaf straightened up, flanking their boss. He glanced at Reggie for support and got a small nod.

Arthur took a brief moment to collect his thoughts. "The Albuquerque Door," he said, "is the greatest thing mankind has achieved since we reached the Moon. Possibly since the creation of the steam engine. It's not exaggeration to say it is going to change everything. Transportation, communication, commerce, the energy industry, space exploration, all of it. Every human being on the planet will have their lives changed by this technology once it's released.

"Until then, we can't risk having it leak out in bits and pieces. You show it to your aides and consultants, they each share it with their own staff, their staff members share it with their assistants and departments. Some of them might even talk about it with friends and family members. That's a hundred people, just off this one meeting, and the more people who have access to that information, the better chances it will get out there. To be blunt," he said, gesturing at Olaf and Jamie, "this is our life's work, and we're not going to risk it being torn apart and fought over by vultures before we're allowed to say anything publicly."

"So this is about recognition," said the colonel.

"Of course it is," said Olaf. "Have you been paying attention? We're going to win every Nobel Prize for the next ten years. Even the ones for Economics, Physiology, and Literature. We're going to get them just on general principle."

"I can understand your concern," the Asian man said, "but this isn't like handing over your college thesis to an old professor who can't work his e-mail. We're talking about the federal government."

"Yes," said Jamie, "exactly."

"You can't keep your own secrets," Olaf said, "but you want us to believe you'll do a better job with ours?"

The colonel's jaw shifted.

Reggie cleared his throat and the athletic woman glanced over at him. "Mr. Magnus?"

"I understand this seems highly irregular," he said, "but it really isn't any different than the numerous high-security programs DARPA has carried out for your branches and departments in the past. On and off the books."

The senator muttered something at her file, and then turned her attention to Reggie. "So DARPA expects us to just funnel an extra three hundred million into this project based on . . . what? No explanations, no status reports, nothing."

"Based on the fact that it works," said Olaf. Arthur hushed him with a wave. Olaf threw himself back into his chair and crossed his arms.

Reggie pointed a finger at Olaf. "The man has a point," he said. "In fact, it's the only point that matters. The Albuquerque Door works. I've seen it work with my own eyes. We're not talking about another year to see if they can get results, we're talking about another year so they can finish testing and have ironclad documentation that no one will question."

"But without knowing what they're doing—"

"We know what they're doing," Reggie said, cutting off the senator. "They've built a system that lets you go from New York to London with one step. That's exactly what they said they were going to do."

The man with the glasses tapped his pen against the file folder. "Even though none of us knows how it works."

"None of *you* know how it works," said Arthur.

Reggie raised two fingers and the athletic woman said his name again. "When we hire the best chef in the world to cater a dinner," he said, "we don't expect him to share his recipes. He's just supposed to serve the food we ask for and make sure that it's exactly what we want. That's what Dr. Cross and his team have done. They're giving us a taste of some great food with the understanding that we'll get even more— and the recipe, too—somewhere down the line, when it's perfect."

The athletic woman leaned over and whispered to the Asian man. He nodded and glanced over at the senator. The Air Force colonel was still glaring at Olaf.

"In addition," said Reggie, leaning forward again, "I'm sending one of my top men to do a full on-site evaluation. He'll be bringing back a detailed report of the project for your examination."

He gestured across his body to Mike.

Everyone in the room followed the gesture. The board members. The scientists. The seven people taking notes. Mike could feel their stares on his skin. Arthur Cross straightened up. Jamie's eyes narrowed. Olaf scowled.

"I haven't agreed to anything," he whispered.

"Too late now," murmured Reggie.

"Well," said the athletic woman, "under the circumstances it seems like the question and answer session we had scheduled for this afternoon is a bit pointless." She closed her file and exchanged a few glances with the other board members. "I think that's that, then. Many thanks to you and your team for coming out this morning, Dr. Cross. You've given us a bit to think about."

He bowed his head.

"Mr. Magnus," she continued, "I think we'll still want a few words with you after lunch."

"I thought you might."

She nodded. "Let's be back here at one-thirty then."

The board members rose, were joined by aides, and broke off into pairs and trios. The scientists huddled together and spoke in low whispers. Their gazes flicked between Reggie and Mike.

"That," said Mike, "was very uncool."

"You've been hanging around teenagers too long."

SIX

"You tricked me," said Mike.

"I didn't trick you," Reggie said, settling in behind his desk. "I just know you."

Mike looked around the office. The ants carried out images from his last visit. A new computer monitor sat on the desk. Two more black poker chips, each with the logo of a different Las Vegas casino, had joined the three around the monitor's base. The walls were eggshell now, instead of stark white. There were nineteen new books on the shelves and fifteen of the old ones had vanished. There was a hardcover and paperback copy of Arthur Cross's *The History of What We Know.* The spine of the paperback was smooth and pristine.

"Once you were down here," continued Reggie, "and heard what the project was, I knew you'd be up for it."

Mike skimmed the other items on the shelves. A framed certificate. A windup robot. A pair of plaques, one brass, one silver. A photo of Reggie in casual clothes smiling with a younger Asian woman. A postcard from Disney World featuring Tomorrowland. The ants cataloged each one under a dozen different topics. "You could've told me before," he said.

"You hadn't been cleared."

"You just said you knew me."

"Do you want an apology?"

Mike flopped into one of the chairs on the other side of the desk.

"I needed you on this. I couldn't afford to have you say no, so . . . I may have stretched the truth and put you in a position where it'd be tough for you to say no." Reggie tapped his palms against the desk. "I'm sorry."

"You know what something like this will do to me. To my life."

"I do. But I really need you on this."

Mike forced a few ants back behind their walls. "You're a jerk."

"Nothing I haven't heard before. Do you want the flight home?"

"And the thousand dollars."

"Yeah, of course. If you're really not interested, if you think you're not up for it . . . I get it."

Mike counted to five. It was a habit he'd developed early in life. Answer too quickly and everyone assumed you hadn't thought about what you were saying.

Reggie tapped the table again. "Is that what you want?"

"No."

"And I'm supposed to be the jerk."

"As long as we're clear on that."

"Can we stop wasting time now?"

"Sure."

"I'm going to have to go back in and face the board again in less than an hour," Reggie said. "You should be with me. What did you think of this morning?"

The ants wiggled loose. They carried out sound bites and images, first impressions and gut reactions. "This is all serious? Cross has made an actual teleporter? A machine that moves matter from one place to another?"

"Yes. Well, you heard them. More of a doorway."

"Like a Stargate or something?"

Reggie shook his head. "Don't say that around Arthur or Olaf. They hate the comparison."

"Noted. How long have they been working on it?"

"Three years on the Albuquerque Door. Before that was two years on SETH."

"I thought DARPA only gave one-year grants."

"Usually, yes, but we're not going to cut off something really promising just because twelve months have passed."

"And there's no question it's real? Not some magic trick or something?"

"I've seen it myself," Reggie said. "Three times. Last time they offered to let me and Kelli do it."

The ants flashed a quick image of Reggie's petite assistant. Her hair was red, but there was an eighth of an inch of brown at the roots. "Did you?"

"Yes. Both of us."

Mike straightened up in his chair. "So it was hers, yours, and another was three times? Or saw it twice then did it once together?"

"You're nitpicking the math?"

"Hell, yes."

Reggie smiled. "I saw a rat the first time. And a baseball."

"A baseball?" The ants assembled a picture before Reggie could take in a breath to respond. "It's an open doorway. They throw the baseball back and forth as a test."

"Right. Second time was a chimpanzee. Last time was nine weeks ago. Kelli and I did it one right after another. Me first, then her."

"What did it feel like?"

"Like nothing," said Reggie. "Like stepping from one room to another."

"Is the Albuquerque Door a Bugs Bunny reference?"

"Yes. Arthur loves the old cartoons. You're the first person who didn't need it explained to them."

Mike nodded. "Okay, don't get me wrong," he said, "but if Cross has done it, what do you need me for? I don't understand why you're having a problem with funding. Hell, I don't understand why you haven't announced it."

"A few reasons." Reggie lifted his hands off the desk and laced his fingers together. "One, as you may have noticed, they're very secretive. Arthur and Olaf have been pretty much obsessive about keeping the whole thing under wraps, and they've got a serious cult of personality going with their team."

"How big's the team?"

"Six people."

"Not much of a cult."

Reggie ignored him. "People in Washington don't like it when things are kept from them. It's a status thing. You saw how the senator and the colonel tensed up at that 'need to know' comment."

"Yeah."

"In this town, that's not just an insult, it's a slap in the face. So a couple of those folks just want to shut him down for ego reasons."

"Stupid, but I guess I can see that."

"Two, it's been a very long project by DARPA standards. If it was anyone except Arthur Cross, it probably would've ended years ago. But he's probably the third- or fourth-best-known scientist alive today, after Stephen Hawking and Neil deGrasse Tyson."

"Is Bill Nye your other possible third?"

"Of course. So I gave Arthur two extensions, he showed some very impressive results, and I gave him a third."

"And this is the fourth?"

"Hopefully."

"Still not seeing anything you need me for."

Reggie unlaced his fingers and picked up one of the black poker chips. He flipped it across his knuckles, threading it between his fingers with a magician's grace. "I think there's something wrong."

"You just said it worked."

"It does."

"Did somebody come through with a giant fly head or something?"

"It doesn't work that way. And the problem's not with the tech." Reggie walked the chip over the back of his hand and shrugged. "Okay, maybe it's with the tech. I don't know. Everything looks fantastic on paper, so to speak, but there's something wrong."

"Something like what?"

"There's a bad vibe out there. They're all on edge. The tone's off on personnel reviews. People are taking a lot of sick days."

"Like the physicist who was supposed to be here today?"

"Maybe. It's hard to pin down. I mean, they're a bunch of reclusive scientists, so, yeah, I expect to feel like a bit of an outsider. I'm used to it with some of the people I deal with. But for the past six or seven months, things just seem . . . wrong."

"Wrong how?"

"That would be point number four," said Reggie.

"Why do I get the sense this is the one you should've led with?"

"Probably. I sent Ben Miles out there two months ago, right after my last visit. He was one of my—"

"I met him last time I was here," Mike said, holding up a finger. "You're using past tense. What happened to him?"

The chip paused in its spiraling trip around Reggie's fingers. "He went out to San Diego for a more formal review. We talked a bit when he got back, and he sounded overall positive. Felt good about the project, good about the people. He kept calling me 'pal,' which I remember thinking at the time was odd for him, but I figured he'd picked it up out there. He said he'd have a full report in a couple of days. Then he went home and called nine-one-one. Said someone had kidnapped his wife and replaced her with an impostor."

The ants carried out an image of Ben holding out his hand to shake Mike's. The other hand had a gold wedding band.

"He deals with a few sensitive projects, so the FBI was involved. Becky, his wife, was a little wigged out, but she passed all her checks. Ben still wouldn't let it go. Accused me of being in on it." The poker chip began to weave between Reggie's fingers again. It did a full circuit around his knuckles. Then another. Then a third. "He's up at Belmont Hospital in Philadelphia. Been there for almost six weeks now. At first they thought it was a Capgras delusion, some sort of brain input-output error, but he failed a couple of tests for it. Now they're tentatively calling it paranoid schizophrenia."

"No sign of mental illness before this? No secret conspiracy theories or anything like that?"

"None. The man was a rock."

"Drug use?"

"Barely even drank. He had a full physical once a year that backed it up."

"So?"

"Arthur says nothing happened out there. Ben seemed fine every moment he was there. A little too aggressive trying to put his report together, but they understood it, even if they didn't like it."

"Then he came home and went insane."

"Something like that."

"And now you want me to go out there."

"Yes."

"I thought we were friends."

"You're not going out unprepared. And we both know you're a lot more observant than he was."

"Stop with the flattery."

"Facts aren't flattery. You go out there, they welcome you into the fold, you learn whatever you can about what's going on, and then give me a glowing report. Done. You're back fixing bumper cars before the Fourth of July weekend. With a much bigger bank balance."

Mike counted to five again. "Can you tell me anything else?" he asked. "Something you've seen? Something you've heard?"

Reggie shook his head. "You know when you're in a rush and you put a T-shirt on backward? Even if there's no tag in it, you don't have to look in the mirror to know it's on wrong. You can just feel it."

"That's all you've got for me?"

"It's just wrong," he replied with a shrug. "That's all I can tell you. There's something so wrong out there that you can almost feel it in the air. And you know what's the weirdest part?"

"What?"

"I think everyone out there feels the same way."

THE LEFT
TURN

SEVEN

Mike drove past the facility in San Diego once, even with OnStar calling out directions to him. The fence out front was old chain-link, with no signs. The guard post needed paint. When he came back around, the lone guard asked who he was and waved him in. There were lots of fresh scuff marks along the fence in a well-marked path, and Mike took that to mean at least one or two other guards were walking the perimeter.

Only one building was visible from the street. It was concrete and gray, with a few windows on the far end; a warehouse that had developed some architectural lesions. The building was flanked on one side by a large patch of overgrown weeds that had hit the point where they could be called small trees.

There was a small parking lot with a dozen spaces broken up by a quartet of large trees in wooden planters. Eight of the spaces were taken. Four were marked reserved and one was marked GUEST PARKING. He pulled into the farthest spot from the entrance.

He walked up a set of concrete steps and stepped inside. An odd mix of framed, poster-sized prints decorated the small lobby. Einstein. Tesla. Goddard. A history of automobiles. The Moon landing. Mike couldn't shake the feeling someone had looted them from a college bookstore.

The woman at the front desk stared at him with large, dark eyes above elegant cheekbones. Dark, straight hair ran over her shoulders and out of sight down her back. Her lips split in the polite, meaningless smile Mike knew from countless parent-teacher meetings. "May I help you?"

"Leland Erikson," he said, "here for Arthur Cross."

She gazed at him for a moment. He heard fingers tap on a keyboard and her eyes shifted to the flatscreen. "You're early," she said.

"I didn't realize there was a set time," he said.

She smiled again. This time it was sincere. "We didn't think you'd get here until the end of the day."

"Is that a problem?"

"Not at all. Dr. Cross?" she said to the air. "Mr. Erikson from DARPA is here for you." She stared into space for a moment. "Of course." The polite smile reasserted itself. "He'll be right out."

"Thanks."

"Will you be with us long?"

"A few weeks, I think. Maybe a whole month."

She nodded. "I'm Anne," she said after a moment. She held out a hand. "Nice to meet you."

"You, too." They shook. "Call me Mike."

Her face shifted just for a moment, and the sincere smile made another brief appearance. "Mike it is."

Mike heard the thump of a cane, and Arthur Cross strode out from the hallway. He was in shirtsleeves, but still wore a tie and also an ID card on a lanyard. "I see you found us all right."

"Yep." Mike held out his hand.

The scientist gave a curt nod and shook the hand once. "So, would you like to get settled first, or . . ."

"I'm ready to dive in, I guess, if you're ready for me."

Arthur's lips tightened. Just for a moment. "Very well," he said. He gestured at the front desk. "We don't allow cell phones past this point."

Mike slid the phone Reggie had given him from his pocket and placed it in Anne's outstretched hand. She slid open a foil-lined drawer and set it inside. "Just stop by on your way out," she told him.

"Right this way." Mike followed Arthur back down the hallway he'd appeared from, past a staircase and a connecting hall to a large door. It was almost square. Mike gazed up at the red light mounted in the wall as Arthur slid his ID card across a reader.

"Warning flasher," Arthur said. "Lets anyone coming in know if we're up and running or not."

"The magnetic flux?"

Arthur pulled open the door. "You've read up, I see."

"Reggie . . . Mr. Magnus gave me all the reports you've submitted to date."

"All of them? And you've read them all?"

"Yep. I read fast."

Arthur guided him around a bank of machinery as the door thudded shut behind them. "I guess you do."

A few yards in front of Mike, a pair of twelve-foot, off-white rings rose up from a solid base, looking more like a futuristic art installation than experimental technology. The rings dominated the gymnasium-sized room.

He glanced at Arthur. The older man nodded. "This is the Albuquerque Door."

Each ring was more round than flat, and Mike put them at about two feet thick. They were parallel, with twenty inches between them, according to the mental measuring tapes the ants overlayed for him. The ivory plating that covered them was made of heavy plastic. A ramp of expanded steel rose up in front of an array of rolling desks and computers, leveling off into a platform. The platform passed through the rings and ended in midair, a foot past the far one. Four bundles of cable ran from each ring, vanishing back into the mass of assembled technology.

White lines, almost a foot wide, circled the huge machine and formed a path out to the ramp. Mike noticed that almost all the equipment was kept outside of the lines. The desks were a good ten feet from it.

The two other people from the hearing, blond Jamie and Bogart-esque Olaf, waited by one of the desks. A large flatscreen loomed behind them, and a younger man stood near Olaf's elbow. Mike's school-trained eye put the man at twenty-six, tops. His brilliant red hair had the precisely messy look of someone who spent a lot of time trying to make it look like he spent no time on his hair.

Against the wall stood a row of six cylinders, each the size of a water heater and wrapped in an insulating blanket. A man and woman with heavy gloves were switching an insulated hose from one tank to the next in line. The hose ran into one of the bundles of cable and vanished beneath the legs and braces that held up the rings.

The man had a thin beard of blond hair that looked even thinner because of its color. His jeans were well-worn and the sleeves of his plaid shirt were rolled up past his elbows. He would've blended in well in a small town.

The woman's hair and eyes were as dark as Mike's own, although her face and body weren't anywhere near as angular. Her red T-shirt had an elaborate logo for "Scotty's Starship Repair Shop," with a list of services provided. He guessed she was a couple years older than him. She stared at Mike across the room while she held the hose and the other man tightened the connector. It was the kind of stare that said, "You're the teacher who gave my little angel a C."

Arthur walked to the trio by the workstation and gestured back at Mike. "Everyone, this is Leland Erikson. He works for Mr. Magnus. He's going to be staying here and observing things for a while."

"You can call me Mike," he said.

"How long is a while?" scowled Olaf.

"I thought Magnus was happy," said the redheaded man.

Arthur ignored them. "You already know Jamie and Olaf," he said. "This is Bob Hitchcock, our junior physicist."

"I get to double-check all the math," he said with a smile.

Arthur gestured at the bearded man. "The gentleman over there is Neil Warry, chief engineer and operations manager. That's Sasha Prestich next to him, our second engineer and resident *Star Trek* fanatic."

There were a few grunts as Mike made eye contact with each of them. Bob shook his hand. Neil kept working and sent a distracted wave in his direction. Sasha looked down her nose at him for another moment and then turned her attention back to the hose.

"Well, then," said Arthur, "I thought we'd start with a demonstration."

"We've got nothing scheduled," Olaf said. "Neil's going to have to make some calls."

"Make them. Who wants to go through today?"

Neil gave a nod of acknowledgment. "Just let me finish this," he said, patting the hose.

"I'll go," said the redhead.

"Christ, Bob." Jamie shook her head. "How many would that make for you?"

"An even eighty-four. I am the most traveled person on Earth."

"Of the nine people who have traveled," sneered Olaf.

"Nine people, two hundred and sixteen rats, six cats, and a chimpanzee," said Bob. "I'm still at the top of an ever-expanding group."

Arthur looked at them. "Does anyone besides Bob want to go?"

"I'll go," snapped Olaf. "Let's just get on with it. I have a conference call at three." He turned his back to them and began typing at a console. Jamie stalked past Mike to the hall, with Sasha a yard behind her.

A low hiss came from the gas tanks as valves opened. A vibration shivered through the floor and two red lights flashed at either end of the huge room. Arthur pointed up at a slanted window fourteen feet above the chamber floor. "Let's head up to the control room," he said.

"Friendly bunch you have here," said Mike as they passed through the square door again.

"Don't take it personally," Arthur said, "but everyone's sort of looking at you as the enemy."

"How could I take that personally?"

"You're the government. You're the man deciding if we get to keep working or not, despite all the progress we've made." Arthur gestured for Mike to follow him up the narrow staircase. "They all resent that. I resent it, to be quite honest."

"I don't make the call, you know. I just have to tell Reggie what I think of your work."

"He must think very highly of your opinion."

"We've known each other a long time. He knows what I can do."

Arthur stopped at the top of the stairs and turned to look down at Mike. "We never cleared that up back in Washington," he said. "What is it that you do for him? What's your title?"

"Ahhh. Well, to be honest, I don't think I have one."

"I find that somewhat hard to believe."

"Outside consultant?"

"And what's your usual position, then?"

Mike tapped his fingers on the railing. "They're waiting for us in the control room, aren't they?"

"Yes, they are." He set both hands on the head of his cane. "It's one of the small perks of being in charge. I can make people wait for me."

Mike sighed. "Well, I teach junior year English."

"You're a college professor?"

"Junior year of high school," clarified Mike. "South Berwick High in Maine."

Arthur stared for a moment, then crossed his arms. "Is this some kind of joke?"

"Not really."

"Magnus thought a high school teacher was the ideal person to evaluate our work?"

Mike took a breath and weighed his words. "I have some abilities that make me a worthwhile observer and theorist. Reggie's been trying to get me on the payroll for almost a decade. Your project's been the only thing he's ever told me about that interested me."

"He said something similar at the budget meeting. Could you be more specific?"

"Do I have to be?"

"Yes."

He sighed again. "I maxed out the only IQ test I ever took. I was given a few extra problems by the tester and she ballparked my IQ at over 180. Granted, I was under the recommended age, and it was the old Stanford-Binet, not the Titan Test or the Mega, so it isn't terribly accurate at that scale, but I confirmed the general range myself. On top of that, I've got an eidetic memory. Complete, instantaneous recall of anything I've ever seen or heard."

"You're joking."

"No."

"I thought eidetic memory was something they made up for science fiction stories."

"There are a few confirmed cases, although it's tough to prove someone remembers everything without having them remember everything for you."

Arthur stared at him for a moment. "Give me a demonstration. Impress me."

Mike mulled it over and let a few ants loose. "When I pulled into the parking lot, there were four cars parked in the spaces closest to the front office. A yellow Volkswagen Beetle, California license plate 2GKD627. A blue Hyundai, Oregon license plate CK96668 with a Darwin fish on the passenger side of the trunk. A black Dodge Durango, California license plate 4OCE815."

"That's mine."

"Are you a *LOST* fan?"

"No," Arthur said, "but I've been told about the significance many times."

"The last car was a blue Mini Cooper, in desperate need of a wash, California license plate 3FKM864. It had a license plate frame with two eight-pointed stars and the words KHARN NEVER MISSES. It's a reference to a character from the game Warhammer 40,000, used in an army called the World Eaters. There was also a decal on the side window of an Internet cartoon character called 'the Cheat.'"

"Impressive, but how do I know you didn't—"

"The day we met in Washington, you were wearing a silk tie with fractal geometry patterns on it. The Lyapunov set. It was available in the two thousand nine Christmas catalog from BBC America. Dr. Johansson had a sterling silver pen in his shirt pocket, and I know his tie was a clip-on because one of the plastic strips was showing under the left collar. Miss Parker was carrying a knockoff Louis Vuitton purse. The print pattern didn't line up on the seam, that's what gave it away. A woman I work with has a real one she got as a Christmas gift three years ago. All three of you are right-handed, by the way. So is everyone I've met here except Mr. Hitchcock and Anne, the receptionist."

Arthur stared at him for a moment, then slowly closed his mouth.

"Sorry," Mike said, "but I can keep doing this for hours. I try not to. It's kind of a hazard, actually, once I get on a roll."

The project leader shook his head. "No need. I think I understand why Mr. Magnus is so eager to get you on his staff."

"Great. Think you can explain to him why I want to be a high school teacher?"

"I'll see what I can do." A smile, a real smile, crept up on Arthur's face. "Well, Mr. Erikson, you've shown me what you can do. Now let me show you what I can do."

EIGHT

The control room was almost level with the top of the rings. A line of windows angled out over the huge lab, offering a perfect view. A half dozen stations dotted the room, with banks of humming computer towers, flatscreens, and monitors. Jamie kicked her chair along from station to station as she checked levels and paused to tap a few keys.

Mike watched Neil, Olaf, and Bob scurry around the device down on the floor. From up here he could see the wide white lines that marked out a clear path up to the rings. "It takes this many people to run it?"

Arthur shook his head. "It takes this many people to monitor everything. Olaf and Jamie are the only ones operating the system, and even she's doing more monitoring than running anything."

"Says you," she snorted. "Try running this place without me."

"We also designed it as a safety system," said Cross. "There need to be at least two people present in order for the Albuquerque Door to work. One up here, one on either side. Any combination of two works."

"Why's that?"

"Because that's how we set it up," said Jamie. She leaned in to the microphone. "Ready in four."

"No, I mean, why set up a safety system at all? What do you need it for?"

Arthur's lips twisted into an unfamiliar shape. Mike realized the man was almost smiling. "It cuts down on joyriding," he said. He leaned his cane against his body, pulled his glasses off, and polished them on his tie. "Once we'd established the Door was safe, more than a few team members decided to try it." He gave a pointed look at Jamie.

"Just once," she said. "Don't act all high and mighty. You did it, too."

Mike smiled.

Down in the chamber, red safety lights flashed over every door. One was just beneath the window. The men stepped back, clearing a space around the rings. A series of relays clicked around the room, followed by a buzz, as they activated the device.

Down on the floor, Olaf set a finger against his flatscreen. His voice echoed through the speakers. "Sasha's on the other side. Power is good. Flux density is steady."

The chair coasted by, carrying the blonde to another monitor. "Ready in three," she announced into her headset. She grabbed a pen from the console and spun it twice around her thumb before shoving it behind her ear. Her fingers danced over the keyboard and she pushed the microphone a hair closer to her mouth. "This is Jamie Parker, it's June twenty-second, twenty-fifteen, and this is run one-sixty-eight. Traveler is, for a change, Olaf Johansson." She pulled the pen back out from her ear, and jotted some quick notes on a clipboard.

A hiss of steam echoed up from the main floor as the heavy hoses frosted over. The buzz became a full hum, shaking the air. Mike watched the set of double rings and waited for them to light up or spin or do something impressive.

"We still get power spikes sometimes," Jamie told him, shifting her attention for a moment. "They don't affect the Door once it's open, but they play hell with the components, especially up here. Every spike costs us about four days of work and something like fifty thousand in replacement parts. Ready in two."

"Closer to a hundred thousand, actually," murmured Arthur.

Mike peered down at the rings. The space between the twin circles seemed to shift and ripple like the air over hot pavement. He took a step to the left and confirmed the effect was only within the rings.

Arthur nodded. "It's also one-sided," he said. "You can see the formation of the Door here, but if you were on the other side of the rings you wouldn't see anything. Perfectly clear."

"Really?"

He nodded.

The ants filed it all away with quick notes and first impressions.

The computer screen in front of Jamie stopped scrolling and flashed a string of numbers. "We've got a solution. Ready in one."

"Power is good," said Olaf down on the floor. "Flux density is good. Opening the Door."

A faint crackle of light raced around the rings, a sparkling St. Elmo's fire. There was a crisp hiss that reminded Mike of a fresh glass of soda being poured, and the sound settled to the constant bubbling of carbonation. Then the sparkle of light faded and the rippling air between the two off-white rings grew still.

"Field has cohesion," said Jamie. "The Door is open."

Two timers appeared on a screen close to Jamie. Each one extended to hundredths of a second, where the numbers flew by in a blur. One counted up from zero. The other counted down from ninety-three seconds.

Nothing happened. Mike stared down at the lab, waiting for a flash or a crackle or a bang. The rings seemed as inert and lifeless as they had when he first saw them.

Olaf stepped away from his station, and Bob slid in to take his place. He walked up to the expanded steel pathway, stood between the two white painted lines, and gave a curt nod up to the control booth. Then he marched up the ramp and through the rings.

And vanished.

"No way," breathed Mike.

Arthur smiled. "Three years now and I still love watching that." He punched an extension number on the phone, tapping the speaker mode button at the end. "Have him, Sasha?"

"Of course." Olaf's sneer echoed over the phone.

"Yeah," said Sasha's voice. "Without a hitch."

Arthur pointed at a bank of monitors. "He's over at Site B, on the far side of the property. You can see him there."

Mike bent to the screen. It showed Sasha in the foreground at another workstation while Olaf stood by an identical set of—

On screen, it wasn't a pair of rings. It was a trio. Behind Olaf, through the three-ringed Door, Mike could see Neil and Bob working at their own stations.

Mike looked down through the window at the two men. He could clearly see two rings on the main floor, but if he craned his head to look through them, he could see the base of a third ring.

He looked at Arthur. "Where does the third ring come from?"

"It doesn't come from anywhere," said Arthur. "There are two rings at each location. You're seeing the point where the sides of the Door connect."

"How far is Site B?"

"About a quarter mile away. The rings are sixteen-hundred and three feet apart."

"Is that significant?"

"No. Just where they ended up."

Mike pointed at the monitor. "This is real time?"

The older man nodded. "You can talk to them through the god-mike, if you want. They'll hear you in both labs."

Mike leaned into the microphone. "Olaf, could you raise your right hand?"

On the screen, Olaf muttered something the speakerphone couldn't catch and put his right hand up at shoulder height in an annoyed salute. Sasha chucked, and her tinny laughter bounced around the control room.

Mike glanced down at the floor. "Bob, could you stand up please?"

The redhead glanced up at the booth and pushed his chair away from his desk. On the monitor, through the rings, Mike saw him rise from the chair before Olaf's body blocked him.

"Olaf, could you lean to the left a bit?"

"No," growled the scientist. "Are we done yet?"

Down on the lab floor, Bob stretched out his arms and did a little dance, rolling his shoulders as he pointed up at the booth, through the Door, and back. On screen, the distant Bob through the rings did the same, but with Olaf hiding him for the most part.

"Forty-five seconds left," Jamie said.

Arthur leaned into the microphone. "Want to do a walk-back?"

"If it gets this over and done with, fine." There was a faint ripple down in the space between the rings, and Olaf reappeared on the walkway. He marched down the steel ramp and back to his station.

"Wait," said Mike. "One more time? Can he go back?"

Arthur smirked and nodded. "Back to Site B, Olaf."

"What? Are you joking?"

"Come on," said Jamie into her headset. "Play nice for the guest."

"This is ridiculous!" Olaf snarled up at the booth. "I have things to do."

"I'll go," said Bob.

Jamie glanced at the timers. "Twenty seconds."

"Olaf, please," said Arthur. "Back to Site B."

The scientist shot an angry glare at the control booth and marched through the Door again. On the monitor he barked an order at Sasha and slashed his hand across his throat. The intercom clicked off and he began to vent at her in silence. She studied her instruments and made one or two gestures of casual agreement.

"It'll take him ten minutes to get back here," said Arthur. "Let's go to my office and talk, if you've seen enough."

Mike stared back at the monitors, soaking up every detail. He gave a nod, which Arthur echoed to Jamie. Her fingers ran across the keyboard and the bubbling noise rose back to a hiss before going silent. Down on the floor the red lights stopped spinning.

NINE

Bookshelves filled most of Arthur's office. About two thirds of the contents were old science books on astronomy, physics, and biology. Many of them had faded spines and cracked bindings. Mike recognized eleven of the authors. One of them was H. G. Wells, printed on four black-bound volumes of *The Science of Life*.

Twenty copies of *The History of What We Know* formed a bright block at the center of the bookshelf to the left of the desk. Ten hardcover, ten paperback. Ten weeks on the *New York Times* bestsellers list, too. All of Mike's fellow teachers had read it and sung its praises.

The rest of the shelf space was filled with binders, random electronics, and a few framed photographs. On a rare section of exposed wall a large poster showed Bugs Bunny, Daffy Duck, Wile E. Coyote, and other Warner Bros. cartoon characters. An overstuffed Bugs Bunny made of smooth fabric and loose stitching was seated on the bookshelf to the left of the poster.

The laptop on the desk was at least three years old. A stack of dark brown file folders was piled next to it. The only other item was a photo of Arthur embracing a woman with strawberry-blond hair.

Across from the desk was a CAD blueprint of the twin rings of the Albuquerque Door, packed with notes and insert diagrams.

Arthur followed his gaze to the blueprint. "Eidetic memory," he said. "How does that work?"

Mike shrugged. "When I was ten I started having this visual of ants carrying around pictures in my mind, like frames of a film. It's like having instant access to a time-stamped DVD of everything I've ever seen.

I can replay it, rewind it, slow it down, freeze frame. The only limit is if I actually saw something or not."

"Ants?"

"My fourth grade science teacher, Mr. Tall, showed a movie about insects in class. There was a war between two ant colonies, and I thought, 'That's just what it's like in my head.' Thoughts and memories pouring all over each other in this big, boiling mass."

"That's an interesting metaphor."

"Yeah. And I can't get rid of it because I can't forget it. Odin has ravens, I've got ants." He saw Arthur looking at the blueprint. "Sorry. That's not really your concern, is it?"

"Not exactly, no."

They studied each other for a moment.

"I'm not here to steal secrets or learn your methods," said Mike. "I could've kept quiet, let you think I was an idiot, and just stored up everything for the trip back. But that's not what this is about. Reggie just wanted someone who'd be able to get a larger sense of how things are going out here. I can take in more and get up to speed faster than anyone he's got on staff."

"Of course."

They stood across from each other for a few more moments. Mike glanced at the picture next to the laptop. "Your wife?"

"Yes."

Mike weighed his options for a moment, then let a few ants loose. "Violet. Married in nineteen ninety-eight, while you were both doing postdoctorate work at MIT. You were already a bit of a scientific celebrity."

"You'd make a fantastic stalker."

"Reggie gave me dossiers and copies of all your files to review. Well, all the files you've given him."

Arthur's shoulders shifted a bit. His lips pulled into another faint smile. "I do envy your memory. I forgot my anniversary last month. Could've sworn I had another week, and now I'm still in the doghouse." He pulled a bottle from his desk drawer. "Scotch?"

"Love some."

"I have options."

"Scotch is fine."

Amber liquid splashed into the glasses. "This has been my life for the past decade. Four years of work before we even started on SETH. Two years of that and then we carried a good chunk of it over to the Albuquerque Door. Three years of testing and refining since then. It's been all-consuming, to say the least."

He handed a glass to Mike. They raised them politely to each other and then each man took a sip.

Mike lowered his glass. "Can I ask you a question?"

"Of course."

"Why do you think Reggie's worried something's gone wrong here?"

Arthur laughed and swirled the scotch in his glass. "Not much for small talk, are you?"

"It comes from spending too much time with sixteen-year-olds." He sipped his scotch. "So, why, do you think?"

The older man shrugged. "Well, you may not have noticed, but we're a bit insular here. You get a group of people like that, put them under a lot of stress—most of it self-imposed, granted—and then start peering over their shoulders. It doesn't help that we actually were hiding a secret for a while."

"The animal testing they mentioned at the review board?"

Arthur settled into the chair behind the desk. "How much do you know about the whole incident?"

"Not much," said Mike. He tugged one of the spare chairs closer to the desk and sat down. The ants carried out the seventeen reports that mentioned the incident and set out the relevant lines and paragraphs. "All the reports seem happy to brush it under the rug, so I just know the very bare facts."

The older man nodded. "I suppose we might as well begin at the low point." He took another taste of his drink. "This was all originally the SETH project, a straight teleport—"

"What the hell is this?" barked a voice behind Mike.

Olaf stood in the doorway, his icy glare shooting back and forth between Mike and Arthur. "Is this another one of Bob's stupid jokes? Where are my things, dammit?"

Arthur looked from the other scientist to Mike, and then to the glasses of scotch. "What are you talking about?"

"What did you do with my computer? And all my files? I swear to God, if that idiot has messed up any of my files, I'll smash his head in."

Arthur stood up. "Bob did something to your office?"

"Don't patronize me! Are you part of this nonsense, Arthur?" He shot a frosty look at Mike. "I thought we were all supposed to be on best behavior."

Arthur locked eyes with Mike for a moment. Then he marched past Olaf to the door across the hall. He swung it open and glanced inside. "Everything looks fine to me."

Olaf glanced over his shoulder. "Switching offices? What the hell! Is this a freshman dorm?"

"Just calm down," Arthur said, walking back into his own office. "Bob knows the rules, and if he did something wrong, he'll be disciplined."

"*If?*"

"You know where the professionalism forms are, Olaf."

"Did I mention I have a conference call? I don't have time for this juvenile crap!"

"Make your call. Let me know if anything's damaged. I'll talk to Bob."

The scientist stomped into the hall and a door slammed.

Arthur settled back behind his desk and had a longer drink of his scotch. "Sorry about that."

Mike looked back at the door. "Is that normal?"

"He's a pain in the ass, but he also has one of the greatest theoretical minds on the planet. I'd put him in a class with Hawking. We're under a lot of pressure here, and sometimes a little mistake can set any of us off. Olaf just goes off more than most."

"Doesn't deal with the stress well?"

"That *is* how he deals with stress. He runs and he complains about everyone. Pretty much the only reason we have professionalism forms is for Olaf."

Mike turned to look at the blueprint again. "Is Reggie after you that much for results?"

"Not that bad, but we're also pressuring ourselves. What we're doing here is going to change the world forever. A lot of people say it, but . . . well, we're actually doing it. And we all know it."

"Understandable," said Mike.

"Where were we?"

"The SETH project."

"Right. At that point we were working on pure teleportation. We had a series of breakthroughs. Some huge intuitive leaps. It was the fastest and furthest our work had gone to date. Over three weeks or so, we became convinced we'd cracked it, that we'd made a true IMT system."

Mike nodded. "So you wanted to start animal testing."

"We couldn't wait. Honestly, we couldn't. After three weeks of nothing but leaps and bounds, the idea of waiting months to get approval seemed ridiculous. After all, we *knew* it would work this time."

He took a sip of his drink.

"Tramp was a stray who'd been hanging out around the trailers. He'd sort of been adopted by the whole team. We fed him and played with him sometimes. He trusted us. And we put him on the platform, turned on the machine, and . . . killed him."

"Just like that?"

Arthur gave a grave dip of his chin. "He looked like . . . like road kill. Just a hunk of gristle and fur spread over the receiving platform. We were all . . . We were so caught up in being right we hadn't considered how dangerous it could be if we were wrong." He paused for another drink. His glass was almost empty. "It was a horrible way for anything to die. Anything."

He swallowed the last of his scotch.

"You tried to hide it," said Mike.

"At first, yes." He reached across the desk and poured another half-inch of scotch for himself. "It was clear to everyone that SETH was going nowhere, so we weren't worried about a bunch of intense scrutiny. As our focus shifted to the ideas behind the Albuquerque Door, though, we realized we had to come clean, so there was no chance of animal-rights groups spinning it into a scandal later on."

"Over one test animal?"

"One that we hid. Too many people would think, 'Who knows how many are still hidden, that died in even worse ways.'" He shook his head. "We wanted the Door to be as clean as possible, so we just confessed to everything. Olaf and Neil insisted on it before we moved forward."

Mike glanced across the hall. "Olaf insisted?"

Arthur nodded. "He doesn't make a good first impression, I know, but he's a good man at heart. I think the whole thing bothered him more than any of us. We had a long talk with Magnus—Reginald, paid some hefty fines, and we each ended up making a sizable donation to the Humane Society. With all that in mind, it's understandable that he'd continue to see problems here. Which just breeds more resentment and pressure from us, of course."

"Of course," agreed Mike.

They sat and looked at each other for a few moments.

"You seem like a decent person," said Arthur. "I'll try my best not to bite your head off when you ask questions. I'll ask everyone else to do the same."

"Thanks."

"But we're still not going to be revealing any technical information. Not one equation, not one line of code, not one blueprint."

"You said the same thing at the review meeting. Exactly the same."

"It's become kind of a mantra for all of us here. And to be honest, everyone's going to be more on guard with you once they hear about your . . ." He tapped two fingers against his temple.

"I get that a lot, don't worry. Again, I don't want to violate your agreement with Reggie, I just want to go back to him with a fair assessment of things."

"Then I think we'll get along just fine."

Mike turned his head to look at a small diorama on another bookshelf. A miniature Wile E. Coyote had a fan and a sail strapped to his back as he roller-skated down a plastic hill, a set of silverware held out in anticipation. "I understand you're also a big Bugs Bunny fan?"

"Now the small talk?"

"Sorry."

Arthur smiled. Another real smile. "Almost any concept or idea in the world can be expressed through comparison with a classic Warner Bros. cartoon."

"Even the Albuquerque Door?"

"Of course."

Mike waved him on.

"Do you remember Foghorn Leghorn?"

The scotch traced a warm path across Mike's tongue. "Think about who you're asking."

The older man settled back into his chair. "One of my favorite cartoons had Foghorn babysitting this tiny baby bird genius to impress the widow Prissy with a nice house. Do you know it?"

"There were a few with the widow Prissy. Her chick was named Egghead Jr. The first cartoon they were all in was 'Little Boy Boo' in nineteen fifty-four."

Arthur arched an eyebrow at him.

Mike's lips pursed. "Sorry. Annoying habit, I know." He tossed back some scotch. "You were saying?"

"I was saying, at one point Foghorn and the chick are playing hide-and-seek. Foghorn hides in the woodbin. Egghead looks around for a few seconds, writes out a page of mathematics, and sticks a shovel in the ground about ten feet away. Out pops Foghorn. He tries to argue that what's just happened is impossible, and the chick keeps showing him the page of calculations."

"And that's what you do?"

"That's what we do," Arthur said. "We take over six hundred pages of math and force-feed it to the universe through an electromagnetic funnel. We tell the universe 'I don't care what you think. I'm lifting my foot *here* and putting it down *there*.'"

"And the universe doesn't object?"

Arthur finished off his whiskey. "Not so far."

TEN

"Here you are." Anne handed Mike a badge on a lanyard. "Your ID card. Dr. Cross gave you full coverage so you can open pretty much every door on campus."

"Pretty much?"

"Some of the hazardous substance lockers need two cards to open," she said. "If you need access to those, I can talk to Dr. Cross and update your privileges."

"Are you this formal with them, too?"

She smiled. "Sorry. Still not used to you. I'll try to be better."

He shook his head. "Whatever makes you comfortable. I just don't want you thinking you need to act this way around me."

She smiled.

"Jesus!" said someone. "You've been here three hours and you're already hitting on my woman?"

Mike turned to see the red-haired physicist at the hallway entrance, smiling. He glanced back, and Anne rolled her eyes. It was a perfect eye-roll, a careful balance of fed up and flirty, seasoned with just enough amusement. "I didn't realize the two of you were—"

"We're not," said Anne, turning back to her desk.

"Another rejection," said Bob. "Y'know, I can only take thirty or forty more."

"Good thing you've got your girlfriend to fall back on, then." Anne punctuated her sentence with a look that said the joke was done for the day. She had very expressive eyes.

Bob bowed his head and shifted his focus to Mike. "Arthur's given me tour guide duty for the day. Ready to see your new home away from home?"

"Actually, can we go see it again? The Door?"

"Sure. We can cut through the lab to the trailer park."

Mike waved goodbye to Anne but she'd already sunk back into work. He and Bob wandered down the hall. Mike took his new ID for its first test drive, and the square door opened with a click.

The air on the main floor was a good five or six degrees cooler than the rest of the building. The huge room was deserted. The silent shape of the Albuquerque Door loomed at the center of the chamber. Mike gazed at the rings as they walked past.

"What does it feel like? When you go through."

Bob said nothing.

Mike glanced at him. "What it feels like is a trade secret?"

"It doesn't feel like anything, to be honest."

"Nothing? No visual effects? No dizziness? Not even a tingle from the electromagnetic fields?"

"Nope. There is one thing, but it's not internal."

"What?"

"D'you ever walk into a big store in the summer, and they've got the air conditioning vents right at the doors, pointing straight down?" He mimed an archway around himself with his hands. "Y'know, you walk in and there's just this instant, blasting temperature change. And then you walk past it and everything's normal again?"

Mike nodded.

"That's kind of what crosswalking feels like, but no temperature change. Just this sudden *whoof* that tells you you're somewhere else now. Even if your eyes are closed, you can tell the moment you've crossed."

"Crosswalking?"

"Yeah. No pun intended, but I think he kind of likes it."

They walked down a passage of electronics and power gauges, past a pair of closet doors to a fire exit. Bob hit the crash bar and glaring sunlight blasted into the lab. "We cut the alarm lines months ago," he explained, nodding at the red and white stickers on the door. "It shaves a few minutes off the trip home every night."

Behind the building was a gravel pit. Eight office trailers stretched across it in a double row. They were gray and bland, and Mike could glimpse curtains and sheets hanging in the small windows. A few hundred yards past the trailers stood another industrial-looking structure, newer than the main building. It looked like a cross between a warehouse and an aircraft hangar. The only thing that made it stand out was the seven foot tall "B" someone had painted along one side.

"That's where the other machine is?" asked Mike.

Bob glanced over. "Yeah. Site B. We've got a couple bicycles and a golf cart that run back and forth between them, if you're ever in a rush. Your card should get you in over there, too. And that's the trailer park," he said, waving at the double row of blocks. "Home away from home for those of us working on the Albuquerque Door."

"They provide living quarters for everyone?"

"Sort of. The trailers were just for storage, or a place to crash if someone worked really late and didn't want to drive home. Then about two years ago, Olaf staked one off as his personal space and just moved in. It gave him two or three extra hours a day, and by the end of the month he was so far ahead, the rest of us did, too."

"How long have you been with the project?"

"Four years," Bob said as they crunched across the gravel. "I joined up about a year before the SETH project folded, right out of grad school."

"And now you all live here?"

"Well, I moved in for real a little over a year ago. Got rid of my place in Pacific Beach and just brought everything here. The trailer's free and it's bigger than my old apartment. Arthur lives up in La Jolla with his wife in his big book-money mansion."

"Really?"

Bob grinned. "No. But it's a real house and it's in La Jolla, so it wasn't cheap."

Someone had rolled out carpets of green Astroturf between the double row. The plastic grass rustled under their shoes. It was a welcome contrast to all the gravel.

"Nice touch," said Mike.

"Yeah. I think Sasha found it somewhere. On the off chance it rains, be careful. This stuff's cheap, so it gets slippery, and it's all just gravel underneath."

"That sounds like the warning of someone who's fallen."

"Twice," said Bob. He pointed at the trailer in front of them. "Neil's is there, but he's got a wife and kids up in Oregon, so he's not really 'living' here." His fingers slid along the row. "That one's me, right behind him. Olaf next to him. Jamie and Sasha have the two on the end, so they can have a bit of privacy."

"Oh," said Mike. "I didn't realize they were a couple."

"They're not, sorry. Well, Sasha is. Not with Jamie, though. Jamie's just . . . well she's a bit . . . abrasive, y'know? Sasha's on the end, Jamie's on the . . ." He paused and shook his head. "Damn, no. Jamie's on the end, Sasha's on the left."

"And one of these is mine?"

Bob nodded. "We had the cleaning crew freshen up the one next to Olaf for you. Congratulations, you're a buffer."

"Lucky me."

"It won't be that bad unless he's listening to opera."

"He's an opera fan?"

"Opera and running, but I'd swear he just does the opera to be annoying." The redhead unlocked the trailer. "You're going to be here awhile, I guess?"

Mike shrugged. "A few weeks, in theory. Maybe a month or two. I guess we'll see."

Bob tossed him the keys. "Magnus wouldn't spring for a hotel?"

"I think he wanted me close to everything."

Inside was gray. Gray carpet holding up gray walls decorated with gray cabinets. Dull bungee cords held a folding cot shut in the far corner. In the nearer one, a gray office phone sat on the floor. The only spot of contrast was an oversized black roach trap halfway along the wall. "You've just got the basics," Bob explained. "If you want a mini fridge or some more furniture, we can probably scavenge something up for you. And there's a few thrift shops up on Clairemont Mesa and a Target on Balboa."

"I think it's bigger than my old apartment, too."

"It's not bad, really, for a free place. Olaf has no life, the rest of the guys are pretty quiet, and I'm gone a lot on weekends."

"Miniature war games?"

"Complete geek, yes," said Bob with a grin. Honest smiles were hard to come by, Mike realized. "Who told you?"

In Mike's mind, a few red ants slipped into the colony of black ants.

"There's some paint under the fingernails of your right hand, but you're left-handed," he said. "That tells me you were painting something while you held it. Two different color paints, both shades of red, implies fine detail work of some sort. I already knew someone here played Warhammer games from the license plates on the Mini out front, so it wasn't much of a leap."

"No, of course not, Mr. Holmes," said Bob. "You want help with your bags and stuff?"

"I wouldn't turn it down, thanks."

"Do you play 40K?" Bob asked as they stepped back out on the deck.

Mike shook his head. "Some of my students do. I looked through a couple of the books, so I could assure parents the afterschool gaming group wasn't some kind of cult or fight club. And it's fun to watch tanks driving over the scale model of the town."

The redhead laughed and guided them across the Astroturf and toward the side of the building. "The door's a pain to open from this side," he explained. "The path leads right up to the lobby entrance and the parking lot."

"What's that?"

Bob followed his eyes. Just past the spare trailer on the end was a small wooden cross. A few stone tiles were arranged in front of it.

"The dog?"

"You heard?"

"Arthur said it died instantly."

"Yeah," the redhead said with a nod. "Faster, if that's possible. We just wanted to do something, make sure he got remembered."

"You always this attached to lab animals?"

"Laika was just a lab animal, if you think about it," said Bob. "People write whole books about her, and she only went into a loose orbit on Sputnik 2. Tramp went through the fabric of reality and came out the other side."

Mike walked over to the grave. The word TRAMP was written in Magic Marker on the pale wood. The soil was loose, as if someone had weeded it out.

The redhead took a few more steps up the path and glanced back. "It was a failure, but if he hadn't died, we'd've never started following this path. We wouldn't have the Albuquerque Door."

He sensed Bob's desperate desire to change the subject. "So they built this whole complex just for you guys?"

"Oh, hell no." Bob shook his head. He waved his hand up at the concrete structure. "They built Site B, but back in the seventies this place used to be a Jack in the Box processing plant. They expanded into a bigger building, and then I think it was used as a warehouse for a while. The government grabbed it up right after Nine-Eleven and it got handed off to SETH back in . . . late two-thousand-eight, I think."

Mike glanced up at the building as they came out into the parking lot. "Jack in the Box? The fast food chain?"

"Yup. Our control room was part of their marketing office or something like that. The main floor was the meat processing area."

Mike smiled. "No symbolism there."

"It's been brought up," said Bob.

ELEVEN

Mike debated leaving everything in his bags, but figured it would make a better impression if he unpacked. It took him half an hour to transfer his clothes into the cabinets and spread his shaving kit around the bathroom sink. He heard footsteps and voices outside, and saw Neil and Sasha. They ignored his trailer and headed for their own.

His stomach reminded him that he hadn't eaten a meal since Logan Airport back in Boston. He'd passed eleven restaurants and franchises on the way to the complex, but the closest one was almost two miles away. He thought about using the new smartphone Reggie had equipped him with to find somewhere closer, but he didn't want to start getting dependent on it. Or addicted. It took him ten minutes to find the Wendy's two streets up. He put lots of salt and pepper on his fries and ate his chicken sandwich alone at a table.

Then he was back at the gray trailer.

Part of him wanted to go through the reports he'd been given and start comparing them to what he'd seen. The ants itched at his mind. They were eager to mix, to bring the elements together and watch them seethe.

Part of him missed his little apartment. And his summer job down in York, doing maintenance work on the rides at the Wild Kingdom amusement park. And nights just staring out at the Atlantic while the tourists walked around him.

Then the computer tablet chimed from his pillow. He sat on the edge of the cot, tapped his thumb against the screen, and was shown a picture of Reggie's face with his office behind him. "Hey," said the picture, "it's me."

"Yeah, I know," Mike said. "I'm looking at you."

"Just trying to be polite."

"You're there late."

"Some of us work for a living. You have a good flight?"

"It was okay. Finally got to see the new *Hobbit* movie. Read some of the files you gave me."

"Some?"

"All."

"Stop holding back. I'm counting on you for this."

"Yeah, I know," said Mike. He thought of his quiet classroom, almost three thousand miles away, filled with books he hadn't read in years. "Trying to break a lifetime of bad habits."

"Got your car?"

"Okay flight, got the car, found the place. I'm here now."

"So, how's it going?"

"Oh, great people. All of them." Mike used his toes to pry off his shoes. "I'm expecting the first brick through the window later this evening."

"That bad?"

"I think Bob Hitchcock is willing to let me crawl out of here with only a beating, so he's probably my biggest fan right now."

"Are you always this pessimistic when I'm not around?"

"Well, I'm in a monotone trailer with no appliances and sitting on my one piece of furniture. It deadens the mood a bit."

Reggie snorted. "You see that Amex card?"

Next to the cot was the briefcase Reggie had given him. The smartphone and computer tablet had been in it, along with some other odds and ends. The ants assembled a complete inventory of the contents. "Yeah."

"It's a prepaid card," he said. "You've got fifteen thousand dollars on it for the next three months. If you want to drop a couple hundred at Target for a few bookshelves and a microwave, knock yourself out. Just save your receipts."

"How long do I get to keep the card?"

"Until you annoy me too much, and I cut you off," Reggie said. "If you need more on it, let me know."

"Thanks."

"Perks of the job. Speaking of which, anything yet?"

"Only been here a few hours. I'm still getting a feel for it. They know you've got worries about them, and they have perfectly rational explanations for your worry."

"Anything odd about the tech?"

"I still don't know enough about what they're doing." Mike set the tablet down, propping it up against the pillow. "Let me ask you something."

"Sure."

"You said you first saw them do this almost three years ago, yeah?"

"Just about."

"They did it again for me today."

"Did you do it?"

Mike shook his head. "Olaf Johansson. I watched from the control booth."

"What'd you think?"

"You're right. It's damned amazing."

"Told you."

"So why does it need more testing? They've had it working for a year and a half. You saw it months ago. Today's run was number 168 with a human subject. There've been no side effects or dangerous technical glitches. I'd say it works."

"And they say it needs more testing."

"But why? I mean, I gather there's still the time limit issue, but so what?"

On the tablet screen, Reggie shook his head. "I've asked Arthur a dozen times since they first showed it to me. He insists it's not ready to be revealed yet."

Mike could feel the ants itching to get at it in his mind. "And you're willing to release it now?"

"Yes. It takes care of the whole funding issue."

"And they know this?"

"They're not stupid. I would've done it the day after they first showed me, if Arthur hadn't been so insistent about the testing." Reggie had never been the type to waste time beating around the bush. He'd been slapped for it more than a few times in college.

"Huh," said Mike.

"Wow," Reggie said. "I am so glad I'm paying top dollar for your insight into this little puzzle."

"I'm holding off diving in as long as I can," said Mike.

Reggie's face shifted. "I know. I appreciate you doing this for me."

"You'd better."

"I do. You still want to do it?"

"Yep."

"If you haven't looked at anything yet, you could still back out. I could have you back in Maine in time to watch the sunrise."

Mike picked up the tablet. "I'm going to do it."

"Good. Now stop complaining."

"Yes sir, mister boss man, sir."

Reggie shook his head. "You know it's three times as offensive when you speak to a black man that way, right?"

"That was my goal. If it's okay with you, I'm going to lay back on my piece of furniture, singular, watch a movie, and go to sleep."

"Jet lagged?"

"Yeah."

"It's worse when you come back. You stay up until two in the morning."

"I do that anyway."

"So you'll be staying up until five."

"I'll call you in a couple days, let you know how it's going."

"Okay." Reggie paused. "I'm glad you're out there. Really. Thank you."

"Yeah, you're thanking me now. Wait until you see my bill."

"What bill? I just gave you a new tablet."

"Oh, that reminds me . . ." Mike swept his fingers across the screen and ended the session. He tossed the tablet onto the end of the bed, then had second thoughts and shoved it in a drawer. Reggie probably had a way to turn it on remotely. He'd have to go through the tablet's system tomorrow and see what kind of extras were in it.

Mike pulled off his shirt and stretched out. The cot squeaked and swayed beneath the thin mattress. After a moment he rolled the wafer-ish pillow into a cylinder and braced it under his neck.

He closed his eyes, blocking off the gray ceiling of the trailer. In his mind, he scrolled back over all the movies he'd ever seen, and decided it might be worth watching *Captain America: The Winter Soldier* again. The darkness behind his eyelids became the flickering Marvel logo.

Mike relaxed into the springy cot and immersed himself in the adventures of Steve Rogers, slowing the images whenever Scarlett Johansson graced the screen to search for any resemblance to Olaf.

TWELVE

Mike found a small kitchenette in the main building with some breakfast basics. It was stocked better than the teacher's lounge at his school, but not as well as the cafeteria. The delivery woman gave him a vague "Good morning," as she opened a box filled with donuts, muffins, and other pastries. He glanced up from his bowl of cereal and examined the selection of pastries.

He was eyeing a sugar-crusted blueberry muffin when Jamie pushed past him to grab a black coffee mug that could hold a softball. THE MACHINE SEES EVERYTHING was printed across its broad expanse in a digitalesque font. "I wouldn't," she said.

"Wouldn't what?"

Jamie emptied half of the coffeepot into her mug. "The blueberry muffin. It's Sasha's. You really don't want to get between that woman and her breakfast."

His fingers shifted targets. "Thanks for the heads-up."

"No, not the old-fashioned. That's Bob's."

"What about the bagel?"

"Olaf's."

"The cruller?"

"Mine," she said, plucking it from the box and setting it by her mug.

He stopped himself from grabbing it back and looked down at the box. "Is there anything here that someone doesn't have dibs on?"

She peered into the box, then tore open three sugar packets at once over her mug. "I think that jelly donut's up for grabs."

"I hate jelly donuts. There's nothing else?"

"Nope." She grabbed the cruller and a napkin in one hand, her coffee in the other, and waved him out of the way. "Guess you should've been here earlier."

"I was the first one here," said Mike.

"I meant earlier in the project," she called back from the hallway.

He finished his cereal, debated the jelly donut, and decided against it. He walked the halls, wondering when the scientists started their day. He wasn't sure if there was any sort of daily schedule. He'd need to ask Arthur about that.

The control room was still locked. His key card didn't work on it. Something else to ask Arthur about.

He wandered down to the main floor and found himself standing before the twin rings of the Albuquerque Door. The only sound was a faint crackle of cold from the nitrogen tanks. A spot of color on the floor moved, a roach scurrying back under cover.

Ten minutes ticked by on the clock in his head.

He walked back to the kitchen. The box of donuts and muffins was gone. The coffeepot was empty, but the machine gurgled as it worked on a new one.

Mike went back to the front desk. The receptionist, Anne, was speaking to someone on the phone. She smiled at him, held up a finger, and finished her call. "Good morning," she said. "Did you get settled in last night?"

He nodded. "All things considered." He glanced around the lobby. "I don't suppose you know where everyone is?"

She glanced past him. "The conference room, I think. They're always in there on Wednesday mornings."

Mike bit back a sigh. "Where's that?"

Anne checked her screen and stood up. "Come on. I'll show you." She led him back down the hall. Her hair reached all the way down her back, he realized. It was smooth and straight, like a silk scarf or shawl. He'd had one or two students who'd tried using their hair as a living accessory, but none of them pulled it off as well. Combined with her eyes, her hair made jeans and a collared shirt look elegant.

They stopped at a door across the hall from the kitchen. Anne rapped twice, and Arthur's voice echoed a greeting from inside. She gave Mike a quick smile and headed back to the front. He opened the door.

The conference room was dominated by a long table and several swiveling chairs. A flatscreen hung on the wall near the door. The far wall held two of the rare windows that marked the front of the building.

The team sat around the table, filling every chair except the one at the far end. Mike glanced at the men and women, then singled out Arthur at the head of the table. "What's this?"

There were a few glances around the table. Bob took a long, slow sip of his water, while Neil became engrossed in the two lines written on his notepad. Arthur cleared his throat. "It's our weekly review and brainstorming session."

"Oh," said Mike. There was another pause. "Am I not supposed to be here for some reason?"

"I'm sorry," Arthur said. "It just slipped my mind. We're not used to having someone watching over our shoulders."

Olaf coughed while Jamie sketched something in the corner of her own notepad.

Mike nodded. "Do you mind if I sit in?"

"We're wrapping up, actually."

"Okay. Anyone willing to share notes?"

More uncomfortable glances flitted around the table.

He sighed. "Look, I know none of you believe this, but I'm on your side. Reggie Magnus doesn't want to see you shut down. He needs an informed second opinion. That's it. But if nobody tells me anything, then I have to go back and tell him I didn't hear anything that reassured me."

"You saw the Door," said Olaf. "It works. What more do you want?"

"I want to know history. Maybe some design. A little bit of the science behind it."

"You wouldn't understand it."

"I might."

"We can get you some of that," said Arthur. "Neil could give you a tour of the machine." He looked to the bearded engineer for agreement.

"No problem," said Neil. He abandoned his notepad and rolled his chair out from the table.

"That'd be great," Mike said.

"Jamie," Arthur said, "could you show him Johnny?"

"Yeah, sure. Find me later this afternoon."

Mike bobbed his head. "What about records of all the crosswalks so far? Could I get those?"

Arthur glanced at Jamie again. She nodded. "I've got the basic reports somewhere, yeah," she said.

"Will that do for now?" asked Arthur.

"That's great," said Mike. "Thank you."

"I'll be in my office if you need anything else. The rest of you have your schedules."

The chairs rolled and spun as everyone got up. Mike caught a simmering glare from Olaf and then turned to find the bearded engineer standing next to him. "Hi," said Mike. "Neil, right?"

"Yep. Sorry we didn't talk yesterday." They shook hands and walked out of the conference room.

"No problem. I'm trying to ease my way in, as you probably noticed."

Neil's lips twisted into a grin. "Good luck with that. You're the enemy, remember?"

"So I've heard. You worked on the Z Machine, out in New Mexico, didn't you?"

He gestured Mike down the hall. "With Gerry Yonas, yeah. You know your big machines, Mr. Erikson."

"Just Mike. One of the only things I had to read on the flight out was everyone's bios and work histories."

"Good memory, then."

"One of the best, so I'm told."

"Yeah. Bob wouldn't shut up about you."

"You guys were talking about me behind my back? How sweet."

The chief engineer swiped his card and pulled open the heavy door. "There's a bar up the street some of us go to after work sometimes. You were the main topic last night."

"Any details left I can fill in for you?"

"Is all the stuff he was saying true?"

"Yes it's true. I've only seen two episodes of *Game of Thrones* and never saw any of *Breaking Bad* or *True Blood*."

Neil smirked. "The other stuff."

Mike shrugged. "That's probably all true, too, but it's not half as interesting, believe me."

They paused, and Mike could see the rings just beyond a rack of electronics. Bob rolled a toolbox toward the rings while Sasha took a socket wrench to one of the off-white panels. The golden text on today's T-shirt proudly declared her to be Starfleet Academy's cadet of the month.

Neil turned to face him. "So how's it work?"

"How do you mean?"

"When I was a kid I read a book about a guy with photographic memory. He described it as this huge set of encyclopedias that he could page through."

Mike nodded. "I've heard it described that way. It's just . . . memory. How do you remember stuff?"

"Usually with a lot of repetition."

"Right," said Mike. "But once it's in there, do you do anything special? It's not in your conscious mind right now, but if I ask you when your birthday is, you know, right?"

"August twenty-third."

"So how'd you know that?"

Neil shrugged. "I just pulled it out."

"That's all it is for me. I just pull stuff out. Except I can pull out anything I've ever seen or heard."

"Can you tell me who won the nineteen fifty-five World Series?"

Mike sighed and black ants skittered around in his mind. "No."

"Why not?"

"I still need to know something first. I'm not a sports guy, and it's not like I try to read every article on Wikipedia in my spare time."

"I would," said Neil with a smile.

"No," Mike said, "believe me, you wouldn't."

Neil clicked his tongue and nodded. "Okay, then. What about school stuff? Who was Zachary Taylor's vice president?"

"Millard Fillmore. He took over when Taylor died in office, so he never had a vice president himself."

"*Hamlet.* What's the first line of act three, scene four?"

"The Queen's Closet scene," said Mike. "Polonius says, 'He will come straight.'"

"The Bible? Book of Judges, chapter twenty-three?"

"Is that a trick question? It's not school stuff, and there are only twenty-one chapters in Judges."

The engineer shrugged and grinned. "I was just pulling numbers out of my butt, to be honest. Ready for your tour?"

"Please," said Mike.

The rings loomed before them. Bob and Sasha had removed a few of the plastic shell sections and were unbolting a large coupling. A replacement sat on the steel walkway near them, glinting in the light.

Mike glanced back. "Can I get closer?"

"Sure. You don't have a pacemaker or any surgical pins, do you?"

"None that I know of."

"Cool. Even shut off, this thing gives off a pretty strong magnetic field. About three and a half Tesla. It'd feel a little weird."

"And when it's turned on?"

"Then there's effectively two fields fighting each other. Remember that scene in *X-Men,* when Magneto rips all the iron out of the guy's blood?"

"Ouch." Mike bit back the instinct to correct Neil and point out the scene had been in the second movie. Fifty-seven minutes into it.

"Yep." Neil swung his hand along the swath of paint on the floor. "It's not quite that bad, but if we're up and running and you step past the white line there, you'll know it. We need to replace components constantly because the fields ruin them."

"How much can you tell me about their construction?"

"What do you want to know?"

"Everything, I guess."

"I can't tell you much about how it works, just about how it's built. Although there's a lot I'll have to skim over because of our agree—"

"I know." Mike waved his hand. "Just tell me what you can."

Neil nodded. "The core of each one of the rings is composed of depleted uranium," he said. "It's a mass-density thing. Not really part of my field, but very important. There's almost a ton of it between the four rings. Can't tell you much more about that."

"Don't worry about it."

"Cool. The core is sheathed in lead, which serves as our superconductor base material. Those silver tubes there and there? That's where the liquid nitrogen circulates in and out."

Neil pointed at the area where Bob and Sasha had removed the off-white plating. "The next layer you can actually see there, right under the carapace. That's the copper wiring. ETP copper, ninety-nine-point-nine-seven percent pure, single strand, four gauge. We have to special order it, and there's almost six miles in each mouth, letting them—"

"Mouth?"

Neil nodded. "These two rings are our mouth. The other mouth, two identical rings, is over in Site B. For the record, the two sets are almost perpendicular to each other, but that has nothing to do with how the bridge forms. It was just space restrictions in each building."

"Got it." Mike nodded. "Why call them mouths?"

"Mouth of a tunnel. You couldn't work that out?"

"Sometimes I just like asking questions."

Neil smirked. "As I was saying, just shy of six miles of copper wire in each mouth, allowing them to generate a continuous electromagnetic field in the forty-six Tesla range, about thirteen times what your standard MRI machine does."

"Is that big?"

"The only comparable magnets are at the National High Magnetic Field Laboratory. They've got a hybrid that's a bit smaller, strength-wise, but it's continuous. The best we can manage with our arrangement is just under two minutes. Ninety-three seconds. When this baby's turned on, it eats up about one-point-four megawatt hours in ninety-three seconds."

"*Megawatt* hours?"

"Yeah. According to Olaf, when the Albuquerque Door is open, it uses as much electricity per minute as the island of Manhattan. I think he's exaggerating a bit, though."

"Not really an energy-efficient way to travel."

Neil shrugged. "Neither are SUVs, but that hasn't stopped anyone. Besides, if Arthur and Olaf are right, energy usage is a constant. It has nothing to do with how far you travel."

"So it costs the same amount to go to Site B as it does to go to Tokyo," said Mike.

"Yeah. Or the Moon. Or the Andromeda galaxy. The only real limit is how long we can keep the rings chilled. If all the funding goes through, we're going to try setting up the other mouth in D.C."

"Jamie mentioned that you get power spikes."

"We did until I built those." He gestured at a trio of solid boxes, each the size of a small refrigerator. "They've cut down on them a lot. Believe it or not, they're just huge resistors. We had to custom build them to keep induction and noise to a bare minimum."

"Why are the rings that size?"

"What do you mean?"

Mike gestured up at the machinery. "The inside diameter's just over seven feet, yes?"

"Two hundred twenty-one and a half centimeters," called out Sasha.

"Right," said Mike. "But why aren't they three hundred or five hundred? Why not build one big enough to drive a truck through?"

She shrugged. "Because that's how big the blueprints said to make them."

"Olaf worked out the math for a larger Door," said Neil. "This size was the most efficient for our work. It's a balance of power requirements for the electromagnets and the size of the field they generate."

Mike nodded. "And you're sure it's safe?"

"One hundred sixty-eight tests so far and not one problem."

"How many jumps with people?"

"All of them. We started from zero again, once we began testing humans."

"So how many tests altogether?"

"About four hundred with animals or people," said Neil. "There were a bunch with test objects, too, and some dry runs. Olaf or Bob could tell you exactly."

"Is it always one of you?"

"At first it was, yeah. As of late, we've been opening it up a bit."

"Yesterday, Olaf said nine people had jumped."

"That could be right."

"The six of you, Reggie Magnus, his assistant."

"Yup."

"And then Ben Miles."

"Yup." Neil examined the floor. "Sad what happened to him."

Mike let the words hang for a moment and gazed over at the big rings. "There's no chance going through did it to him?"

"Going through . . . the Door?"

"Yeah."

Neil shook his head. "No. None at all. It's perfectly safe. Everyone has multiple exams after every crosswalk."

"You've got a doctor on staff?"

"Local doctor," said Neil. "Just down the hill from us. He doesn't know what we're doing, but he's still signed a bunch of nondisclosure forms."

"Did Ben get checked out?"

Neil nodded. "I drove him down there, in fact. Nice guy. His tests all came back good here. He had his second set done back in Washington just after his . . ." He searched for the right word. "His breakdown?"

"Yeah," said Mike.

"He had a full physical done out there and all the results sent to us. I think they've done it two more times since he's been in the . . . the hospital. All clean, all good, as I understand it."

"Is that normal? That many tests."

"They did an extra set because of the circumstances. Everyone gets checked out within six hours of going through, then two more times in the next two weeks and once more at two months. We had everyone under forty-eight-hour observation at first, but Arthur's cut it back since we've had a hundred crosswalks with no side effects." He gave Mike a pointed look. "Think he saved about four hundred thousand in the budget when he did."

"As I understand it," said Mike, "the amount of the budget isn't the big issue they're having back in Washington."

"Well, you could still bring it up."

Mike smiled as they circled back around the machine to Bob and Sasha. They'd disconnected one of the hoses running from the tanks and were working on the connector with a set of ratchets. "One other question, if you don't mind?"

"Sure."

"Why are you replacing that?"

"What?"

Mike pointed at the component in Sasha's hand. "That connector. Socket. Whatever you call it. Why are you replacing it?"

"It's on the list," she said.

"But why?"

Sasha sighed and stepped away to pick up a clipboard. She skimmed through a few pages and then shrugged. "Reason's left blank," she said. "It was probably leaking."

Neil looked at Mike. "Is there a problem?"

He shook his head. "I'm just curious why you're replacing it."

Bob shrugged. "Things wear out. It was probably leaking."

"It wasn't leaking," Mike said.

"No offense," Sasha said, "but how would you know?"

He glanced up at the double rings. "Because I was watching when you turned it on yesterday. There wasn't anything."

"You might've missed it," said Neil. "You were up in the booth."

Bob glanced down at the coupling in his hand. Sasha shifted her feet and crossed her arms. Neil rolled his shoulders. The three of them exchanged looks.

Mike looked at the coupling for a minute. The ants churned in his brain, but he forced them apart. "Yeah, sorry," he said. "Sorry. You guys know this stuff better than me."

Bob smiled. "Well, I don't know about that."

Sasha tapped him on the back of the head. "Speak for yourself."

THIRTEEN

Jamie unlocked the deadbolt, then swiped her key card. The door clicked and she swung it open. A gust of cold air rolled out and chilled Mike's legs. "Meet Johnny," she said.

The room was eight feet on a side. The walls were lined with industrial shelves, the Erector-set looking ones from stores like Home Depot. Computer towers filled each shelf. Cables ran back and forth behind each one. The air in the room shivered from the constant hum of fans and the buzz of the air conditioner.

"Six units on each shelf," said Jamie. "Twelve shelves total. They're all overclocked, so we're effectively running at ten trillion operations per second."

"Why Johnny?"

"*Johnny Mnemonic*," she said. "Old Keanu Reeves movie I saw in high school. It doesn't hold up well at all, but I loved the name."

"TriStar Pictures, nineteen ninety-five. Based off the William Gibson novella. Didn't do well at the box office, or with most critics, but I thought Dina Meyer was pretty hot in it."

"Whatever. Anyway, the system was designed to run at eight hundred teraFLOPS, but I've made some tweaks over the past three years so I think we're actually closer to one petaFLOP. I wanted to submit it for the Linpack Benchmark Top500, just to get a solid measurement, but Arthur didn't want the publicity."

"Must've been a little frustrating."

She shrugged. "He pointed out that once we go public, Johnny's going to become the most well-known computer on Earth anyway."

Mike looked around the room. Most of the towers were the standard flat white, but a few tan and black ones were scattered through the room. He resisted the urge to find a pattern in their placement. He asked Jamie instead.

"We had to do this on the cheap," she said. "It was just whatever housings I could find." She watched his eyes. "Are you memorizing all of this?"

He glanced at her. "I can't switch it on and off. It's just the way my brain works."

Her lips tightened. "So you can't help spying on us?"

"I'm not here to spy on you," he said.

She looked away. "Any other questions?"

Mike gestured at the shelves. "So all this runs all of the Albuquerque Door?"

Jamie shook her head. "No, all it does is the math for each trip."

"That's it?"

"The Door program is over two million lines of code. The folding equations alone are over a thousand pages if you printed them out. Over five hundred thousand lines of math, most of them depending on a number of variables in the system."

He smiled. "Are you supposed to tell me all that?"

"If you can figure out our code from the page lengths, you deserve to bust us."

"Bust you?"

"Find out our secrets," she said. "Steal our tech. However you want to put it."

"I'm not going to steal anything. Honest."

She waved him out of the room. They stepped back into the hall and she locked the deadbolt behind them. "Can I get back to work now?"

"Why the extra lock if it's already got the key card?"

"To keep out government guys who might want to look at our code," she said. "Also because Bob plays too many practical jokes for his own good. Every day he can't get at Johnny is a day I don't need to beat him to death."

"So, what's the answer?"

She blinked. "What do you mean? Answer to what?"

"The answer to the equation," he said. "Is it forty-two? Is it four-eight-fifteen-sixteen-twenty—"

Jamie cut him off with a wave of her hand. "We never see the answer. Even if we did, it's just another equation about a hundred pages long. That's what gets fed into the Door."

"But what is it?"

She stared at him for a moment. "In simple layman's terms," she said, "it's a mathematical representation of an alternate quantum state or 'dimension' that meets our requirements."

"And in non-layman's terms?"

"You'd need to ask Arthur or Olaf. I'm just the computer chick." She turned and walked down the hall.

He stepped quick to catch up. "If you've never seen it, though," he asked, "how do you know it's solving the equation?"

"Because the Door opens. Are you always this difficult?"

Mike shrugged. "Only when I'm trying to get answers."

"Well you're not getting any more from me," she said.

"Actually, Arthur said you had copies of the trial reports."

She sighed. "Yeah, he did, didn't he?" She veered into a side hall, not asking him to follow and not looking to see if he did.

They headed out of the main building and down to the trailer park. "So," he said to her back, "how'd you get involved with this?"

She glanced back. "Huh?"

"The Albuquerque Door. Did you answer an ad or did you know someone or what?"

"Arthur recruited me. Which you know from my files."

"You like working with him and Olaf?"

"Beats working at a bank."

"Do you guys all tend to eat lunch together, or do you—"

Jamie stopped and turned on him. Mike tipped forward but stopped himself before he ran into her. "What's this about?"

"What's what about?"

"All the questions you already know the answers to."

"I'm trying—"

Her eyes flashed. "Are you trying to get me to implicate Arthur or something, because I won't—"

"I'm just trying to make small talk," he said. He gave her the Look. It almost faltered when he realized he was using teacher-student tactics on a woman only three years younger than him.

Jamie fought the Look, but it hit a nerve somewhere. She seethed, but she backed down. "Sorry," she said, not sounding that sorry.

"Don't worry about it," he said. "I'm sorry if you thought I was questioning your loyalty or something. I was just trying to be friendly. And find somewhere to have lunch. That's all."

They stood there for a minute.

"We're not doing anything wrong," she said.

Mike considered a few possible ways to respond. He weighed them against what he knew so far about her. It felt lame, but the best he could come up with was, "I know."

"Don't screw us over."

"I'm on your side, remember? I'm here to make sure you get funding."

"Then make them understand that this is going to change everything," she said. "We know it. Magnus knows it. You know it. That's why it has to be perfect."

"I get that. I'm just trying to . . ."

Jamie turned and continued down the path past Tramp's grave. Their feet crunched on the gravel, rustled against the fake grass, and led them to her trailer.

"More locks," he said as she unlocked the door.

"Yeah, I'm old-fashioned that way."

"No, I mean . . ." He paused. "I get the security up in the lab, but why lock up down here?"

"I know you probably leave everything unlocked back in New Hampshire, but this is a city."

"Maine. And this isn't really a city. It's a fenced-off government facility with guards. It's not like random muggers or thieves are going to get in here."

"It's my home," she said. "Why wouldn't I lock up my home?"

"I . . . never mind. Sorry."

She turned her back to him and vanished inside the trailer. He took the open door as an invitation.

The small space was a flurry of paperwork and technology. Notes, memos, and reports rested in great dunes across her desktop, spilled off the two large, flanking corkboards to cover the walls, and formed small drifts across the floor. She'd hung a few curtains to separate her bed from the rest of the room, but he could see more loose papers scattered there as well. The pressboard bookshelves were stacked haphazardly, with only the barest attempts at organization. Random sheets of paper were sandwiched between the various volumes. A hardcover copy of *The History of What We Know* was flanked by Douglas Hofstadter's *Fluid Concepts and Creative Analogies* and a sun-faded *Machine Man* graphic novel. An old book with gold print on a leather binding was wedged into the shelf on top of them, *Electric Currents—Their Generation and Use*.

Mike glanced at the two computer towers lying half-autopsied on her kitchen table. One had a bag of chips in it, the top held shut with a binder clip. A stack of motherboards rested on the chair in Mylar bags.

"Maid's been on vacation, I see," said Mike.

"Yeah. She ran off with the guy who writes your jokes."

"Ouch."

"There's a postcard from them here somewhere. Want me to look for that instead?"

"No, no. Just the logs will be fine."

Something twitched and stretched on top of the bookshelf. A white paw reached out and spread, flexing an array of sharp, untrimmed claws.

"Glitch," said Jamie, following Mike's gaze. "He was here when I moved in, and he decided I could stay after his first can of tuna."

"Glitch?"

"Second day I was here, he ran across my keyboard and ruined forty-two lines of code."

Mike nodded. "Glitch it is."

The cat blinked at him, focusing its bright green eyes for a moment, and then went back to sleep.

Jamie yanked a dozen sheets of paper from her desk, then a few more from the walls. She thumbed through them, marched back to her bed, and crouched down to dig through the papers there. Her jeans slid down a few inches in the back, revealing a skintight pair of high-waisted blue bicycle shorts. Her backside was nothing but glossy blue spandex.

She glanced over her shoulder. "You want animal tests and simulations, too?"

He shrugged and tried not to look at her ass. "I'll take whatever you're allowed to give me."

She straightened up and returned with two dictionary-sized bundles, adding them to the pile. "I think that's everything except Olaf's trip yesterday. That one's still up in the lab or in Arthur's office." She half-shoved, half-dropped the lot into his arms.

"Thanks." He stood there for a beat and the ants catalogued the files. "I'm surprised how much paperwork you use here. I mean," he hefted the logs, "actual paper."

"It's a security thing," said Jamie. "People can't hack a manila folder."

"No, I get that, it just seems a little . . . I don't know, inefficient? Especially with the size of some of the stuff you're talking about."

"It is what it is. Did you need something else?"

"No, this should do it."

"Okay. You can go now." Her arm swept toward the door.

"Right. Sure. Thanks for the files."

Jamie closed her eyes. "Sorry. Again."

"Don't worry about it. Again."

"I know this is your job, and I'm sure you're a nice guy—"

"You know, those words always hurt."

She smirked. "—but we don't need this right now. We don't deserve it. We haven't done anything wrong. The Door works. We just need more time for testing."

"So everyone keeps telling me," he said.

FOURTEEN

Mike stepped into his trailer and realized he had nowhere to put the armload of reports. He'd assumed he'd be able to rough it in the Spartan apartment for a few weeks, but that wasn't going to be possible. If nothing else, his back wasn't going to take more than two or three nights on the cot.

He set the stack of files on the thin mattress and made a quick mental list. Table. Two chairs. Small bookshelf. Small refrigerator. Toaster. Microwave. A small bed or maybe a futon that could double for a couch. Sheets and maybe a blanket. He could fit some of it in his rental car, but not all of it. He'd have to hope for delivery.

Mike turned his attention back to the files. The red ants and black ants were swarming in his mind. They'd been scratching since the meeting in Washington, since they'd heard the first theories and ideas. Seeing the machine and the blueprints had only excited them more.

It could wait. He could go find a store, get some dinner, and spend the evening setting up his temporary home. Dive into the files in the morning.

The ants itched at the inside of his head.

He headed back out and up to the parking lot. Bob had mentioned some shops in the area, and he'd passed a few on his way in from the airport. He was sure he could find something.

The redhead was standing by the front gate talking with the guards. He gave Mike a half wave, finished up with the uniformed men, and sauntered over. "Olaf drive you away already?"

"Haven't dealt with him one-on-one yet."

"So it was Jamie, then."

"Actually, it was you," said Mike. "You were right. I need some furniture if I'm going to live back there for a few weeks."

"Need some help?"

Mike raised an eyebrow. "Are you offering?"

"Nah. I just like to ask people if they need help and then watch their hopes get crushed."

"Thanks."

"I kid, I kid," Bob said. "Did you want to get something big, like a couch or a bed? I could check out the pickup we use for hauling stuff between the main building and Site B."

"That would be fantastic. Thank you."

"Don't mention it. I'm just sucking up so you'll give me Olaf's job when you get everyone else fired."

"I'm not getting anyone—"

Bob held up a hand. "Relax, man. It's just a joke."

"Sorry."

"Let me go sign out and grab the truck. I'll meet you back here in . . . ten minutes?"

Twelve minutes later they were rumbling down the road. The pickup was a huge, rusted beast, a relic of a time before the term "fuel efficiency." According to Bob, they'd picked it up for under a thousand dollars. Mike didn't find it hard to believe.

"So, I have to ask," said Bob, "how often do you hear the 'young Alan Rickman' thing?"

"Often enough," he said, "although it's mostly kids, so it's usually phrased as 'young Severus Snape.'"

Bob laughed.

"How often do you hear 'Ron Weasley'?"

"Not as much as I did in high school, thank God." He shook his head. "I shaved it all off junior year, about five years before bald became trendy. Spectacularly bad decision for a kid heading for class salutatorian." He flipped the directional and swung them into a turn lane. "Six months of everyone calling me Lex Luthor."

Two and a half hours later, Mike had a truckload of new furniture pieces with quasi-Swedish names to assemble. Bob helped him pile it all in his trailer, then loaned him a small toolbox to help assemble the futon frame.

Mike looked at the pile of bags and boxes. The reports still sat on his cot, and the sight of them made the ants seethe in his mind. He brushed them away. "I think I owe you dinner, at least."

"Nah. It was no big deal. And if it puts you in a better mood while you're here, it works out for everyone."

"I insist. Besides, I need someone to show me a few good places to eat."

"I can go with you, but don't worry about feeding me."

"Technically," Mike said, "Reggie's feeding both of us."

"If you put it that way," said Bob, "I wouldn't want to risk offending the man in charge."

They ended up at a pizza place just down the street from the main building. It was a strip mall restaurant with bare-bones Italian atmosphere. Menus were examined, orders placed, and they sat back in their booth to wait for their drinks. Bob studied Mike across the table.

"So why are you here?"

"You said the pizza was good."

Bob smiled. "Why are you *here*? What are you really looking for?"

Mike shrugged again. "What do you think I'm going to find?"

The waiter came back with a lemonade for Mike and a Pepsi for Bob.

"I think," Bob said, "that a person can always find what they're looking for, whether it's there or not. They'll just see what they want to see."

"Fair point," said Mike, "but all I'm looking for are ways to reassure Reggie so he can reassure all those other people who need to sign off on your budget."

Bob put his glass up to his lips and swallowed twice.

"Is there some reason I wouldn't find that?"

Bob shrugged. "What did Magnus tell you to look for?"

"Nothing," said Mike. "Everyone in Washington was already on edge when Ben Miles had his . . . breakdown. Reggie just wants me here so I can confirm everything's going great."

Bob took a noisy sip from his straw and stared at Mike some more. "Really?"

"Yeah."

"Cool."

"You believe me?"

"We're not doing anything wrong," said Bob. "We've got nothing to hide."

Mike felt the corner of his mouth twitch. "Except all the stuff you insist on hiding."

"Look," said Bob, "I'm not going to give you my ATM code, but that doesn't mean I've got a ton of drug money or something in my account. Everybody's got secrets, and they've usually got perfectly good reasons to keep them."

"True."

"We all know this isn't the normal way things get done," he said, "but this isn't a normal project. You saw it. This changes everything. Is it that weird that we want to keep an iron lock on everything until we're one hundred percent sure it's ready to go?"

"What if someone jumps the gun and just announces it?"

"If they're not going to fund us, why would they announce it?"

"Just a hypothetical situation."

"None of those suits or soldiers are going to go public without solid proof. They'd take a huge credibility hit, probably end up running a Taco Bell or something."

"What if they force you to reveal it?"

"Arthur's got a team of lawyers on speed dial, just in case. Unless they send in the Army—like, actual guys with guns and tanks—they can't force us to do anything."

The pizza arrived. It was a good size for the price. The waiter added a basket of bread and apologized that he hadn't brought it sooner.

Mike freed a pair of slices and slipped them onto his plate. "Can I ask you something?"

"Sure."

"Straight question, straight answer?"

Bob smiled. "I'm still not giving you my ATM code."

"Who put you up to this?"

The smile faltered. "I don't know what you—"

"Come on," said Mike. "Straight question, straight answer."

Bob's smile returned. It wasn't quite as wide, but it was more honest. "Arthur," he said. "Although Neil suggested it."

"Not so hard, was it?"

"What gave me away?"

"Oh, come on. You offered to spend your free time helping me move furniture. There are people I've worked with for years who won't do that."

Bob chuckled. "Yeah, I guess it was a little much."

"Did they give you a list of things to casually drop into conversation?"

"Nah. They just wanted me to be friendly."

"Really?"

"Yeah. Neil was worried we'd gotten off on the wrong foot with the maintenance thing this morning."

"Ahhh. Thanks for helping," said Mike, "regardless."

"No big deal," said Bob. "Straight question for you?"

"Go for it. My pin number's nine-seven-one-three."

"Why you?"

"Reggie's been trying to get me to do some work for him for ages. This was the first thing he ever told me about that interested me."

"Yeah," Bob said, "but why *you*? Even with Miles out of commission, he's got to have a couple dozen guys already working for him who'd be interested in what we're doing. And—no offense—I'd bet half of them have more of the background they'd need to evaluate the project."

"None taken. Like you said, no one's ever done anything like this before. He was probably thinking I'd be able to take in a lot and approach it all without any preconceptions."

Bob used a pizza crust to wipe up some oil on his plate. "Meaning you'll remember everything you see and you've got the brainpower to analyze all of it."

"You could put it that way, yeah."

Bob bit off the end of the crust. "I know he's your friend and all that," he said, "but did you ever think maybe that's the reason he sent you here?"

"That I could steal all your work passively?"

"Yeah."

"Of course I did," said Mike. "But it won't happen."

"Why not?"

"Because that's not what he hired me to do, and I wouldn't do that anyway. I'm just supposed to analyze and make a recommendation."

Bob popped the rest of the crust in his mouth and crushed it between his teeth. "Cool," he said. "If you're just here to reassure Magnus it's all good . . . then we're good."

"Good."

They each ate a slice in silence.

"Actually," said Bob, "can I bounce something else off you?"

"Sure."

Bob set his fingertips on the table and bounced his hands up and down. He bit his lip. "Has Arthur said anything about me? Officially?"

"What do you mean?"

"It's just . . ." Bob's hands shifted. Ten fingers tapped on the tabletop. "Look, in the big scheme of things, I'm still the new guy. I get that. But for the past two weeks or so, everyone's been—"

"Bob," said a dry voice. "Shouldn't you be working on the new ring algorithms?" Olaf stood a few feet away holding a Kindle.

"We finished early," said Bob. He gestured at Mike. "I've been helping him get moved in."

Olaf made a grunting noise.

"Do you want to join us?" asked Mike. He shuffled over a bit in the booth. "We just got our food a few minutes ago."

Another grunting noise from Olaf, this one followed by a sharp sniff. "No, thank you. I prefer to eat alone." He took a few steps across the room and sat at another booth. He put his back to the window so he could stare at them over his e-reader. The waiter brought him an iced tea. He sniffed again and dabbed at his nose with a paper napkin.

"I'm not sure if he's the friendly one or Jamie is," Mike said.

Bob chuckled. "They're not so bad, once you get to know them."

"You play a lot of jokes on him? That's what Arthur says."

The other man shook his head. "Not really. Just one or two. But he got it stuck in his head, and now anything that goes wrong in his life is an elaborate practical joke from me."

"I know a couple people like that. So, you were saying?"

"About what?"

"The past two weeks," said Mike. "You wanted to know if Arthur had said something."

"Oh," said Bob. He glanced over at Olaf. "Yeah, it was probably nothing. Don't worry about it."

FIFTEEN

Mike heaved the futon up and let it drop down onto the frame. The metal pipes rattled. He tossed the pillow at one end, unwrapped the blanket, and called the bed done, for now.

The furniture filled the space just enough so it didn't feel empty. He'd chosen bright appliances deliberately to add some color. The noise of the little fridge and the smell of leftover pizza gave it some life. He'd need to see if there were any spare roach traps, just in case the food attracted them.

The files were on the table now. They were still closed. He'd moved them there when he folded up the cot and pushed it over to the door.

He glanced at his phone. Not even ten o'clock. He was going to be up for another two hours. Maybe more.

Time to start earning his pay.

The geometry teacher at his school, Jack Casey, was a self-confessed alcoholic. Six years sober this summer. He'd told Mike about standing outside bars for half an hour, arguing with himself about going in for "just one drink." He wasn't afraid of drinking, he explained, he was afraid of not being able to stop. It was like a constant stress dream of driving and not being able to hit the brake pedal, no matter how many times he stomped his foot down.

Mike knew just what he meant.

He closed his eyes and took a few breaths to calm his nerves. He found the first report with his fingers. He opened the file and his eyes at the same time.

Mike flipped through the first report. Eight pages. Three and five had text on both sides. Plus notes on the inside cover. Signatures from Arthur, Olaf, and Neil on different pages.

The second report was nine pages. Two double-sided again. Page seven was folded on the upper left corner. The same three signatures.

The third report was eight pages. Four double-sided this time, although one was only three handwritten lines. There was a Post-it note on page six with two lines about processor power, signed with a capital J. Mike flagged the handwriting as Jamie's.

The fourth report . . .

The fifth report . . .

The sixth report . . .

He opened each file, turned each page over, and set it aside. It gave him a steady pace of about two files every minute. His mind worked slower than his eyes took things in, but not by much. Patterns began to develop. He arranged the reports in mental rows and columns. He called up the reports Reggie had given him, the ones he'd read on the flight out to San Diego, and his chart expanded into three dimensions.

The fourteenth report was the first one to not include Arthur's signature.

The fifteenth report . . .

The sixteenth . . .

The seventeenth . . .

There were scattered pictures and diagrams in the reports. Mike constructed a mental model of the main floor with the Albuquerque Door components. He labeled many of them and began tagging them in relation to the different files. He'd need the maintenance logs, too. He could ask Arthur for them in the morning.

The twentieth report . . .

The twenty-first . . .

The twenty-second . . .

The twenty-third report had an extra two pages from Jamie about speeding up calculation times. The forty-second was signed by Sasha instead of Neil. The fifty-first had a coffee-cup stain on the upper right corner. The brown ring matched the circumference of Jamie's oversized mug.

The black ants and red ants roamed free in his mind. Thought and memory. Huginn and Muninn in Norse mythology. They charged at each other and became a seething mass of red and black static. Images and patterns rose and fell in the cloud as Mike made more and more and more connections.

The fifty-seventh . . .

The fifty-eighth . . .

The fifty-ninth . . .

The sixty-third report had a note in the margins from Neil. Bugs were getting into the machinery. Actual bugs. He'd found a few dozen of them in the Site B rings. Mike had never heard of green cockroaches before, and he wondered if they were native to San Diego.

The sixty-fourth . . .

The sixty-fifth . . .

The sixty-sixth . . .

BUGS IN THE SYSTEM

SIXTEEN

Arthur found Mike waiting outside his office door. "Good morning," he said. "Waiting long?"

Mike shook his head.

"Good."

"Sorry to ambush you like this," Mike said, "but I had some questions for you."

Arthur nodded and unlocked the door. "Of course. I'll answer whatever I can, within the limits of our . . ."

Mike waved his hand in the air as they stepped into the office. "I know," he said. "You have a contract with DARPA. I'm not asking about any of that."

"What can I do for you, then?"

"Do you mind if I close the door?"

Arthur's face hardened. It hadn't been soft to begin with. "Why?"

"You're the one who's big on keeping secrets."

He looked at Mike for a moment, then nodded at the door. Mike gave it a nudge and it swung shut, closing with a click.

"So," Arthur said, "what's this about? Another problem with the maintenance schedule?"

"Funny you should ask," said Mike. "At first, I thought this was a big embezzlement scam."

Arthur paused halfway down into his chair. He glared at Mike. "What?"

"Well, half embezzlement, half kickbacks. I'm not sure if there's a legal distinction there."

"You'd better have something to back up these accusations," said Arthur, "because I can assure you being friends with the director won't protect you from—"

"All the maintenance you've got them doing on the floor," Mike said. "Changing tanks and couplings and everything else. But nothing needs to be replaced. You're just switching out one set of working components for another one. Replacing gas tanks that are still three-quarters full."

Arthur shook his head. "All this because they replaced a leaky coupling."

"It wasn't leaking," Mike said.

"No offense," Arthur said, "but how would you know?"

"Because I was watching when you turned it on the other day. There wasn't a leak."

"You might've missed it. We were both up—"

In Mike's mind, yesterday's experiment played out again frame by frame, a procession of black ants carrying pictures. He watched through the windows of the control room and in his peripheral vision he could see three different camera views of the main floor on monitors. Two cameras covered the coupling. He watched it play out again four times, focusing on a different part of the image with each repetition.

There was nothing coming from the connector.

"—in the booth."

Mike tapped the side of his head. "If it happened, I couldn't miss it."

Arthur simmered in his chair.

Mike sat down in the chair across from the physicist. "In a way, the fact that you only use paper for your work would help out a lot in something like that. Everything gets entered piecemeal into a Washington computer, so no one's ever seeing all of it at once, except a few interns who've probably gone numb from the mindless labor."

They stared at each other for a moment.

"I think," Arthur said, "I should have a talk with Mr. Magnus." He reached for his desk phone.

Mike shook his head. "Don't bother. I said I thought it was an embezzlement scam, but it's not. I talked with Reggie first thing this morning, Washington time. I asked for copies of your budget for the past two years. It's shrunk over the past six quarters."

"I know, believe me."

"I also went back over the budget, taking into account the idea that you're just recycling the same components, and everything lines up."

"That must've been some impressive math."

Mike shrugged. "You also have an out-of-date laptop and you drive a cheap car."

"It's not that cheap."

"It is for someone stealing tens of millions. Just the fact that you automatically think of a Dodge as a not-cheap car tells me you don't have piles of cash in your mattress."

"So you decided to dramatically announce that we're *not* stealing millions from DARPA?"

"No. I wanted to make it clear to you that I'm not going to jump the gun and incriminate you or your work."

"But you called Magnus."

"I called him and asked for the budgets. He sent them. That's all."

Arthur leaned back in his chair. "You didn't tell him why you wanted them?"

"No," said Mike. "Here's the catch, though. It's not embezzlement, but it's something. And unless your engineers are a lot dumber than they look, they're all in on it, too. Which means there's something going on here."

Arthur's face hardened again.

"I'm just trying to make a point. You need to start being honest with me, because I will figure out what's going on. If it's something harmless, fine. Reggie won't care. Or maybe he doesn't even need to know. But if it's not . . ."

"Yes?"

Mike leaned back in his own chair.

"Thank you," Arthur said after a moment, "for not running to Magnus with your initial theory."

"You're welcome."

"I know he's worried about things here, and the last thing we need is more suspicion." He leaned forward and tapped his fingers on the desk. Then he leaned back again. "This project involves . . . well, a lot of math. Calculations. Code. Minor engineering tweaks. Most of the people we're reporting to are bureaucrats. Lawyers, businessmen, former military officers. Many of them don't have an appreciation for how much work these things can be."

"I can understand that."

"So we do constant maintenance. Yes, about ninety percent of it is busy work at this point, but it gives us paperwork and material we can wave to prove we've been doing something. It also gives me a reason to keep most of the senior engineering staff on payroll."

"Awfully generous of you."

"The hell it is," said Arthur. "They've signed nondisclosure forms, but people's attitudes change a lot when they're downsized. I don't want to give them all a chance to rethink their loyalties."

"Do you think they would? Rethink their loyalties?"

Arthur thought about it for a moment, then leaned forward again. "I don't know," he said. "A few years ago, I would've said not a chance. Olaf and I have known each other for almost fifteen years at this point. Jamie and Neil have been working with me for eight. But after all these . . . all this secrecy . . ." He looked past Mike to the diagram of the Albuquerque Door on the wall. "Half the time I feel like I'm surrounded by strangers."

"The secrecy was your choice," Mike said after a moment.

Arthur blinked and looked at him. "Not really," he said. "Sometimes things just have to happen a certain way. You know that."

"Maybe."

Arthur shook off his mood. "So, if you're convinced I'm not an embezzler, what can I do to get you out of my office so I can start my day?"

Mike stood up. "When you gave me access to the trial logs, Jamie said they were the basic reports. Are there more detailed versions?"

"Yes, the full travel reports. They cover everything except internal mechanics. Times, power usage, flux measurements. I think we even noted sunspot activity on some of them. There's almost six hundred of them, going all the way back to the first runs with test objects and rats." Arthur reached out and adjusted the plastic Wile E. Coyote on his desk, turning the carnivore's head to the left. "I'll make sure you get them as soon as you're done with the human trials."

"I finished them last night."

Arthur raised an eyebrow. "All of them?"

Mike shifted his shoulders in a half shrug. "There were only a hundred and sixty-seven of them."

"And you reviewed our budgets this morning?"

"Just back to two thousand eleven, but yeah."

"If I didn't know what you could do," said Arthur, "I'd be tempted to call you a liar."

"You still can, if you like. You wouldn't be the first." He shoved his hands in his pockets, then pulled them out. "It's a memory thing. Once everything's in my head, I don't have to deal with any input or output limitations. No turning pages, no eye fatigue, I can just go through all of it as fast as I can think."

"When you're done with this assignment, I really might try to steal you away from Magnus."

"Good luck with that."

Arthur smirked. "I'll ask Olaf to get you the travel reports. Anything else?"

"I think that'll do it for today."

"Good. We were going to run another trial tomorrow, if you'd like to watch."

"Yeah, thanks. Who's going through?"

"I think it's going to be Bob."

SEVENTEEN

"Really?" said Mike. "Never?"

"No," Olaf said. "I've never felt the need."

The room was lined with file cabinets. Ten stood against the north wall, each one four drawers high, and another ten against the south. Three of them stood across from the door, placed not to interfere with the others. A clipboard with half a dozen dog-eared sheets of paper hung on the wall next to the door. A small table sat at the center of the room, but no chairs.

"Are you serious?"

"Yes." Olaf flipped to the next key on the ring and tried it in the lock. The tumblers clicked inside the cabinet, and he slid the drawer out an inch to check. He nodded to himself, and inched the key back around until it popped free of the lock. It had DO NOT DUPLICATE stamped into it.

"You must've been tempted," Mike said.

"Not really."

"Not even *Casablanca*? It's one of the greatest films of all time. It's won piles of awards. Made it onto hundreds of lists."

Olaf fit the key back onto a second ring with six others. "How high is your IQ? Supposedly?"

"Pretty high."

"Then this shouldn't be too hard to understand. I'll even say it slowly for you." He stared Mike in the eyes. "No."

"Sorry."

"Don't apologize. Just stop making all this wasted time even more irritating." He slapped the smaller key ring into Mike's hand. "These will open the room and all the relevant cabinets. Files can't leave campus. Log it if you take them out of this room." He pointed at the clipboard.

"Thanks."

"Don't lose those keys."

"I won't."

"You'd better not."

"It's really hard for me to lose things."

Olaf shook his head and muttered something under his breath. He gathered up the small bundle of files he'd walked in with and set his Kindle on top of it. "If you need help, don't hesitate to call someone else."

"Okay," said Mike. He pointed at the Kindle. "Reading anything interesting?"

"*Physics in the Nineteenth Century*," Olaf said. He stalked out of the room and back toward his office.

"Thanks again," called Mike.

He looked at the wall of file cabinets. The ants paced back and forth in his mind. After setting them loose the other night, it was tough to keep them under control. Even more so, since he knew he'd just be setting them free again.

Despite Olaf clutching them for twenty minutes, the keys were cold in his hand.

The individual drawer labels were clear in his mind. The first one he wanted was second from the end on the far left of the east wall. The west wall had blueprints, design specs, and other schematics. It was off limits to him.

Mike sighed and unlocked the first file cabinet. He pulled out a half dozen folders and set them down on the desk. The ants teemed and swarmed out as he swung open the mental doors.

The travel logs were standard to the point of boring. Eleven pages of raw facts and numbers. Another seven or eight pages of written reports from every department followed. The early ones were loaded with a glut of detail, describing everything that went wrong, went better than hoped, or went exactly as expected. There were veterinary reports for all the animals, and doctors' reports once human testing began.

Number 192 made him pause. He went over it three times before shifting focus to 193. Then he compared them. Several of the numbers he'd grown used to were zeroed out. There was no test animal or object listed. Both tests had taken place at midnight. The same with 194.

But 195 was a normal one. Two of the rats had gone through side by side at ten-twenty in the morning. Then there were four more reports at midnight with no numbers. Then normal reports resumed.

Arthur had been the first person through the Door. Report 425/1. Report 426/2 was Olaf. Jamie was next. Hers was just marked 3.

The elaborate chart in his mind grew as he developed new methods of arranging the data. Symbols, colored bars, new axes. He expanded it into a series of three-dimensional graphs that he could cycle through, and overlap at will.

After four hundred and fifty reports, Mike's stomach growled too loudly to ignore. He thought about going to get lunch, but the ants were making too much static. He settled for a walk down to the kitchenette. There was an apple and three cans of soda in the fridge. The pastry box was on the counter, emptied out except for the latest jelly donut. It sat alone in the crumb-filled box.

The ants urged him back to the files. There was still more for them to fight over. He sighed and grabbed the jelly donut with a paper towel. He took a tentative bite in the hallway and artificial raspberry syrup hit his tongue. He made himself take three more bites and felt the sugar buzzing between his teeth and gums. He shoved the last of it in his mouth, licked his fingers, and opened the next file.

As successful human jumps became the norm, the written reports became shorter and more casual. The recent ones were almost-blank pages with a few quick sentences. As far as Mike could tell, the last noteworthy thing had been a series of tests where the travelers carried different timepieces with them. That had been almost seven months ago.

Olaf had immaculate penmanship. Neil dotted his lowercase i's with a horizontal dash. Bob kept a tally of the total distance he'd jumped in the margins of every report he wrote. He wrote it in pencil and then erased it, but the impressions were still there.

Mike closed the last file. His stomach growled again. It had been growling for almost an hour this time. The hallway outside the room was dark. No one had activated the energy-saving lights in a while.

He gathered up the folders on the table, put them back in the drawer, and locked the cabinet. The file room door locked behind him with a thump of steel and magnets. He walked through the hall to the front of the building. The sun was low in the sky. Anne glanced up from the front desk. "All done?"

"I think so. Have you been waiting on me?"

She smiled and looked down at her desk.

"They don't trust me at all, do they?"

Anne smiled again. This one didn't feel as practiced. "If it makes you feel better," she said, "I've been here for almost two years and they barely trust me."

"Worlds better."

She lifted a purse that had been ready to go for at least an hour up onto the desk. "Is there anything else you need?"

He shook his head. "I think I've got everything for the night."

Anne tapped a few more keys. "Okay, then," she said.

"Did you at least get overtime for being stuck here?"

"Of course," she said. "One minute for the alarm."

She waved him to the entrance. They stepped outside, and she locked the door behind them. "I'll see you in the morning," said Anne.

"Two years, and they don't trust you, either?"

"I said they *barely* trust me," she said. "I've got a general idea what's going on here."

"Really?"

She considered him for a moment as they walked down the steps. "There are some advantages to being the pretty woman," she said. "Sasha and Bob come up with reasons to talk to me all the time."

"Ahhhhh," he said.

She smiled again. Another less-practiced one. "They haven't told me anything important," she assured him. "Or if they did, I didn't realize it."

They strolled across the small parking lot, and Mike realized he was walking her to her car. "So how'd you end up here?" he asked. "Did you know somebody or . . . ?"

Anne shook her head. "Temp agency placed me," she said. "I'd just moved down here from LA, and I'd done a lot of work for them up there. Data entry at a magazine, another receptionist gig, that sort of thing. So the local agency gave me this. I was here for about three months, and Dr. Cross hired me full time."

"Los Angeles?"

"Yeah."

"Why'd you move?"

She unlocked her car door and considered him again. Her dark eyes studied his face. "He said we should be careful if you start asking too many questions."

"Sorry," said Mike. "Was he worried I'd find out why you moved?"

She laughed. It was a perfect laugh. Quick, honest, full of life. It was easy to see why Sasha and Bob came up with reasons to talk to her. "I suppose not," she said. She tossed her purse onto the passenger seat. "I lost my brother."

"Oh," he said. A dozen teacher-student protocols flooded his head. "I'm sorry."

Anne saw it in his eyes. "We weren't that close," she said. "Hadn't talked in years, to be honest, even though we lived in the same city. He called me that night, wanted me to join him for a family thing, and I kind of brushed him off. And then he was gone."

There was more to it that that, he could tell, but he knew better than to push. "I'm sorry, again," said Mike.

Her head went up and down once. The practiced nod of someone who'd told a story a few times. "I left LA about a week later. Didn't want any reminders. It was kind of freeing, actually, just dumping half my stuff and moving to a new city."

"I'll have to try it some time."

She glanced down the path toward the trailers and gifted him with one last smile. "Didn't you?"

"I guess I did."

"Good night, Mike."

"G'night, Anne."

She drove off with a wave, and he wandered down the path to the trailers.

He reviewed the logs again in his mind while he microwaved a Lean Cuisine sandwich. He summoned up his ant-constructed model of the Albuquerque Door and added seventy-six new labels. The microwave beeped at him.

He ate his chicken club panini as the trailer got dark. He didn't bother turning the light on. He knew where everything was in the room. And it made it easier to concentrate.

He broke the data down into categories. Every scrap, no matter how mundane it seemed. He organized it in spreadsheets and graphs and columns.

There was a hole in the middle of his data with a spike in it. Three empty reports, one normal, four empty.

Jamie had signed off on all of the empty ones.

The gray phone was still on the floor in the far corner. A plastic menu slid out from beneath it with a list of extensions and names. He shoved the list back, picked up the receiver, and pressed three digits.

The line rang thrice. "Yeah?"

"Hi, Jamie, it's Mike."

"What do you want?"

"I'm fine, thanks. I was going over the logs and I noticed a discrepancy."

"Where?"

"On one ninety-two through one ninety-nine. The numbers seem a bit . . . off."

"Off how?" He could hear her frown.

"Well, they're all blank. There are no numbers."

"What the hell are . . . Where are you?"

"I'm over in my trailer. Are you—"

Jamie hung up. A moment later he heard the muffled crunch of gravel and a fist pounded on his door. He almost reached the door before she barged in. She was dressed in crimson sweatpants, despite the warm night, and wore a hooded MIT sweatshirt with the sleeves pulled down. "Why are your lights off?" She reached past him and flipped the switch.

"I was thinking."

"Think with the lights on, like a normal person. What do you mean, they're wrong?"

"I didn't say wrong. I said off. Aren't you kind of warm in that?"

She ignored the question. "What reports are you talking about?"

"In the one-nineties. I saw them earlier. I was just charting all the data for the trials, and it stood out again, so I thought I'd—"

She glanced around the sparsely furnished trailer and focused on the tablet computer. "Where are those? Let me see it."

"Those . . ."

"Your charts. Spreadsheets. Whatever you did. I need some context."

"Oh," said Mike. "Well, I just did it all in my head."

Jamie's brows relaxed, but her eyelids sank down. "In your head?"

"Yeah."

"Are you fucking with me?"

"No."

"You made charts for six hundred runs in your head?"

He shrugged.

She reached up and covered her eyes for a moment. "Wait." Her hands dropped. "Three blank and then four blank? One in the middle?"

"Yeah."

"That's the timer experiments."

"Okay."

She shrugged. "We were testing a timed operation. It didn't work."

"Timed how?"

"On a timer. It was a dry run on automatic to see how stable the system was."

"Dry run?"

She sighed. "We'd just open the Door. Nothing was going to go through."

"Okay."

"Anyway, whenever we tried to use the timer, we couldn't get the Door to open."

"Hardware or software issue?"

"Hardware."

"What was it? Causing the problem."

She shrugged. "We'd pulled the automatic tests forward. We had enough other work to do, so we just shelved the whole thing to deal with later. Never looked at it. Haven't even thought about it in close to a year."

"So it might be a software issue."

"Noooo," said the programmer, "it couldn't."

"But if no one looked at it—"

"You think I screwed up coding a timer?" Her chin went down.

"No, no, of course not," said Mike. He took a half step back and bumped his new table. "But, no offense, if the Door worked the rest of the time, isn't the timer program kind of the obvious place to start looking?"

Jamie glared at him. Then she turned and stalked out of his trailer. He waited for a moment and then followed. He stepped outside just in time to see her vanish into her own. She left the door hanging open.

A moment later she emerged holding a sheaf of papers. She slapped it against his chest, and one page flipped away and floated to the ground. "There," she said. "Try to find a mistake."

"I didn't mean to—"

Jamie stalked back to her door. "Don't call me after office hours again," she growled over her shoulder as she stepped up into her trailer. "And if you want to play scientist while you're here, at least write your goddamned work down to show people."

Her door slammed behind her.

He heard a creak to his left and saw Neil peering out. Their eyes met. "Sorry," said Mike.

The engineer nodded. "She's going easy on you. It's a good sign." He waved. "G'night."

His door clicked shut and Mike stood alone on the plastic grass.

EIGHTEEN

"So it was a dead end?" Reggie asked.

"Pretty much," said Mike. He tossed his towel over a chair and pulled on his shirt. "She was right. It should've worked."

"You sure?"

"It's a fifteen-page program. A little overcomplicated, really, for what it does. I'd think with her experience she could've pared it down to four or five with no problem."

"Yeah?"

Mike nodded. "It's all C++. And it's a simple program."

"You understand C++?"

"I learned it last night. It's just another language. I found the basics on a few websites, figured out the syntax, grammar, vocabulary." He shrugged.

On the tablet screen, Reggie shook his head and smiled. "Well, I haven't seen any complaints, so I guess you weren't too rough on her. Still wish I'd seen it."

"I thought I was kind of gentle, all things considered."

"So what do you think?"

"About her?"

"About all of it."

Mike buttoned up his shirt. "How much of this have your people gone over? The basic ideas behind the Albuquerque Door?"

"None of it," said Reggie. "There's nothing to go over until Arthur releases it."

"But he and Olaf and the others . . . They've talked about it in meetings and phone calls, right?"

"Yes, of course."

"Have you gone over the transcripts?"

"We've had people diagram the sentences, just to see if we could squeeze a little extra out of their word choice. Nothing."

"Doesn't that strike you as odd?"

"They don't want to tell us anything. They haven't."

"Yeah, but to be able to have numerous conversations and let absolutely nothing slip. Doesn't that seem unusual to you?"

Reggie rubbed his chin. "Maybe."

"If you and I were talking with someone, how long do you think we could hide the fact that we knew each other?"

"How smart's the other person?"

"As smart as you."

"Not too long. I'd pick up on something."

"Right. But you've been talking to these people for years now and you haven't picked up any details about what they're doing. This project is everything, and they've never let a single thing slip that you've been able to catch."

On the tablet screen, Reggie's face grew still. "Are you going somewhere with this?"

"I'm no expert," said Mike, "but it feels like they're playing fast and loose with a lot of their terminology. That might be why you can't get anything from them."

"How so?"

"A lot of the terms they're throwing around—dimensions, quantum states, realities—they use them like they're interchangeable, but I don't think they are, scientifically speaking." He shrugged. "Again, not my field of expertise. That's why I was wondering if any of your people had seen any connections. Or lack of connections, I guess."

Reggie nodded. "I'll have my people check again. Anything else seem odd?"

Mike rolled his neck. "I don't know. Everyone feels a little . . . rehearsed."

"How so?"

"It's like a kid who hasn't done his homework, and he's spent the whole school day planning out what he's going to say as an excuse."

"Canned responses are pretty normal," said Reggie. "I get that a lot."

"It's more than that, though," said Mike. "I had a professor in college who taught a course on the Brontës. He was talking one day about *Villette* and—"

"*Villette*?"

"It's a novel by Charlotte Brontë. I'm making another analogy. Be patient for a minute."

"Charlotte Brontë," muttered Reggie.

"One of the characters in the book spends all her time saying 'I'm fine, I'm just fine, I'm really fine, I'm fine.' And the professor pointed out that anyone who says they're fine that many times is probably really not fine."

"Okay."

"Everyone out here keeps telling me they're not hiding anything," said Mike. "All of them. The only person who didn't try to tell me they're not hiding anything was Anne."

"Anne?"

"The receptionist."

"Ahhhhh," said Reggie. "Okay."

"I think Bob was going to tell me something the other night at dinner, but he closed up when we ran into Olaf."

"Any idea what he was going to say?"

"He asked if Arthur had talked to you about him."

"To me?"

"Yeah."

"No more than anyone else. Did he give you any sort of context?"

"It probably ties to something they were talking about a few weeks ago."

"They meaning Bob and Arthur or meaning the whole staff?"

Mike replayed the conversation in his head. "I'm not sure," he admitted.

Reggie shook his head. "Could be anything, then. Did it match anything in the records?"

"Nothing I've seen, but I haven't gone through the maintenance logs yet."

"Let me know what you find."

"Yeah, of course. Question."

"Shoot."

"Why'd you pick me for this?"

"What do you mean?"

"Why am I here instead of someone else?" asked Mike. "I'm not a physicist or a rocket scientist."

"Says the man who taught himself C++ in a few hours."

"You've got at least eleven people on your staff who are security-cleared and fully qualified to be here. Why me and not one of them?"

Reggie's face shifted. He leaned back in his chair. "Where'd you get that number from?"

"The reports you gave me have already been approved on your end. They've all been signed and half of them have e-mail addresses tagged onto them. Eleven distinct people. They wouldn't get the reports if they didn't have clearance and they wouldn't be reviewing them if they didn't have the background."

"I thought we agreed you'd only use your powers for good?"

"You know the rules," said Mike. "If you don't want me to know something, don't show it to me."

"Fair enough."

"So why me?"

Reggie stared at him through the monitor. "You alone there?"

"It's six-thirty in the morning. Who else would be here?"

"I'm giving you the benefit of the doubt. Answer the damned question."

"Yes, I'm alone."

"You're there because we couldn't find anything."

The ants scurried about with images of reports and memories of Reggie talking and arranged all of them in new patterns. "They're not paranoid," said Mike. "You *have* been trying to steal their tech."

"I can't *steal* it. I'm the one who paid for it. Besides, imagine if Arthur and Olaf died in a car crash or something? I would've been pouring hundreds of millions down a hole with nothing to show for it. Not to mention the greatest invention in human history—gone, just like that."

"You wouldn't get their work?"

Reggie shook his head. "Arthur's contract is ironclad, legally. Nothing about the Albuquerque Door can be released without his approval. That approval isn't transferable or inheritable. An asteroid hits him tomorrow, the project is over."

"How'd your people get into the computers? There's no wireless in the main building."

"They don't have the wireless turned on," corrected Reggie. "It doesn't mean it's not there if you know what you're doing."

"And you couldn't find anything," said Mike. It was a statement.

"Not a thing," agreed Reggie. "No in-house files, no cloud backups, no e-mails, no Facebook posts. They've hidden everything. That's high-level paranoia, even for government employees."

"So I'm here to find a back door for you?"

Reggie shook his head. "You're there to evaluate it, just like I said. And *if* you end up with three-quarters of the project in your head, and *if* something ever happened to Arthur and Olaf . . . then we might have another talk."

"You're going against the contract."

Reggie bit down on a response and took a breath. "I'm not stealing anything," he said, "and I don't want you to steal anything. I'm not releasing anything to anyone, not even to my own staff. I'm bending the terms of the agreement, yes, but I need to know there's a way to get at all this data in a worst-case scenario. That's all. Even if you can just confirm he's writing everything down somewhere and not doing it all in his head, that'd be fantastic."

"Why is everyone against people doing stuff in their head?"

"Because you can't share anything that way."

"True," said Mike. Neither of them spoke for a moment.

"Are we good?"

"Yeah. Sorry I doubted you."

"I'm sorry I didn't explain everything."

"Well, I'm supposed to be the smart one."

"True," Reggie said.

"Is there anything else you need to tell me?"

"About?"

"About all of it. Anything else you're keeping from me or forgot to mention or think you're going to slip past me?"

Reggie smiled and settled back in his chair again. "I've known you too long to slip anything past you."

"Not an answer."

"No, there is nothing else I'm keeping from you. I want you to spend the month there and come back assuring me that I have nothing to worry about with the Albuquerque Door. Or its future."

"Okay," said Mike. "I don't want to lie to anyone."

"Your integrity's safe," Reggie said. "Or as safe as it can be for any government employee."

NINETEEN

"Good morning," Arthur said, looking up from his desk. "I was about to call you."

"Sorry," Mike said. "Talking with Reggie. Mr. Magnus."

"All good things, I hope."

"Some good, some bad."

Arthur waited a moment, and when Mike didn't continue, he nodded. "We're going to be up and running in about half an hour. Bob's already over at Site B."

"He's coming through the other way?"

"There's no difference. None we've ever been able to detect, anyway. It's the same doorway either direction. We just change it up so we have records of all possibilities."

"Ahhh."

"I need to check in with Jamie in the control room and then we can head out onto the main floor." Arthur locked the office door behind them and they headed down the hall toward the stairs.

"I've got a few questions," said Mike, "if you don't mind."

"Go ahead."

"You told the board the Albuquerque Door has never failed."

"It hasn't."

"But what about—"

"You want to know about the one-nineties? Jamie mentioned you'd talked last night."

Mike nodded. "It reads like seven failures to me."

Arthur shook his head. "It didn't fail. We couldn't even get the system to activate."

"Again, that sounds kind of like failure."

"For the Door, failure is a collapse of the magnetic field or a technical glitch. You can't lose a race if your horse was never on the track."

"You can if it was supposed to be out there," Mike said.

"Now you're arguing semantics."

"Pot, meet kettle."

Arthur chuckled. "Point taken." He swiped his keycard and the control room door buzzed open.

Jamie glanced over her shoulder at them, then turned back to her monitors. "I'm defragging some of Johnny's drives," she said. "We should be ready to go on schedule."

"Excellent." He handed her a flash drive. "The changes we talked about."

"I'll get them in as soon as I can."

Mike looked down at the main floor. Olaf and Neil were discussing something in front of the mouth. The godmike wasn't on, so he couldn't hear them. Olaf threw back his head to growl at the ceiling and saw Mike watching. He muttered something to Neil, who looked up over his shoulder at the control booth. They split up. Olaf went to his station, Neil headed across the room to check the oversized resistors.

He turned back just as Jamie held up a finger for silence. "This is Jamie Parker, it's June twenty-fifth, two thousand fifteen, and this is trial run one hundred sixty-nine. Traveler is Bob Hitchcock, which I'm sure comes as a complete surprise to everyone listening to these." She tapped her keyboard.

"Are you good?" asked Arthur.

"Yeah," she said, "I've got everything up here."

He glanced at Mike and gestured at the door. "Shall we?"

"I'll catch up with you," said Mike. "I've got another question or two for Jamie."

She glanced at him and sighed.

Arthur's shoulders hunched a bit. Then he nodded and turned. The door thumped shut behind him.

She turned back to her screens. "What do you want now?"

He bit his lip. "Do you do all the hardware work on the computers here?"

"I work on Johnny, sometimes on the system up here. Sasha or Bob help sometimes, depending."

"What about the office computers?"

She turned to him. "D'you have another problem with something?"

Mike took a slow breath. The ants scurried out with a collection of images and sounds. The student code of conduct. Lecturing his school's quarterback about plagiarism. Slipping Reggie the answers for a pop science quiz junior year. Teachers in the staff room talking in an uninformed way about surveillance and phone lines.

"I think," he said, "you should disable the Wi-Fi on all the computers here."

"It's already turned off."

"Disable it," he said. "Unplug the hardware. Physically remove it."

Jamie studied his face. "Why?"

He pressed his lips together. They looked at each other for a moment. "You were right, by the way," he added. "Your timer wasn't the problem. It was fine."

She furrowed her brows. "Thanks?"

He headed back out into the hall.

Arthur was waiting for him at the bottom of the stairs. "That didn't take long."

"I didn't have much to ask her."

They headed out onto the main floor. The twin rings loomed in front of them. The large flatscreen was on, and showed Sasha and Bob over at Site B. It struck Mike that he still hadn't gone over to examine the other space.

"*Defrag's done,*" boomed Jamie's voice from a speaker. "*We'll be up and ready to go in about five minutes.*"

"Excellent," said Arthur.

"Hey, Mike," said Bob from the flatscreen. "This is your first time seeing the Door work up close, right?"

"Yep."

"Arthur," said the redhead, "can we do a physics test?"

"I think so." He glanced at Olaf.

Olaf grunted and pitched it high enough to sound affirmative.

Mike looked from the screen to Arthur. "Physics test? I saw that on a few dozen reports."

Arthur walked over to the other desk and tugged open the bottom drawer. He removed something and tossed it at Mike, who caught it one-handed. It was a baseball. Not a high-end one. It was dirty, but not scuffed. Dropped, but never hit with a bat.

"*We are up and running,*" Jamie said. "*Ready in four.*"

"It was Bob's idea," said Arthur. "One of those faster-cheaper-better things the government's so fond of."

Mike nodded. "Reggie mentioned this. Mass, acceleration, momentum, angle of descent. Tons of math in every throw and it's apparent if any of it changes in midair."

"Exactly."

"Gauss field is steady," Olaf told his microphone. "Power is good."

"That ball's gone through the Door more than anything or anyone else," said Arthur. "Throw it back and forth with Bob a few times."

"Yeah, c'mon, Dad," Bob said from the flatscreen. "Let's have us a catch before you go to work."

Mike smiled. "So," he asked, "whatever happened to all the test animals?"

Arthur blinked and Olaf looked up from his console. On the flatscreen, Bob's smile cracked and he glanced back at Sasha. "What?"

"All the animals that went through the Door. Two hundred and sixteen rats, six cats, and a chimpanzee, yes?"

"Something like that," said Arthur. "Why do you ask?"

"Just curious."

They all looked at Mike.

"A third of the rats were dissected to check for any structural or anatomical issues," Arthur said. "A third of the others were kept under observation for three months each before dissection. The remainder were allowed to live out their lives. None of them ever showed any signs of damage, even on a cellular level."

"Who did the observations?"

"Graduate students at San Diego State. Double-blind observations. They knew nothing about the Albuquerque Door."

"Statistically," said Olaf, "the Door rats had lower cancer rates than the control group."

"Not notably," said Arthur. "It could've been a fluke. The cats went to a shelter after six months of observation."

"I found homes for three of them," Bob said. "People I knew, so we could check on them, if we ever needed to."

"*Ready in three.*"

Mike glanced up at the booth. "Is Glitch one of them?"

"*No.*" Olaf, Neil, and Bob all answered, but the speakers let Jamie's voice dominate. They glanced at one another.

The hoses from the tanks hissed and frosted over. The temperature in the big room dropped by a few degrees. Mike wasn't sure it was from the liquid nitrogen.

"And the chimpanzee?" he asked.

"Six months of observation," said Olaf. "And then Magnus had him sent to a farm up north."

Mike blinked.

"No, really," said Neil, leaning back in his chair. "There's a big wild-life farm for retired movie animals and some test animals up by Los Angeles. I've gone up to see Caesar twice."

"Caesar?"

On the flatscreen, Bob smiled. "What else do you name a chimpanzee who changes the world?"

Olaf sent a stare at Mike. The temperature went down a few more degrees. "If that's all, we're trying to run an experiment."

"Sorry. Didn't mean to distract you."

"*Ready in two.*"

"No worries," said Sasha from the screen. "Everyone gets a little nervous first time they're near it."

Bob waved at Mike. "You still want to throw the baseball?"

"Yep."

"They don't talk about this part," said Bob, "but I think there's something very soothing about tossing a ball back and forth. I call it the Hitchcock Effect. I think it helps the brain cope with the idea of a fold in space, on a psychological level. That's my opinion, anyway."

"You're not a psychologist," said Olaf. "Your opinion's worthless."

"Olaf's jealous because the effect won't be named after him," Bob said.

"Bob," Olaf said without looking at the flatscreen, "how long has it been since I asked you to shut up?"

"A few hours, at least."

"That explains why it's worn off."

Mike tossed the ball from hand to hand and took a few steps toward the mouth. The air around the rings seemed to waver and twist. Even though the room was cool, it still looked like heat haze. The rear wall blurred. It was still clear at the center of the rings, but the ripples were spreading inward.

"*We've got a solution,*" boomed Jamie. "*Ready in one.*"

"Mike," called Neil, "watch the line."

He glanced down at the white lines. "Am I safe here?"

"You can be standing up on the pathway when it opens, if you like. Just don't cross the line."

The circle of still air inside the ring shrunk more and more. Mike estimated it was two feet across at the most. Then eighteen inches. Then less than a foot. The faint hiss of carbonation began to grow. He couldn't tell where it was coming from.

"Power is good," said Olaf. "Flux density is at full. Opening the Door." He tapped three buttons and the rings sparked and shimmered.

One moment the heat-haze view through the mouth was the back wall of the main floor, about twenty feet past the second ring. It was cinder blocks with at least two coats of white paint. He could see a few conduits running high along the wall and a fire extinguisher hanging on a square hook.

Then, like a television switching channels, a third ring appeared and Bob stood ten feet away, grinning. The pathway stretched back beneath his feet to another ramp. The wall behind him was almost fifty feet away, and now it was sky blue. Equipment and desks filled the space between them. Sasha sat at one of them, checking her own instruments.

"*Field has cohesion,*" said Jamie. "*The Door is open.*"

Bob waved to them from Site B. "Hey."

Mike glanced down at the white lines, then leaned to the left.

"Careful," said Neil.

"I see them." Just past the rings Mike could see the rear wall of the building, right where it was supposed to be. He looked the other way, through the metal and ceramic rings, and saw the wall of Site B twice as distant. "It's amazing."

"Yes it is," said Arthur.

"Hey, rookie," Bob said, smiling. He held up his hands and flexed his fingers. "This is the big leagues now. Show me what you got."

Mike looked at the ball in his hand. "Just toss it?"

"Yep."

He lobbed it through the rings. His eyes followed it through the air, watching for a waver to show him when it went through the Door. He couldn't see anything.

Bob caught the ball with both hands. "Not bad," he said. "Try this one." He lifted the baseball for an overhand throw.

Mike studied its path through the air again. He waited for a glitch, for the arc to shift, for something to happen. Nothing did. The ball bounced off his fingertips and rolled across the floor.

Arthur and Bob chuckled. Olaf smirked. Neil scooped up the baseball and tossed it back to Mike.

"Don't overthink it," said Bob. "It's just throwing a ball."

Mike sent the ball through the rings again. Bob plucked it out of the air and threw it straight back. Mike caught it. It was just like catching a ball tossed across the room. A ball tossed a dozen feet at most. He lobbed it through again, and it slapped against Bob's palm.

"Now you're thinking with portals," Bob said with a grin. "For the record, this ball's going sixteen hundred feet every time we toss it. That's about fifteen miles a minute, so you're pitching a nine-hundred-mile-per-hour fastball."

"What's the world record?" asked Mike. He tried an underhand pitch and watched Bob catch it. Still nothing.

"Depends on how they measure it," said Neil. "Nolan Ryan hit a hundred and eight back in the seventies, but most people say Chapman's hundred and five is more accurate, so he's got the current record."

"Only until we go public," said Bob. He tossed the baseball back to Mike.

"*We have thirty-five seconds left,*" Jamie said from the booth.

"Copy that," said Bob. He gestured to Mike and cupped his hands to catch the last throw. He raised his head as the ball smacked into his hand. "For the record, this is now my eighty-fourth time through the Door. That means half of all the crosswalks made by human beings have been made by me, if you round up. I am guaranteed a place in every history book on Earth."

"Are you coming through?" said Olaf. "If not, I'd like to close the Door so I don't have to listen to you."

"That's your jealousy talking again," said Bob as Mike glanced back at Olaf. "It really—"

Olaf's face shifted. Neil screamed. So did Sasha. And Arthur. Mike spun back to the rings, bumped into the other man on the walkway, and stepped back in surprise. He didn't compensate for the ramp and his foot found empty air. He fell back on his ass and slid to the floor, and the figure on the walkway stepped forward to loom over him.

TWENTY

Mike's first thought was that Bob had rolled his eyes up to show the whites. Students did it in the hall or in class as a joke, sometimes with groaning voices or zombie moans. It was hard to do for more than a few seconds.

He could see Bob's irises because his eyes were wide open, not half-lidded. They were pale and lifeless. The pupil of the left eye was a cloudy blur. The right eye looked around the room. It stared at Mike and dilated wide open. He'd seen the same look from terrified animals.

Bob's skin was yellow, the color of Post-it notes or old pencils. His mouth was a chapped, cracked gash. Half of his nose was gone, and the nostril left behind was a slit at the center of the face. A few patches of red stubble were all that remained of his hair.

Nothing was left of his clothes but rags. His left arm had been twisted into a knot of muscle and bruised flesh. It hung from the shoulder in an odd way. The hand at the end was blurred by a collection of scars. Glistening trails led up his yellow body to open sores.

His left side was soaked with blood. The ragged shirt and pants were almost stained black with it. The mutilated arm was pressed against his torso, covering a wound. Drops of blood splashed against the pathway or passed through the expanded steel to the concrete.

Bob let out a low moan. It stretched out and mixed with Arthur's scream. Sasha yelled something on the other side of the Door. The ants ran it back in Mike's mind three times before he combined the sounds with some basic lip-reading.

Not again!

"Call nine-one-one," shouted Neil. "Somebody call nine-one-one!"

Bob wailed again. The awful sound echoed through the concrete room. He took a few strides down the ramp as he gazed around the chamber.

Mike kicked against the floor and pushed himself away from the scarred man.

Bob lumbered after him. Every step threw him off balance and almost toppled him. His good arm swung up as he staggered forward.

Alarms bleated. Mike looked over and saw Olaf's hand pressed against the panic button. There was a deep thump, a shockwave that rippled through the air as the Door slammed shut and Sasha vanished from sight.

The thing that had been Bob turned its good eye to Mike. The bleached iris shrunk, tried to focus, and relaxed. His knees folded and the yellow man collapsed. He dropped down onto his knees, then tilted back. His skull cracked against the steel ramp. More blood poured out onto the floor.

Arthur stopped screaming. He stood with his hands at his mouth. His eyes went from Bob to the rings and back.

"First aid kit!" bellowed Olaf. He ran to Bob. Neil lunged for the white box mounted behind one of the workstations and ripped it from its bracket.

Bob twitched on the floor. His limbs thrashed, went still, and thrashed again. He took a few quick, rasping breaths. Mike and Olaf tried to hold him steady.

"Jesus, that's a lot of blood," Neil said.

"It's a head wound," said Mike. "Head wounds bleed a lot. It's probably not that bad."

Neil pulled a handful of gauze pads from the first aid kit, tore them open and shoved them at Olaf. They lifted Bob and placed the pads behind his head. They turned red. Olaf applied pressure. Bob opened his mouth wide and hissed.

Mike counted seven sockets where teeth had been just a minute ago.

Neil stared at Bob's arm. "What happened to his skin?"

"It's just the light," said Olaf, glancing at his own tanned fingers.

Bob coughed and looked up at Olaf. He moaned again, and the moan became recognizable words. "No," he said. "No, no, no."

"What happened to him?" Neil's question was tinged with desperation this time.

"It's just the light!" snapped Olaf.

"*We need an ambulance!*" boomed Jamie. "*There's been an accident. We're in the complex on the west side of—*" There was a rumble and a crash as she tossed her headset aside.

Four different first aid classes ran through Mike's head. He wrapped his arms around Bob's legs and lifted them off the floor. "Cover him," he said. "Keep him warm."

"Hang on," said Olaf. "Just hang on."

Bob's gaze slid off Olaf and landed on Mike. His good arm twisted up to grab the other man's sleeve. Their eyes met.

"He's still bleeding," said Neil. "He's bleeding a lot."

"You have to stop them," Bob hissed at Mike. "Don't let them . . ." He coughed on the words and freckles of blood appeared on his lips and remaining teeth.

Mike ignored the blood and leaned in. "Don't let them what?"

Bob kicked again. His other arm yanked away from Neil. His knee slammed up into Mike's armpit. Then his legs tensed up and went board straight. Short breaths whistled in and out of his mouth.

Mike looked over at Arthur. "Chair," he yelled, jerking his chin at one of the workstations. "Get me a chair for his legs."

The project head kept looking from Bob to the rings and back.

"Arthur!"

His eyes locked onto Mike.

"Chair. Now."

Arthur nodded and ran.

The speakers boomed and rattled. "*The ambulance is coming,*" said Jamie.

"We need a blanket," yelled Mike. "Something to keep him warm."

Bob's dead eye stared between Mike and Neil. The good one flitted between each of the three men. When it reached Olaf, it opened wide again. He hissed out a sound. A last word. But it was too faint, too whispery, to be heard.

Then both his eyes rolled up and back.

TWENTY-ONE

"He died in the ambulance," Mike said. "Dead on arrival at the hospital."

Reggie's face frowned on the tablet. It was propped up on the counter so he could look out at most of the trailer. He didn't look like he'd been awake for twenty-two hours. "You heard a cause of death yet?"

Mike paced back and forth. "As of three hours ago, according to Arthur, they're considering it an accident. Blood loss. They said he never regained consciousness, so he probably wasn't in any pain. Any more pain, I guess."

"How did they . . ." Reggie paused. "Did they have any thoughts about his condition?"

"I don't think . . ." Mike stopped pacing, but didn't turn to look at the tablet. "They don't seem to understand that his condition was new. They think he always looked like this."

"That won't last," said Reggie. "As soon as someone looks at his medical records they'll realize something's wrong."

"Hell, as soon as they look at his driver's license."

"Have they called anyone?"

"Arthur said his family's just up in Anaheim. I think the hospital's already informed them. Or the police. Probably the police. That's the procedure when a student gets hurt. I'm guessing they've got something similar."

"I'll hold them off as long as I can," said Reggie.

Mike watched his friend think for a moment. "I guess . . . Should I just go book a flight or do you need to do it?"

Reggie's brow furrowed. "A flight?"

"A flight home."

Reggie stared at him through the tablet.

"I'm done here, right?"

"No, of course not. I thought you were supposed to be the smart one."

"So did I. Between this and Miles, I assumed funding goes away now for sure. At the very least, everything goes on hold for a while."

"Well, you know what happens when you assume."

"Really? You're going to keep it going after all this?"

Reggie shook his head. "There's too much at stake here to just shut it down. And even if they deny further funding, Arthur has enough to keep working for another few months."

Mike sighed. "Great."

"I want you to talk to the coroner. Or the medical examiner. Whoever does the autopsy."

"I'd really rather not watch that."

"You don't have to."

"Thank you."

"But I might ask you to take a second look afterward."

"It's not my field of expertise."

"I'm not one of the rubes. Everything's your field of expertise." Reggie rubbed his temples. "So what the hell happened?"

"I don't know."

"Why not?"

"Because I looked away for one and a half seconds." He closed his eyes and replayed what he'd seen of the crosswalk for the eighty-seventh time. The only view was his own. He hadn't been able to see any of the monitors from up on the pathway, playing catch with Bob. It still felt too soon to be asking the others for the video records.

"Was it because of how often he's done it? Crosswalked? He's done more than all the others, right?"

"Olaf's next closest with thirty-one. But they've all been checked out. If it's a cumulative thing, I have no idea what could be accumulating. Which would mean it's a random thing that's never happened before in over four hundred tests."

A sigh echoed up from Washington, bounced off a satellite, down to a signal tower, and out of the tablet. "So can you tell me anything?"

Mike closed his eyes and replayed Bob's jump again for the eighty-eighth time. "Not right now, no."

"Well, let me ask the ugly question, then."

He opened his eyes. "Was it an accident?"

"Yes." Reggie's eyes flitted to another screen. "'You have to stop them. Don't let them . . .'"

Mike paced back and forth again. "I considered it. Arthur gave Jamie some kind of changes just before they opened the Door. If it was something to kill Bob, they're both idiots for talking about it right in front of me." He shook his head. "I don't think it was deliberate. As far as I know, everyone liked Bob, except Olaf, and even Olaf didn't hate him."

"But Bob was going to tell you something over dinner, and Olaf shut him up."

"That isn't how I'd put it, but yeah."

"Did he ever get back to you about it?"

"No."

"Maybe someone wanted to make sure Bob didn't talk to you. Would kind of fit with him saying, 'You have to stop them.'"

"Maybe. Olaf's got a stick up his butt, but I don't get the sense he's a killer. Plus, there were three other people monitoring the experiment."

"Assuming they weren't all in on it."

Mike replayed the scene again. He started with the last toss of the baseball. Looking away at Olaf, seeing his eyes go wide and his jaw drop. In his peripheral vision, Arthur's eyebrows and hands going up. Hearing the reactions. Swinging his head around and seeing the pale yellow skin and the eyes. Sasha in the background leaping out of her chair.

"Everyone was freaked out and panicking," said Mike. "They didn't know what was going on. If they were acting, they're all in the wrong line of work."

"Maybe they didn't expect it to be so . . . messy."

"For someone who wants this project to go on, you're finding a lot of reasons to shut it down."

"I'm just asking the questions I know the board's going to ask me," Reggie said. "Washington One-Oh-One."

"Maybe that's what he was talking about," said Mike with a shrug. "Stop the board. Don't let them . . . shut us down?"

"Loyal to the very end?" Reggie rubbed his chin. "That's good. I could work with that."

"We don't really know that's what he meant."

"We don't know that it isn't."

"He said something else, too."

Reggie's brow went up. "That's not in your report."

"Because I'm not sure what he said. I didn't want to guess."

"Feel free to guess, as long as it improves our chances of funding."

"I think he said 'mobster.' Maybe 'mobsters,' plural."

"What?"

"That's just it. I'm not sure. His lips were fluttering, he was losing consciousness."

"But he said it to Olaf?"

"He was looking at Olaf," said Mike, "but I'm not sure he was seeing anything at that point."

"And you're sure it was 'mobster'?"

"No. That's why it wasn't in the report. I wasn't sure. Maybe he was calling for his mother. Maybe he was calling Olaf a monster. I'm just not sure."

Reggie rubbed his chin again. "You were right to keep it out of your report for now."

"Thing is, from everything I understand about how the Door works, this shouldn't've happened."

"Are you sure? It sounds like he . . . what did they call it? Humpty Dumpty-ed."

"That was the old project," Mike said, "back when they were working on teleportation."

"Are we sure they're not working on it?"

"Wouldn't make sense. Why declare on the record it can't be done, then do it and claim it's something else?"

"Modesty?"

"Have you listened to these people at all?"

"So he didn't HD?"

Mike shook his head. "The Door doesn't do anything to the traveler. That's why the wound doesn't make sense."

"How so?"

"He had an actual wound. A puncture or a cut in his left side, just under the ribs. I never had a chance to look at it. I think that was a lot of the blood loss."

"What caused it?"

"I don't know."

"Because you weren't looking."

"Don't be an ass. Partly that. But I have no idea what could've injured him. There weren't any jagged edges around him. I was the closest person. Sasha was over on Site B with him, and she didn't say anything. Arthur was next closest and he was five and a half feet from me."

"Could there've been someone else over on Site B? Someone you didn't see?"

"Just beyond the Door? Maybe. They'd have to be really fast to stab him and get out of the way. Not to mention timing it as I just happened to look back at Olaf."

"Deliberate distraction?"

Mike shook his head. "It was just sheer chance I looked back. And that still wouldn't explain everything else that happened to him." He closed his eyes and watched again as his field of vision shifted around onto Bob. Watched the yellow man with pale eyes stumble forward. Heard him moan and collapse.

He opened his eyes and Reggie was staring at him.

"You okay?"

"It's two in the morning and I'm exhausted," said Mike. "And this isn't what I signed up for. Not remotely."

"I'm sorry."

"You know this is ruining my life on a bunch of levels, right?"

"I do."

"It happened right in front of me. Six feet in front of me." The crosswalk played again in his mind. Ninety-one times in just over six hours. Once every four minutes on average.

"I'm sorry," Reggie said again. "I really am. But I need you on this."

"Dammit," said Mike. "I'm an idiot."

"That's reassuring."

"I missed something. We all did, we were so focused on Bob."

"What's up?"

"Let me check this out first. I'll call you tomorrow."

The face on the tablet blinked. "*You* need to double-check something?"

"I told you, I wasn't looking at him when he went through."

"What do you think happened?"

"I'm not sure," Mike said. "But I think I might've just found a clue."

TWENTY-TWO

The sun was peeking over the horizon when Mike went over to the main floor. He found half of the Albuquerque Door team there. Most of the panels had been pulled off the back ring. Neil and Sasha examined components and cables one by one. Neil's eyes were puffy.

Olaf stood behind them and looked over their shoulders. He glanced over at Mike. "Do you need to be here?"

"Just doing my job," said Mike. He looked up and saw Arthur speaking to someone just out of sight—Jamie—in the control booth. "I'm kind of surprised to see you all working."

"We need to find out what went wrong," said Sasha, "before those idiots in Washington decide to shut us down."

"Then we're all on the same page," said Mike. He walked around the rings and studied the floor. There were still dark spots of blood on the pathway, caught in the corners of the expanded steel. There were thin swipes and trails in it where the puddle had been wiped up.

"Hey," he said, "is it safe to get close?"

Neil looked up from the rings and nodded. "We're powered down." He pointed off to the side where five thick connectors had been pulled apart.

"Thanks."

Mike crouched down to look under the ramp. Then he crawled forward. He reached out and swept his hand back and forth in the dim space under the walkway.

"Looking for something?" asked Olaf.

"Maybe," said Mike. He straightened up and dusted his hands on his jeans. "Did you pick up in here at all?"

"What?"

"Did you move anything? Clean up anything?"

Sasha's eyes dropped to the dark spots. "What are you looking for?"

He told them. Neil and Sasha traded a confused glance and both shook their heads. Olaf rolled his eyes. "Is that important?" asked Neil. He reached up to wipe his eyes with the heel of his hand.

"No," muttered Olaf.

"I'm not sure yet," Mike replied. "Has anyone else been down here since . . . well, since it happened?"

"Arthur and Jamie were both down here for a while," said Sasha.

"Did they move anything?"

"I don't think so," Neil said.

"No," snapped Olaf.

Mike counted to four. "Do you have any idea what happened to Bob?"

Olaf flapped his lips for a moment. He tensed, and Mike was sure the other man was going to swing at him. Then his shoulders dropped—not quite a slump—and he shook his head. "I don't know," he said. "It . . . it makes no sense. It shouldn't've happened."

"He HD'd," Neil said. "It's the only answer. He got scrambled somehow. Just like Tramp."

"You can't HD in the Door," said Olaf. "There's no point when the traveler is broken down, so it can't be a reintegration issue."

"What about the magnetic field?" asked Mike. He tugged open a workstation drawer and peered inside. "Neil's told me it can be pretty dangerous."

Sasha nodded, but Olaf shook his head again. "Everything was balanced. There was no flux. And he never crossed the lines."

"Besides, it wouldn't mess him up like that," said Sasha.

"What about his clothes?"

Olaf bit back another snide remark. "We don't know," he said. "Like I said, none of this should've happened." He waved a hand back at the rings. "The levels were all good, power was steady, nothing's misaligned. Everything checks out. It couldn't've happened."

"But it did," said Mike. "So how?"

"It had to be a programming issue." He jerked his chin toward the control booth. "The computer messed up one of the variables."

"And that would . . ." Mike glanced at the Door.

"I don't know!" Olaf threw his hands in the air. "All I know is we can't find anything wrong with the tech." He turned and half-stomped back up the ramp to loom over the two engineers.

Mike took a last look around the floor, then headed for the control room.

Jamie was hunched over a monitor, scrolling through lines of code. Arthur stood a few feet behind her, both hands on his cane. His eyes were red.

"Hey," said Mike.

"How are you doing?" asked Arthur. "This whole thing must've been a shock for you."

"I'm okay. Thanks for asking."

Arthur looked at him for a moment. "Is there something we can do for you?"

Mike nodded at the screens. "Any idea yet what happened?"

"Hardware problem," said Jamie. Her eyes never left the screen. More lines of code scrolled by.

"Olaf seems pretty sure it's a computer problem," said Mike.

She spun. Her eyes weren't as red as Arthur's, but they weren't far from tears. "Did you just come up here to stir things up?"

"No," he said. "Sorry. I was just trying to—"

"It's hardware," she said. "It has to be."

"If it was the program or the equations," said Arthur, "the Door couldn't've opened."

"Are you sure?" said Mike. "There's no way it could've opened . . . wrong?"

Jamie made a noise that sounded like a snort cut off before it could get free. The corners of Arthur's mouth trembled, as if his lips were fighting to form either a faint smile or frown and were too evenly matched. "No," he said. "I don't think so."

"That doesn't sound too certain."

Jamie tapped a key, freezing the scroll. She looked up over her shoulder at Arthur.

"I . . . this is why I told Magnus we need more testing," he said. "There are still a lot of things we don't know." Arthur hooked his cane on his pocket, pulled off his glasses, and pinched his nose. He took a few deep breaths. A few more moments passed before he pushed the eyeglasses back onto his face.

A moment passed.

"The day after I arrived," said Mike, "Bob asked me if you'd been talking about him."

Arthur blinked. "Me?"

"Yeah."

"Talked about him how?"

Mike counted to three and then raised his shoulders in a casual shrug. "I don't know. We were out having dinner, Olaf showed up, and he changed the subject."

Arthur and Jamie traded a look. "To be honest," he said, "we'd all noticed that Bob had been acting a little odd lately."

"Odd how?"

"Just not like himself," said Jamie. "Kind of . . . well, paranoid."

Mike counted to three again. "Like Ben Miles?"

Arthur shook his head. "Nothing like that. He just seemed like he was hiding something."

"Any idea what?"

"I couldn't say."

Another moment passed.

"Could the accident have anything to do with that flash drive you gave Jamie just before Bob went through?"

Arthur set his cane back down on the floor. "What are you implying?"

"I'm not implying anything," said Mike. "I'm asking a question. You introduced a new element and something went wrong. I'm wondering if there's a connection."

"We didn't introduce anything," said Jamie. She reached across the desk and picked up the flash drive. "I haven't even plugged it in yet."

She and Arthur shot dark looks at Mike.

"So what's on it?" he asked.

"Suggestions for an algorithm update," Arthur said.

"What kind of update?"

"I'm afraid that falls under things we don't have to share with you."

"And it's moot," said Jamie, waving the drive, "because I never did anything with them." She tossed it back onto the desk. It clattered against some equipment and fell to the floor. She didn't move to pick it up.

Arthur tapped his fingers on the head of his cane. "Did you need anything else, Mike?"

Jamie looked back and forth between them.

He let a few moments of his own pass. "Yeah," he said. "I was wondering if either of you took anything from the main floor."

Her eyes focused on him. "What do you mean?"

"After Bob . . . after he came through the Door, did either of you pick up anything?"

Arthur peered over his glasses. "Like what?"

"The baseball."

Jamie blinked. "The baseball?"

"The one Bob and I were tossing back and forth."

"Yeah, I figured that's the one," said Jamie. "What about it?"

"It's gone. Vanished."

Arthur frowned. "Are you sure?"

"Pretty sure."

"Neil or Sasha probably picked it up," said Jamie. She turned back to her screens and the text scrolled. "They probably don't even remember doing it."

"I asked," said Mike. "Unless they picked it up and put it somewhere else altogether, it's not down there."

"You were right there," said Arthur. "Didn't you see where it went?"

"I wasn't looking when he stepped through."

Another moment passed.

"So?" asked Jamie.

"So," said Mike, "maybe it's a clue. Maybe if we can find it, it'll help us figure out what happened."

Arthur hooked his hands in his pockets again. "We already have a lot to do, Mike," he said. "We're stripping the Door down to the wires and going over every line of code."

"It'll just take a minute to look at the video, though."

The older man cleared his throat. "We don't have the time."

"You don't have the time to find out what went wrong?"

"We have an established method for hunting down problems. I'll consider your idea and add it to the schedule."

"So just let me look at the video. I won't get in the way."

"I'd rather you not look at something that may give away insights into the workings of the Albuquerque Door."

"Are you serious?"

"Of course. That's one of the conditions of your being here."

"I was standing right there watching it," Mike said, gesturing down at the main floor, "but you won't let me watch the recordings?"

Arthur said nothing.

"It'd go ten times faster if you let me help."

Jamie stabbed at her keyboard and stopped the scroll again. She glared at Mike. "You think you can go through this faster than me?"

"I didn't mean it like that," he said. "I just meant—"

"No, please," she said. She rolled her chair back a foot and opened a path to the monitors. "Tell me what I'm missing. Tell me how I screwed this up."

"No one thinks you screwed up," said Arthur.

"If he can do it so much faster, let him," she said. "I'm halfway through, but God knows I don't want to be doing this right now."

Mike waited a moment, then stepped forward and bent to the screens. He set one hand on the back of Jamie's chair. His fingertips brushed her shoulder and he felt her tense up.

Jamie twisted out of the chair and sucked a breath between her teeth. Her eyes flashed as she spat the air back at him. "Don't!"

"Sorry," he said. "I didn't mean to—"

"Don't you FUCKING TOUCH ME!" she roared, stalking past him and out of the control room.

The room settled and Arthur cleared his throat. "I'm sorry about that," he said. "I don't think Jamie's personal space issues have come up before, have they?"

TWENTY-THREE

The bartender, a thick-armed woman with a dyed-black topknot and red lips, glanced up as light from the parking lot followed Mike inside. As promised, the place was narrow, with the actual bar itself running half the length. The stools were free standing, not bolted to the floor, and some of them formed small clusters and knots. A pool table and jukebox filled the back third, and a dart board was set up where it would be far too dangerous to use.

Two men watched ESPN with the volume at a murmur. An older woman drank at the bar with one hand up, holding the memory of a cigarette. A man in a business suit studied a whiskey. Jamie sat at the far end of the bar nursing a beer. Mike hesitated, three steps into the bar, still close to the door. Then she held up the beer bottle and gestured him closer with it.

He walked over but didn't sit down. "How goes it?"

"Carly," she called to the bartender, "give the government jerk a drink. On me."

"You're too kind," he said.

"It's a bar," said Jamie. "People come here to drink, not to talk."

"What'll it be?" asked Carly.

"Rum and Coke." He sat down next to Jamie. The stools had a good distance between them. "Can we talk at all," he asked, "or do I have to have a drink in my hand?"

She killed her beer and let the bottle clunk on the bar. "Will the drink make you more bearable?"

"The first one won't, but probably the second one."

"Well," she said, "that answers that, then."

The topknotted bartender set down a large glass for Mike and another bottle for Jamie. She lifted the beer and held it out without looking at him. He tapped his drink against hers. She took three long swallows before setting the bottle back on the bar.

"Thanks for telling me about the wireless yesterday," she said. "Stupid mistake. I should've done that a year ago."

He pulled the straw out of his drink and had a sip. "You're welcome."

"Why'd you tell me?"

He shrugged. "Just the decent thing to do."

Jamie coughed and took another hit off the bottle. She set it down. "His girlfriend called this afternoon, looking for him. No one had told her. Anne had to break the news."

Mike decided to have another sip of his drink rather than say anything.

"I finished going through all the code," she said, "and I've run fourteen different simulations. It couldn't've happened. The accident."

"It did."

She shook her head. "Not because of me."

He waited a few moments to see if she had more to say. "You're sure?"

"Positive. Numbers don't lie, and nothing was wrong with the numbers. If something went wrong, then it's been going wrong every single time we've used the Door and nobody ever noticed anything."

"Or something else failed somewhere in the calculations," said Mike. "One of the science teachers at my school told me that on every test she usually has one or two kids who get an equation wrong but still get all the math right."

"You think we've had the equations wrong all this time?"

Mike shrugged and had another drink.

She snorted. "There's nothing wrong. Besides, the Door's always worked."

"Except when you tried to put it on a timer."

"Yeah, whatever. Don't nitpick. It works. The equations work. The math works. The Door opens. We go through it. It has to be something that went wrong with the hardware."

"And Neil and Sasha say it's not the hardware. So there has to be something else."

She made a rude noise and drank half the remaining beer.

"Have you considered it might be something cumulative?"

"You better finish that," she said to Mike, waving to the bartender. "You're going to have another one in a minute."

"You always drink this much?"

"Only when people I know die in front of me." She finished the bottle and set it down on the counter.

He gave a slow nod and took another drink. "That's kind of impressive."

"What is?"

"Going through all the code already."

"Y'know, for a supposedly decent guy, you're kind of a cold bastard, aren't you?"

"Me?"

"Bob's been dead a day and a half, and you're still talking about work."

Mike downed the last of his drink in one swallow. "I don't have anything to say."

"That's what I mean," she said. "Cold bastard."

Carly set down another glass and another bottle. She looked at Mike, then Jamie. "He still on your tab?"

Jamie nodded. She didn't bother holding the beer out for a toast this time. She swallowed twice and set it down on the bar. "So," she said, "why is Leland 'Mike' Erikson, sometime decent guy, such a bastard?"

"You really want to know?"

"No, but it beats anything else we could talk about."

He took a hit off his drink. Then another. "Did you have a pet die when you were little?"

Jamie wrinkled her brow. "What?"

"A cat? A dog?"

"Are you comparing Bob to a cat?"

"I'm trying to make a point."

"Yeah, of course I did."

"You said cat. What was her name?"

"His. Spock."

"Did you cry when he died?"

She tilted the bottle back. "What's it to you?"

"Did you?"

"Yeah, okay, I was eight, and my cat died."

He swallowed some more rum and Coke. "You're not crying now."

"It was almost thirty years ago."

Mike nodded. "Lose any of your grandparents?"

"Both on my mom's side," said Jamie. "One on my dad's."

"You're not crying for them, either."

She banged the bottle down loud enough to draw attention. "Is this some super-genius analogy, where you try to prove I'm as big a bastard as you?"

"No," he said, "just making a point."

"Okay. What?"

"What I keep telling you. I remember everything. My memories never fade. They never get soft or blurry. Never."

Jamie blinked.

"My dog, Batman, was hit by a car when I was six," said Mike, "and I cried for four hours. I lost my granddad on my mom's side when I was nine, and my nana on my dad's when I was eleven. We had to put down our cat, Jake, the morning of my sixteenth birthday. My mom died my junior year of college, and I was there in the hospital with her. And every single one of them could've happened a minute ago. I can tell you what everyone around me said, every thought in my head, every sight and sound and smell. I remember every second of them all dying with perfect, crystal clarity. Everything's always raw. It's always 'too soon.'"

She lowered the bottle. "That sounds like hell."

"It's not great," he agreed. "And now I get to have Bob dying right in front of me every day for the rest of my life. I'd be lying if I said I haven't had a few nights where I wished for early-onset Alzheimer's, because I don't want to think about how much'll be in my head by the time I'm sixty or seventy."

"That's messed up."

"Yeah," he said.

Her chin dipped toward the bar. "I never thought of it like that."

"No one ever does." He tilted his glass back and swallowed twice.

"Did you really have a dog named Batman?"

"You had a cat named Spock."

"Yep."

Mike sketched lines around his eyes with his fingers. "He had black fur on his face like a mask. I thought he went out at night and fought crime."

Jamie's lips twitched into a faint smile. "So the whole super-brain thing didn't kick in until later?"

"Batman was a great dog. He could've been fighting crime while I was asleep."

Her lips got dangerously close to a smile again. A moment later she held up her half-empty bottle. A moment after that he tapped it with his glass.

"I'm sorry if it seemed like I didn't care," Mike said. "I liked Bob. He seemed like a decent guy."

"He was," she said. Her tongue slipped and it came out sounding like "wash." She shook her head and rolled her shoulders. They popped twice.

He tapped his fingers on his glass and nodded at her shoulder. "Sorry about this morning."

"About what?"

He gestured with his chin again. "Touching you."

She frowned, then shook her head. "Don't be. I was angry. I needed to blow off some steam. I overreacted."

"It wasn't appropriate."

"Oh, for fuck's sake," she said. "You touched my shoulder by accident. It's not like you slapped my ass or something."

"It bothered you."

"Because I have issues. My issues aren't your problem." She raised her beer and tilted her head back.

He finished his own drink. His throat was warm, and a pleasant tingle ran from the back of his skull down into his chest. Jamie downed the last of her bottle and waved for the bartender. "How many is that for you?" he asked.

"Enough that this is her last one," said the bartender.

"How many?" asked Mike.

"This one's ten in about two hours."

"Fuck," Jamie said. "Bob's dead, Carly."

"I know," said the topknotted woman. "Give me your keys and you can have two more for him before I call you a cab."

Jamie dug in her coat pocket and slapped a mess of keys on the bar. "Give me three more, and the government jerk can walk me home."

Mike raised his eyebrows.

"Oh, don't get your hopes up," she told him.

"D'you actually know this guy?" asked Carly. "He looks kind of . . ."

"Like a government jerk?"

"I was going to say kind of like Snape in *Harry Potter*."

"Sitting right here," said Mike.

"He's fine," Jamie said. She tapped the key ring. "Drinks."

Carly gave Mike a look. He returned it. She sighed and scooped up the keys.

"I don't usually drink this much," Jamie told him.

"Well, you're doing it like a pro."

She snorted, but it turned into a chuckle at the end. "Bob was always telling me to loosen up. I never listened."

"Issues?"

"Yeah."

Carly returned. She set a fresh glass in front of Mike and put a beer in Jamie's hand. A third of the bottle was already empty. Jamie didn't seem to notice.

He slid the straw out of his drink and dropped it on the bar. "Anything you want to talk about?"

"What?"

"Your issues?"

She straightened up and stared at him. "Are you serious?"

Mike shrugged. "Part of the teacher thing."

She shook her head. "I'd think it'd all be in those great personnel files you saw."

"Believe it or not, even these days, government files aren't as in-depth as most people think," he said. "I did some stuff as a kid that I was sure would be in mine. It was a bit disappointing."

She smirked. "Not that special after all. Must've been a blow."

"I've had worse."

Jamie took a quick drink. "You know I'm a speed junkie, right?"

"Yeah, that's in there." The ants carried out her dossier pages. "Twenty-three speeding tickets in four states over five years. Eight driving to endanger. It raised a lot of flags when you were vetted for the

SETH project, even after Arthur vouched for you and got them to overlook your hacker history. It's a miracle you've still got a license."

"Traffic school. It doesn't mention the crash?"

Mike shook his head. "Crash?"

She sighed. "All that brain power and it never occurred to you why a cheerleader turned into a computer geek?"

"I just figured you were some Internet male fantasy come to life."

She made an unpleasant sound and hefted her bottle again. "I was sixteen," she said. "Dating this guy from the next town over. Kevin Ulinn. Kev. He only had two things going for him. He was a college freshman, and he had a motorcycle. Drove my parents nuts. I'd sneak out at night and we'd drive around. Get out on the highway and push it up to one-ten or so, then fuck wherever we ended up. Perfect high school summer relationship."

"I've seen a few like that."

Jamie nodded. "I bet you have, Mister I'm-just-a-high-school-teacher." She swallowed two mouthfuls of beer, then raised an eyebrow at the mostly empty bottle. She made two attempts to line it up with the wet ring on the bar napkin, then gave up and set it down. Her eyes were glassy.

"One night he hit a wet spot, lost it, and dropped the bike. We were going about ninety-five. They said he died instantly. Hit the ground just right and snapped his neck, even with the helmet. I got thrown off and skidded almost a hundred feet down the road on my back. He'd given me his leather jacket. Without it the pavement would've ripped me to shreds. They say it was just rags when the paramedics got there. Serious miracle I didn't end up in a wheelchair. As it was, I woke up in the hospital with a broken arm and three fractured vertebrae. Wore a halo until Christmas." She reached up and gestured at the two scars on her forehead.

"That must've been terrifying."

"Oh yeah. Lucked out that I didn't end up with a bunch of surgical pins or any of that, but I had to get skin grafts over most of my back, sides, and this arm." She picked up the bottle with her left hand and toasted, but didn't drink. "They didn't take well, and it ended up scarring a lot. A complete mess. So ended my days as a cheerleader. No more halter tops or short sleeves. Had to wear this awful, high-necked dress to the prom. You know it's bad when an eighteen-year-old boy doesn't want to have sex with his date on prom night."

Mike looked at her shoulder. "So your back's still sensitive?"

"Nah," said Jamie. "It's completely numb. The crash grated off pretty much every nerve ending from my neck to my ass. Haven't felt anything in almost seventeen years."

"So what's the—"

"I just don't like being reminded that I'm disfigured."

"I'd hardly say that," he said. "If you don't mind me saying it, you're one of the most beautiful women I've ever met."

She waved the words away. "Yeah, that's what they all say. Then they see me naked." She downed the last of her beer. The bottle hit the bar hard and loud.

Mike looked at her. "Can I ask you a question?"

Her head went side to side. "No, you cannot see my scars."

"Not that. I was just wondering how you read all that code today."

"What?"

"Over two million lines of code. How'd you go through all of it in one day?"

She looked at him for a moment. She took in a slow breath. Then her eyes got watery and trembled. "Oh, you poor bastard."

"What?"

"I'm going to throw up all over you on the way home."

TWENTY-FOUR

A dark-haired woman with owlish glasses and a white coat leaned into the lobby. "Leland Erikson?"

Mike straightened up. "Yeah."

"Phoebe Forrester." She held out her hand.

"Dr. Forrester?" he repeated with a faint smile.

"Believe me," she said as they shook hands, "I heard it all through med school." She studied his face for a moment, then gestured him through the door and into a white hallway. "I've been expecting you. Someone from the Defense Department called, said you'd be stopping by."

He bit back a yawn. "I hope it's not too inconvenient."

"It's not a busy day, and it's a break in the routine. Are you okay?"

"Sorry. Late night dealing with a drunk friend."

"Ahhh. You were one of the ones who found the body, right?"

"It wasn't a body then."

"Right. Sorry." She stopped by a wide door. "How do you want to do this?"

"To be honest, it's my first autopsy. What do you recommend?"

"Do you want to see the body or just hear the results?"

"I know which one I want," he said, "but I think I need to see the body."

Forrester gestured him to the next door. "He's cleaned up. It won't be that bad." She pushed open the door. "Did you know him?"

"Kind of. We'd hung out a couple of times."

"Just remember to breathe. Speak up if you need a minute."

The cold smell of polished metal and chemicals hit his nose. He'd seen morgues on television, but he still paused for a moment in front of the wall of steel doors. Phoebe walked to the far corner and double-checked a clipboard. "This was an odd one."

"Odd how?"

"Better to show you." She pulled a pair of latex gloves from a box. "You want a pair?"

"Hopefully, I won't need them."

She held the box for another moment. He tugged out a pair of gloves and held them in his hand. She snapped hers on. "What's your field of specialty? Your people didn't say."

"Early American literature."

"Sorry?"

"It's a joke," he said. "Don't worry about me. Feel free to be clinical. I'll ask if I don't understand something."

"Okay."

She yanked on the handle and slid the body out. There was no sheet. Both of Bob's eyes were cold and white now. His yellow skin had faded to a pale, waxy color. A large Y of stitches stretched out across his chest. The ragged wound in his side had been cleaned. He'd been a big believer in manscaping.

"My official ruling," said Forrester, "going off the scalp wounds, is that the underlying cause of death is sharp force trauma. Accidental. That's what's going to be on the death certificate."

"But you're saying it like that because . . . ?"

"Because there's a lot wrong with this guy. But trying to pin down all the contributing factors for the chain might take a few weeks. Maybe even months. There's the obvious stuff," she said, pointing at the wound below the ribs. "He's got a nice gash on the back of his skull, too. Between them, they account for the blood loss. Less than three pints in him when he got here. I'd guess one, maybe one and a half pints of what he lost ended up on his clothes, but they still need to be tested."

"Dammit," said Mike.

"What?"

"His clothes were already bloody."

"I'm sorry?"

"It can wait." He nodded at Bob's—at *the body's* wound. "Do you know what that is?"

"It's a puncture wound," she said. "I'd be tempted to say it's ballistic trauma—a gunshot wound—because it goes straight through the soft tissue, but it's too clean to be point-blank. This . . ." She shrugged. "Maybe a very fast stab or thrust of some kind?"

He gestured at the malformed body. "So you think all of this might've contributed to his death?"

Forrester shrugged. "Maybe. I don't think he would've lived much longer, even if he hadn't bled out. Three or four months, tops."

"Why?"

"He had cancer."

"What kind?"

"Lots of kinds." She waved a hand across his body. "His skin's like that because of pancreatic cancer. In some cases it causes painless jaundice. I heard about a patient this bad once when I was a resident, somebody with skin like the Simpsons, but I've never seen it before."

"And you're sure it's cancer?"

She nodded and gestured at the Y incision. "His pancreas was just a mess of tumors. Same with his liver, lungs, colon, and prostate. A few small ones in his brain, too. Spleen and bone marrow show signs of leukemia. Except for the pancreas, none of it's that advanced, but I don't think he was getting treatment for any of it. No sign of chemo in his system, but . . ."

He looked at Forrester. "But what?"

"Nothing."

"I need to know anything you found."

Forrester tapped her fingers against each other. "There's not going to be any trouble about this, is there?"

"What do you mean, trouble?"

"I'm not going to get black-bagged for figuring out too much, am I?"

Mike blinked three times. "What?"

"You know. Black sack over the head. Whisked away in an unmarked van, never seen again."

"You watch a lot of television, don't you?"

"I just . . ." She shrugged. "This whole thing is a little weird, and then the DOD calls, and then you show up . . ."

"You're safe," Mike said. "Honest. Believe me, if I could get somebody black-bagged, there are four or five people who'd be on the list ahead of you."

She exhaled and her shoulders relaxed.

"So what'd you find? What's so weird?"

Forrester gestured at the scarred hand. "See that?"

"Yeah."

"That's a burn." She pointed at another scar near the elbow. "So is that. I'd guess maybe a year or so old. You can tell by the way they flatten out against the skin."

"Okay."

"This guy has a couple of old burns and a lot of cancer. One thing causes both of those."

Mike felt his brows go up. "Radiation?" He looked at the body. "Those are radiation burns?"

"No such thing. Burns are burns. If you don't know the cause, you can't always pin it down from the wound itself, despite what you may have seen on television." She shot a quick smirk at him. "Combined with all the cancer, though . . . I'd be willing to bet a few bucks on it."

"How many?"

Her mouth twitched side to side. "Maybe fifty."

"That sounds like a pretty confident bet."

"I'd go higher, but there's a bit of a conflict. Burns mean intense radioactive exposure for a very brief time. But cancer's a result of long-term, low-level exposure."

"How long term?"

"It's not really something you can work backward to figure it out. It usually takes years for radiation cancers to manifest, but there are cases where it's taken a lot less. My assumption was it was tied to everything else."

He looked at Bob—at the body—again. "Everything else?"

"Well, look at him. He's had the shit beat out of him a couple times over the past few months."

"No," said Mike. "That's all . . . pretty recent."

Forrester bit her lip. She shook her head. "This is all old damage."

"It can't be."

She ran a finger along the body's bubbly jaw line. "See this? That's scar tissue. Old scar tissue. Again, I'd guess a year, at the most."

He crouched and peered at the line of pale ripples in the skin. "You're sure?"

"Yeah. And it's a mess. Looks like half his face was ripped off and he didn't get any stitches. I don't even think it was taped. I'd say he just held it in place for a couple of hours until the blood clotted and it all healed by secondary intention."

Mike frowned.

She pointed at his arm. "Same with this. That twist? That's a broken humerus that wasn't set. Well, wasn't set right, anyway. Probably hurt like hell all the time."

"Broken when?"

"A little over a year. Again, all consistent."

Mike crossed his arms.

"Something wrong?"

"Very wrong. How old's the puncture wound?"

"I'd say an hour before death."

He frowned again. "Are you sure?"

"Yeah. There was a lot of tissue damage, but it didn't hit any major arteries, so that's consistent with blood loss. A few inches higher, closer to the armpit, that'd be a different story."

"Is there anything else you can tell me?"

"Two more things. They almost seem minor compared to everything else."

"Shoot."

"Secondary symptom," she said, "most likely a contributing factor to his death, is dehydration."

"Dehydration?"

Forrester nodded and touched the body's face. "Look here, how chapped his lips are. Also notice the nostrils and the skin around the tear ducts. It was really obvious once I checked the vitreous fluid from his eyes." She tapped Bob's chest. "I'd say he's been getting, at best, just under half a gallon of liquids a day for two or three weeks."

"Not possible. He was a caffeine addict. He was always drinking something. Coffee, soda, energy drinks."

"I never met the guy. I can only tell you what I found on the autopsy."

Mike rubbed his temples. The ants were swarming on both sides of his brain. They wanted out. He was tempted to let them go. "What was the other thing?"

"I checked stomach contents. It's a standard thing. His had some raw meat, dirt, and just over three ounces of grass."

"He swallowed his stash?"

She shook her head. "Not pot. Actual grass, like from a lawn. A lawn that was in pretty crappy condition, because the grass is long and mostly dead. And the meat . . ."

"What about it?"

"We probably won't know for sure until next week, but . . . it had fur on it." She tapped her fingers against each other again. "My daughter has three pet rats. It looked like rat fur."

A few ants got out. They carried hypotheses and ideas and wild guesses. He looked Forrester in the face. "Are you sure it's him?"

She looked at the body. A few moments passed.

Mike studied her expression. "You saw his driver's license?"

She nodded and cocked her head at a pair of file cabinets. "His personal effects are in there. They haven't been processed yet. He had an old gym ID, too."

"So," he said, "what do you think?"

"I half-figured you were here to claim the body and tell me there was some kind of mix-up, that this guy had been living in a cave outside Fukushima for the past ten years."

"Or black-bag you?"

"Maybe."

"Do you think it's a mix-up?"

Forrester shrugged. "Hair and eye color are right, even though his IDs don't show the bad eye or the scarring. Height's correct, blood type matches. We could try dental but he's got seven teeth missing and two broken, which also doesn't match either photo. I don't see any fillings so we'd just be hoping for a lucky match. There were four positive identifications. You were one of them."

"DNA testing?"

"Again, not a television crime lab."

"Could you do it?"

"I'd need a sample to run it against."

"I think I can get one for you. He had physicals pretty much every month or so. There should be some blood samples somewhere."

"It'll probably take a week or two. Maybe even a month."

"I'll see if there's anything I can do to rush it a bit."

"Good luck with that," she said. "You're only the government."

"Can I ask you another question?"

"That's why you're here."

"How old would you say he is?"

One side of her mouth pulled up. "I had the same thought when I was thinking this might be mistaken identity. But he checks out. There's some malnutrition, but the curve of his spine, his joints—they're all just what they should be for someone his age. And in his condition."

"One other question."

"Okay."

Mike frowned at the corpse. "You didn't find a baseball somewhere in him, did you?"

TWENTY-FIVE

"No baseball?"

Mike shook his head. "Not even scraps. She even did another set of X-rays to double-check for me. It's vanished into thin air."

Three thousand miles away, Reggie leaned back in his chair. "Or it got picked up by an EMT who wanted a free baseball for his kid."

"That I would've seen."

"Is it really that important?"

"I think it is." Mike crossed his arms and tapped his palm against his elbow. "His clothes were torn up, too."

"What?"

"I saw his personal effects. Flipped them over, saw them from every angle."

"That's good, yes?"

"Yeah. They were frayed and crumbled in a couple of places. There were three distinct tears on his pants, two on his shirt."

"Okay. And . . . ?"

"The fraying and crumbling could be written off as a result of the crosswalk. I'm not sure how, because I still don't know enough about the Door, but it's not hard to imagine a powerful electromagnetic field having a general degenerative effect on materials. That's something else to run past your experts." The ants carried out images of the clothes spread out on the chrome table and lined them up in his mind. "Tearing's a physical action, though, like the wound. It's inflicted damage."

"The machine gave him cancer, and you're focused on his pants."

"He didn't catch his pants on something stepping through the rings and tear one of the cuffs half off. But the cuff is torn. And he got shot or stabbed with something." Mike flipped the clothes in his mind and examined the burst stitching and the broken weave of the fabric. "They were dusty, too. In one step he accumulated about four ounces of dust, spread all through his clothes."

"I saw a mattress commercial once that said most dust was human skin cells," said Reggie. "Might explain his condition if a quarter pound of skin went 'poof' when he stepped through the rings."

Mike closed his eyes and tried to recapture the sensation of rubbing the fabric between his fingers. His memory was strongest with sights and sounds. His other senses were still recorded, but they weren't any sharper in memory than they were in real life. "The dust was gritty," he said. "More like sand than . . . well, dust. Plus, there was the blood."

"What about it?"

"There was blood soaked into his clothes. It was down his side and all over his left arm where he was trying to block it."

"You said he had a good-sized hole in him."

"Yeah," said Mike, "but his clothes were *already* soaked as soon as he stepped through the Door. Almost two pints. And if he lost a quart of blood that fast, he should've been dead in seconds. That's losing-a-limb bleeding."

"Maybe it wasn't his blood?"

Mike shook his head. "She tested it there. The blood type's right." He opened his eyes and paced in the trailer. "Everything about Bob's body says that he gained at least a year's worth of experiences in less than a second. But the medical examiner's pretty sure he isn't any older than he should be."

Reggie shifted his jaw. "Time dilation? The Door lets people cross big distances very fast. Physics says that should be a time shift, right?"

A few more ants spilled over the walls in Mike's mind. "Not exactly," he said. "Again, not my field, but I'm pretty sure time dilation depends on speed. If Arthur's telling the truth, the Albuquerque Door covers distance by bending space, not rushing through it. Bob was moving a mile and a half per hour, tops."

"Ahhh."

"Even if he wasn't, moving faster would've meant time passed slower for him, not faster. A minute for us would've been a second for him."

"And it didn't even take a second to get through the Door."

"Not even."

"So he's the right age for that."

"It's not time dilation. I know that much."

"Are you sure?"

Mike uncrossed his arms. "I'm not really sure of anything out here."

"You're still sure no one caused it, though?"

"Sabotage?" Mike shook his head. "No real motive."

"It got rid of Bob."

"It got rid of Bob and shut the whole project down. Nobody here wants that."

"Are you sure?"

Mike paused. "Pretty sure," he said.

Reggie shifted in his chair. "Have Arthur's people found anything?"

"No. They've taken the whole system apart and put it back together again. They can't find anything that explains Bob's injuries. Not even a loose wire."

"Could it be something they're hiding?"

"I think they're hiding a lot of things."

"About the accident?"

"About the Door itself. They're just . . ." Ants streamed through his brain and piled into two or three minor skirmishes. "I think we might be coming at this the wrong way."

Reggie started to speak, but Mike waved him quiet.

"Your people haven't been able to find anything because they're starting under the assumption Arthur and his team have what they want, the answer to a specific question."

More and more ants had joined the battle. They struck at one another with images and sounds and ideas. The inside of his skull blurred with images.

"It's not making any sense because we keep putting all the random snippets and clues in the same pile when there should be two or three. They're not hiding one thing, they're hiding a couple things. There's stuff they know that they don't want to share quite yet, but I think maybe there's things they don't know, either, and they're trying to keep that ignorance hidden, too. Which means there's probably still facts about the Door none of us even realize we're looking at."

"What they know," said Reggie, "what they don't know, and what they don't know that they don't know."

"Yes, exactly," he said. "The Door works, but I don't think it works the way they're telling everyone it does. But however they got it working, it does work. And they're going to change the world and get a ton of recognition for it. So what are they worried about?"

Reggie cleared his throat. "It might all be moot," he said. "I've been talking with some people. The board's leaning toward denying the new budget."

Mike shook the ants away. "I thought they were waiting for my report. Your report."

His friend shrugged on the screen. "With Bob Hitchcock and Ben Miles, I think we're looking at a two percent failure rate, yes?"

"Close enough."

"That's equal to three or four jumbo jets dropping out of the sky every day. How popular do you think air travel would be with that kind of survival rate?"

"You're giving up?"

"I'm not doing anything except waiting for a full report from my man in the field. Show me it's safe, that this was just a fluke, and it's not going to give anyone else cancer, and I'll make sure Arthur keeps getting checks." Reggie's eyes darted to the left. "I'll talk to you later." He reached forward and the tablet blinked back to its default screen.

Mike stared at it for a moment. Then he watched Bob die for the 234th time. The ants had a swarm of images and theories for him. None of them fit together well.

He headed back up to the main building. Anne smiled at him from the desk as he walked past her. He swiped his key card and walked out onto the main floor.

Olaf and Neil were there, each sitting at their stations. Olaf had a simulation running on his screen. They glanced up as Mike walked across the floor to them.

"How goes it?"

Neil looked at Olaf. "Fine," said Bogart's twin. "Is there something we can do for you?"

Mike stepped over the cables. "I was just wondering where Arthur is."

Neil opened his mouth, but Olaf cut him off. "He was up in the booth about fifteen minutes ago. He might be in his office now."

Neil turned back to his screen. He made a point of looking nowhere else.

Mike studied the two men. "Anything new on the . . . incident?"

"No," said Olaf.

"Did I do something wrong?"

"No," he said. "We're just busy. We're in the middle of a simulation."

"Of the incident?"

"Of something related to it, yes."

"What?"

Olaf straightened up and turned from his station. "Weren't you looking for Arthur?"

"Sorry."

"Not a problem."

Someone coughed over the speakers and Mike glanced up at the booth. "If you need any help," he said, "just let me know."

"Of course," said Olaf.

Mike wandered back out into the hall and up the stairwell. He swiped his card again and unlocked the control room door. "Hey," he said, "I was . . ."

Sasha looked over her shoulder at him and held up a finger. "Ready in two," she said to the microphone.

"Oh," he said. "Sorry. I thought Arthur was up here."

She shook her head. "He's over at Site B."

Mike felt his brows furrow. "He's monitoring a simulation from the other lab?"

"Simulation?"

He looked past her to the screens. The ants carried out the images from Olaf's monitor a few moments ago. "You're doing a full run? Even though we don't know what happened last time."

"That's why we're doing it," said Sasha. She turned back to the screens. "We need data."

He glanced around the room. "Wait a minute . . . why are you up here?"

"Someone's got to monitor the system." An icon on one of the monitors flashed, and she leaned toward the microphone. "Johnny has a solution. We are ready in one." Her eyes glanced down at the lab and the shimmering rings.

"Why isn't Jamie—"

The scurrying ants put the picture together in less than a second. Mike yanked open the control room door and dashed for the stairwell. He pushed past Anne in the hall, spilling her coffee, and ran for the big door. He swiped his card too fast. The reader didn't get it until the second pass. The lock clicked and he yanked the door open.

Olaf made three quick keystrokes. "Power's good."

"No!" shouted Mike.

Threads of static electricity lashed around the rings, whipping back and forth between each one. An acid hiss echoed across the main floor. The air inside the rings thrashed and boiled.

And then it all grew still.

Mike ran past the workstations and up onto the ramp.

"*The field has cohesion*," boomed Sasha's voice. "*The Door is open.*"

The third ring appeared. Jamie stepped up onto the ramp at Site B. Her hair hung around her face. Her clothes were rumpled. Mike could see Arthur behind her at one of the stations. The older man locked eyes with him, then looked away.

Jamie stood six feet and half a mile away from him. "Don't do this," said Mike.

She shook her head. "It'll be fine."

"Olaf," he called out, not looking away from her, "shut it down. Now!"

"We know what we're doing," he snapped.

"Like you did with Tramp?! Shut it down!!"

He heard Neil wheeze, and Sasha gasped over the speakers. Jamie took a few steps down the pathway toward him. She was inside the first ring, inches from the threshold. "It's going to work," she said. "There's nothing wrong with the code. There's nothing wrong with the tech. What happened to Bob was just a fluke."

"You don't know that."

"We do," she said. "I do."

"Jamie," he said, fighting the urge to glare at Arthur, "none of you know what happened. You don't—"

"It's going to be okay," she said. "Really."

She took a deep breath and stepped through the Door.

TWENTY-SIX

Jamie bumped into Mike and they stood nose to nose. She stayed there, pressed against him on the pathway. He could feel the warmth of her body. Her hair smelled like talcum powder.

"It was sweet of you to be worried," she said. Her words carried the smell of sweetened coffee. "But you didn't need to be." She swept her hair away and it fell back in front of her face.

"Are you all right? Do you feel okay?"

"I'm fine. It worked. No problems."

"That was stupid," he said.

"Trust me. I'm not as dumb as you feel right now."

"*We have forty seconds left on the Door,*" said Sasha. "*Are you going back, or is that it?*"

Jamie smiled at him. A real smile. "Well," she said, "am I going back, Mister Government Jerk?" She bounced on her toes. For a moment Mike had the odd thought that she was going to kiss him in front of everyone.

"No," he said. Then he looked over his shoulder and raised his voice. "No. Shut it down."

Neil glanced at Olaf, then bent to his station. Mike saw Jamie nod from the corner of his eye. Olaf reached down and stabbed at his keyboard.

"*Closing the Door,*" boomed Sasha. "*Stand clear.*"

Jamie put a hand on his chest and guided him a few steps back. He looked past her and glared at Arthur. The project head ignored him.

Then the air between them rippled and a hiss of radio static echoed out of the rings.

"That was amazingly stupid," said Mike.

"Seriously," she said. "Unclench. Everything went fine. I'm okay."

He turned around and gave Olaf and Neil the Look. Neil cowered from it a bit. Olaf straightened up.

"What the hell is wrong with you?" Mike asked. "The last time someone went through there he died."

"And over a hundred and sixty times before that," said Olaf, "someone went through and nothing happened." His smug tone was back. Mike hadn't missed it. "This is what science is all about. Taking bold steps and not stopping the moment you hit a setback."

"A setback?" Mike marched toward Olaf, waving his arms back at the rings. The other man clenched his fists. "What happened to Bob was a setback?"

"We couldn't find anything wrong," said Neil. "We had to run a test to see if it was a fluke."

"There's a pet store down the street," said Mike. "You could've sent a rat."

"No," said Olaf, "we couldn't. Going back to animal testing would've sent up a huge red flag. It'd be declaring a failure."

"That's because it failed!"

"No, it didn't," said Jamie.

Mike turned on her. "Bob is—"

"We don't know what happened to Bob," Neil said, "but we can't find anything that says the Door was at fault. We needed more information."

"We had to run another test," said Jamie. "So I volunteered."

The big door hissed open on its piston and Sasha walked out onto the floor. Her eyes darted between them. She moved to stand near Olaf.

Mike looked at Jamie. "You could've been killed."

"But I wasn't."

"It made sense for her to go," said Olaf. His fingers danced on his phone.

"How does volunteering to get killed make sense?"

"Because I had the least to lose," said Jamie. "Everyone else has family or other commitments. I don't. It made sense."

Mike shook his head. "Nothing about this made sense." He looked around at the team members. "Seriously, what were any of you thinking?"

"I was thinking it's my life's work," said Jamie, "and I didn't want to see it get flushed away."

Her words echoed in the big room.

"We'll need to get you checked out," said Olaf. "Full physical and X-rays, first priority. CT scan too, just to be sure."

She nodded. "Of course."

He pointed at his monitor. "Arthur's bringing his car around to take you. Do you feel okay to walk?"

"I feel fine," she said. "There's nothing wrong with me."

"You can't just ignore this," Mike said to them. "This was insanely dangerous."

"Bob wouldn't think so," said Sasha. "He knew what this meant. He'd want us to keep working."

The door hissed open again. Arthur walked in, car keys in hand. "I'm right by the entrance," he said. "Ready to go."

Mike glared at him. "I can't believe you allowed this."

"Why not?"

"You could've had another body on your hands."

"Or we could've proved the Door works." He waved a hand at Jamie. "And we did."

"I have to tell Reggie what you did."

"Unfortunate," said Arthur, "but not unexpected."

"You know this is the nail in the coffin. Even he'll agree they have to shut you down for this."

"No," Arthur said, "he won't. At this point he's depending on this project as much as us. He's invested too much. The Albuquerque Door is going to make or break his career, too, and if he has a choice, I'm confident which way he'll go."

"Someone died," said Mike.

"And we've shown that was a fluke. The Albuquerque Door project works as promised. That's what matters."

"Can we put this on hold for now?" asked Jamie. "No matter how we look at this, the best thing is for me to go get checked out, right? So let's get that done and then we can argue about if this was a mistake or a bold step."

Mike looked at her. "And if it's a mistake?"

She spread her arms and then gestured up and down her body. "For the third or fourth time," she said, "fine."

"Well, let's be sure," said Arthur. He gazed at Mike. "Unless you have any other objections."

Mike turned his back on them and paced back and forth in front of the rings.

"Let's go," Arthur said.

"Back soon with a clean bill of health," said Jamie.

Their footfalls faded and the door hissed again. It closed with a thump. Olaf and Sasha spoke in quiet tones. Neil moved to join them.

Mike stood alone and took a few slow breaths. He stared up at the rings. There was a certain logic to what Arthur had said, but Reggie would shut the project down. At the very least, he'd put someone new in charge. The next time they opened the Door, who knew what would happen to the person who walked through it?

He turned and headed for the door. An insistent ant held up an image in his mind. Something he shouldn't see. He rewound it even as he turned his head to look again.

The twin rings stood up on the walkway. He'd moved so far to the right they were almost edge-on. He took a few steps until he could see the far side and the two inside edges of the rings there.

Then he took another step and saw the third ring.

He glanced over at Olaf, Sasha, and Neil. They were debating some point. None of them were near their stations. Behind them, the red light was dark.

Two rings close to him.

Three rings on the far side.

He took a few steps back, then walked behind the platform. From behind, there were only two of the big off-white rings. He traced them with his eyes. Then he walked out to the front again. He stepped to the left and looked through the Door.

Three rings.

His movement caught Neil's eye. "What's up?"

Back to the right. Two rings.

Mike cleared his throat. "Guys . . ."

They all looked up.

"Is the power on?"

"Yes," smirked Olaf. "That's why there's no sound at all."

Three rings.

Two rings.

He snapped his fingers twice and pointed at the rings. "Is the power on?"

The smirks vanished and Neil shook his head. "No, of course not."

"We've got a problem," said Mike.

TWENTY-SEVEN

Neil and Sasha walked to the Door with long strides. Three quick steps brought Olaf back to his station. "We're shut down," he said. "No question about it."

Mike stepped up onto the platform and looked through the rings. From this angle, he could see into Site B. Jamie's sweatshirt was still balled up on one station. Arthur's chair was still pushed out. The back wall was twenty feet farther away than the one he saw in the corner of his eye. The red light wasn't on there, either.

Sasha and Neil moved in on either side of him. "Oh, fuck," said Sasha. "What the fuck's going on?"

Neil reached out a hand toward the Door, but Mike slapped it down. "What?"

"Do you know how long it's going to stay open?"

The other man looked at his fingertips and shuddered.

Sasha stared up at the rings. "We've never managed to keep it open longer than ninety-three seconds."

"It's *not* open," Olaf called from behind them. "Power's down, the system's down, it's not—"

"It's open," said Mike.

"Maybe it just looks open," said Neil. "This might be some kind of afterimage or something."

Sasha pulled something from her pocket. She showed a handful of coins to Mike and Neil, then flung them through the rings. They chimed off the ramp in Site B. One quarter wedged itself into the expanded steel walkway. A pair of dimes rang on the concrete floor and rolled off out of sight.

"Fuck," she muttered.

Mike dug around in his own pocket and found another quarter. He held it between his finger and thumb, and then flung it like a miniature Frisbee. The coin sailed through the rings and across the other room. It hit the floor, skidded, and pinged against the far wall.

"Are you sure it's open?" asked Olaf. He was poring over the data on his screen.

"Positive," said Mike. "We just threw about a buck in pocket change over onto Site B."

Olaf shook his head. "It can't be. There's no power."

They stared at Site B for a moment. Then Neil stepped back from the rings. Mike and Sasha followed him. They gathered by Olaf's station.

"It could just be an . . . an aftereffect," stuttered Olaf. "It's possible the magnetic fields have somehow created a . . . some sort of a lensing effect, like a gravitational lens, and we're just seeing an afterimage."

Mike ignored him. "Is anyone still over in the other building?" he asked Sasha.

She shook her head. "Shouldn't be. Arthur was running things alone."

"Neil, get over there. Fast. See if it's open on that end. Don't get near it."

"Okay." He made a wide arc around the rings and headed for the back door.

"And don't touch anything," Mike called after him. "Not the controls, not the coins, nothing."

"You taking charge?" asked Sasha.

"Just trying to make sure no one gets hurt," said Mike. "Figured someone should."

"We had good intentions."

"Just like you did with Tramp?"

Sasha winced.

Olaf's eyes were still locked on the rings. "We could just be seeing a delayed image, one that's a few moments off from—"

Mike shook his head. "It's not a gravitational lens, Olaf. The Door is open."

"It can't be." Olaf shook his head. He had the wide eyes and slack jaw of a man who'd been slapped hard and hadn't quite accepted it yet. "I mean . . . I mean Occam's razor. The power isn't on, so it can't be—"

"How the hell do you get to gravitational lensing by using Occam's razor?" asked Sasha. She walked over to check the readouts from the other station.

"Well, I mean . . . there's no other way."

"The Door's open," said Mike. "The power's off, the program's not running, and the Door is still open. Why?"

"I . . . I don't know."

"Did something like this ever come up in your theories?" asked Mike. "Even the possibility of it?"

He shook his head. "I don't think so."

"You don't *think* so?"

"No," snapped Olaf. Getting defensive put him back on familiar ground. "No, it never came up."

"Get Arthur back here."

Sasha glanced over from the other station. "What about Jamie?"

Mike paused. So did Olaf. The three of them exchanged looks.

"How far's the doctor?" asked Mike.

"Not far," said Olaf. "They're probably halfway there."

"He'll turn right around if he thinks the project's in trouble," said Sasha.

"I'll send him a text," Olaf said. "Tell him there's an issue and he should come straight back as soon as he drops Jamie off."

Mike looked around. "I thought phones weren't allowed in here?"

"Your phone's not allowed in here," said Olaf. His finger moved across the touchscreen. It made him look old. Mike was used to students texting lightning-fast with their thumbs.

Sasha stared up at the rings. "What's powering them?"

"No idea," Mike said.

She took a step forward. "The energy has to be coming from somewhere," she said. "Something like this can't happen without—"

"Sasha," Olaf said, "watch the line."

The tip of her shoe was inches from the white paint. "It's not . . ." She glanced at the rings. "Fuck. Is it safe?"

"Let's not find out the hard way," said Mike. "We need to make sure everyone knows it's open. Until we figure out what's going on, treat this like a standard run."

Olaf tapped out on a code on his keyboard. The red lights ignited and began to spin. Through the rings, they could see shifting red shadows over on Site B. It made Mike think of Bob sprawled on the floor in his own blood.

The phone fired off a handful of quick violin notes. The ants identified it as part of the "Russian Dance" from Tchaikovsky's *Swan Lake*. Olaf tapped at the screen. "Jamie. They want to know what's going on."

"What are you saying?"

"That Arthur should drop her off and get back here."

"It's a wound," said Sasha.

"What is?"

She stared up at the rings. "We've been ripping and tearing at space-time so often, we made a wound. But we kept ripping, so when it scarred, it didn't scar shut. It scarred open. Somewhere along the way, the Door became permanent."

"And we never noticed?" scoffed Olaf.

"You wouldn't," said Mike. He pointed back at the spinning red lights. "The Door's never open without all the warning lights on. They became part of it. You didn't see the lights, so you didn't look to see if it was actually closed."

"But it has to be recent," said Sasha. "We were looking at it just the other day. It wasn't open when we stripped the whole thing down."

"And it wasn't open when Bob died," added Olaf.

"It closed after Jamie came through," said Mike. "I was right up there on the walkway. So it just happened now. Why?"

"The last straw?" suggested Sasha. "If it was going to happen, it had to happen sometime. Why not now?"

They heard the echo of the door hiss. Olaf glanced over his shoulder. Mike looked at the rings. The sound had come from the other side of the room.

From the *other* room.

Quick footsteps echoed from Site B. Neil appeared on the far side of the three rings. "Oh, hell," he said.

Mike toed the ramp. "You see us?"

"Clear as day. It's just like the Door's open, except . . ."

"It's open," said Mike. "What do the instruments there say?"

Neil slid into the chair at a workstation and his eyes flitted back and forth across the screen. "Everything here says the Door is shut down. Power's at zero, field is at zero, no program running, nothing."

"Fuck," Sasha said again.

"What," said Olaf, "did you think everything there would say it was turned on?"

"Maybe," she said. She tapped her own screen with two fingers. "It could've been an instrument problem."

Neil was looking at them through the rings. "So," he said, "definitely not an afterimage."

Mike pointed at the ramp. "You see the coins?"

Neil's eyes flitted to the quarter, then around the floor. "A couple of them."

"They look okay?"

He shrugged. "They look like coins. I can't really tell from here." He took a step toward one of the dimes.

"Don't touch them," said Mike. "Not yet."

Sasha's back pocket let out a musical chirp. Mike recognized it as the Star Trek communicator sound. She tugged out her phone. "Arthur," she said. "Asking what's going on. Should I ignore it?"

"If you ignore it, he'll think something's wrong," Olaf said.

"Something *is* wrong."

"Just ask him if Jamie's with the doctor," said Mike. "And then get up to the control room. See what everything says there."

She nodded and walked away, head bent to her phone. Mike noticed she typed with her thumbs. The door hissed open and thumped shut.

"Neil," said Olaf.

"Yeah?" Neil raised his head up and peered through the rings.

"I want you to count with me, just to make sure this isn't some kind of residual image on either side. Count to five, one Mississippi between each number, starting right now."

"One," they said in unison. "Two. Three. Four. Five."

"Damn," Olaf said.

Mike looked at him. "Any other ideas?"

"A few," said Olaf. His mouth was a flat line below his eyes. They flitted from the Door to his screen and back again. "We're going to need to run all our basic tests again. Baseball. Maybe even animals."

"Once we hear back about Jamie," said Mike. "Once we know it's safe."

TWENTY-EIGHT

"Well," said Arthur. "This is quite interesting."

He crouched at the top of the ramp in Site B and looked through the three rings at Mike and Olaf. He'd insisted on checking all the readings himself, in the control room and at each Door. Neil sat at one of the stations behind him. The one with Jamie's sweatshirt on it.

On the floor by Neil were the ends of the power cables. He'd disconnected all five in each building and dragged the ends away. The bulky connectors looked like soup cans with spikes sticking out of the center. The Door hadn't even flickered.

"You never thought something like this could happen?" asked Mike.

Arthur traded a quick look with Olaf. "Never."

Mike closed his eyes and sighed.

"Sorry," said Arthur. "It's just force of habit. Anything that touches on our core research."

"I think it's time to forget about keeping secrets."

"I'm not sure I agree."

"In the past week, you've had one person die, one person risk her life, and I think it's safe to say you've now messed with the structure of reality," said Mike. "No more secrets."

"Don't be melodramatic," Arthur said. "It doesn't suit you."

"He does have a point," said Olaf. "Maybe it's time we come—"

Arthur glared at him and raised a finger. "No."

Mike looked between them. "Come . . . clean? About what?"

"A poor choice of words on Olaf's part, I'm sure," Arthur said.

Olaf pressed his lips together and nodded. He turned and walked back to his station.

Mike looked through the rings at Arthur. "So how do you want to do this? Olaf suggested going all the way back to basics, but I thought we should wait until we had more news about Ja—"

Arthur reached out and plucked the quarter from the walkway.

"Jesus," said Mike.

"Is there a problem?" asked Arthur.

"Seriously, do you have any concept of safety at all?"

"It's just a quarter." He straightened up and held the coin between his finger and thumb. George Washington's profile gleamed in the light. It was one of the old ones, before they were state themed.

"Which could be radioactive, for all you know."

"Unlikely."

"Not according to Bob's autopsy."

Arthur gave Mike a look. *The* Look. Mike used it as a teacher, but Arthur wielded it at professor-strength levels. He tossed the coin in his hand. "No burns," he said. "No heat at all. It's a bit cool, in fact."

"We should still examine it."

"We will." Arthur glanced up. "How many other coins did you toss, Sasha?"

Her voice thundered down from the control room. *"I think there's three or four more. Two dimes, a nickel, two or three pennies. Plus Mike threw one, too."*

"Another quarter," said Mike, rubbing his temple. "It should be against the far wall."

"We'll collect them all and check them for . . . well, everything. Olaf," he called out, "we still have a Geiger counter somewhere, don't we?"

"I think so."

"I've got it," Neil said. He pointed at the rings. "It's in the supply closet back on the main floor. We were using it to check for leaks in the shielding after Bob's . . . after the incident."

Arthur nodded.

Mike looked around the platform. "Maybe we should establish a safe distance from the rings."

"We've done that," said Arthur. He closed his hand around the quarter and gestured at the white lines.

"Maybe we should establish a *new* safe distance," Mike said, "while we figure out how this is happening."

Arthur's eyes flitted from the lines up to the rings and back. "You may be right," he said.

"Thank you." Mike turned to look at Olaf. "Do you think you could map a new safe zone?"

Olaf nodded without looking up from his station. "I'll figure something out."

Arthur traced the rings with his eyes. "Fantastic."

Mike looked at him. "Sorry?"

Their eyes met across ten feet and half a mile. "Don't misunderstand me," said Arthur. "This is a crisis, and we need to understand what happened. And how. But at the same time . . . it is a fantastic sight. A stable gateway across space-time."

"We don't know that it's stable."

"We don't know that it isn't. Our power limitations meant we were able to keep the Door open for ninety-three seconds. This has been open for over two hours now."

Mike took a breath and counted to three.

Arthur looked down at the white line again. "I wonder how safe it would be to examine the components. It'd be interesting to see if they're still active, despite what the instruments say."

Over Arthur's shoulder, Mike saw Neil's eyebrows go up. "We'd need to do a lot of tests before I'd be willing to risk that," said the engineer.

"*Same here*," said Sasha.

Arthur glanced back and up. "When did you become timid?"

Neil shook his head. "Since this all started going wrong."

"What's gone wrong?"

"Bob," said Mike.

"That was a freak accident," Arthur said. "I think we've proven that at this point."

"Arthur, this isn't right," said Neil. "Even if you ignore what happened to Bob, there's no way this should be happening. It *can't* be happening."

"It's a new science," said Arthur.

"Yes," Olaf stated, "it is. And we shouldn't assume we understand it."

A few moments of silence stretched out. Arthur's phone beeped. "It's

Jamie," he said, skimming the text. "Her first round of tests all came back with no problems. Physical, X-rays, CT scan. She looks fine. They should have basic blood work in the morning."

"Good," Mike said.

"Olaf," said Arthur, "if you could join me in my office, we'll start working on a testing routine. We can go over the originals, and between us I'm sure we can come up with an accelerated schedule."

He waited to see if anyone else had a comment, then continued.

"For now, we should keep it under direct observation, even when we're not testing it. We can work in, say, six-hour shifts. Mike, if you're still willing to pitch in that would help."

Mike nodded. "Of course. Someone on each side?"

"While the Door's open, it's effectively one room. We can probably make do with just one side. And Sasha?"

"Yes?"

"You're closest to a hard line. See if Anne can order us a late lunch. I don't know about the rest of you, but I haven't eaten in about seven or eight hours at this point."

Neil's shoulders relaxed in the background. "Probably dinner, too. It'll be a long night."

Arthur turned his back to Mike and walked down the ramp, away from the rings.

TWENTY-NINE

The morning pastries were still sealed in their box. Neil used his finger to break the tape and freed his banana-nut muffin. Mike glanced at the box. "Is it too soon for me to take Bob's donut?"

"Probably," said Neil, "but it's not here anyway. I think Anne might've canceled it. She's good about stuff like that."

Mike bit back a sigh and nodded. "I thought Arthur didn't have you on watch duty until tonight."

"He doesn't, but I still need to do my job. You taking a shift?"

"He paired me up with Jamie. Half because I don't know enough about the project to be left alone, half so she can assure me she's fine."

"You don't want the jelly donut?"

"Not really, no."

"What about this chocolate thing?"

"What?"

Neil pulled on the back flap and tilted the box up.

Mike took two steps to the box and eyed the mixture of dark chocolate and flaky pastry. "I love chocolate croissants," he said. "Does it belong to someone?"

"New to me," said Neil. "I think it's yours. I'll back you up if anyone complains." He sliced the top off his muffin and scooped up a blob of butter with the knife.

Anne walked in and headed for the coffee. "You," said Mike, "are my new favorite person."

"Thanks," she said with a smile. "Why?"

He held up the croissant. "How'd you know I liked these?"

Anne shook her head. "Wasn't me."

"No?"

She shook her head again and filled her mug.

Neil let his knife clatter in the sink. "Could be a thank-you from Arthur for not saying anything to DARPA."

"It's not much of a thank-you. Plus, he and I talked to Reggie yesterday afternoon."

"How'd that go?"

"He was right," said Mike. "Not even a slap on the wrist for letting Jamie crosswalk."

"Stop taking my name in vain," said Jamie. She swung past them and around Anne to land in front of the coffee. Neil leaned out of the way as she reached back to grab her cruller and snatch up her oversized mug.

"Do you know anything about the croissant?" he asked.

"Chocolate croissant." She glanced back in the box. "Yeah, it's Mike's. I added it to the order."

"You did?"

"Told you it wasn't me," said Anne as she walked out the door.

Mike looked from the pastry to Jamie. "How did you know?"

She shrugged. "Magnus called about a report the other day and I asked him. He said it was all you ate for breakfast in college."

"It was."

"You added it to the order," repeated Neil.

She nodded and ducked back out the door. Mike stared after her. "Is it just me," he said, "or is she a lot more pleasant since her visit to the doctor?"

The engineer took in a slow breath. "Maybe they gave her a bunch of great painkillers."

"For what? She didn't have anything wrong with her."

"You have a better idea?"

"Maybe she's starting to like me."

Neil bit back most of his laugh and pulled a cup out of the cabinet.

"It sounded better than suggesting brain damage."

"Arthur said her CT scan was normal."

"It was normal in the general, quick check sense," said Mike. "The brain's a very sensitive thing. One little tweak here or there, a few pathways realigned, and you get a different person."

Neil reached for the coffee. "That's not what the Door does, though."

"Isn't it?"

The other man glanced away from the coffee and furrowed his brow.

"No screwing around," said Mike. "What are you all hiding? Did you all make a deal with the devil, and it runs on the blood of orphans or something like that?"

Neil laughed. "No," he said. "No, of course not."

"That wasn't a very sincere laugh."

"Well, I'm the one who has to kill all the orphans. It's not a funny business." He poured a quick shot of milk into his coffee. "Look," he said, "have you ever kept a secret?"

"Yeah, of course."

The engineer waved his free hand in front of him, trying to sweep the right words out of the air. "You know how, after a while, it just hits the point that you *have* to keep the secret? That you've been hiding it for so long the reason you were hiding it doesn't matter anymore?"

The ants lunged at one another. It was a furious war of red versus black, thought and memory. The roar of noise in his head almost made him wince.

And when they were done, he was left with the image of a mousy, flat-chested girl with wire-rimmed glasses.

Cheryl Woodley. Class of 2012. Just a hair off being salutatorian. Mike had her in his class from 2010 to 2011, when college applications went out and came back. She'd been accepted to every school she tried for and offered enough financial aid to afford most of them. The PTA had her earmarked for their annual scholarship, too.

But as graduation came closer and closer, she'd become more and more skittish. In the teacher's lounge there was talk of drugs or a bad home life. Possibly an abusive boyfriend. It was more common in high school than most people liked to think.

The Friday before Easter weekend, she'd come to Mike after school, close to a breakdown, and confessed. She'd screwed up. She was going to lose everything. Someone would trace her achievements back to a paper she'd written in sophomore year.

At least, one she said she'd written.

"Is this your work?" asked Mike.

"The coffee?"

"The Albuquerque Door. Did you . . . Did Arthur get this from some-one else?"

"Don't be ridiculous."

"Am I? Being ridiculous?"

"Have you heard of anyone else ever working on a project like this?"

"No, but no one's heard of this project, either."

"It's Arthur's idea," said Neil. "Arthur and Olaf."

Mike studied the other man's face. The ants were seething. "You said 'ever.' So it's not something current."

Neil shook his head. He made a point of staring into his mug while he stirred his coffee.

"Are you building off Nazi science or something? Something no one's supposed to use?" The ants rushed past his eyes with memories of Arthur's bookshelf, Jamie's old electronics book, Olaf and *Physics in the Nineteenth Century*. "Is it something Arthur discovered for his book, something that no one uses anymore?"

Neil's coffee spoon clattered in the sink. "Sorry," he said. He didn't look Mike in the eye. "You're starting to sound like one of those conspiracy theorists."

He walked out and Mike was left alone with his ants.

THIRTY

Mike leaned forward in his chair. "I had an interesting talk with Neil."

"Yeah," Jamie said, "I know."

"You do?"

"Neil went right to Arthur. He was worried your nonsense about Nazis and Arthur's book was some clever ruse, that you'd tricked him into saying something important."

"I think I did."

"So we're all secretly Nazis?"

"I never said that."

"Hail Hydra."

"You seem pretty eager to turn it into a joke."

"Or," she said, "it *is* a joke and you're the biggest part of it." She flexed her fingers. The ones on her left hand crackled and popped.

"Are you sure you're feeling okay?"

"I swear to God, if you ask me that one more time, I'm going to slap you."

Mike shrugged and settled back in his chair. "I just want to be sure you—"

"I might slap you anyway, just as a preventive measure." She stepped over the bundle of power cables and walked past his station to check the liquid nitrogen tanks. She'd checked them twice already, and they'd been checked yesterday.

He looked down at his tablet and flipped through the next ten pages of *The History of What We Know*. It walked the tightrope between informative and entertaining, and made that walk look easy. He was halfway through the book and hadn't seen a single thing that looked potentially Door-inspiring. It was doubtful Arthur would be so blatant about something he'd copied, but sometimes people did dumb things.

Jamie marched back to her workstation. She kicked one of the power connectors on the way and swore at it. She checked the monitor.

"Tanks the same?"

"Yes," she sighed. "This makes no sense."

"Yeah," Mike said, "that's what we all said yesterday while you were being checked out."

Jamie walked past her station to his, elbowed him out of the way, and leaned over the terminal to double-check something. Her shirt drooped open to reveal a wide swath of cleavage. Mike was suddenly aware of how few buttons were done on her shirt.

She met his eyes and followed his glance down to her chest. "Don't get any ideas."

"What?"

"We're not here for a nooner."

He coughed. "I beg your pardon?"

She pulled the sides of the shirt together and fastened a button one-handed. "Don't lie. You were thinking it."

"I couldn't've been. You told me the other night how unattractive you are."

She gave him a thin smile. "All that brainpower and you can't figure out when a girl's playing hard to get?"

"No, usually I can. I can also tell when she's close to demanding a restraining order. That's more what I was leaning toward."

She laughed.

"Since you brought it up, though," he said. "About the other night. You mentioned something at the bar."

"Ahhh," she said. She walked back to the other station and dropped into her chair. "I was wondering when that was going to come up again."

"You said you'd gone over all the lines of code looking for an error that could've caused Bob's accident."

She blinked. "What?"

"The code for the Door." He gestured at the rings. "D'you remember saying that?"

"That's what you want to talk about?"

"Was there something else?"

Her brow settled over her eyes. "I guess not."

"So you'd gone over all the code at that point?"

"Yeah. That's why I went to get a drink."

"How?"

"I got in my car, drove to the bar—"

"How'd you go over two-million-plus lines of code in thirty-six hours?"

Jamie opened her mouth, then closed it and shook her head. "You must've heard me wrong," she said.

"So you didn't finish going over the code?"

"Of course I did."

"When? Because I couldn't've done it in that time, and I can pretty much guarantee my reading speed's faster than anyone you know."

She smirked. "Now you're just trying to get me turned on."

"Don't dodge the question."

"Seriously, all the things we talked about that night, and this is what sticks in your mind?"

"What are we supposed to talk about? Why you named your cat Spock when you were little?"

Jamie shook her head. "See, that's how drunk I was. My cat's name was Isis. My parents made fun of me because he was a boy cat and Isis was a girl's name."

"You're still avoiding the question. Did you go through all the code or not?"

"You're being a pain and you're asking about things you're not allowed to know about."

"Technically, I'm just asking about your job performance."

"That doesn't mean you're not being a pain."

He put his hands up. "Just a guy trying to do his job."

She leaned back in her chair and tapped her foot on the floor, swinging it side to side. "Okay," she said. "What's your deal?"

"What do you mean?"

"Why do you keep up this whole 'just a normal guy' thing? Between your memory and your IQ, you're probably one of the most intelligent people on the planet."

"Well, that's up for debate."

"See?" Jamie kicked at the floor and her chair rolled away from the workstation. She pointed at him. "That's what I mean. You know you're in the top point-zero-zero-one percent of humanity, but you laugh it off and try to ignore it. You've got more potential than anyone I've ever known, and you're a small-town schoolteacher. Why haven't you been working for Magnus all along? Hell, why aren't you his boss or running NASA or JPL or something?"

He shrugged. "I'm not interested."

"That's not a real answer."

"It's real enough."

She smirked. "Do you want real answers from me or answers that are real enough?"

Mike sighed. He turned away and made a point of studying the rings. The red lights on either side of the Door were still out of sync. He kept the monitor in his peripheral vision, but none of the numbers or readings even flickered.

"Okay," she said. She tugged her chair back to the station and turned to her own terminal. "Just remember, I offered."

"You ever met any high-IQ people, the ones with insanely high IQs? Or read interviews or articles about them?"

"My question first."

"I'm trying to answer your question."

She shrugged without looking up. "Counting you?"

"Sure."

Jamie spun her chair toward him and swung one foot up onto her knee. "Four or five, I think. Olaf's 165 or something like that."

"What's the one thing they all have in common?"

"Besides being really smart?"

Mike shook his head. "When I was thirteen," he said, "when we got the results back from the IQ tests, I was excited as hell. It's every kid's dream, right? To find out you're special? It's Harry Potter and Spider-Man all wrapped up in one."

"So what happened?"

"Everyone started treating me different. All the other kids already thought I was some kind of brainiac, and now they had proof I was strange. All my teachers were either second guessing themselves around me or giving me extra work and getting annoyed that it didn't slow me down."

He looked through the rings at Site B. The red light flashed by again, like a fast wave of blood washing in across the beach. He remembered what Sasha said about a wound.

"I did my own study," he said. "I reached out and found other high-IQ people online. It was just basic stuff back then. Bulletin boards. CompuServe."

"I remember."

"But I was smart and I found people. Little proto-web online communities. The Mega Society. I talked to people, asked questions, basically studied every person I could find with an IQ over 150. And you know what I found out?"

She shrugged.

"Almost all of them have some kind of social problems. Relationship issues, emotional issues, superiority complexes. The more I looked, the worse it got. Most of them are isolated and lonely. The divorce rate looks good until you realize how few of them ever get married. Pound for pound, it's one of the unhappiest subsets of people you can find."

"Why?"

"Because they know they're different. They know they're smarter than everyone around them, everyone in the building, usually everyone in a thirty- or forty-mile radius. It's like spending your whole life as a doctoral student stuck in a kindergarten class, forced to do single-digit addition and writing the alphabet every day."

She sat back and digested the idea.

"I already knew my memory made me different. Now I had pretty solid evidence I was going to be miserable for the rest of my life, and I wasn't even old enough to shave yet. So I decided to be normal."

"How?"

"By not feeding it. Until then, I'd read everything I could get my hands on. I watched tons of shows about history and science. And at thirteen I stopped. I didn't give my brain more to work with.

"That's why I never had another IQ test. It's why I didn't study physics or astrophysics or biochemistry or anything like that in college. It's why I didn't want to work for Reggie. I don't want to know how much smarter I am than everyone around me. I didn't want to 'expand my potential' or use 'the full scope of my phenomenal intellect.' I wanted to teach high school English, help kids get into college, direct the fall musical, and live a normal, happy life like everyone else."

Jamie's lips curled into a smile. "So, basically, you're telling me ignorance is bliss?"

"You have no idea."

"There are just all kinds of levels to you, aren't there?"

"Not by choice."

"What's the musical?"

"*Little Mary Sunshine.*"

"Seriously?"

"Yeah."

"Is that a real thing or did you make it up?"

"It's real and it's cheap," he said. "I wanted *The King and I*, but it's crazy expensive."

"I was in *West Side Story* when I was a sophomore. My mom thought it'd be good for me to try something new."

"How'd that go over?"

"I hated it. I'm not good at pretending to be someone else." She looked at him for a moment. "You've learned a lot here, haven't you?"

He made a point of focusing on the rings again. "Yeah."

"Lots of physics. Programming. Electronics."

"Yep."

Her smile dimmed. "You're not going to be able to go back, are you? Back to being a teacher?"

Mike looked at the monitor. "I sent them my resignation two days ago. My contract was up for renewal anyway."

"Just like that?"

"Feeding the ants is a one-way street. I can't forget any of it, so I can't stop myself from thinking about it. That's why I kept turning Reggie down for years."

"But you signed up for this."

"He kind of tricked me into it, but how could I pass it up? Like you all said, it's going to change the world."

"So where do you go from here?"

"I don't know." He shrugged. "Maybe I'll try running NASA or JPL or something."

The smile returned to her face. "I'm glad you came here."

"Thanks. Have I answered your question?"

She straightened up in her chair. "I believe so," she said.

"How did you go through all the code so fast?"

She studied his face for almost a minute. Once her eyes darted to the rings. Twice to the computer screen. She bit her lip, looked at the Door, and the lights flicked on in the control room. Her eyes widened, just for a moment, even as her shoulders relaxed. "I think that counts as another question you're not supposed to ask," she said.

Mike sighed.

"My turn," she said a little louder. "Which one of us is paying for dinner?"

"What?"

"Dinner," she said. "Someone has to pay. You or me?"

"Why don't we just each pay for ourselves?"

Jamie shook her head. "You're kind of missing the point," she said. "If I don't have to say 'buy me dinner first,' it's your big chance to look like a gentleman."

He stared at her for a minute.

"Okay, fine," she said. She fished a quarter out of her jeans and flipped it into the air. "Call it."

"Heads."

Her fingers snatched the coin out of the air and slapped it onto the back of her palm. "It's your lucky night," she said. "You're buying dinner."

"Ahhh." He looked away and bit his lip.

"Something wrong with that?"

Mike studied the rings. He watched the lights. He checked the readings on the screen. They still hadn't changed.

"Well?"

"Did Arthur put you up to all this?"

"What?"

"You've become a lot more friendly toward me ever since I threatened him." He ran through a list of potential words and phrases. "Some might say aggressively friendly."

Jamie studied his face for a minute. "Are you politely asking if Arthur's pimping me out to you in exchange for your cooperation?"

"I thought I'd done a fairly good job of not saying that."

"Did it occur to you that this could just be a woman attracted to a coworker in a very normal part-admiration, part-lustful way?"

He shook his head. "I can honestly say it did not."

"You weren't kidding about the social problems and relationship issues, were you?"

"Apparently not."

The control room light blinked out.

"No, Arthur did not put me up to this. I am asking you to take me to dinner all on my own."

"Telling me to, really."

"Well, clearly if I waited for you to ask, I'd starve to death."

They both made a point of studying their monitors and checking the rings.

"Was there someplace you'd like to go?"

"Go?"

"For dinner."

"Oh, gosh, I thought you'd never ask."

THIRTY-ONE

Mike's fingers wiggled on the steering wheel. "So, where am I going?"

"Is there anything you don't like?"

He shrugged. "There's a lot of stuff I haven't tried."

"Thai? Italian? Mexican?" Jamie paused and frowned. "You're not one of those people who thinks Taco Bell is real Mexican food, are you?"

"I was able to figure that one out on my own."

She stretched in the passenger seat and put her feet up on the dashboard. "So what do you want?"

"We're in San Diego," he said. "I'm guessing there's good Mexican food?"

"Great food," she said. "I know a little hole-in-the-wall place. You'll love it."

"Where am I going?"

"Freeway. Go left."

Mike flicked the directional, changed lanes, and made the turn just as the light flipped to yellow. She waved him onto a southbound ramp. "How far are we going?"

"I'll let you know."

He nodded, and they drove in silence for a moment. "You want to talk some more about the code?"

"Not really," she said.

A few dozen responses flitted through his mind. He could push her for more information about the Door. He could be subtle about it and see what she let slip.

Or he could try to let it slide for a night and just enjoy being out with her.

"Here." Jamie gestured at another ramp. "Stay in the first lane."

"Okay."

"So what's up with Mike?"

He glanced away from the road. "Sorry?"

"Your name's Leland, right?"

He sighed. "Yeah."

"I'm guessing one of your parents was drunk when picking baby names?"

"Family name. Grandfather and great-grandfather were both Leland. Mom insisted."

"How do you get Mike from Leland?"

"You don't."

She pointed at a sign. "South again," she said. "Where'd it come from?"

"Why are we talking so much about me?"

"Because I spilled my guts the other night at the bar and all you want to talk about is work. Where'd Mike come from?"

"Reggie gave it to me back in junior high, about a year after we met."

"Mike? That's the best nickname he could come up with for you?"

"It's a nickname for a nickname."

"Now this sounds kind of dirty," Jamie said with a grin.

"It's short for Mycroft. Mycroft Holmes."

"Related to Sherlock?"

"His older brother. Mycroft was introduced in 'The Adventure of the Greek Interpreter.' We had to read six of Arthur Conan Doyle's stories for English class in tenth grade. Mr. Jones. Most boring teacher ever."

"I'm still not getting it."

"Mycroft was the superior Holmes. Smarter, more observant, better at deduction. But he never did anything with it. He didn't study or sharpen his gifts, he just used them as a party trick now and then. He was the embarrassment who always frustrated Sherlock."

"So Reggie called you Mycroft?"

"Everyone else called me Mycroft," he said. "They'd all been in classes with me for years. Even after I decided I didn't want to be special, I still couldn't help blowing the bell curve. And they all knew I wasn't trying at that point, which made it even worse. We read that story, and they all had me pegged. Hell, two of the teachers slipped and used it in class when they called on me."

"Ahhh. No offense, but it sounds like a lot of your formative years sucked."

He shrugged.

"Get off here," she said, pointing at another sign. "East exit. The ramp's almost going to go around in a full circle."

Mike tugged the wheel and a car behind them honked. He glanced in his mirror and the other driver flashed lights. The car accelerated and pulled around them, roaring off down the freeway.

"So everyone called you Mycroft," Jamie said.

"Yeah. It went on for about a week and then Reggie put a stop to it. He just started calling me Mike. And, well, he's one of those guys who can get people to do what he wants, so three weeks later everyone was calling me Mike."

"Just like that?"

"Just like that. It was kind of a double blessing. I didn't have to deal with Mycroft *or* Leland."

"Follow the road around the curve," she said.

"Okay."

"You're going to turn left at the light up there."

He glanced over his shoulder and tapped the directional again.

"I would've figured you as one of those guys who'd make a name like Leland work for you," she said. "That you'd just own it and make it cool."

"There is no way Leland would ever be a cool name. I say this as someone who grew up in the decade of *Twin Peaks*."

"That's what people thought about Hugo," said Jamie. "And then Hugo Weaving came along and suddenly there's a hundred kids named Hugo."

"Really?"

"I don't know. Maybe. I'd name a kid Hugo."

The area looked more residential, but with lots of smaller businesses. They passed a coffee shop, a bookstore, and a small garage. "Where am I going now?"

"Go about two more blocks and then start looking for a space."

"They don't have parking?"

"I told you, it's a hole-in-the-wall."

The car came to rest at a stop light. There was another coffee shop, a corner store, and a Laundromat. He could see a few bars and restaurants ahead, past a street-spanning sign shaped like a trolley car. "Around here?"

She nodded. "It's right up there on the left. If you see a space, grab it."

He slowed a bit. Both sides of the street were packed. A few cars crowded driveways. "So why are we here?"

"Because I'm guessing you've never had good Mexican food."

"No," he said, "seriously. Why are we here?"

Jamie sighed. "Again?"

"Sorry," he said. "This just doesn't feel right."

"How so?"

He turned right onto a side street. "I've been here a week, and now out of nowhere you want to know all these little details about me."

"I'm old-fashioned," she said. "I don't like to sleep with strangers."

"And that," he said. "The over-friendliness. I just don't buy it."

"Oh, for Christ's sake," she said. She undid her seatbelt and threw her leg across his waist. The car jerked to a halt as she rolled into his lap, wedging herself between his body and the steering wheel. "Stop talking."

"Are you—"

Jamie leaned into his face and kissed him. Hard. The tip of her tongue darted out to tap his. She found his wrists, pulled his hands up, and pressed his palms against her breasts.

Then, just as fast, she slid off him and back into her seat. "Okay," she said, "do you still think I'm here just because Arthur asked me to be friendly?"

He pressed his foot down and the car rolled forward. "No."

"Do you think I have any ulterior motives?"

"Well," he said, "not the same ones I thought you had a minute ago."

"Are you hungry?"

"What?"

"Do you still want to get dinner?"

"Does it make me shallow if I say no?"

The corners of her mouth twitched into a grin. "If it does, I'm shallow, too."

THIRTY-TWO

They didn't speak at all on the drive back to campus. Jamie gestured at road signs and made a point of not looking him in the eyes. He drove around the main building and parked his car by the trailers.

Mike shut the engine off. "Mine or yours?"

"Mine," she said. "I don't want to be worried about Magnus spying on us."

"I don't think he randomly checks in."

"You're talking again," she said with a smile.

They kept their hands off each other until it was clear there was no one else around the trailers. Then she was kissing him and pulling at his belt, even as his hands slid around her back and beneath her shirt. They paused so she could fumble with her keys and they stumbled into her trailer.

Glitch the cat let out a confused meow. It turned into a hiss as they walked past his food bowl and bumped into the table. He danced around their legs and vanished.

Mike's heart pounded, and he could feel his pulse in his fingers and his face. He kissed her mouth, her chin, her cheeks, and her ears.

Jamie yanked her own shirt open and then pulled his over his head. She pressed herself against him and kissed him hard. Her kiss was filled with lust and hunger and desperation. They wrestled with each other's jeans and tangled themselves in the curtains that divided the room.

The back of his legs hit her bed and he fell backward onto the blanket. She didn't let go, riding him down. The springs squealed under their combined weight, and Glitch threw himself off the bed with another hiss.

Mike rolled on top of her and pulled away the last bits of her clothing. Her skin was like silk against his. She was warm and moist and wrapped her legs around him. He bent his head to her chest and she gasped and grabbed a fistful of hair.

It was very hard for Mike to get lost in the moment. So many things could set off memories and comparisons, spurring the ants into action. More than a few times he'd had the mood ruined by a deluge of images and sounds inside his head.

This time his mind was blissfully silent.

Half an hour later he heard a thump. A few moments later, Glitch hopped onto the bed, and shoved his head into Jamie's arm. He meowed, shifted his paws, and leaned his forehead against her shoulder.

"He has no boundaries," said Mike.

"He's a little perv," she said. "He watches me in the shower sometimes."

She twisted beneath him, and he slid behind her. His arms wrapped around her. Glitch sat on the bed and watched them.

"Does he want to be fed?"

"He wants his treats," Jamie said. "Whenever I come home late, I give him some extra cat food or Greenies or something. He's a creature of habit."

"Sorry to mess up the schedule."

"It's okay," she said. She reached up and held his arms. "I didn't want to wait on *my* treats."

"Clever."

She chuckled and tugged his arms a little tighter around her. "Are you staying for the night?"

"Do you want me to?"

"I wouldn't complain."

"We wouldn't get much sleep."

"Oh, really?"

"Just being honest."

"You ready to go again?"

"Give me a few more minutes to catch my breath."

"I'm not so sure I'm still in the mood."

"Really?"

She half-turned to him and her teeth gleamed in the darkness. "You can try to change my mind, if you think you can."

"I think I could make a few compelling arguments."

"Go for it."

He kissed his way down her back, tasting her sweat on his lips. She sighed. He stopped at her tailbone and reached up to run his fingertips across the smooth glistening skin of her shoulders, tracing lines alongside her spine.

Then he paused, and frowned.

"Jamie?"

"Mmmmmm?" She closed her legs around his left thigh. She was still wet.

He squinted at her in the dim light of the bungalow. "There's nothing wrong with your back."

"Great to know," she said. "Did you have a problem with the front?"

"No, seriously, where are your scars?"

She twisted around, smiling. "My what?"

He set his hand on her shoulder and gently rolled her onto her stomach again, pushing her into the thin shaft of light that seeped around the blinds in her trailer. He ran his fingers down her spine and looked at her skin. Her flawless skin. There were faint tan lines framing her ass and another one across her back. "Your scars," he said. "You told me your back was a mess."

She turned to face him. "What?"

"The motorcycle crash in high school. The awful prom dress. Apologizing for freaking out on me when I touched your shoulders."

Jamie's smile dipped at the edges. She shook her head. "What are you talking about?"

He rolled onto his knees. "You're serious? You don't remember telling me all this at the bar?"

She sat up and leaned against the wall. "I told you about Tramp at the bar, and then we flirted for almost an hour. I thought I freaked you out being so forward, and that's why you've been kind of distant."

"And you don't have any scars?"

"Have you noticed any?"

The ants got out.

They carried out pictures and sounds and associations. Jamie in Washington the first time he saw her. Nine other women he'd been casually naked with (seven girlfriends, two friends with benefits). Jamie bending over and showing off the biker shorts under her clothes. Jamie in the bar talking about her cat dying and the motorcycle crash. Taking his own cat, Jake, to be put down. The baseball. Jamie standing on the other side of the three rings, about to step through, knowing she might be walking to her death. His mother dying. Bob dying. Jamie standing in front of him on the pathway, unharmed and uninjured.

The baseball that wasn't there anymore.

Bob with cancer from months of radiation exposure.

Jamie standing in front of him with no injuries.

Talking about her cat in the bar.

He replayed her crosswalk in his mind. She'd come through okay, so he'd barely studied it. Not the way he'd obsessed over Bob's. He pulled up before and after images. Her in Washington. The first time he saw her in San Diego. In her trailer. Watching the rings. Driving on the freeway.

"Oh, hell," he said. The ants carried out Reggie's words from the other day. What they know, what they don't know, and what they don't know that they don't know.

"What? What's wrong?"

Mike took her by the hands and tugged her toward the center of the mattress. She rolled onto her knees and shuffled where he guided her. He turned her toward the window. Her skin gleamed in the light.

He brushed her hair away from her face. He shook his head. "Hell," he said again.

Jamie reached up to feel her cheeks and nose and forehead. "What is it?"

He rolled out of bed and searched for his boxers. "Don't take this the wrong way," Mike said, "but you're not the woman I thought I was going to bed with."

THIRTY-THREE

"All right," Arthur said from the conference room door, "please tell me what is so damned important that I had to drive back down here at midnight instead of hearing it in the morning."

"No idea," said Olaf. He sat at the table across from Neil and Sasha. Jamie was in a chair by the corner, wrapped in her sweatpants and a long-sleeved T-shirt. Mike stood at the head of the table, close to her. He stared at Arthur for a moment. The older man's returned look was close to a glare. It was the first time Mike had ever seen him without a tie.

"Well?" asked the project head.

"We've been waiting on you," said Mike.

"How gracious of you." He looked around the room. "Is anyone monitoring the Door?"

Jamie shook her head. "Cameras are all on."

"I think it's best if everyone hears this at once," said Mike.

Arthur simmered for a moment. He glanced at his usual seat, then pulled out the chair near Olaf.

They all stared at Mike. He gazed at each of them. He'd been going over this in his head for almost an hour, since he tumbled out of Jamie's bed.

"I know what happened to Bob," he said. "And I know what the Door does."

Eyes went wide around the table. They shifted in their seats. Sasha looked at Arthur. Arthur and Olaf exchanged a few unspoken words. Neil closed his eyes and sighed.

Jamie kept her eyes on Mike. She'd been annoyed that he wouldn't talk to her, but she was still giving him the benefit of the doubt. He wondered if she still would when he was done.

"I don't know what you think you've learned," Arthur said, "but our contracts with Magnus are quite specific. If you breathe a word of what you've learned—"

Mike waved him to silence. "I don't know *how* it works," he said. "I just know it doesn't work the way you've been telling everyone."

More uneasy glances from Arthur and Sasha. Olaf shifted in his seat again. "What do you mean?"

Mike waved a hand at the wall, toward the main floor. "You've all been assuming that you're creating a bridge across space-time," Mike said. "A fold, you called it. The traveler steps through this set of rings and comes out of the one over in Site B."

Arthur nodded. "That's a simple way of putting it, but that's what it does, yes."

"The Door lets us locate an appropriate fold in space-time," said Olaf, "and we use that to open a tunnel that extends across another quantum state."

"No," said Mike. "That isn't what it does."

Olaf crossed his arms.

"If I'm right, and all the evidence says I am, the Albuquerque Door doesn't extend across alternate quantum states. It extends *into* them."

Neil straightened up. "That's not how it works," he said.

"Yes it is," Mike said.

"No," said Arthur, "it isn't."

Sasha scowled at Mike. "What the fuck are you talking about? It's been working fine for over a year."

"Again, I don't know enough about the physics of it to explain it technically," said Mike. He held up his hands and moved the left one toward the right. "It's more of a thought experiment. When we open the Door, subject A steps through the rings into a quantum state we'll call X. An alternate reality, for lack of a better term. Subject A enters this other reality and knocks A-X, his or her alternate self, out through the other rings into *our* reality." His left hand tapped the right and it moved off, continuing the path. "A goes in, A-X comes out."

"No," said Arthur with a shake of his head. "Impossible."

"It's not impossible."

"It's nonsense is what it is," Olaf said.

"It's what's happening."

"Prove it," said Arthur. "Where's this evidence that says you're right? Did you bring any of it?"

"Almost all of it," said Mike.

"Is this another one of your mental spreadsheets?" asked Jamie. "That's not going to make you popular."

"No, it's physical evidence," he said. "Right here."

Arthur gestured at the empty table. "Where?"

Mike looked at Jamie. "Can you pull your hair back?"

She blinked. "Why?"

"It'll make sense in a minute. Just pull it all back away from your face."

She raised an eyebrow at him, but she gathered her hair into a loose ponytail. Mike reached out and touched her forehead on either side. "Here and here," he said. "Anyone see anything?"

Jamie tried to look up at her forehead. "You're starting to freak me out," she said.

"I don't see anything," said Neil.

Olaf rolled his eyes. "What's this supposed to prove?"

Mike took a slow breath. "Her halo scars are gone."

Jamie pulled away from his fingers. "My what?"

Arthur frowned and leaned forward. So did Neil. "It might just be the light," said Sasha.

"They're gone," Mike repeated.

"Is this supposed to be some kind of 'angel' joke?" Jamie asked.

"Medical halo," he said.

She blinked and opened her eyes wide.

"Scars can fade over time," Olaf said.

"They were there four days ago," said Mike. "Scars don't fade that fast. Case in point." He touched Jamie on the shoulder, guiding her up and out of the chair. "Can you pull your shirt up?"

Her eyes went wide. "What?"

"Just in the back."

She leaned in to Mike, breathing in his ear. "I don't have anything on under this."

"Even better."

"Seriously," she said, "what the hell does my back have to do with Bob?"

"Just . . . just trust me, okay?"

"You're lucky you're cute."

He looked at the others. "You all know Jamie's got a thing about her back, right? And why?"

She was the only one who didn't nod in agreement. Olaf shrugged. "What's your point?"

"All of us were so busy looking deep for problems, we didn't see the ones right on the surface." He touched her arm "Go ahead. All the way up, if you don't mind."

Jamie reached back and grabbed the shirt between her shoulder blades, gathering it up in two handfuls. She slid it up and shrugged it over her shoulders, crossing her arms over her chest. Her tan lines stood out in the bright lights of the conference room. Mike glimpsed the swell of her breast and felt his pulse jump.

A series of gasps and mutters leaped from the team. Sasha punctuated it with "Oh, fuck."

"How?" Arthur stared at her bare back with wide eyes.

"It's not just the scars, though," Mike said. "She didn't even argue much about pulling her shirt up, did she? Does that seem normal for her?"

"Stop talking about me in the third person," Jamie chided him. "I've always been a little bit of an exhibitionist. What's the big deal?"

Neil frowned. Arthur took off his glasses and rubbed his temple.

"The big deal is that Jamie never would've shown us her back because it was a mess of scars."

"That's what you said back in my trailer."

Sasha's eyebrows went up. "Back in the trailer?"

Mike held up his hand to the others. "Who was Kevin Ulinn?"

"Kev . . . oh, Christ." A touch of pink colored her cheeks. She rolled her shoulders and shook the shirt back down over herself. "How do you even know about him?"

"You told me about him at the bar."

"I did?"

"Yep. Whatever happened to him?"

She frowned. "I don't know. We dated for about four months. Wasn't even dating, just a lot of teenage sex. I kept it a secret because he was three years older than me. I lost touch with him pretty quick after we ended things."

Mike nodded. "It might take a phone call or two, but I think we can prove to you that Kevin died in a motorcycle crash seventeen years ago. The girl he'd been seeing was injured in the same crash. She ended up with scars all over her back. Her name was Jamie Parker, a cheerleader from the next town over."

"No." Jamie shook her head. "No, that didn't happen."

He took her hand, applied a careful amount of pressure, and then let go. "It didn't happen to you," he said, "but that's what happened here."

"Here?" echoed Arthur.

"Here. In this reality." He looked at all of them. "Jamie, this Jamie, is from another universe."

"How?"

"I already explained it," Mike said. "She came here through the Door."

"Okay," said Jamie, "not really sure what you're trying to prove here, but you can stop now. This isn't funny."

"I'm sorry," said Mike.

"This could just be some sort of renewal effect," said Olaf. "Her cell structure could've been—"

"The Door doesn't do anything on the cellular level," Mike said. "That's what you all keep telling me."

"There has to be another . . ."

"This is what happened to Bob," said Mike. "Our Bob, the guy we knew, went into the rings and knocked another version of himself out. A version from a world, a reality, where things have gone very bad, I'd guess. Maybe there was some kind of war, a full-on nuclear one. Bad enough that he'd be dressed in rags and suffering from dehydration and radiation exposure. That's why we couldn't find the baseball. That Bob, the Bob who died here, never had one."

They looked at one another. They looked at Jamie. She looked at Mike and at all of them.

"You haven't made a doorway," said Mike. "You've created a huge, interdimensional croquet set."

"Fuck me," said Sasha.

Olaf snorted. "There's a problem with your multiverse hypothesis," he said. "Why doesn't it happen all the time? If this is how the Door works, then every single person who goes through should've traded places with an alternate self." He gestured at the room. "We've all gone through. Everyone here should be from a different universe."

Mike shifted on his feet and counted to five. "That's my point," he said. "You are."

ID ERROR

THIRTY-FOUR

Olaf opened his mouth, then closed it with another snort.

"No," said Neil. "No, no, no."

"All of us?" Sasha looked at Neil, at Arthur, and then at Mike. "How can you be sure?"

"Because you've all been through the Door," Mike said. "Just like Olaf said, anyone who's gone through would have switched."

"This is nonsense," said Olaf, and for a brief moment he sounded like Bogart, too. "We were all given multiple exams."

"The exams were all looking for something that had gone wrong," said Mike. "Nothing else. And they still missed something important, something you wouldn't've thought to test for."

"What?" Jamie's eyes were calm, but still wide.

"Disease," Mike said. "Each of you is carrying different versions of the flu, the common cold, and probably some other stuff that never took hold. And you've all got different resistances. That's why there've been so many sick days." He shrugged. "I'm tempted to say that's what caused the last two or three flu scares here in San Diego."

Olaf brushed the words out of the air. "The many worlds interpretation is nonsense," he said. "It's a mathematical party trick, nothing else."

"We would've noticed," said Neil. "How could someone be replaced without everyone else noticing?"

"You did notice," Mike said. "All of you did. You just didn't understand what you were seeing."

Arthur furrowed his brow.

"When I first came out here," said Mike, "most of you mentioned memory problems. Arthur, you told me you'd forgotten the date of your anniversary. Bob was confused about which trailers Jamie and Sasha lived in. Olaf thought his office was on the other side of the hall."

"My office *is* on the other side of the hall," snapped Olaf. "It was another one of Bob's stupid jokes."

"We've been busy," Jamie told Mike. "Forgetting things isn't that surprising."

"Except none of you actually forgot anything, did you?" He looked at each of them. "None of you ever drew a blank, you all just remembered something different. Something from your native reality."

"I don't remember anything different," Sasha said.

"Neither do I," said Jamie.

"It wouldn't be different to you because it would line up with your experiences. But those experiences don't always line up with the facts here." He looked at Jamie. "When we were at the bar, you told me you had a cat named Spock growing up."

She shook her head. "No, I told you, my cat's name was Isis."

"*Your* cat was named Isis," said Mike, "but I remember Spock because you aren't the Jamie I was talking to in the bar."

"You were right next to me."

"Not me," he said. "Another me on another world. The experiences don't line up." He glanced at each of them in turn.

Sasha looked around the room. "So this is the mirror universe?"

Mike nodded. "From your point of view, yeah."

"But you're not all evil?"

He shrugged. "No more than usual, I guess? I don't know what you think we're supposed to be like."

Neil looked at his hands. "You're saying I'm from another dimension? I'm not from here."

"If it makes a difference," said Mike, "the Neil you replaced wasn't from here either. According to the reports, Neil made his first crosswalk last January. He's been gone ever since."

"Not necessarily," said Arthur. "There's a chance the native Neil could've been shifted back the same way this one was."

Mike shook his head. "You're talking about millions of potential

realities. Billions. The odds of finding the same one again are astro-
nomical."

"How can you know it's not the same one every time?"

"Because you're not all like Bob. If you were all from the same place,
you'd all be from there. And you're not."

Neil was still studying his hands. His wedding ring. "So my wife . . .
the woman I've been sleeping with for the past year and a half . . . isn't
my wife?"

"Sort of," said Mike. "She's the same person. You probably still have
a lot of the same experiences together."

"But she's not *my* wife," said Neil. "She's not the woman I married.
She married some other me."

Mike didn't say anything.

Arthur's eyes went wide. "Ben Miles."

Mike nodded. "He didn't have a breakdown. He doesn't remember
his wife because the Ben who came out of the Door married someone
else. His wife really is a stranger to him. An impostor."

"They locked him up for nothing."

"I'll talk to Reggie in the morning," said Mike. "We'll get him out."

"Oh, Jesus," said Neil. "I've been cheating on my wife."

"You've been cheating on her with her," said Sasha. She rubbed her
chin. "It's not that bad."

"Yes it is."

She looked Mike up and down. "You're not the guy I was flirting
with back in Washington?"

"Definitely not," he said.

She turned to Arthur. "And you're not the man who recruited me at
DEF CON?"

He shifted his feet. "Apparently not, although I remember recruiting
you there."

"It doesn't seem to make that much of a difference," Sasha pointed
out. "I mean, we've all been functioning fine. It's been six weeks since
my last crosswalk, and I haven't had any problems. None I've noticed,
anyway."

Neil grabbed a handful of hair above his ear. "How can you all be so
calm about this?"

"It would stand to reason," mused Arthur, "that with the number of potential realities, there would be an almost infinite amount with negligible differences. We step through the Door and there's a small change. Something that either slips by or we brush off as a minor mistake of some sort. The date of an anniversary. The name of a cat." He glanced at Olaf. "What side of the hall your office is on."

Olaf didn't say anything. His stare was focused just past Jamie's shoulder. Mike wasn't sure if he was trying to keep an angry outburst in check or if he was deep in thought.

"Eventually, though," said Mike, "you'd end up with an undeniable difference. Someone comes through from a more divergent reality."

"Someone like Bob," said Jamie. "Or Miles. Or me."

"You're not quite as extreme a case as Bob," said Mike, "but, yeah." He considered taking her hand, but decided he shouldn't. Under the circumstances, with all she was getting hit with, it needed to be her choice.

"And would we have even known about Jamie if . . ." Arthur looked at the table. "Forgive me for being blunt, but it seems you two are sleeping together, at least."

"Neither of us slept," Jamie said. She managed a half-smile. "And I thought he was somebody else at the time."

Mike's cheeks warmed. He tried to tighten his lips and push past it. Sasha chuckled.

"My point is," continued Arthur, "there may be several differences that just haven't come up for the rest of us because there's nothing to put them in context. How long would your lack of scars have gone unnoticed if, well, someone hadn't seen you . . . naked." He looked down at the table again on the last word.

"I'm sure I would've worn something revealing sooner or later."

"You've been happier," said Neil. "I just figured you were so relieved that nothing went wrong when you crosswalked."

Sasha nodded. "It's been a little weird. I just figured . . ." She glanced at Mike and smiled. "Well, I figured you two slept together that first night."

Jamie raised an eyebrow. "Are you saying you thought I just really needed to get laid?"

Now they all chuckled. Even Neil made a tight grin.

"I'd guess," said Mike, "this might be one of the reasons you've all been tense. Everyone's body language is wrong. Each time someone went through the Door, he or she ended up surrounded by people whose movements and gestures all felt off. And he or she would seem wrong to everyone else. Just little things, on a subliminal level." He looked at Arthur. "You told me that half the time you felt like you were surrounded by strangers. In a way, you were right."

They all looked at one another. Studied one another.

Mike took another breath. "And I figured out something else, too."

Neil sighed. "More bad news."

Mike crossed his arms, stared at Arthur, and counted to five. "None of you actually know how the Door works, do you?"

Arthur took in a breath and raised his hand. Now that Mike was looking for them, he could see the way all the facial muscles shifted in time with the movement, how the lips formed words that came quick but with no urgency. It was a practiced motion, something prepared and rehearsed.

Then someone cut him off.

"No," said Olaf. "No, we don't."

THIRTY-FIVE

"Olaf, you've signed a number of—"

"Give it up, Arthur," he said. "It's over."

"We all agreed—"

"It's over," Olaf said again. "He figured us out."

Arthur made a point of not looking at Mike. "You and I both agreed that we wouldn't—"

"You and I didn't agree to anything," said Olaf. He waved his hand at Mike. "He's probably right and I'm not the guy who discussed anything with you."

"But you know what we discussed."

"Fuck it," said Sasha. "Olaf's right."

They all traded glances for a few moments. Neil played with his wedding ring. Jamie squeezed Mike's hand, then let go and settled back into her chair.

Another moment of silence passed.

"So," said Mike, "should I keep making educated guesses, or does someone want to explain how you built this thing?"

More looks went between them. Then Olaf cleared his throat. "The SETH project was a disaster," he said. "On every possible level. We'd been kidding ourselves for ages, and then we were just in deep denial, even after the failure with the first two test blocks. After Tramp, we knew it was all downhill. Especially for me and Arthur. No more grants, no more research. For the rest of our careers, we were going to be the idiots who killed a dog trying to teleport it. If we were lucky, we'd end up teaching Physics 101 at some community college."

Olaf paused to rub the bridge of his nose. "I came up with the idea of the Door as a way to stall the inevitable. We thought we might get an extra year or two before anyone realized we weren't producing anything. Enough to maybe dim the memory of SETH a bit."

Arthur coughed into his hand. "There is some real science behind the Door," he said. "It wasn't a complete hoax. It was just decades, maybe centuries past what we actually knew how to do."

"It was like NASA's warp drive project," said Sasha. "It's hypothetically possible, we just don't know how to make it work in practice."

"But it does work," said Mike. "How'd you do it?"

Arthur and Olaf glanced at each other.

"Well?"

"We got drunk," said Olaf.

"Beg your pardon?"

Arthur pulled off his glasses. He reached for a tie he wasn't wearing, sighed, and polished them on his shirt sleeve. "We managed to hold off Magnus for fourteen months," he said. "And then he demanded to see something. Some scrap of proof that we were making progress. If not, he wasn't going to renew our funding. And we had nothing. We'd constructed the rings, the whole system, but without the equations to make it all work it was just a very powerful, very expensive electromagnet. We'd hit the end of our careers.

"Olaf came to my office, and we each had a double whiskey. Then another one. And a third."

"Then we sent someone out to get more," said Olaf.

"Me," Jamie said.

"Was it you? I don't even remember anymore."

"I think it was," she said, "but I guess who did what is up for debate now."

Olaf snorted.

Arthur straightened up in his chair and looked around. "Most of us were there at that point, and we were all pretty drunk. We started talking about how we were going to go down in history as a bunch of crackpots. Maybe mad scientists if people were feeling particularly kind. And we were right there in my office. With my book collection.

"One of them," Arthur said, "is a treatise by a man named Aleksander

Koturovic. Limited run. I think only two or three hundred were ever printed, and most of them were destroyed. I found it in a used book-shop in England while I was doing research for *The History of What We Know*."

Mike waited a moment for him to continue. Everyone was staring at Arthur. Olaf made no move to pick up the thread.

"Koturovic did a lot of early work in neuroscience and biochemistry back in the late eighteen eighties, but he also dabbled in physics, math-ematics, a bit of everything. Dabbled being the key word. Half of his ideas were brilliant, even by today's standards. The other half . . ." Ar-thur pushed his glasses back onto his face. "Well, I didn't even bother to include him in my book. Let's say that."

"He was a doomsday nut," said Sasha. "He thought someday hu-manity was going to form some kind of telepathic gestalt, a collective unconscious, that'd open a dimensional breach between worlds. And then monsters from those other worlds would come attack us."

Mike glanced at her. "You've read it?"

"We've all read it at this point," said Jamie. "Two or three times."

"If he was alive today," said Neil, "he'd be showing up on the History Channel all the time, talking about mermaids and pyramid power and Bigfoot and all that crap."

"Or he'd have a movie deal with SyFy," Sasha said.

Arthur cleared his throat. "Olaf made some comment, something that reminded me of the treatise," he said. "I can't remember what. But we pulled it off the shelf and read some passages out loud. A large part of Koturovic's work is his doomsday theory, and he had a lot of math backing it up. It was all nonsense, of course, and we imagined people reading about us the same way in a hundred years. Then we reached a few pages of his raw calculations for breaching dimensional barriers. I stumbled over them for a few minutes, and then Sasha said we should just use his equations to run the Door."

She shrugged. "I'd had three or four drinks at that point," she said. "It sounded like Koturovic had a better grip on how to create a dimen-sional breach than we did."

"We were all drunk," said Olaf. "Drunk enough that it made sense to try it, not so drunk that we couldn't do it."

"We took a pair of bottles down to the main floor," Jamie said. "Arthur read off thirty-seven pages of equations and I typed it all in."

"Jamie's the fastest typer," said Neil. He twisted his wedding ring off and flipped it back and forth between his fingertips. "Our Jamie was, anyway."

Her lips twitched and her gaze dropped to the table for a moment.

"I think," said Arthur, "on some level I was hoping it would destroy the system. That it would all overload, seize up, short out, something. That was my high hope, that we could just end in failure rather than disgrace. Jamie entered the equations, we all made one last toast, and we turned it on."

"And it worked," said Mike.

Arthur nodded. "Yes. And to this day we don't know how. We all stood there and stared at it. It stayed open for fourteen seconds before we blew a fuse."

"We caused a blackout," said Neil. "Everyone for half a mile lost power."

"The next morning we weren't sure if it really happened or not," Arthur said, "but there were too many things we all agreed on. So we spent two days replacing everything that had burned out and tried it again. And there it was.

"We agreed to keep it secret right then and there. We didn't know how it happened, just that all our careers were saved. At least for a while longer. I approached Magnus with our requirements for complete secrecy. He saw one test and agreed. We all signed the nondisclosure agreements and there it was." He looked around the room. "We had a conspiracy."

Jamie and Sasha nodded. Neil bowed his head.

"Over the next few months we improved the tech side of it, made it more energy efficient, and doubled the time. Then we tripled it and eventually got it to where it is today." Arthur pulled his glasses off again, remembered he still wasn't wearing a tie, and pushed them back on. "But we still don't know why or how it works."

"You've had almost three years to study it," said Mike. "You must have figured out some of it."

"There's nothing to figure out," said Olaf. "The man's hypotheses were—are—gibberish. Even back then, people said they were gibberish. Psychic energy and dimensional barriers and giant alpha predators. His science is weak at best and a third of his equations aren't even finished. He published a volume of loose premises with nothing to back them up except a few mathematical coincidences."

"And yet," Mike said, "it works."

Olaf managed a bitter smile and nodded. "It works."

"Why didn't you just say something? Come clean and get some more people in here?"

Arthur took a deep breath and sighed. "Pride," he said. "Ego. We were so sure we could crack it, then too embarrassed that we couldn't."

"Suddenly we'd go from being the people who created the Albuquerque Door to a footnote," Olaf said. "We'd just be the people who laid the groundwork for someone else to figure it out."

"Nothing wrong with that," said Mike.

"You don't publish a lot, do you?" smirked Olaf.

"We kept running trial after trial, hoping to learn something," said Arthur. "Olaf and I spent weeks combing through the treatise and going over every crosswalk again and again. It gave us material to feed to DARPA. If nothing else, we hoped an overwhelming series of successful tests would deflect attention away from the fact that we didn't understand why they were successful."

"Really?"

"Lots of inventions went public before people fully understood them," said Neil. "Three-quarters of the pharmaceutical industry is just mass-testing random compounds and seeing what kind of effects they have. When the United States bombed Hiroshima and Nagasaki, there were less than two hundred people in the world who understood all of the science and engineering behind the atomic bomb. No one in Washington did. But everyone understood the explosion."

"We've made almost no progress," said Arthur. "There's something missing. Some element that's just beyond us."

Mike raised a brow. "How do you mean?"

"I have a premise," he said, "a bare-bones one for another book, that certain ideas can only happen at certain points in history. We don't see the sun the same way the ancient Egyptians did. We don't see the night sky the same way the ancient Greeks did. We don't see the ocean the same way the Vikings did. The scientific views of a time shape how people view things enough that once society gets past a certain point, it's almost impossible for us to think in the same way."

"I've heard similar ideas," said Mike.

"Some key paradigm has shifted in the hundred-plus years since Koturovic wrote down his theories," Arthur said. "Something about how we see the world. And it's keeping us from fully understanding what he was saying."

"It probably didn't help that every now and then one of you came through the Door with slightly different research priorities," Mike said. "Just enough to keep throwing things off, and adding to the sense of memory issues."

Arthur raised his shoulders, and let them slump back down.

"Still, though," Mike said, "three years? How's that possible?"

"Fermat came up with his 'last theorem' in sixteen thirty-seven," said Olaf. "It took three hundred and fifty years for someone to solve it again. That was a scribble in a margin. We're dealing with almost nine pages of equations."

"With nothing to back them up," Arthur added. "As I said, most of his work was destroyed. I'd be amazed if there were thirty copies of his treatise left in the world. There's no early research or further studies or later experiments. Koturovic's almost a nonentity, historically. He dropped out of sight in England, reappeared briefly in America, and died in eighteen ninety-nine."

"We just needed more time," Jamie said. "We figured if we had more time, if we could run more experiments, eventually we had to find a pattern. We'd figure out how the equations work."

Mike looked at her, and the ants carried out more images. Computer towers. Talking about code. Pages from different reports.

"Johnny doesn't just run the crosswalks," he said. "It's analyzing them. It didn't take you long to go over the code because most of his functions don't involve running the Door at all."

Jamie and Arthur both nodded.

Another moment passed.

"So," Arthur said, "now you know everything. What happens next? Are you going to turn us in to Magnus?"

Mike shook his head. "I think the Door itself is the big issue right now." He looked at each of them. "No one else should go through it, and we need to figure out how to shut it off."

"Tough," said Olaf, "since we don't know how it works in the first place."

THIRTY-SIX

"Okay," Jamie said. "I might regret this, but can I ask you a question about her?"

Mike looked away from his terminal. "Her?"

"The other me?"

They were watching the Door again. Olaf was at Site B. Sasha was with them, checking the cables and hoses for the ninth time, to make sure something hadn't been left connected.

"You can ask," said Mike, "but I don't know if I can answer."

"I might be able to," Sasha said.

"Why would she name the cat after a doctor?"

"What?" Mike yawned. They were all working on five hours of sleep. He hadn't been too surprised when Jamie spent it alone in her trailer.

"Spock," she said. "Why would a kid name their cat Spock?"

"I thought it was the *Star Trek* character," said Mike, "not the doctor."

"Pretty sure it was," said Sasha. "You . . . she was a fan of the original series."

Jamie looked at Sasha, then over to Mike, and back. "What's *Star Trek*?"

There was silence on the main floor.

"You are fucking kidding me," said Sasha.

"What?"

"'Space, the final frontier . . .'" said Mike. "Captain Kirk, Mr. Spock, the *Enterprise*."

Jamie shook her head.

"Okay," he said, "where'd you come up with Isis?"

"*Assignment: Earth*," she said. "I loved it when I was little. I named him after the cat on the show."

"*Assignment: Earth*?"

"Yeah, you know. The old sci-fi show. Gary Seven. Isis." She tilted her head to the left. "'Our mission is to guide mankind into the twenty-first century. . . .'"

It was Mike's turn to shake his head.

She stared at him. "Robert Lansing, Teri Garr, Julie Newmar. It ran for six or seven years. They made movies out of it. And a spin-off series."

"Wait." Sasha furrowed her brow. "You're talking about the old *Star Trek* episode, 'Assignment: Earth'?"

"Yes!" Jamie snapped her fingers. "That's right. I always forget it was a spin-off."

"But you've never heard of *Star Trek*?"

"No, no, no," she said. "I remember it now. It was that spaceship show Roddenberry did for two seasons before *Assignment: Earth* replaced it."

"So no Captain Picard?" asked Sasha. "*Deep Space Nine*? *Wrath of Khan*?"

Jamie straightened up. "*The Wrath of Khan*, yeah, of course."

Sasha put her fists on her hips. "How do you have *Wrath of Khan* but not *Star Trek*?"

"It was the second *Assignment: Earth* movie, when they tried to stop the Eugenic Wars. Ricardo Montalban came back and played the same character from that *Star Trek* show. They had to dye his hair black so it'd match the old episodes."

Another moment of silence spread itself thin across the main floor.

"The universe you come from sucks," said Sasha. "I'm going up to the booth to check the main readings again."

Jamie settled back in her chair and sighed. She flipped a quarter off her thumb, caught it, and worked it back to her thumb again. It spun into the air two more times, and she blew air out of her nose.

Mike glanced at her. "Problem?"

"Well, yeah. Apparently I'm stuck in an alternate universe where there's no *Assignment: Earth*."

"That's all?"

She looked at him. "What are we doing?"

He tilted his head. "Us?"

"It's not on!" she said, waving a hand at the rings. "The power's not on, the coils are cold, there's no magnetic flux past the standard residual. We can't shut the Door down when everything already says it's shut off."

Mike shrugged. "And yet . . ."

"It's open," she agreed. "We didn't know why it opened at all, and now we're trying to figure out why it's staying open, even though we've got no idea what made it happen." She waved a hand at the screen.

He studied her face. "And . . . ?"

"And the only damn thing I can think of is that I'm not smart enough to figure this out, but she'd probably know the answer already."

"She?"

Jamie smacked the quarter out of the air with two fingers, and it clattered onto her workstation. "The one who had a cat named Spock. The one who's supposed to be here. The . . . the real one."

He shrugged. "You're not that different."

"You're not really good at this whole comforting thing, are you? You're just supposed to hug me, maybe squeeze my butt, and—"

"Not different in the important ways," said Mike. "The Jamie I met, the one who was here before you, she could be a little bitter. I think she thought that motorcycle crash was the defining moment in her life, that it was why she ended up working with computers rather than doing, I don't know, something else. I think she regretted it sometimes. Like she'd been forced down a path instead of having a choice."

"Yeah?"

"Yeah. But you didn't have the crash. And you still went into computers. You still decided using your mind was the best way to go in life. Because that's who you are."

She swept up the quarter and flipped it into the air again. "I take it back," she said. "You're better at this than I thought."

"I have moments."

"You do."

"If it's any consolation, I think you may be a bit smarter than her. You seem to get your mind around things a lot faster."

"My 'mind.' How polite of you." She took the quarter between two fingers and flung it at him. It whizzed through the air, hit him in the arm, and chimed to the floor.

"Okay," he said, "I deserved that." He bent down, scooped the coin off the floor, and pushed it into his pants pocket.

"Hey," she said. "Quarter. Mine. Give it."

"You gave it to me."

"I threw it at you."

"Same thing," he said.

"Not quite."

"This is not the way to get your butt squeezed."

"If I have to pay you to squeeze my butt we're both doing something wrong."

He slid the coin free and tossed it to her. She caught it one-handed, switched it to her thumb, launched it back into the air, and caught it again. "Is Mike sleeping alone tonight?" she asked the quarter. She glanced at him. "Call it."

"There's more to this than a coin toss, right?"

"I don't know. We'll see what the coin says."

"In that case, tails."

"An ass man. Good to know. Don't get your hopes up." She flicked the quarter into the air, snatched it as it dropped, and slapped it onto the back of her hand. "Tails?"

"Still, yes."

"Are you using super-memory powers?"

"Yeah, they let me predict it before you tossed the coin."

"Wiseass." She looked at the coin. "And a thief. Give me my quarter back."

"What?"

"You're sleeping alone." She held up the quarter. "Fake."

He peered at it. "It is?"

"New Amsterdam?"

Mike frowned and held out his hand. She reached out and pressed the coin into his palm, letting her fingers glide back along his.

The quarter showed the familiar outline of New York and the Statue of Liberty. The curving text was identical to all the other state quarters he'd seen, except this said NEW AMSTERDAM.

"Where'd you get this?"

She smiled. "You just pulled it out of your pocket, Mister Photographic Memory."

"Is this one of the quarters we threw through the Door?"

Jamie shook her head. "It's just pocket change. I've been carrying it around for a couple days now."

"Did it come through the Door with you when you crosswalked?"

Her brow furrowed. "I don't think so. Pretty sure I got it over at 7-Eleven yesterday morning."

He reran the past few minutes in his mind. The coin had been facedown on the floor when he'd picked it up. It had said NEW YORK then.

When he pulled it out to toss it to Jamie it had been in his peripheral vision. His fingers blocked some of the surface, and the diffuse light of the main floor made it hard to pick out details. But he could see enough. NEW YO was visible for almost a tenth of a second. The ants moved forward with a dozen slices of time until he caught a glimpse of the Statue of Liberty as the coin spun toward Jamie.

"This isn't the coin I threw you," he said.

"Yes it is."

"No," he shook his head, "it isn't. I gave you a New York quarter."

"That's the coin you gave me."

Mike frowned. He set the quarter down on the workstation. Tails up, so NEW AMSTERDAM was visible.

He looked up at the rings. The red lights were still out of sync. His eyes drifted down to the white lines painted around the platform. Olaf hadn't been able to draw a new safe zone because there was no magnetic field to measure.

Jamie held her hands out, palms up. "I couldn't've switched it. It was in plain sight the whole time."

"I don't think you did," he said. He slid the coin back into his hand and stood up. "I think we need to get off the main floor."

"Why are you whispering?"

"Because I'm nervous, and I think we need to get away from the rings right now." He moved away from his workstation and tugged her out of her chair.

Her eyes went from the rings to the line and ended on his fingers wrapped around the quarter. "Oh, shit."

"Yeah."

Inside the rings, Site B flickered. Then the room beyond the Door went dim. Red light continued to pulse out from the other side of the rings.

They reached the big door. He pulled it open and pushed it shut behind them. "Is there a way to disable the card reader?"

"I don't know."

"Wait here. Don't let anyone go in."

Mike ran to the front desk. "Hey," said Anne. Her hair was pulled back in a flawless braid today. "What can I do for—"

"We need to make a sign. Right now."

Her mouth twitched. "I can make something up in Office and—"

"No. Right now."

Her eyes brightened a bit. She tugged open two drawers. A collection of Sharpies came out of one, a cardboard envelope for Priority Mail came out of another.

"Tape?"

Anne reached back into the second drawer and came out with a heavy roll of packing tape on a red spindle.

Mike tore one of the envelopes open along its seams. He flattened it out on the desk, blank side up, and wrote DANGER with one of the markers. He underlined it three times and then added DO NOT ENTER. "Thank you."

"No problem."

He scooped up the sign and the tape and jogged back down the hall to Jamie. He covered the card reader with the sign and held it in place while she taped. She leaned back, took in a breath, and shouted "Arthur!"

He appeared out of the cross hallway as she finished taping. "What—" He paused to wheeze out a breath and suck in more air.

"Problems," said Mike.

"It's growing," Jamie said.

"We need to seal off the other building," said Mike.

"What do you mean? How are the rings growing?"

"Not the rings," said Jamie. "The Door."

"The Door," said Arthur, "is inside the rings."

"Not anymore," she said. She stuck her hand through the packing tape and wore the roll like a bracelet.

Arthur shook his head. "That's not possible. It has to be contained within the rings."

"Why?"

"The field's generated within the rings, so it can only . . . Ahhh." Arthur bit down on his tongue.

"Yeah," said Mike. "We need to find Olaf and Neil. We need to make sure all the doors onto the main floor and Site B are locked solid."

"I think Olaf's already over at Site B," said Arthur. "He was going to check readings there."

Jamie glanced at the stairs. "What about the control room?"

"I don't know. It's probably safe." He looked at the big door. "If the field's reaching the control room, it's reaching out here into the hall."

"How do we know it isn't?"

Mike glanced at her. "For now we just have to hope."

THIRTY-SEVEN

Arthur spread the blueprints across the conference room table.

Mike sifted through them. "This is for both sets of rings?"

"The two sets are identical," said Sasha. "We used the same blueprints for each one."

"Are they?" asked Mike. "No other little secrets or hidden changes?"

Arthur shook his head. "We might not know why the Door works on a scientific level," he said, "but the engineering behind it is honest."

He nodded. "Did Site B get locked up?"

"I thought Olaf did it," said Neil. "He was over there, too."

Olaf shook his head. "I didn't."

"Are we sure it's dangerous?" asked Sasha. "I mean, swapping quarters, that's more of a party trick, right?"

Mike looked at her. "You want to end up wherever radioactive Bob came from?"

"No."

"Then it's kind of dangerous."

"How can it be growing bigger?" said Jamie. "I mean, it took me two days to wrap my head around the rings working without any power."

"It can't," said Neil. "That's the whole point of the rings. They focus the fields."

"But the rings aren't doing anything as it is," said Jamie.

"Hang on," said Mike. "Safety first, yes?"

"Yes," said Arthur after a moment. "Of course."

"Who wants to go make sure Site B's locked up?"

"I'll go," said Sasha.

"No," Neil said, "I'll do it."

"You should be part of this discussion," Arthur said.

Neil shrugged. "Anything I know Sasha knows. Besides, I could use the fresh air."

"Are you okay?"

"No. Not sick. Just . . ." He looked at the blueprints. "This is all making my head spin a bit. The fresh air will be good for me."

"Okay, then."

"I'll take one of the bikes. I'll be back in ten minutes, tops." He stepped out into the hall. A moment later the sounds in the hallway shifted as the front door opened and drifted closed.

Mike closed his eyes. The large blueprints called the ants out like a picnic. They added the new design specs to the model of the rings he'd built in his mind, filling in final details and labels. "Let's forget how," he said. "For the moment I think we can all agree *how* is beyond us, yes?"

"We can figure it out," said Arthur. "Nothing's unknowable."

"Except all those things men weren't meant to know," said Jamie.

Arthur glared at her. Mike held up his palm. "Forget how. *Why* is it growing bigger?"

"What's the difference?" said Sasha. "We don't know either."

"How might be beyond us, but we should be able to come up with a why. Something's changed. There's a new variable that's causing all this."

"Weak logic," said Olaf. "Whatever caused the Door to stay open this long could also be what's causing the expansion."

"They're two different things, though," said Jamie.

Olaf shook his head. "They appear different because they seem to be two separate effects, and we don't know what's causing either. It's just as likely this is the same effect, building in force or intensity."

Mike looked up and took in the room. The five of them were standing around the table. Him, Jamie, and Olaf on one side, Arthur and Sasha on the other. A chair lurked by each of them, plus the ones on either end. An image blossomed in his mind, his first time in the conference room, the Albuquerque Door team filling every chair except the one at the far end. The one beneath the clock with its ticking second hand.

There was only one spare chair.

Arthur had omitted Koturovic from his book because of the early scientist's bizarre theories.

"How much time did Ben Miles spend here?" he asked.

Arthur and Olaf traded a look. "Four days," said Arthur.

"But how much of it was *here*? Was he staying in one of the trailers?"

Sasha shook her head. "He had a room at a hotel down in Mission Valley. The Sheraton, I think."

"So he wasn't here a lot of the time?"

Olaf shook his head. "It was more like two days here, with a travel day on either end. On the first day he stopped by for about an hour, just to meet everyone."

"The other days he spent maybe eight or nine hours on site," said Jamie. She looked at Arthur. "I don't think he actually came here on the last day."

Arthur shook his head. "He and I had breakfast together at his hotel and talked a bit. He had a morning flight out of Lindbergh."

"The guys at the gate would probably have his exact in and out times," Sasha said, "if that's important."

The ants took note but he waved it away. "Who watched the timer tests?"

Arthur looked up from the blueprints. "Timer tests?"

"When you tried to run the Door on automatic," Mike said, "was anyone watching?"

Arthur, Jamie, and Sasha passed a confused look back and forth among themselves.

"Simple question," said Mike. "Was anyone on the main floor or Site B when you ran the tests?"

"No," said Sasha. "We just watched the video logs the next morning."

"We ran them at night so we could get more work done," said Olaf. "The whole point was that it was an automatic test."

"And you never found out why it didn't work." It wasn't a question. He stared at the blueprints.

"To be fair," Jamie said, "we didn't try that hard."

"I looked at your code for the timer," Mike said. "There was nothing wrong with it."

"Thanks."

"It didn't work," said Arthur, "because of how it interacted with something else."

Mike shook his head. "It wasn't the timer. It was the Door itself. It was missing one key element."

Sasha frowned and looked at the blueprints. "What?"

"People. The Albuquerque Door only works when there are people around it."

"Again, weak logic," Arthur said. "That's like saying the refrigerator only works in the kitchen because you've never seen it work in my office."

"Except we all know the refrigerator would work in your office," said Mike, "and you can't get the Door to open if there's no one around."

Sasha put her fists against her hips. "Are you trying to say it *knows* when there are people around it?"

"No," said Mike, "no more than a flashlight knows it has batteries in it. But it still won't work if they're not there. It's not a consciousness thing, it's just mechanics. A boat doesn't know it's in the water, but it only works there, not on land."

"That's kind of a big leap," said Jamie.

He looked at Sasha, then Arthur. "You said Aleksander Koturovic had a hypothesis about gestalt minds. That's why you didn't use him in your book, because his ideas sounded too crazy."

"Not exactly a gestalt," said Olaf. "More of a mental energy-critical mass issue. It was nonsense."

"Did it relate to the equations you used for the Door?"

Olaf stared down at the blueprints. Another look passed between Jamie and Sasha. "Yes," Arthur said. "All of his work was based around the same ideas."

"So you got the Door working by programming it with equations that somehow involve levels of mental energy, and when there's no one present, the Door won't work." He looked at each of them. "Does that still sound like much of a leap?"

Arthur's eyes fell to the blueprint.

Mike waved his hands around the room. "There's only one spare chair," he said. "It's just for visitors, right? You've been so secretive, you'd never have any sort of temps or extra personnel. Except for an odd day now and then, like with Ben Miles, there's never been more than the six of you around the Door for any length of time."

"No, not until Magnus sent you," Arthur said.

"It was me," said Mike. "I was here long enough and helped the Door hit critical mass, or some level of it. Now there were seven people here all the time." He glanced toward the front of the building. "Maybe eight if Anne's desk was close enough to count."

Olaf shook his head. "It's nonsense," he said again. "There's no such thing as 'mental energy.' The brain gives off weak electrochemical signals that barely reach a few inches."

"But you can build voltage by connecting weak sources in series," said Sasha. "That's basic electronics."

"This is a bunch of unconnected guesses based off the ravings of a Victorian madman."

"A madman who you proved right," said Mike. He tapped the Door blueprints. "At least partly. We know there's something to his ideas about other dimensions. And it would explain why you lost control of the Door after I arrived."

A loud honk came from outside the conference room. It rose and faded, then rose again. If it had been from the other direction, Mike would've assumed it was passing cars blaring their horns out on the street.

Arthur's brow wrinkled up. Then his eyes went wide. His eyes flitted from Jamie to Sasha.

"What?" asked Mike.

Arthur strode out into the hall, with Olaf a few feet behind him. Sasha followed, pushing past Mike. Jamie grabbed him by the arm and dragged him along.

THIRTY-EIGHT

The sirens were louder in the hall. The emergency lights had switched on. They made bright patches in the already-lit hallway.

Arthur was at the front desk looking over Anne's shoulder. There was a flashing icon on the screen. "It's at Site B," she told him. Her eyes were wide.

Olaf and Sasha ran past the desk and out the door.

Mike looked at Jamie. "What is?"

"Hazardous material leak," she said. "Coolant, welding gas, radioactive material. Something bad's happened and it's warning us all to stay out of the area if we're not in hazmat suits."

They headed out the door and caught a glimpse of Sasha sprinting down the path toward the trailers and the golf carts. Mike and Jamie dashed after her. Olaf was already around the corner and out of sight. Some of the overgrown branches along the path reached for them, pushed out by the wind.

The sirens were sounding outside, too.

They ran around the corner and collided with Sasha. Jamie caught Mike before he fell. Mike grabbed Sasha. The older woman regained her balance and pointed across the gravel lot. "What the fuck?" she yelled over the building wind.

They followed her gaze and her finger.

Olaf had made it halfway across the lot before stopping. Past him Mike could see the bulk of Site B. It was shaking. The corrugated sheets that made up its roof rippled and buckled. One of the domed skylights shattered. The cinder-block walls trembled and cracked.

Sasha lunged back into action, running across the lot. Mike and Jamie followed. Their feet crunched in the gravel, then scuffed on the dusty supply road. They were five hundred feet from the building, then four fifty, and then four hundred.

This close, Mike could see even more fractures on the walls. What he'd thought were cracks at a distance were large breaks up close. Another one formed while he watched, crisp and clean even at this distance.

The black ants brought out a few memories, but the red ants overwhelmed them.

Olaf grabbed Sasha's arm as she tried to pass him. "Wait," he yelled. She yanked it away but now Mike was close enough to grab her. "Wait, goddammit," Olaf snarled.

"Neil's in there!" She waved her free arm at the bicycle parked by the door.

"Where's the dust?" asked Mike.

She stopped, just for a second. The groan of the flexing metal roof echoed over the wind. "What?"

"There should be dust," he said. "From all the breaking cinder blocks."

Sasha gazed past him, and then her head tipped back and up. "Oh, fuck," she said.

Mike and Olaf looked up. Clouds were gliding across the sky. Not rushing, but their movement was apparent. They were closing in from every direction, moving with the wind.

The wind was blowing toward Site B. All of it.

Arthur and Anne caught up with them just as the roof of Site B buckled again. One section sank low, as if an invisible weight was pushing it down. The bolts snapped with a gunshot noise and the section of roofing tumbled away inside the building. Two more panels broke free and vanished, then a third. The low roar of the wind became a howl.

"Is it a hurricane?" asked Jamie.

"We don't get hurricanes in California," said Anne.

A shriek of metal came from the building. They looked back in time to see Site B's security door crumple inward and vanish. Clouds of loose sand and leaves raced after it through the door frame. A moment later two more roof panels tore loose and plunged inside.

"I think we should back up," said Arthur, taking a few steps away and leaning on his cane.

"I agree," said Mike.

"What about Neil?" asked Sasha.

Mike glanced at her and gave a small shake of his head.

"Half the building just collapsed," Olaf said.

Mike took a few steps back. Jamie followed him and pulled close, calling into his ear over the tumult. "What is it?"

Mike opened his mouth and thunder rumbled above them. They all looked up. The clouds were building up, blocking the sun. Drops fell on their faces.

"What the fuck is going on?!" shouted Sasha.

"It's raining," said Olaf. It was more a general statement than a response. He sounded confused.

"I think it's decompression," said Mike.

"What?"

He raised his voice over the low howl. "The whole building's getting sucked into the rings. Everything is. It's creating a huge low pressure zone in the atmosphere." He gestured up at the sky. "It's changing the weather."

The wind rippled their hair and clothes. Arthur stepped back again. Mike and Jamie did the same. Anne stumbled after them. Sasha and Olaf stood where they were, staring at Site B.

Then it stopped, like a fan being unplugged. The wind died down. The air grew still. The rain continued to patter down, slowly darkening the pavement.

What was left of Site B stopped shaking. Concrete dust and gravel poured from the cracks in the wall. A section the size of a small car slid free and crashed to the ground. It took half of the green letter "B" with it. One of the surviving roof panels squeaked as it swung back and forth on its last bolt.

They stared at the remains of the building for a moment. Then Sasha ran forward. "Neil," she yelled. "Neil, are you okay?"

They headed for the building. Anne stayed where she was, staring at the ruin. She had the blissful but vacant look of soldiers after surviving an artillery barrage.

Sasha paused at the doorway and then headed inside. The others stopped to look at the damage. Mike touched what was left of the hinges. Two of them had torn free of the door and swung loose. The third was twisted and snapped at the pin.

Jamie stepped inside. "All the wiring's gone," she said. "The conduits are stripped right off the walls."

Olaf's head craned back. "The lights are gone, too. Hell, almost everything's gone."

"Neil," shouted Sasha. Her voice echoed in the cavernous space. "Neil, where the fuck are you?"

Arthur walked forward and looked at a fallen piece of machinery. It was one of the huge resistors. He tapped it twice with the end of his cane. There was a path of scratches in the concrete behind it.

They walked deeper in. Only the heaviest and most solid items had made it through the incident. Anything small or loose was gone.

The rings stood in the center of the barren space. Patches of frost covered the steel ramp. It let off puffs of steam as raindrops hit it through the open roof. All but one of the carapace sections had been stripped away, exposing endless loops of copper wire. A few cables hung loose. The connecting hoses were gone.

"I don't see anything," said Arthur. He pointed at the rings. "On the other side of the Door, I mean. I don't think it's working anymore."

Mike looked. The view through the rings was the side wall of the ruined building. He took a few steps and checked from a different angle. The view stayed the same.

Sasha finished her circuit of the room and joined them. "I can't find him," she said. She gazed at the dead rings.

"Let's not give up yet," said Jamie. She looked at Mike. "Do you think he's still here somewhere?"

"I hope so," Mike said. "I don't want to think about where else he might be."

THIRTY-NINE

They didn't find Neil.

Arthur reported the building collapse to DARPA. He said nothing about Neil's disappearance. Then Mike talked to Reggie and tried to get him as caught up as possible.

"So Ben's not crazy?"

"No," Mike said, "he isn't. But Becky isn't an impostor, either. It's a point-of-view issue." He settled back in his chair. He'd propped the tablet up on the table so most of the trailer would be visible behind him.

"Which means what?"

"Going through the Albuquerque Door changed him," said Mike. "Just not in the way we've been thinking."

"So he's changed, but not crazy?"

"Yeah. This Ben had slightly different memories and experiences."

"*This* Ben?" Reggie looked at him for a moment. "I take it there are a few things you're not telling me."

"For the moment, lots of stuff," Mike said. "There've been some . . . developments."

"Are they cloning people or something?"

"No."

"Seriously, is everything okay out there?"

Mike didn't look at the screen. "It's what you were worried about."

"I was worried about a couple of different things."

"There are some complications with the Albuquerque Door. With the Door itself."

"What kind of complications?"

"I'd rather not say at the moment. We're still trying to figure them out."

"We?"

"Yeah. Me, Arthur, the rest of the team."

On the tablet, Reggie leaned in close. "You haven't gone all Stockholm Syndrome on me out there, have you?"

"Cute."

"Answer the question."

"No, I have not."

"You're okay? No stress? No pressure?"

"No more than you'd expect in this situation, I guess."

"So what's going on?"

"I don't think I can really explain it like this."

A scowl washed across Reggie's face and was gone. "Why not?"

"Because it's complicated and because I know you," said Mike, "and I know how you react to things. Charging in with a lot of people and micromanaging isn't going to help anything right now."

"And you think that's what I'd do." It wasn't really a question.

"I know that's what you'd do."

"So why shouldn't I? You're telling me a building's collapsed, a bunch of very expensive equipment's been destroyed, one of my assistant directors isn't crazy, but he's been changed into a different person somehow. And that charging in would be my normal reaction at this point."

"Because you told me to take care of things out here," Mike said. "I'm taking care of it, and then I'm going to tell you everything. Just like we talked about when you hired me."

They stared at each other through the screen.

"I need you to find a way to salvage this," said Reggie.

"I'm not sure that's possible, at this point."

"You've got until the end of the week."

"Okay," Mike said. "Thanks."

"And you'd better have a ton of answers by then. Or else."

"Or else what?"

Reggie didn't smile. "Or else." He reached out and the screen went dark.

In the kitchen area, Jamie sighed. "That could've gone better."

Mike flipped the tablet down on its face. "Better than I thought it might."

"Yeah?"

He dipped his head at the tablet. "Worst case, I could've seen him taking control, ordering us all off campus, and launching a full investigation."

"He can't do that."

"With his connections? Sure he can. I bet he could arrange some kind of 'security drill' that would drop a hundred Marines from Camp Pendleton here in the next half hour or so. And then we'll never find out what's happening here."

Jamie scowled.

"So," Mike said, "we've got until the end of the week. We should get back to work."

"Yeah," she said. "You want to have sex?"

He looked at her. "Right now?"

"Yeah."

"Why?"

"Because it was a lot of fun the first few times," she said, "no matter who you turned out to be. And it means we can put off watching the security footage for a while longer."

"We need to."

"I have needs, too."

"And I'll gladly try to satisfy them, if that's what you want," he said. "Believe me. But we need to do this."

THE SECURITY FOOTAGE was custom-encrypted. It would only play in the control room. Jamie was pretty sure she could write up a patch that would let it play in the conference room, but they all agreed it wasn't worth the time. If the control room was dangerous, the conference room was, too.

Arthur leaned on his cane behind her chair. Mike noted that it had gone from mild affectation to an actual support for the man.

"Fuck," Sasha said, staring down at the main floor. "We've got a serious roach problem."

"They get brave when there's no one around," said Mike. "Didn't take them long."

Olaf looked down through the window. "Must be a hundred of them down there."

Mike stood next to Sasha and peered down through the window. Dozens and dozens of tiny spots moved across the floor like drifting motes of dust. "Probably more that we can't see. My mom used to say there were ninety-nine cowards hiding for every brave one that came out in the light."

She shook her head and stepped away from the window. "Little fuckers."

"How do we want to do this?" Jamie glanced up at them from her chair. "Work backward? Start at the top?" There were three gray squares, each on its own screen. The security cameras inside Site B had stopped filming at some point. Two of them had died almost simultaneously, the other had lasted fifteen seconds longer.

Sasha rested her hands on the back of the chair. "Do we know when 'the top' was?"

"Let's start thirty seconds before the alarms went off," Arthur said.

Jamie set her hand on the track ball, shifted it, right-clicked, shifted, and clicked again. Her fingers came back to the keyboard and danced on the number pad. The three squares filled with images. Site B from different angles. "Okay," she said. "Everyone ready?"

Mike stepped back and found a sweet spot that let him see all three screens. "Good."

Arthur nodded. Olaf crossed his arms. Sasha just bit her lip.

Jamie tapped the mouse. The images came to life, although the only real movement was the constant sweep of the red warning light. The time code spun away in the corner.

Camera two looked straight at the rings. They could see through to the main floor and its own flashing light. Mike remembered the angle from the first time he watched Olaf crosswalk.

Nothing happened. From three different angles.

"The alarms should go off any second now," said Arthur.

On camera one, a shaft of light appeared.

"The Door," said Mike. "Neil's checking things out before he locks it up."

Sasha's eyes went wide and she put her hand over her mouth.

Jamie reached out and tapped the mouse. All three images froze. "Do we really want to watch this?"

Sasha closed her eyes and whispered into her hand. It sounded like "Fuff Vee."

"We owe it to him," Arthur said. "He worked on this project almost as long as you. He wouldn't want us to get weak over this."

"I think what he'd want is to be standing here with us," said Olaf.

Mike set a hand on Jamie's shoulder. She reached up and squeezed it. The ants pulled out the image of the last time they were in this configuration. Him. Her. Arthur. His hand on her shoulder. Her shouting at him.

He set the ants to new tasks. Cataloging. Filing.

Jamie reached for the mouse.

The images came to life and camera two went black. White lines of static flickered across it.

Arthur leaned forward. "What happened?"

Jamie's fingers danced between the keyboard and the mouse. The images rewound, then began to crawl forward at quarter speed. There was no sound. She tapped something and the image from camera two expanded to fill its screen.

"There," said Olaf. He reached out and almost touched the screen. "Do you see it?"

"Move your hand," said Sasha.

The air was rippling. It was the familiar summer-heat haze that meant the Albuquerque Door was about to open. But the blurry air spilled out around the rings by at least five or six feet. It almost covered the screen.

The air shifted and the screen went black.

"Dammit," said Jamie.

She reached for the controls again but Mike stopped her. He moved his hand to point at the bottom of the screen. The concrete floor was there, complete with painted lines. His finger slid up and circled the base of the ramp, just visible through the batch of blackness. A little higher and he traced the dim outline of the rings. "It's all still there," he said.

Sasha reached out her own hand. "Are those stars?"

There were over a hundred of them, at least. Crisp and clear, like photos from the Hubble. They were brightest toward the center of the rings.

The ants swarmed in Mike's head, bringing out hundreds of images until they had the right one. "That's the Northern Hemisphere," he said.

Olaf glanced at him. "Are you sure?"

Mike tapped the side of his head. "I've looked up at night a couple of times."

"So now the Door's going out into space?" said Jamie.

"No," said Olaf. He ran his finger across the screen. "See it?"

Mike peered at the screen and saw the gray line Olaf had caught. It was hidden in the fuzziness at the end of the void. A barren horizon of gray soil marked by a few low hills and rocks.

"It's the Moon," said Sasha.

"It can't be," said Olaf. "The Door opens here. Right here." He pointed at the floor.

Jamie shook her head. "Not this time."

Something fluttered at the edge of the screen. At quarter speed, the lines of static were visible as pieces of paper from the workstations. They zoomed into the rings—into the area where the rings should've been—and vanished. A moment later, something red whipped out from under camera two and disappeared into space.

Jamie blinked. "Was that . . ."

"Fire extinguisher," said Olaf. He pointed at camera three's screen. "The one from the main support."

The shaft of light vanished from all the images.

"The door," said Sasha. "It was closed when we got there."

"Probably slammed shut by the air pressure," Mike said.

On the screen the fire extinguisher bounced and tumbled across the barren landscape and came to rest a few yards from the Door. Mike frowned. The ants scurried in his mind.

The lights in the room shifted again. "There's the alarm," Arthur said. "Emergency systems are reading this as a hazardous materials leak."

The images continued to crawl forward. Another fire extinguisher flew into the rings. One of the chairs worked its way around the workstation and rolled to the base of the ramp. It tipped over and flipped up into the starry void. Fluorescent tubes dropped from the ceiling to shatter on the ramp or the platform. Their shards vanished into space.

A white line shot across all three monitors, coming from somewhere behind camera two. It wobbled like a sound wave. "What is that?" Arthur leaned in close. "Is that some kind of static?"

"Might be a digital artifact," said Jamie. "The magnetic fields may be affecting the cameras."

A single laugh slipped past Mike's lips. Barely a chuckle.

Jamie glanced at him. "What?"

"It's toilet paper."

The white line wavered again.

"It's from the bathroom in the back of Site B," he said. He pointed at the camera two footage, where the white line extended off into deep space. "We're watching a hundred feet of toilet paper unwind in slow motion."

The line twisted and wobbled some more. A few seconds later it was gone, a dim thread in space. A few more scraps of paper and loose items flitted across the screen and disappeared. A cable slithered across the floor like a black snake and into the rings.

A tiny movement caught his eye. He focused his attention on it. "There," he said.

He pointed at camera three. Just visible in the dark corner was the shadowy figure of a man. He seemed to be pushing on the wall next to the door.

"He's hanging on to the conduits," said Sasha. "Why doesn't he just grab the door handle and get out?"

"The wind might be too strong," Mike said. "He could just be too scared to let go."

"Like when drowning swimmers take the lifeguard down with them," said Jamie.

"Something like that, yeah."

The workstations were moving now, scraping across the floor. Their assorted cables lifted off the floor and grew tighter and tighter. The other chair rolled free and shot across the open space into the Door. It tumbled across the gray soil and kicked up clouds of dust.

The ants seethed. Mike felt his brow furrow.

Olaf noticed it. "What?"

"It should've gone farther," said Mike. "With that amount of momentum, it should've gone a lot farther."

"How is this happening?" asked Jamie. "Explosive decompression doesn't just go on and on like in sci-fi movies. That's why it's explosive. It just happens all at once, like a balloon bursting."

"Normally, yeah," agreed Mike, "but this isn't normal. We had a hole in space. A doorway into outer space right here, deep down in the atmosphere."

Olaf nodded. "Every ounce of air on Earth is pushing those things into the rings. This isn't breaking a water balloon, it's turning on a fire hose."

Light spilled across all three screens. Something big dropped from the ceiling and blocked camera one for a moment. It bounced off the concrete, slid across the floor, and spun up into the rings. It wheeled through the lunar sand and fell over.

"The roof panel," said Sasha.

On camera three, Neil was moving. He stayed low to the ground, but moved toward the lens. His feet entered the frame on camera one.

Camera one flickered to black, then white, and then went dead.

A nitrogen tank rolled across the floor on its side. A dozen feet of hose whipped at the end, twisting in the air to point at the rings. The tank was too wide to go through the rings, but it rolled into the rift and bounced once before coming to rest on the dusty ground on the other side.

The air spiraled into thin whirlwinds that vanished into the rings. Two cables popped loose on one workstation, then a third, and then the whole thing lifted into the air. On camera two, they could see the equipment piling up on the dusty surface. Another roof panel struck the steel ramp and tipped over into nothingness. A few moments later, a section of metal roofing sliced through the cables of the other station. It all slid forward and went in. The last piece of metal never even touched the ground. It curved in midair and swung into the rings.

Camera two died. No flicker or static. It just went black between digital frames.

Neil grabbed at one of the flailing cables from the workstation and missed. He slid another few feet and rolled over to claw at the concrete. At one quarter speed, his screams distorted his face.

His feet grew dark as they hit the bottom of the ramp. It was as if a shadow stretched over them in the bright room. On camera one, they just vanished into the void. He tried to pull them out of the darkness, but the dragging winds forced him to keep them braced against the ramp. Neil screamed again. It lasted fifteen seconds in slow motion.

"His feet are in space," said Mike.

Camera one flickered. There was one last image of Neil trying to turn, to find something to grab. And then the camera shut off.

FORTY

They stared at the dark screens for a moment. Jamie wiped her cheeks. Sasha closed her eyes.

"It wasn't that bad for him," Arthur said without much conviction. He pulled off his glasses and cleaned them on his tie. A drop fell on the lenses while he did. "The slow speed made it seem worse. It was . . . I'm sure it was quick. That was barely thirty seconds."

"Just shut up," muttered Sasha.

They stopped looking at one another. Jamie spun her track ball and cleared all the monitors back to bare desktop. Sasha tapped her head against the window. Olaf stared down at the remaining set of rings.

A swarm of ants raced in Mike's head. They brought out hundreds of images from the footage he'd just watched, and hundreds more from memory. He made comparison graphs and drew conclusions.

And then he reviewed the footage and drew new conclusions.

"That wasn't the Moon," he said.

They turned to look at him. Jamie smudged one last tear from her face. "What?"

"Where the Door opened up to. It wasn't the Moon."

"It sure the fuck looked like it," said Sasha.

He shook his head. "The Moon's our only reference for images like that—a world with no life and no atmosphere. But the gravity was wrong."

Arthur wrinkled his brow for a moment. "On the Moon," he said, "all those items should've gone for a hundred yards or so."

Mike nodded. "The lighter ones at least, but even the heavier ones should've gone farther than they did." He pointed at the screen. "That was Earth gravity. One g. Everything was just moving a little strange because there was no air resistance."

"So that was . . . what?" Sasha glanced from the screen to the rings. "A world where Earth was just some rock in space?"

He counted to three. The ants carried out numbers for him, like tiny ring girls at a sporting event. "No," he said. "Well, sort of."

Olaf frowned at him.

Mike turned to Jamie. "Can you bring the camera two footage back up. Time-stamp thirteen-eleven-twenty-three."

She tapped the keyboard. "How fast do you want it?"

"Just freeze it there."

The screen filled with the starry void. The dim image of the rings were visible behind it, and the gray horizon past that. The red fire extinguisher and the chair had both already come to rest. The first roof panel was a blur of motion, still up on its side like a wheel.

"Full screen?"

Two more clicks and the frozen image leaped to fill the flatscreen. Mike reached out and ran his fingers along an outcropping of rock on the left side of frame. "See that? How straight it is?"

Arthur squinted. Jamie pulled up the image on the screen in front of her and stared at it. "Okay," said Sasha.

Mike traced a few faint vertical lines along the outcropping. They were straight and evenly spaced. "See these? This is the only point they really stand out. The light's reflecting off the roof panel just right."

"What's your point?" asked Olaf.

"Those are cinder blocks," said Mike. "That's what's left of the south wall of the main floor. Back there—" He pointed at a faint ripple in the gray sand past the fire extinguisher. "—that's the west wall."

Arthur pushed his glasses tighter against his head. "Are you sure?"

"Positive," said Mike. He tapped the side of his head. "They all line up with the regular view through the Door. I even overlapped it with previous crosswalks to be sure."

"Fuck me," said Sasha. She glanced down at the main floor and shook her head.

"That doesn't make sense," said Olaf. "If the main floor's there, and presumably a Door, that means we were there working on it."

"Maybe you were," Mike said.

Jamie leaned back in her chair, still staring at the smaller screen. "So what happened?"

Mike counted to four this time. "There's nothing there. No old weeds or vines. No sign of life at all. Sometime between finishing the Door and now, maybe in the last year or two, something wiped out all life on the planet. It even sucked away the atmosphere. And it did it fast."

"A war?" asked Jamie. "People always say we had enough nukes to destroy the world a hundred times over, or something like that."

Sasha frowned. "Could that burn off all the air?"

Mike shrugged.

"It looks too complete," said Arthur. "Unless a warhead struck the lab dead center, we should see more than this."

"There's also the bigger picture," said Mike.

They all glanced at him, then back to the screen.

"Metaphorical picture this time." He waved his hand at the rings outside the window. "When all this happened at Site B, nothing happened here. This mouth was normal. Which would mean the Door only opened on one side. Or, at least, the two sides were open to two different realities."

Arthur's mouth flattened into a line. Jamie's eyes went wide.

"Which means," Mike continued, "we still don't know how it works."

"Or it's working differently now," said Sasha.

Arthur shook his head. "Nothing else has changed. Why would it be working differently?"

"Why would it be open when there's no power?" she asked. "How the fuck should I know?"

Olaf gazed at the rings below and stiffened. He took a step to the left, then back. "Jesus," he muttered.

Sasha pressed her head against the glass. "What? What is it?"

"The Door," he said. He glanced back at Arthur, then at Sasha, and then back down to the main floor. "The damned thing's still open."

"It can't be," said Arthur. "The other rings were destroyed."

They all moved to the glass and craned their necks. Jamie and Arthur slid to the side, pressing against the others to get a better view.

The rings stood still and quiet. From the high angle, another two feet of the pathway could be seen continuing on through the Door. The base and bottom section of a third ring could be seen curving up and around the pathway.

"Fuck me," said Sasha. "Does this mean there's another Site B over there? On the other side?"

Jamie lunged back to her chair and stabbed at keys. The monitors lit up with new camera feeds, showing the floor, the stations, and a high view from just below the window. The last monitor let them see another fifteen feet through the rings.

All three of the rings.

Through the open mouth, the red light flashed across the walkway and ramp of a whole, undamaged Site B, complete with a white paint line marking off the safe zone.

"If each set of rings opens to a different reality," murmured Arthur, "it may have been doing this all along."

"You might have something there," Mike said. "I wonder how many discrepancies we'd find if we went back over the video logs and compared what one camera saw through the rings to what another camera saw directly. Things you might've written off as little glitches or time lags."

"Your red hair," Olaf said to Sasha.

She blinked twice and her eyes went wide. "Oh, fuck," she said.

Mike looked back and forth between them. "You saw Sasha with red hair once?"

Olaf nodded. "About six months ago. We'd just changed out some of the overhead lights and were doing a random physics test. I was at Site B, she was over here. Her hair looked deep red. I remember saying something to her about it while we tossed the ball, how the lights made her hair look red, and she laughed it off."

"But I didn't remember it," said Sasha. "The comments or anything. We talked later, face-to-face, and I just thought he'd been thinking of something else." Her gaze drifted back to the rings.

"I thought you were being absentminded," Olaf said.

"There are probably even more examples," said Mike. "Times the difference was just too slight to notice."

"So," said Sasha, "what now? Do we go say hello to ourselves?"

"We have to shut this thing down," said Mike. "If it's opening onto random realities, it's too dangerous to spend any more time trying to study it. It could flip back to the airless world again. Or worse."

"It might not," said Olaf. "In three years of operation, it's the first time something like this has happened. I'd say the odds are low."

"Three years of operation that don't even add up to eleven hours altogether," said Mike as the ants added up hundreds of timed reports. "The odds don't seem so low when you look at it that way."

They all looked at one another for a moment. They all looked at Arthur. And then, one by one, their gazes all slid to Mike. Jamie was first. Then Sasha. Then Arthur himself. Olaf was last.

"Well," said Arthur, leaning forward on his cane, "what do you suggest we do?"

Mike counted to five while the ants carried out images, sounds, and predictions.

"The set of rings on Site B shut down after they were damaged," he said. "We should try the same thing here."

"But we don't know why they shut down," said Olaf. "We still don't know how the Door is staying open."

"I still don't care about the why or how," said Mike. "I just want to turn this thing off before someone else gets killed or hurt."

Sasha cleared her throat and tapped two fingers on the window. "What if we just took it apart?"

Arthur blinked. "What?"

"Take it apart," she said again. "Since we can't shut it off."

"Could we do that?" asked Mike.

"The actual construction took about two months once all the components were fabricated. We could have the rings disassembled in a day or two, tops." She gestured at the rings down below. "Heck, we could break it down into larger components and drag them off the main floor one at a time. Then we can take 'em apart in the hallway or in here."

"What if that makes it even bigger?" asked Olaf. "This area of . . . instability? Right now we're relatively sure it's still around the rings, but if we start spreading the ring components out, what then?"

"If it does that," said Arthur, "then we should be able to go the other way. We can make a pile of everything and contract the area a bit. But I believe Sasha's right. Based on the evidence, taking them apart seems like our best bet to collapse the fold."

"How do we do that," asked Jamie, "if it's dangerous to have people near the rings?"

"We risk it," said Mike. He looked at Arthur and was relieved when the older man gave a nod of agreement. "We'll try to be quick, go in with specific goals, and get out."

"We should go over the design specs," Arthur said to Sasha. "Determine the fastest way to pull things apart."

She was staring out at the rings again. She looked back at Arthur and took a breath. "Yeah," she said. "Yeah, we should. I can do that."

Mike looked out the window again. On the floor, the roaches were weaving back and forth. "How long, you think?"

Sasha and Arthur exchanged a look, then included Olaf. "A few hours," said Arthur. "We didn't design it with rapid disassembly in mind. There may be a few snags." He tapped his cane twice on the floor. "I won't be much good for the physical work, but I think we can come up with a few ways for the four of you to make some quick headway."

"Five," said Jamie. "We could bring Anne."

"She's not cleared for the main . . ." Arthur shook his head. "Sorry. Old habits. Still, we shouldn't assume. She's not paid for these kinds of risks."

"None of us are, really," said Sasha.

FORTY-ONE

"Do you have everything?" Arthur asked.

"Yes," snapped Olaf. "For the third time, we have everything."

There wasn't much to have. Mike was a bit surprised at how few tools they'd need to disassemble the rings. A few socket wrenches and screwdrivers. Sasha had outfitted each of them with a full set. They didn't know if the tools on the main floor would still be there. Or if they'd still fit the hardware if they were.

Anne had offered to help while Arthur and Jamie were still explaining what was happening on the main floor and what they needed to do. Her offer didn't change when they finished explaining. She'd shown up in heels and a dress, but it turned out she kept a pair of running shoes in one of her desk drawers. She'd copied Jamie and tied her hair back. Her dress didn't have any pockets, so Sasha had strapped a tool belt on her.

Arthur went up to watch them from the booth. The five of them stood by the door beneath the flashing red light. "Everyone ready?" asked Mike.

They nodded. "Right side first," said Sasha. Her T-shirt showed a group of zombies in Starfleet uniforms below the logo THE WALKING RED. "We're going to start with the bolts at points six, seven, and eight. I'll get the ones at six. The four of you should be able to reach the others without getting up on the walkway. That'll get those carapace sections off and let us get at the coils."

"Do we need, I don't know," said Jamie, "a safe word?"

Anne laughed. Even Olaf smirked. "A what?"

She smiled herself. "Not like that, pervs. Some sort of code word or something that we can say in case . . ." She glanced at Mike. "So we can prove who we are."

"I think if anything happens," he said, "it'll either be very obvious, or it won't matter. Not for what we're doing, anyway."

"The safe word is Isis," said Sasha. "Work for you?"

Jamie nodded.

Olaf peeled the homemade DANGER sign off the card reader, and waved his ID over the panel. Magnets clicked and the door lock thumped. Its pistons hissed as they dragged it open.

The only sound on the main floor was the low rasp of the warning lights as they spun in their housings. The ants scurried out with image after image, comparing them to the current room. He couldn't see anything that had changed.

"I don't see anything different," said Jamie. She walked next to Mike, studying the room. Anne followed in their footsteps, looking at everything with her wide eyes.

"Me, neither," he said.

Sasha waved them away from the door. They walked around a tool chest and onto the main floor. Something crunched under Jamie's shoe. She glanced down and lifted her foot. One of the green cockroaches dragged itself away on its front legs.

"Hope nobody's got a thing about bugs," Mike said.

Roaches covered the main floor. A few hundred of them scurried back and forth. They darted out from under the workstations and toolboxes and the oversized resistors. Some of them crawled over the ramp and the platform. As the red light passed over them they turned black, then back to green.

"Fucking roaches," said Sasha. "They'll even survive a hole in reality."

Anne raised an eyebrow.

"We should be grateful they're not carnivorous or something," said Jamie. "Zombie roaches."

"Thanks for putting that out to the universe," Olaf said.

"Multiverse," said Mike.

"Even better."

One of the roaches stopped in front of Mike and Anne. It wiggled its antennae in their direction. The tips seemed to glow, like fiber-optic threads. Then it dashed away.

They stepped over and around the roaches and moved toward the rings. Mike watched for any ripples in the air, but there was nothing.

He couldn't shake the feeling that the rings were waiting for them to get closer.

THE RINGS LOOMED over Sasha up on their platform. They'd never looked quite so big before. She thought about how they called them mouths, and then about how she was standing in front of a huge, open mouth of copper and steel.

She set one foot on the ramp and paused. Mike had offered to do the high bolts, but as the only engineer left, she'd insisted. She counted to three, hoped she wouldn't end up like Bob, and took two quick steps up onto the platform.

Sasha stood there for a moment, feeling the dance of static electricity on her skin. The warning light from the other Site B flashed in her eyes and she stared through the Door at the other room. "So do you think . . ." She glanced down at the others. "Is Neil still alive over there?"

"Don't get distracted," Olaf said.

"He might be alive."

"He might not be," said Mike. "And it doesn't matter, because he still wouldn't be our Neil."

"I don't think any of us are 'our' people anymore," said Jamie.

Sasha tore her eyes away from the sights on the other side of the rings. "Okay," she said, "there and there." She used her socket wrench to point at a hex nut for each of them. She settled her tool over a higher one and cranked it four-five-six times. The sound always made her think of New Year's Eve noisemakers. Always. Even when she was little and her father worked on cars. He'd give her a small socket wrench and she'd spin it in the air.

That's my memory, she thought. *All mine. So I'm still me.*

She spun the nut off the last half inch of threads with her fingertips. Then she popped the thick washer off and dropped both bits in her pocket. Odds were they'd never be reassembling the rings, but old habits were tough to break.

She glanced down. Mike and Jamie almost had bolt seven off. Olaf had eight, one of the tough ones that had to be wrenched off all the way to the end of the bolt. Anne was holding the other side of it still with her own ratchet.

Over on Site B, the sun moved out from a heavy cloud to a thinner one, brightening the room by a slight amount. Sasha's eyes flicked up, and for a moment she thought someone had left the blinds open on a window, because she could see straight through the other building to the field of sand and scrub behind it. Although there were very few plants growing, and the few she saw were withered and gray. It looked like everything behind Site B had been dead for ages.

Then she realized that Site B didn't have a window. Definitely not a panoramic one that gave the outside world a view of the rings. And it crossed her mind that the view had switched to the real Site B, a wreck of a building filled with gaping holes that was going to be condemned as soon as someone official saw it. But just as fast, she realized the rings on Site B no longer worked, and she was looking somewhere else. Somewhere where something else had destroyed the other building but left the rings standing.

And then something beyond the shattered wall moved. Something tall and lean, wrapped in a ragged cloak. There was a flash of eyes beneath a rough cowl.

Sasha took in all of it between two heartbeats.

Then she blinked, and when she opened her eyes Site B—the un-damaged Site B—filled her view. She glanced down and saw Anne staring at the rings. *Through* the rings. Her eyes were wide, her lips hung open. "Did you see that?" Sasha asked.

Anne's brow wrinkled. Her head went up and down once, as if she didn't want to end the moment by speaking or looking away. She stared through the Door, willing the ruined world to appear again.

Sasha's eyes drifted back to her own bolts and she blinked. The inside nut was still in place. She thought it had come off a little too easy. Her wrench had just been spinning air and she was too on edge to notice.

Or had it? The matching bolt on the other side of the plastic carapace was gone. Had she pulled that one and moved on without thinking? She didn't think she'd done two already. But she patted her thigh and felt hardware.

She fitted the socket over the bolt, checked to make sure it was solid, and cranked the handle back and forth. The wrench clattered and pulled, clattered and pulled, and then the resistance faded and she tugged it free. She grabbed the nut between her thumb and two fingers, spun it off the threads, and dropped it in her pocket.

It slid against her thigh and clunked against the other bolt. They felt too heavy. Something wasn't right. She scooped everything out of her pocket and looked at it.

She had three of the heavy silver hex nuts, even though she'd only taken off two of them. She looked at the bolt she'd just freed up. The one she thought she'd done before.

It had a silver nut on it, backed with a washer.

The air tingled and her pulse jumped in her chest, hard enough that she felt the shift. The hair on the back of her neck stood up.

Sasha set the wrench over the bolt. She tugged the lever, felt the nut loosen and give, heard the ratchet *click-click-click* as she swung it back to tug again. The wrench turned again and again, moving the nut along the threads toward the end of the bolt. She pulled the socket away and worked it off with her fingers. The washer bumped off, shaking along the threads.

Behind the washer was another silver nut. And another washer. She glanced over at the matching point. It was bolted again, too.

"*What's taking so long?*" They all jumped at Arthur's booming voice. Sasha glanced up at the booth.

Below her and to the left, Jamie coughed. "I don't know about you guys," she said, "but I think I've got a problem."

Sasha looked down. "Fuck," she said. "I think we do."

Jamie looked up and their eyes met. "What's wrong?"

"Your hair," Sasha said. "It's changed color."

Olaf looked over at Jamie and frowned. Jamie grabbed a lock of hair and pulled it around in front of her face. She squinted. "It has?"

"Yeah," said Sasha.

"No," said Anne. "It hasn't."

"Yes, it has. It's platinum blond."

"It was always like that," Jamie said. "Always has been."

Sasha shook her head. "You just switched." She glanced at Mike. "Tell her."

Mike pressed his mouth into a line. "Jamie didn't change," he said.

"Yes, she did." Sasha stopped and stared past Mike. The warning light was still spinning on the main floor. But it had changed color. Instead of a deep, orange-amber, it was fire engine red.

She looked at Jamie again. "The safe word," she said. "It's Spock, after your cat, right?"

Jamie didn't answer. Neither did Mike or Olaf. Anne stared at her.

"Ahhh, fuck," Sasha said.

FORTY-TWO

They stared at Sasha and the bright streak of white running through her hair. The Rogue stripe, Mike had heard kids call it. It started above her left eye and stretched back across her scalp.

Sasha looked back at them. Her eyes were wide, but her breathing was still even. She studied each of their faces in turn.

Mike gave her a moment. "You going to be okay?"

She focused on him. "Yeah," she said. "Yeah, I'm okay."

"Not to sound cold," Olaf said with a glance at the others, "but I think this emphasizes that we shouldn't spend too much time in here." He gestured at the bolts. "Is anyone having any luck with these things? I can take them off, but new ones appear right under them."

"Same," said Jamie.

Anne nodded, but her gaze was focused through the rings again.

"I've taken off three," said Sasha, double-checking her hand.

"I think they're bleeding through," Mike said. "Overlapping. We're taking off bolts from every version of the Door."

Arthur's voice rang above them. "So we can't disassemble it?"

"Maybe not this way," said Sasha. "We could try the other side. It might be a localized effect."

She stepped across the platform while the others worked their way around the ramp. Sasha slipped her socket over the nut at point eleven and the wrench chattered while she levered it back and forth. It was one of the stiffer ones, and she had to use the wrench the whole way. It inched out to the end of the bolt and she shook it free of the socket.

"Fuck me," she said.

Another hex nut held the washer in place.

"*The same?*"

She looked up at the booth and nodded.

"Is there something else we can do?" asked Mike. "Some other way to remove them?"

Sasha shook her head. "We'll have to break them off."

"Is that safe?" Anne asked.

"Should be." Sasha banged her wrench on the off-white carapace. "None of this was intended to be high-end protective. It's just enough to slow people down if someone tried to sneak in and get a look at the tech."

Jamie glanced around. "Cables we could unplug? Fuses we could pull? Anything?"

"We did it all a couple days ago, when the Door first stayed open," Sasha said. "The only things still hooked in are the feeds to the computer."

"*Without those, we'll have no way to monitor the Door except looking at it.*"

"It won't change anything," said Jamie. "All our readings have been flatlined for days."

Mike stared out at the room. Then he looked left and right, craning his head around equipment. Jamie watched him and followed his gaze. "What's up?"

"All the roaches are gone."

They looked around. Every one of the green bugs had vanished. The floor was empty.

"We must've scared them away," said Olaf. "So?"

He glanced at the barren floor again, then up at the booth. "Unless you've got an idea," he said to Arthur, "I think we should get out of here and regroup. We shouldn't just stand here next to it."

"*Fine. We should—LOOK OUT!*"

Something moved in Mike's peripheral vision. A splayed shape. It lunged fast. Jamie and Sasha turned to look. Olaf and Anne leaped back.

It had leaped from nowhere, appearing out of . . .

It had appeared out of the Door.

It landed on the floor by Jamie with a noise like pasta breaking, a baker's dozen of hard clicks in a row.

The figure straightened up as Mike turned his head. It was tall and thin, dressed in a one-piece garment of pale leather that seemed to be half tunic, half cloak. One of its shoulders sat higher than the other, like a hunchback without the hunch. It held a long thin spear in both hands. The ants pulled out a series of images comparing it to a javelin, or maybe a harpoon. He swept them away. The hands were shiny and gray. They reminded Mike of raw oysters.

It had bare feet with the same wet-gray skin. Its toenails were thick and pale. The ends were cracked and jagged. They looked bloody in the red light. The nails curled around the figure's toes like claws, or maybe hooves.

The figure pointed at him and let out a hard, stuttering breath, the sound of wet lungs. The death rattle of something angry, fighting with its last breath. The black ants presented a set of sound clips for comparison, the most prominent one from the movie *Predator*.

How was it pointing at him if both its hands were holding the spear?

The figure swung its free arm, there was a sound of a baseball bat hitting meat, and Jamie went flying. The movement shifted its hood back, and the loop of ragged fabric slid down onto its shoulders.

Mike, instincts honed by too many cafeteria fights and hallway brawls, started forward as soon as he saw the arm swing at Jamie.

As the creature's hood dropped, the ants swarmed out with pictures and images in a desperate attempt to find some condition or deformity to explain the figure's face. The closest was a collection of deep-sea fish with glasslike tusks and dead eyes. And even those weren't that close.

It had three eyes. The largest one didn't seem to have any lid. It just bulged on one side of the face. The other two, stacked one above the other, were small and dark, like spider eyes. Its nose was a pair of slits in the clay-colored skin.

Arthur made a sound that echoed over the godmike. Sasha shrieked out a "fuck." Anne stood frozen, staring at the creature. Olaf froze, too, and it lashed out at him with the spear. The shaft caught the physicist across the face with a crack, and sent him stumbling away.

The creature saw Mike coming and hissed out a series of clicks, like bubbles popping from the mouth of a drowning man. Its legs shifted beneath the cloak and its feet clacked on the floor. It spread its arms wide, and the two hands on the right flexed. They had fingernails like claws.

He looked at the extra arm and froze.

The creature lunged at him.

Sasha swung one of the chairs around in a wide arc. Anne screamed. The metal casters smashed into the creature's skull and sent it staggering back. The spear clattered to the ground. The impact jarred the chair out of Sasha's hands and it crashed to the floor.

The creature rolled over on its stomach. Two of its arms pushed at the floor, its legs shifted beneath the cloak, and its spine folded back like a circus contortionist, lifting its head up high. It took three scuttling steps toward Sasha on all fours before it straightened up onto two legs again. Anne was still as a statue, her eyes locked on the monster.

"Hey," shouted Mike. He waved his arms. "Over here!"

Its swollen eye glanced at him. The other two stayed on Sasha. It growled again, and the sound built into a roar that echoed across the main floor.

It went after Sasha.

Mike charged.

The creature slashed at Sasha with one hand. She jumped back and threw her arm up. Four slashes of red appeared on her arm. The tall thing followed up with a backhand across her jaw that sent her sprawling.

Then Mike slammed into it. The impact was like tackling a scarecrow made of two-by-fours. The creature staggered, tripped, and fell. Mike's face was pressed into the cloak. It smelled like dust and leather and sweat.

The creature swiveled its head around and glared at him. Its teeth gnashed together. An elbow slammed back into his ribs, and then another one. The cloak twisted and thrashed beneath him. Mike pushed himself up and threw a punch as the creature turned. His fist struck the garden of teeth and the points tore at the skin on his knuckles.

One of its arms twisted back—*how did it* bend *like that*—and grabbed his wrist. The creature wrenched itself around so it could look him in the face. This close he could smell its meat-breath and see the glistening of its eyes and the tiny scales that made up its skin.

He tried to throw a punch with his free hand, but the creature grabbed it, too. Its fingernails bit into his skin. The third hand—*it had three arms!*—lashed up and grabbed him around the back of the head.

The spidery fingers twisted themselves into his hair. Its teeth spread, its bear-trap jaws opened wide, and it pulled him down. Mike's pulse made another leap, blood trickled on his wrists, and Jamie smashed a fire extinguisher down on the creature's elbow.

She heaved the canister up and brought it down again. Something cracked in the arm. The creature howled.

It hurled Mike aside, and he slammed into the legs of a workstation. The creature folded itself onto four limbs again, the extra arm hanging limp on its high shoulder. It snarled at Jamie.

She swung the extinguisher back for another blow, and Anne's paralysis finally broke. The receptionist grabbed Jamie's arm and spit out some panicked, incoherent syllables. The drowning swimmer taking the lifeguard down with her.

The creature glared at the two women for a moment, then stalked forward on all fours. Jamie managed to shake Anne off. She swung the fire extinguisher around in a wide arc.

The monster reared back and up. The red cylinder swept past it and momentum made Jamie stagger forward. The extinguisher twisted in her hands and she fumbled. It slipped from her fingers and left her and Anne unarmed in front of the creature.

Its head swung between them and one of its arms lashed out. It punched Anne square in the chest, its knuckles landing right on her breastbone, and she flew back. The creature watched her crash to the floor, then reached for Jamie.

A socket wrench smacked into its shoulder blade and hit the floor with a clank. The creature turned, and Mike smacked it across the face with the flatscreen. The LCD cracked, but so did a few teeth. Plastic and enamel rained on the floor.

Anne screamed again.

Mike swung the screen back, but the creature had an arm up. It batted the weapon from his hands, and one of its feet lashed out to hit him in the gut. He'd never been hit so hard in his life. He felt the jagged toenails rip at his flesh as the impact knocked him back. He hit the ground and grabbed at his stomach. It was hot and wet. Gut injuries were supposed to be a horrible way to die.

The creature roared again, its clicks bouncing off the walls.

Another roar drowned out the creature. And another. And another. It twisted with the second gunshot, shrieked at the third.

Arthur limped forward with the pistol held firmly in both hands. It was black with a barrel that was squared off instead of round. He squeezed the trigger again and again. One round passed through the creature's cloak to spark against the steel ramp. Another made it jerk. It raced toward him, covering the distance with terrifying speed, and he shot and shot and shot.

It lunged at Arthur and he flinched away, but there was no strength left in it. A feeble swing of its claws missed him and it crashed to the floor. He fired another shot, one-handed and half-looking, but it would've been hard to miss at this range. The cloak twitched and the slide of the pistol slammed back and locked.

The creature let out a low, bubbling moan that trailed off into a wheeze. It settled against the floor. Its outstretched hands relaxed.

Arthur looked at the figure for a moment. He looked at the pistol. Then he took two uneven steps to the left and threw up.

FORTY-THREE

Mike twisted his head around to find Jamie. She was curled in a ball near the ramp, arms wrapped over her head. Anne was shrieking and crying and rocking back and forth on the floor, but didn't seem to be injured. Olaf sat near the base of the Door, cautiously touching the side of his head. Sasha was sprawled by the far wall.

Mike's fingers probed his stomach. He had some cuts with a lot of blood, but they didn't seem to be serious. He crawled to his feet, and a few drops of blood pattered to the floor. His fingers pressed a little harder, and he counted to five. His gut ached, but everything was staying in place.

Arthur threw up again. This time was more of a retch. A thin line of drool stretched down from his lip. He staggered over to grab his cane where he'd dropped it.

Jamie lifted her head and glanced around. Her eyes fell on the cloaked body. "Is it dead?"

Mike staggered over to her, one arm wrapped around his stomach. "I hope so."

"You're bleeding."

"I think Sasha's bleeding a lot more. Arthur!" He waved the other man to her.

Jamie wrapped an arm around Mike and helped him toward Sasha. They stepped around the fallen chair, keeping the creature in their line of sight. It didn't move. He saw a reflection on the floor next to it that looked like blood.

Anne's shrieks faded into a muffled sobbing. She stared at the dead thing on the floor and trembled. Her eyes were glazed. She muttered a few random sounds and seemed to think they were words.

Jamie and Mike reached Sasha just as Arthur did. Jamie gave Mike a squeeze and released him, making sure he could stand on his own. Then she doubled back to check on Anne.

Sasha groaned, stretched her leg, and then leaped up with a shout.

"It's okay," said Mike. He settled her down. Blood had soaked her forearm. At least two of the gashes were deep enough to show muscle.

Her eyes darted around. "Where is it?"

Mike pointed. "Arthur shot it."

"What?" Sasha stared at the pistol in the older man's hand. "Where the fuck did you get that?"

"Top left drawer of my desk," said Arthur.

Mike glanced at the weapon. It was stuck open, which he knew meant it was empty. The ants carried out a series of images from television shows and movies and a small sequence of Tommy Lee Jones explaining the wonders of the firearm to Robert Downey Jr. in *U.S. Marshals*. "You keep a Glock in your desk?"

"Of course I do. I'm the head of a highly classified Department of Defense project." He looked over at the body. "Did anyone see where it came from?"

"It came out of the Door," said Olaf. The split across his cheek streamed blood down onto his chest. A huge bruise was blossoming along his jaw.

Jamie shook her head. "We were right there," she said. "Nothing came out."

"I think he's right," said Mike. "It came out of the rings."

"I saw something in there," said Sasha. "I think I saw it. It saw me."

Mike prodded her arm and she yelped. "Sorry."

Sasha flexed her hand and winced. Her cheek had faint hints of red and purple across it. "Am I going to live?"

"I think you're going to need stitches," said Mike, "but it doesn't look too bad." He glanced up at Arthur. "Your doctor trustworthy?"

"How so?"

"Can he keep this quiet? If this is an attack, I think he needs to report it to the police."

"So?"

Mike gestured at the corpse with his chin. "You want to explain that to the police? That's before we try to explain that you shot and killed it."

Arthur looked at the pistol in his hand. "I see your point." He crouched and set the weapon down on the floor. "I've known David for years. I think we can trust him to be discreet."

"Then let's get her to the doctor."

"Yes," said Sasha, "let's." Her cheek was all purple now, and the color was spreading along her jaw. She winced as they helped her up, and bit back a yell when Arthur grabbed her arm by accident.

"You, too," he said to Olaf.

"I'm fine."

"You're bleeding like crazy," said Jamie.

"It's just a flesh wound," Olaf said. "I'm fine."

"It hit you in the head hard enough to knock you ten feet," said Mike. "You need to get checked for a concussion, at the least. Probably an X-ray to be safe."

Jamie wandered back with Anne. The receptionist had calmed down, and wrapped her arms around herself. Jamie cast her eyes on Mike's bloody shirt and hand. "What about you?"

"I'm okay. It looks worse than it is."

"It doesn't matter, if it was carrying an infection," said Olaf.

"That's a happy fucking thought," Sasha muttered.

Mike glanced over at the first aid kit attached to the workstation. He was pretty sure it hadn't been restocked since Bob's accident. His mind flitted through images of the building and picked out three other kits.

"Can you get me a first aid kit?" he asked Jamie. "Maybe the big one from the kitchen? I'll use up all the hydrogen peroxide and antiseptic ointment before I bandage myself up. Then I can have some of whatever antibiotics they give Sasha."

"You scared of the doctor?"

"No, I'm scared of leaving this thing alone and having it be gone when we get back. Or of leaving you alone with it while we all go to the doctor, and then *you're* gone when we come back."

"I'm pretty sure it's dead," said Arthur.

Mike glared at him. "Do you know what it is?"

"No, of course not."

"Then maybe we shouldn't assume it's dead."

Arthur bowed his head. "Of course."

Anne bit back another sob. Her eyes were locked on the creature.

"Can someone please just get the fucking first aid kit so we can go?" growled Sasha.

Jamie vanished into the offices, dragging Anne with her, and returned alone a few minutes later with the red canvas case. Arthur, Sasha, and Olaf were waiting at the big door when she returned. They slipped out and the door thumped shut behind them.

Mike pulled his hand away from his stomach. It was sticky with blood, but the actual bleeding seemed to have stopped. He loosened the first button on his shirt. "Where's Anne?"

"I left her in the kitchen with some coffee and a bunch of Advil."

"She okay?"

"I think she might have a few bruises. Nothing that'll show."

"No, I mean . . . is she okay?"

"I don't know. I'll let you know when I'm done freaking out." Jamie crouched a few feet from the creature. "You really think it might still be alive?"

"Maybe." He pushed the last button through its hole. One side of his shirt fell open. The other side stayed stuck to his body.

"He shot it a dozen times."

"Ten, and only five of them hit."

"Y'know, that can be annoying."

"Tell me about it." He gritted his teeth and peeled the shirt off.

Jamie righted one of the chairs, set the kit down, and unzipped it. It was an oversized thing intended for earthquakes. She pulled out some alcohol swabs and a box of gauze.

"This is going to sting," she said.

"I thought it might."

She used half a dozen swabs cleaning off the blood. He winced a few times. She tossed the swabs in a pile on the floor. "It doesn't look too bad," she said. There were three gouges in his stomach and a long scrape, deep enough that it had bled a bit. "I think only the big one broke the skin."

"Lucky," said Mike. He looked at the body again. "The roaches are back."

The green bugs were creeping out from beneath equipment, making small circles on the floor. Their antennae waved back and forth. Two or three of them scurried up to the dead creature and then darted away.

"Looks like they didn't like him either," Mike said.

"I don't blame them." She tore open a pack of gel caps, popped them in her mouth, and swallowed them dry.

"They have an extra limb, too."

"What?"

"The roaches all have an extra leg on the right side. Just like this thing." He dipped his head toward the body.

"Really?" She twisted the cap on a brown bottle and the seal popped. She peeled it away.

"You never noticed?"

She glanced over at the bugs and the body. "I don't spend a lot of time looking at cockroaches. Lean back."

He rested his hands on the desktop and she poured hydrogen peroxide across his stomach. It sizzled on the wounds. Mike took in a sharp breath and banged his hand against the desk.

"Stings?"

"Yep."

Jamie splashed more of it on him. The cuts foamed and hissed. She rinsed his wounds one last time and a few more bubbles danced on his skin. "Almost done."

"Good. My pants are soaked."

"You'll live."

"Other parts of me are tingling."

"That's just because I'm touching you."

"Hah."

She pulled the cap off a yellow tube and squeezed ointment over the gouges. Mike went to spread it around, and she slapped his fingers away. She tore open two packs of gauze at the same time, pressed them over the wounds, and had him hold them while she peeled off some tape. Then she found a bandage in the kit and wrapped it four times around his stomach.

"I think that's enough," he said.

"You sure?"

"How are you? That thing hit you pretty hard."

She reached back and touched her head behind her ear. "I've got a lump and some sore ribs. I'll live."

"You sure?"

"I got off easy. The rest of you took the beating." She gestured at the body. "So . . . what now?"

"We should lock it up somewhere," he said. "Maybe clean out one of the hazmat lockers?"

She looked past him. "The closest one's way over there. We wouldn't be able to watch it and empty the locker."

"Maybe tie it up?"

"It's a high energy physics lab. We don't have a lot of rope laying around."

He shivered.

"You sure you're okay?"

"I'm kind of cold."

"Really?"

"I've lost some blood, my pants are wet, and I don't have a shirt. Yes, I'm cold."

"Okay, then," she said. "We can't leave it alone. We can't lock it up." She glanced over at the rings. "And we can't stay here."

He nodded. "So we make sure it's dead."

Jamie found two big wrenches in the toolbox. Each one was only a foot long, but they were steel and solid and had a good weight to them. There were a few utility knives, but the blades were too short to be of any use.

They approached the body. Its blood was dark red. A few more roaches circled the creature, but none of them moved closer than a few inches before skittering away.

He could see the back of the creature's head. It had a loose circle of gray-black hair. The strands were close to dreadlocks in places, thinning and patchy in others.

The cloak was coarse leather that had been bleached by the sun. Not even leather, just hides that had been worn and bent enough to stay soft. Some of it was hairless, some had bristly patches of fur. The whole thing was held together with broad stitches of thick cord. Mike had a feeling it was dried muscle sinews. He knew Native Americans and some other cultures used sinews for threads and bowstrings.

"I think that's a good sign," he said, pointing his wrench at the roaches circling the body.

"You think they're going to eat it?"

"No clue. But they were mobbing this place until it showed up and now they're all coming back. I think they know its dead."

"Does that mean we're done?"

He shook his head. "We've got to be sure."

Jamie looked at the two right hands sticking out from under the cloak. One was palm up, the other palm down. Two of the long fingers curled under the left hand. "You want to take its pulse or something?"

"I guess. It's a start."

"Wish I'd kept the fire extinguisher."

"You want to go grab it?"

"No."

"You sure?"

"Believe me," she said, "if it moves I'm beating its head in with this wrench."

Mike reached over the puddle of blood and touched the creature's left wrist. Hot pinpricks of pain sparked under his bandages as he stretched. He tried to ignore them.

The skin looked like wet clay, but he felt dozens of tiny scales shift under his fingertip. He counted to five. When the body didn't move, he lifted the hand. The bent fingers uncurled, and he heard the rustle of Jamie's clothes as she tensed up. He let the wrist settle against his fingers and counted to ten. Nothing. No throb or rhythm or tremor. Drops of blood beaded up on two of the long nails and plopped to the floor.

"Well?" asked Jamie.

He counted to ten again. Still no pulse. "I'm going to try to roll it over," he said.

"Why?"

"To get a better look at it."

"You're hurt," she said. "Why don't I roll it over?"

"Because I'm hurt," he said, "and if it jumps up and grabs me, I want somebody healthy trying to beat its head in."

She managed a tight smile.

The easiest way to flip the body, Mike decided, was to move the single arm in close to the torso and then roll the creature from the other side. He tucked his wrench into the back pocket of his jeans, slid his hand along the cloak to the elbow, and pushed. The joint was more flexible than he expected. The loose material of the cloak, half stuck to the floor by blood, rolled and flopped under the arm.

He shifted his feet, leaned a little farther, and pushed the arm up against the body. The fingers left trails of clean floor in the puddle, and then the blood oozed back in to fill the trails and erase them. The cloak dragged out flat.

Mike looked down and screamed. He pushed himself back, the pin-pricks of pain in his stomach became razors, and he slammed into Jamie. She saw the cloak and made a sound that could've been a loud groan or a muffled shout. She slapped her free hand over her mouth.

Mike's mind was a blur of static. The ants had hundreds of facts and images for his comparison. What kept rising to the foreground was another fact about Native Americans, an old grade school maxim.

They used every part of what they hunted.

FORTY-FOUR

The eye sockets were ragged. Mike wasn't sure if it meant the cloak was well-used, or if the skinning had been a sloppy job. One of the holes went right up to the eyebrows. The mouth and nostrils were still plain, even though they'd been stretched flat. He could even see pores and a few whiskers on the cheeks.

Jamie made another sound. It was muffled by her hand. She took a step back. "What the fuck is this thing?" she hissed.

Mike straightened up and took a few steps around the body. The blood puddle was still creeping out. He didn't like the idea of putting himself by the double arms, but he was feeling more confident that the creature was dead. He also knew that in most horror movies that confidence marked the moment the monster got back up and killed the guy poking it with a stick.

He glanced at Jamie. "You ready?"

Her grip tightened on the wrench again. She pressed her lips together and nodded.

Mike crouched and reached for the cloak. He shuddered as his fingers touched it, and he tried to think of it as a collection of hides and leather. He felt the body through the material and found the double shoulder. He set his hands against it and pushed. The creature was heavy.

He braced his feet, ignored the pain in his gut, and heaved. The head twisted around and the swollen eye glared at him. He almost lunged back again, but there was no life behind the stare. The pupil was wide and gazed past him at the wall.

Mike heaved again, and the creature flopped onto its back. He overbalanced, slipped, and landed on his knees in the blood puddle. He shuffled backward, leaving sticky tracks on the floor.

One of the small eyes was closed, the other half-lidded. The large one stared up at the ceiling. A dozen of its teeth were broken. Half of them oozed dark blood.

Mike picked out all five bullet holes in the cloak. Each of them was ringed with blood. One high enough that it almost skimmed the raised shoulder, one where the thigh met the hip, and three scattered across the torso. One of them might've been in the heart, but the creature wasn't humanoid enough for him to be sure.

He wondered if it was one of Koturovic's alpha predators.

He slid out his wrench, held it over the body for a moment, and then whacked one of the gunshot wounds.

Nothing.

He smacked the bloody hole again. Then he jabbed it with the pointed tips of the wrench. He poked his way across the body to one of the other wounds.

Nothing.

Jamie leaned over him. "Now what?"

He looked past her to the rings. "We need to get out of here." He looked down at the body. "We should get *it* out of here, too. Do you have the keys to the spare trailers?"

"They shouldn't be locked."

"I say we stick this thing in one of them for now, crank the air conditioning up all the way, and then call someone to come take it off our hands."

"You know someone to call for that?"

"I know someone at DARPA," said Mike, "and I'm betting he knows a lot of people who'd fight to get this thing."

"So how do we move it?"

"I'll take the heavy end."

Jamie looked down at the body. "You want me to touch it?"

"I wanted you to say 'you're hurt' again and then offer to take the heavy end."

She shoved her own wrench in her pocket and crouched to grab the ankles. "It feels like fish," she said.

"I thought it was more like snakeskin," said Mike. He tried to figure

out a way to reach under the body's crooked shoulders without smear-
ing blood on his hands. After a moment, he grabbed two big handfuls
of the cloak. "You ready?"

"I guess."

He heaved on the cloak and she pulled on the legs. The creature's
knees bent back and its shoulders rolled too far forward. The hood
slumped back over its face. The body lifted a few inches off the floor.
Jamie wrestled the ankles up higher, almost into her armpits. Mike set
his end down and gathered up more of the cloak. Some of it was sticky
with blood.

They shuffled past the rings to the back door. The cloak dragged and
left streaks on the concrete. Jamie took short steps to avoid tripping on
the fabric. She tried not to look at the swath of material with the face
sewn into it.

Mike hit the release with his elbow and pushed the door with his
back. The cuts in his stomach were burning. The bandages were wet.

They struggled with the corpse down the rear staircase. The cloak
snagged on the corner of a step and almost yanked the body out of
Mike's hands. He teetered on the step for a moment.

"Set it down," said Jamie. "I need a break, anyway."

He nodded. It was going to be a pain to pick up the body again on
the stairs, but his knuckles ached from holding the gathered-up cloak.
He lowered his end of the body and tried to stretch out his fingers.

She shook out her own hands. "You're bleeding again."

He glanced down. Red blobs spotted the gauze. "It's not bad," he
said. "It'll hold until we get this thing locked away."

They wrestled the body back into the air between them. They lumbered to the bottom of the stairs and started across the park toward
the trailers. Mike aimed them at the back of the double row, straight
toward the empty one. The gravel crunched under their feet and made
a whisking noise as the cloak dragged across it.

Jamie flinched and turned away from the body.

"What?"

She dipped her head down without looking in that direction. The
tunic-cloak had slid halfway up the creature's thighs. The creature's
legs were almost white in the sunlight. "I think it's some kind of her-
maphrodite or something, maybe. It's going commando, whatever it is."

"Ahhh."

"I'm going to take a long shower after this."

Mike glanced at his trailer. "Me, too."

"Don't get your hopes up," she said. "I'm not thinking sexy shower."

"Neither was I."

"You have no idea, believe me." She glanced at the pale thighs and shuddered.

"Very, very unsexy," Mike agreed.

"Later maybe. When this thing's out of sight and all that shit's off you. And I've had three or four good, mind-erasing drinks."

"Just let me know."

They shuffled a few more feet closer to the end of the trailers. "Hang on." She shifted her arms. "It's slipping."

Mike opened his mouth to suggest setting the body down again, but his hands weren't aching as much. He had a better grip, or the cloak had settled into a better position to take the weight. He held his end and waited for her to adjust.

Jamie heaved up one ankle so she had it between the crook of her arm and her armpit. Something crunched and her eyes went wide. "Oh crap," she said. "I think I just broke its foot."

He shook his head. "Probably just feels that way. Come on, we're almost there."

They carried the body another few yards. Mike stepped onto the green Astroturf, and they worked their way around the corner. Mike glanced over his shoulder and saw the steps to the last trailer just a few feet away.

Jamie rolled her shoulder, then shook her head. "It's broken. I can feel it."

"We can deal with it later." Mike looked between the doorknob and the body. The corpse was balanced so well right now, he almost thought he could gather the cloak in one hand and hold it while he opened the door.

"You got it?" asked Jamie.

"Yep." He didn't move.

"Something wrong?"

"Is it just me," he asked, "or does this thing feel a lot lighter than when we picked it up?"

"Yeah," she said. "I thought it was just me."

He lifted his arms. Lifted, not heaved. The corpse went up. It wasn't as easy as lifting an empty box, but it wasn't much harder, either.

"Set it down for a second," he said.

He lowered the double-handful of cloak. Jamie tried to release the legs and they made a rustling noise, like flipping through dry old books. Tiny scales flaked off them like dust and settled on her hands and arms and chest.

The left leg broke off at the knee with a sound of snapping twigs. Jamie shrieked. Bits of skin and bone scattered in the breeze. She dropped the calf and it hit the Astroturf with a dry sound, like a bag of leaves.

Mike crouched and pulled back the hood. The creature's swollen eye was gone. A dry crater gaped in the head. The two small eyes had vanished, too, leaving bullet hole sockets in a sagging patch of flesh. The gray skin was tight around the nostril slits, and the lips were gone.

"It's mummified," said Jamie.

The gums receded before their eyes, showing the roots of the needle-like teeth. More scales dropped away. The cheekbones pushed their way out of the skin. The fingers became claws that became knotted sticks.

She looked up. "Is it the sunlight?"

"It was wrapped in the cloak."

"The legs weren't."

"The face was." He pointed at the skin-wrapped skull. "It's just as far gone as the legs."

"Oh, shit." Jamie wiped her hands on her jeans, then kneeled and rubbed them on the plastic grass.

"Nothing happened until it died," said Mike. "I think you're okay."

Jamie looked over her shoulder, over at her trailer. "I need to go wash off," she said.

He nodded.

"I'm sorry," she yelled as she ran off. She unlocked her door and yanked it open. She ran inside and left it swinging. A minute later Mike heard running water and splashing.

He watched the body shrivel and fall apart, moving his head to get it from multiple angles. The cloak shifted as the body beneath it grew thinner and thinner. The ants carried out grade-school science films about decay and childhood images of raking dry leaves that crumbled between the tines of the rake.

By the time the water stopped running, there was nothing left but bones.

FORTY-FIVE

Mike unwrapped the cloak and looked at the skeleton. Gloria Barker, the biology teacher, had a poster of the human skeleton up in her classroom, complete with labels. Mike had seen it twice. More than enough to give him a basis of comparison.

The creature's skeleton was more or less humanoid. An extra bone ran along the back, something flat and wide where the extra arm attached. The sternum was peaked along the front instead of flat. The ribs were asymmetrical, with fewer on the side with the extra arm. The knees and elbows were an odd arrangement, not quite hinges, not quite ball and sockets. It had an extra toe on the left foot, the one that had broken off.

He examined the skull. Forty-nine teeth, eleven of them broken. Twenty-four on top, twenty-five on bottom. The large eye had its own socket, but it looked like the two small eyes shared one. He couldn't even guess how something like that evolved.

The ants carried out pictures of Bob, the wasteland Bob, and he wondered if the creature had developed naturally.

Mike looked at it all and had the ants file it. Dozens and dozens of images, all stored alongside frames of the creature alive. The contrast gave him a better sense of muscle structure, but not much.

He held up his hands. The blood from the cloak had dried and flaked away. There was almost no sign of it on his fingers, arms, or body.

The cloak was spread out. There was another broad patch with a nipple on it, but past that he couldn't see anything to hint at the origins of the material. Maybe just those two patches were human skin. Maybe it all was.

How could there be recognizable humans in a world that had allowed this thing to develop?

He folded the cloak around the body as best he could. He made a point of hiding the face inside the layers. Then he gathered the whole thing and put it in the trailer. The bones barely weighed forty pounds. There was no meat left on it, but he twisted the air conditioner knob to HIGH just in case.

Mike went to Jamie's trailer. She sat on her bed in her underwear, eyes closed. She was still wet from the shower. He let her have her moment. He knew how important such moments could be.

He grabbed jeans and a shirt from his trailer, then walked back up to the main building. The first aid kit by Anne's printer wasn't as well stocked as the big one. It had more gauze pads and tape, but no actual bandages. He glanced at the hall, toward the door that led out onto the main floor. Tape and pads would have to do.

He passed the kitchen and saw Anne sitting at the small table. She had a cup of coffee in her hands with no steam coming off it. Three packets of Advil sat near her wrist.

"Hey," he said. "You okay?"

She stared past him with wide pupils. "Yeah," she said. "Yeah, I'm fine. I just . . . I'm fine."

A squad of ants ran by with memories of *Villette* and his conversation with Reggie held up for view. "It looked like it hit you pretty good."

"I'm fine. Just a few bruises." Then she blinked twice, focused, and saw him shirtless and bloody. She looked at the bandages on his stomach. "Are you? Okay?"

"I think so. I just need to wash up and change these."

She opened her lips to say something else, but changed her mind. Her gaze drifted back to the wall, in the direction of the main floor.

There was a fresh box of pastries on the counter. He wondered when they'd been brought in. He pushed the box aside without opening it. It felt heavy and he realized he'd been riding an adrenaline high for almost half an hour. There was a crash in his very near future.

He headed into the bathroom.

Mike washed his hands, wiped them with a couple of alcohol swabs, and unwrapped himself. The gauze was all red under the bandage. Red blood seemed reassuring. Almost cheerful. He tugged at the tape, and his stretching skin reminded him there wasn't anything cheerful about it. Threads of gauze clung to the wounds, and he winced as they popped loose one by one.

He looked at his gut in the mirror. The skin around the gashes was shiny from all the ointment Jamie had slathered on. The cuts were wet, but the bleeding seemed to have stopped again. If there had been any of the creature's blood near his wounds, it had vanished with the rest.

Just a few more millimeters and the talon-like nails would've left three big rents in his skin. His intestines would've pushed out, forced the wounds even wider. If the creature had stretched its toes, his guts would've spilled onto the floor.

The room lost focus for a moment. The walls tilted. He'd reached the crash. He braced his hands on the sink and forced himself to take a few slow breaths. He counted to ten, then opened the first aid kit. Fresh gauze was taped into place. This roll of tape was thinner, and it took half a dozen pieces to make each pad feel secure.

He glanced at the bathroom door, then unbuckled his belt. The hem of his jeans was still sticky with blood. So was the front of the crotch and a few spots on the legs. He pried his sneakers off, pushed the jeans down, and kicked them off. There were a few spots along his boxers, too. The creature wouldn't be the only thing going commando today.

Mike caught sight of himself in the mirror. The gauze across his stomach was brilliant in the bathroom's light. His hair was a mess. Shock and a bit of blood loss made his skin pale. With the tired rings under his eyes, the transformation was complete. A very skinny Severus Snape stared back at him from the mirror.

He shook his head and chuckled.

He pulled on the clean clothes, wiped down the belt, and threaded it through the loops. The sneakers were too tight to slip back on, so he untied and retied them. He sealed the first aid kit back up and tossed the bloody clothes in the trash.

Anne hadn't moved from her chair in the kitchen. She still held the cold coffee. Her eyes flitted to Mike as he entered, and she managed a weak smile. "Much better."

"Thanks. I feel a lot better."

He dropped the first aid kit on the counter and tore open the pastry box. The room wobbled, just for a moment, from the effort. He tossed a scrap of paper tape in the trash and a green roach skittered away from the plastic barrel.

The box was packed full of donuts, muffins, and other pastries. Mike saw two of all the usuals. He picked up one of the chocolate croissants, and then eyed the second one, wondering if he could eat two without making himself sick.

"Do you want anything?" he asked Anne. "Might help settle your nerves."

"I'm good."

He tapped the box lid. "Looks like someone screwed up the order. Double everything if you change your mind."

"It wasn't me," said Anne. She managed another weak smile.

Mike took a bite out of the croissant, and the butter and sugar and chocolate melted on his tongue. He pictured it rushing into his bloodstream to help stabilize him and calm his overtaxed system. He slumped against the wall, closed his eyes, and took another bite.

The front door hissed open in the distance. Footsteps echoed in the hall. He opened his eyes in time to see Anne straighten up.

Jamie appeared in the doorway. Her hair was still damp, and her T-shirt had wet spots on it. It was inside out, and stitches wrapped around her shoulders. There were wet trails on her cheeks that stood out against the dampness from the shower.

In her arms was something bundled in a towel. It twisted for a moment, then settled down in her hands. He caught a glimpse of tan fur and a thick claw. She marched forward and set it down on the table in front of Anne. Anne pushed herself away, and Mike had to set a hand on her shoulder to keep her from tipping over backward.

"It's still spreading," Jamie said. She took a step back from the table. The bundle shifted and wiggled.

Mike put the pieces together, but needed confirmation. "The instability?"

"Yeah."

"How far?"

The bundle yipped and shook itself. The table rocked a bit. The towel slid and fell away to reveal even more fur.

"Pretty damned far," announced Jamie. "The trailers. Which means it's hitting most of the campus. Glitch is gone."

"He got out?"

"He's gone," she repeated, looking anywhere except at the animal on the table.

The mutt was small, fifteen pounds, tops, with floppy ears. It eyed Mike and Anne curiously, yapped at her twice, then got distracted by the coffee cup on the table. Its tail wagged back and forth.

Mike stepped past Anne and crouched down to look the dog in the eye. It glanced up at him, then pressed its wet nose against the table and snorted up a few stray particles of food.

"I was getting dressed in the trailer," said Jamie, "and Glitch was on the bed, and then I turned around and . . ." She shook her head and nodded her chin at the dog.

Mike reached out and took the nylon collar in his hand and worked his way around to the bone-shaped tag. He already knew what it was going to say.

Jamie leaned her head against the wall and crossed her arms over her skull.

"Hello, Tramp," murmured Mike.

MOUTH

Mike opened the door and found Jamie in the hall, leaning against the wall. She'd turned her shirt right-side out and pulled her hair back again. "Hey," she said.

"Hey. How are you?"

"Now that I've had time to think? Even more freaked out."

"Yeah, me too."

He glanced back into the conference room as the door eased shut on its hydraulic arm. Olaf and Sasha were checking over Tramp. Both of them still looked more than a little ill at the dog's reappearance. Arthur stood at the head of the table, leaning on his cane. He stared at the dog with flat eyes.

After a few hours, Anne had still seemed to be in shock from the creature's attack. Arthur had called a cab and sent her home. She'd flinched away when he touched her arm to say goodbye. She'd glared at him and climbed into the cab without a word.

Jamie glanced at the book in Mike's hand. It was half an inch thick, with a dark cloth binding and ragged pages. "Koturovic?"

"Yeah. I got it from Arthur when they came back."

She looked at his stomach. "Did you get fresh bandages?"

"Yep."

"Good," she said. "I threw up in the shower. Twice. And I think I took off a layer of skin."

"Did it make you feel better?"

"A little."

He tilted his head over at the bathroom door. "I came pretty close in there when I was getting cleaned up."

"Are you hungry, too?"

"I had a couple mouthfuls of croissant before you showed up with . . . with the dog."

"It's Tramp," said Jamie. "I get it. I think dicking around about it is just going to waste a lot of time."

"Agreed."

"And I'm starving."

He nodded. "Probably crashing like I was after, well, after everything. You had more shocks than me."

She shrugged and managed a smile. "Disemboweled by a monster versus finding a dog. I don't know."

Mike glanced at the conference room door. He was tempted to say the small dog bothered the scientists far more than either the fold in space or the three-armed monster. He wasn't sure if that was funny or disturbing. Probably a little of both.

Jamie nodded at the door. "How's it going?"

He weighed his words. "It's creepy and fantastic that Tramp's back, don't get me wrong. But you're right. He's distracting us from the big issue." He held up the book. "You've read this, right?"

"Yeah."

"I think I've figured a bunch of stuff out."

Her stomach rumbled.

"Speaking of distractions . . ."

"Sorry," she said. "Just let me grab a cruller or something before we go back in. I'm going to pass out if I don't eat something in the next five minutes."

They wandered to the kitchen and Jamie rooted through the box of pastries. "Double donuts," she said. She pulled out the two crullers and wrapped them in a paper towel. "Thank God for screwups," she said.

"It's not a screwup."

"What?"

"Anne didn't double it. It's more bleed-through, like when we tried to pull the bolts on the ring housings." He pointed at her small bundle. "We could call those quantum donuts."

She studied the cruller for a moment, then shrugged and took a bite out of it. "I'm starving," she said. "I'll deal with it if I grow another arm."

"It's just from an alternate universe, it's not magic." Mike pulled open the fridge. "There. See?"

On the top shelf was Anne's usual apple and lunch Tupperware. Except there were five apples piled on the shelf. Four were red, although the produce sticker on one was written in German. The apple farthest to the back was green. The words on its sticker were in Japanese.

"Great," she said. "So if we don't figure out how to shut it off, we'll be smothered in donuts and apples."

"And maybe dogs," said Mike. "It could be a self-correcting problem."

She snorted out a laugh and he pushed the fridge shut.

Unbidden, the ants pulled up his layout of the complex and added labels for the donuts, the refrigerator, Glitch's disappearance, and the reappearance of Tramp. A thought crossed his mind, and they added distances. A red circle blossomed on his map, centered on the remaining set of rings.

One last ant skittered out and placed a label just outside the circle. He focused on it, and it set up a trail of time stamps from the rings, through the label, and into a trailer. More ants carried out memories to fill in the path.

"Huh."

Jamie swallowed a second mouthful of cruller. "What?"

"I used your trailer and the donuts to mark out an area of effect. A map of how far away from the rings things are changing."

She raised an eyebrow. "My trailer?"

"For Glitch and Tramp. The bugman's corpse started to shrivel up as we got it near the edge of that area. And it fell apart just a few yards past your trailer."

"Really?"

Mike studied the layout and the trail of images. "Yeah. Not sure what that means. Maybe it's tied to the rings somehow."

"We're not. We've all left campus."

"You're still alive. And you're not a bugman."

"Thanks for noticing."

He shrugged.

Jamie filled her massive coffee mug, and they headed back to the conference room. Tramp barked at them and wagged his tail when they opened the door. She managed to hide most of her cringe at the sound.

Sasha and Olaf stood on either side of the table. They were at the end farthest from the door, farthest from the rings. Spread out across the table were blueprints and mathematical models.

Arthur hadn't moved. Both hands were still on the head of his cane. Behind his glasses, his eyes focused on Tramp.

Sasha tapped one of the blueprints. Her arm had half a dozen stitches and some bandages that looked much more professional than the ones Mike had taped into place on his stomach. "Maybe it's tapping into the Earth's magnetic field, somehow?"

"That's sci-fi nonsense," Olaf said. A line of small butterfly bandages stretched along his cheek. They made the side of his face stiff when he talked.

"It's what an electrodynamic tether does," Sasha pointed out.

"Hypothetical science at best, sci-fi nonsense at worst."

Mike waited for them to finish and set the book down on the table and counted to five. "I think we may have a big problem. Really big."

Tramp leaped to his feet, yipped, and spun in a circle. He flopped back down, and his tail thumped against the table leg.

"When the Door opens," said Mike, "it reaches into a 'nearby' universe. By nature of being close to us, so to speak, they're less divergent. That's why all of you were able to get by without too much trouble once you switched universes. There were only minor differences."

"Except for other-Bob's world," said Olaf. "And the dead world."

Mike raised a finger. "But they weren't that divergent, either. We know this building existed in both of those worlds. We know teams existed there that built Albuquerque Doors. Which means they were near-parallel until the past year or two."

"And then one world started a war and the other one was wiped out," said Arthur. He balanced his cane against the table and tugged his glasses off. "That sounds somewhat divergent to me."

Mike shook his head. "Not if whatever caused those changes came from outside of the given universe."

They all stared at him. Olaf shook his head. "What the hell are you talking about?"

Mike reached down and tapped the book. "Koturovic," he said. "Appendix three."

Sasha nodded. "That's where he starts spouting all the History Channel stuff about dimensional barriers and the end of the world, right?"

"All the things that got him tossed out of his university," said Olaf.

"Yeah," said Mike, "except I'm not so sure it's that crazy. In fact, a lot of things start to make sense when we take all of his theories into account."

He slid a piece of paper toward himself and scooped up a pen. "Say this is the multiverse," said Mike. He drew a dot at the bottom of the sheet, and then a dozen quick lines coming out from it in a tight fan. "It's our local cluster, if you will. A bunch of realities that only recently split apart, in the big scheme of things. We've got a lot of common history. Enough so that if someone crossed from one to another, they might not even notice any major changes. Think of the lines as branches in a tree."

He glanced around the room. They all seemed to be following him. Or, at least, humoring him.

"Now something comes along with a set of clippers or one of those big buzzsaw things."

"Hedge trimmer," said Sasha.

He nodded. "A hedge trimmer. And it starts cutting through the branches." He drew a horizontal line halfway across the fan. "The Door is doing what it's been doing all along—opening to another branch close to this one. But we're seeing universes that were hit by the trimmer. So they look different."

Olaf tapped his fingertips on the table. His jaw shifted and the bandaged side of his face shifted with it. "And what's the trimmer represent in your clever metaphor?"

"Just what Koturovic said." Mike tapped the book again. "Some kind of super–alpha predators that eat everything. Something that would break through the dimensional barriers, hunt us, and wipe out humanity. An interdimensional locust swarm of some kind. He said they were from a universe outside our own, but if we accept that there are multiple universes, what makes ours so special? Wouldn't the conditions that attract them exist in all those realities, too?"

Sasha crossed her arms. "So you're saying something . . . what, *ate* the Moon-world?"

"Maybe," said Mike. "I don't know that it's true, I just know that it fits all the evidence."

"Wait . . ." Jamie glanced toward the main floor, then to the trailers.

"You mean there's more of those bugman things?" asked Sasha.

"Maybe a lot more," said Mike. "I think the rings punched a hole in that dimensional barrier he talks about. And if Koturovic's right about everything, the more people there are around the hole, the bigger it gets."

"And the more bugmen come through," Jamie said.

Arthur pulled off his glasses, and reached for the tie he wasn't wearing. "We're in the middle of a major city," he said. "We're in a relatively deserted area, but if the instability keeps growing . . ."

"Yeah," Mike said. "San Diego's got a population of a couple million, right?"

"Yes," said Arthur. "And then there's Orange County, Baja, Anaheim, Los Angeles . . . we're talking about ten or twenty million people, depending on how far it reaches."

"And how many bugmen would that set loose?" asked Sasha.

"I don't know," said Mike. "Koturovic seemed pretty sure the alpha predators could wipe out humanity, and it seems like he was right about a lot of this."

Arthur tapped his cane on the floor. "That creature was fast and strong," he said, "but I can't imagine even hundreds of them could stand up to a few platoons of Marines from Pendleton."

"You have to stop them," said Olaf.

Sasha glanced between them. "What?"

"Bob's last words," said Olaf. He glanced at her, then Mike. "The other Bob. He was terrified of the monsters. He said we had to stop them."

Mike bit his lip and nodded. "I think other-Bob came from a world the alpha predators had already reached. And the people there fought back with everything they had. And it wasn't enough. For all we know, maybe the Moon-world is the same one. They just finished eating."

"They can't eat everything," said Olaf. "It's just . . . it's not possible."

Arthur's cane rocked back and forth under his hands. "A small locust swarm can strip a field bare in hours," he said. "A large one can eat over a million tons a day. I suppose it's not impossible."

"I'd rather not find out," said Jamie.

"We stick with our original plan," Mike said. "We know the fold collapses if there's enough damage to the rings. That's what happened on Site B."

"But we can't take them apart," said Sasha.

"Right, so let's just go with primitive basics. We can't take it apart, so let's just smash it."

Arthur winced. Olaf raised a skeptical eyebrow.

"I'm not sure we can," said Sasha. "The rings are pretty solid, even without this other-dimensional reinforcement. The carapace is half-inch polystyrene, and past that the rings are almost solid metal. Steel frame, copper coils, lead plating." She shrugged and winced as her arm moved. "We could work on it for hours with sledgehammers, and not even dent the frame."

"Then we hit it with something bigger," said Jamie. "We drive a truck into it."

"Again, steel frame," said Sasha. "And I don't think we could get a truck up onto the main floor anyway."

"What if," Mike said, "we freeze it with the liquid nitrogen first?"

Arthur and Sasha both shook their heads. "The rings get bathed in it every time we open the Door," said Arthur. "It will boil away long before doing any structural damage."

"At best, we might be able to crack the carapace sections," said Sasha. "And then we're back to solid metal."

"Could we make a pipe bomb or something?" Jamie asked. "What do they call it, an IED?"

Sasha shook her head again. "We don't have anything to make it with."

"None of the chemicals in the storage lockers?" asked Mike.

Sasha shrugged and looked from Mike to Arthur. "I'm not a chemist. I don't know if any of that stuff mixes to make explosives."

"Coffee creamer," said Jamie. "I think I saw a thing on television once where they used coffee creamer to make a bomb."

"I still don't think that's strong enough," said Sasha. "And I don't think we have powdered creamer, anyway."

"I'm also not sure we should be going back in there unarmed," said Olaf. He reached up to touch his cheek. "If just one of those things did this to us, I can't imagine what a few dozen of them could do."

"I have another magazine for my pistol in my office," said Arthur. "And half a box of ammunition at home."

"So we need guns and explosives," said Mike. "Let me make a phone call."

FORTY-SEVEN

"So, to recap," said Reggie from the tablet, "yesterday half the complex was destroyed, but everything was under control. Today, Neil Warry is dead."

"We're pretty sure he died yesterday," said Mike. "The circumstances were just a bit tough to explain."

Mike stood at the end of the trailer park. He held the screen so Reggie could see the remains of Site B. Arthur sat a few yards away on the steps of Olaf's trailer. Olaf stood by him, arms crossed and ready to offer support if needed.

He turned the tablet around, and Reggie scowled at him. "So, having confessed all this, now you want to blow up the other building. Does that cover it?"

"Not the building," said Mike. "Just the last set of rings on the main floor."

"Ahhh, right. The rings that I've paid about a quarter-billion dollars for in the past year alone."

"This is bigger than a budget line," said Mike.

Reggie shook his head. "Give me a minute to process all this."

"It'd be better if you just took my word for all of it."

"That's asking an awful lot right now."

Mike turned the tablet away from the ruined building and set one of the trailers in his background. "You know how you're always telling me to trust your gut?"

"Yes."

"Well, your gut should've exploded a few hours ago from everything happening here. So now you have to trust me. Your top man in the field."

They stared at each other through the screen. Reggie set his hands on the desk in front of him. "What can we salvage from this?"

"This?"

"How much did you get? Files, blueprints, design specs?"

Mike stared at him.

"You're talking about blowing the whole place up," said Reggie, "so we need to talk about rebuilding."

"We can't rebuild it," Mike said.

"We'll be a lot safer this time," said Reggie. "No more of this half-a-dozen cowboys stuff. We'll set up in Virginia or something."

"No, seriously, we can't."

"We can. Even if you've only got partial information, I can throw enough people at this to fill in the gaps."

"Have you heard anything I've said? About what happens to the people who go through? You need to shut this whole thing down and run all the files through a shredder. We blow it up, bury it, and it never comes up again."

Reggie shook his head. He lowered his chin. "Arthur's okay?"

Mike nodded and jerked his head to the left. "He's about fifteen feet that way. With Olaf. Want me to get him?"

"No. He'll agree with everything you've told me?"

"Yeah. He can probably do it with bigger words, too."

"Not now," said Reggie. "No smart-ass stuff now. From what you're telling me there's a chance this is my career-ending day if I mess up one thing."

"I told you, it's a little bigger than that."

"Fuck you. And shut it."

"Sorry."

Reggie's fingers made tiny movements on the desk. Mike realized his friend was pressing them against the desk to keep from making fists. "Okay," he said. "Okay, I know a colonel at Pendleton. I think we're tight enough that he'll make this happen and ask for details later. I should be able to have a demolitions team down there in an hour or so. Maybe an hour and a half."

"There's a chance we'll have to defend ourselves. You should get them to send as many soldiers as possible."

"Never call Marines soldiers," said Reggie.

"I thought we weren't being smart-asses?"

"I'm not." He lifted his hands from the desk and rubbed his eyes. "What do I tell them they're fighting?"

The ants presented dozens of responses. "Tell them it's war," said Mike. "Tell them there's a chance they'll be fighting a war."

"Against what?"

Mike counted to three. "Honestly," he said, "you won't believe me."

Reggie scowled again.

"I'm sorry," said Mike. "I can explain all of it in more detail later. Me, Jamie, Arthur, everyone. You can debrief us or whatever. But right now I cannot stress how important it is that we destroy those rings."

"I can't ask them to mobilize a platoon of Marines without more than that."

"I'm sorry," Mike said again.

"You know what this sounds like, right? If I hadn't known you for most of my life I'd probably be calling Homeland Security right now."

"I know. And you still might need to if this doesn't work."

Reggie pressed his hands against the desk again. "What you were talking about the other day with Ben. The reason he was messed up. It's true of everyone who went through the Door, isn't it?"

Mike glanced over at Arthur and Olaf. He took a few steps away. "Yeah," he said to the tablet. "Yeah it is. Everyone who went through the Albuquerque Door was swapped with a counterpart."

"Which means me, too."

"Yeah. And Kelli, your assistant."

Reggie coughed. "So I'm from another universe."

"Yeah. And her, too. I think you might be from the same one, since you both went through in one session."

A long moment stretched out between them.

"I was going to tell you after all this," said Mike. "I just thought it might be better in person. Maybe over drinks."

Reggie's chin made a slight up and down motion. His fingers flexed against the desktop. "So I don't know you."

Mike counted to three. "No," he said. "Not really, no."

Reggie studied his desktop for a moment, then looked around his office. His gaze slid back to the screen. "Well," he said, "you're still a jerk. So don't get too full of yourself."

Mike smiled.

"Let me call in some favors," said Reggie. "I think I can have some boots on the ground there inside of ninety minutes. I'll ask them to defer to you on everything, no questions asked."

"That would be fantastic."

"I can't make any promises."

"Believe me, anything will help. Make sure they know they're blowing up something very solid. Assume it's a tank, just to be safe. And they'll probably need some kind of timers or remote-control detonator."

Reggie nodded. "Are you going to be okay?"

"Honestly?" The ants carried out images of the bugman and passages from the Koturovic book and the view he'd glimpsed through the Albuquerque Door. "I don't know. This could go really bad. For all of us."

"And here I am worried about if I'll have a job in a few days."

"Yeah, well . . . if they fire you, dinner's on me next time."

"If I get thrown under the bus for this, I'm taking you with me. And beating you senseless next time."

"Well," Mike said, "I really hope I'm around to be beaten senseless."

Reggie bit off a response. "Take care of yourself, jerk."

Mike shrugged. "We're trying to save the world. It comes with some risk."

FORTY-EIGHT

Jamie leaned against the guard hut. "Are you okay?"

Mike looked back at her. "How so?"

"Arthur says you had to tell Reggie he was from another universe."

"He'd figured it out on his own. He handled it well."

She nodded. "All the cool people do."

He turned to the road again.

Jamie nodded and flipped her quarter. "Think he's going to blame all of this on you?"

"Pretty sure, yeah. He needs to pin it on someone. Arthur's too famous, and they need him. He can target me but then protect me from the worst of it."

"Will he?"

"Yeah. I think he's used to doing it. Protecting me."

She raised an eyebrow.

Mike shrugged. "Some things he said. He kept asking how I was doing, if I could handle this. I think his Mike's a bit more fragile."

"Maybe he won't need to pin it on anyone."

He glanced at her. "Did you meet the board?"

"Yeah. Bob had the flu, remember. Other-dimensional flu."

"Just checking. How do you think they're going to respond when Reggie tells them we're shut down and they can't salvage anything because we blew up the Door to stop an invasion of locust-men from another dimension?"

She managed a weak smile. "So you're really unemployed now. No high school, no DARPA."

He chuckled. "Yeah I guess so."

"Arthur would probably hire you."

"That'd be great, if we weren't about to blow up his life's work."

She smiled and flipped her coin again.

"And look at that," said Mike. "Eighty-eight minutes exactly."

A quartet of Humvees roared down the street. Each one was painted in desert camo patterns. Mike had never understood camouflage as a kid. Even then, his pattern recognition skills were too strong for it to confuse him in the slightest.

The heavy vehicles turned into the entrance and screeched to a stop. Two of them flanked Mike and Jamie on either side. The other two stopped in front of them blocked the northbound lane of the road.

It struck Mike that it could be an offensive or defensive formation, depending on which side of it someone ended up on.

Four Marines piled out of each Humvee. Each one was dressed in full combat gear, with body armor, helmet, and a weapon that was held ready, if not up. Patches on the center of their chests gave their name and rank. Mike felt an odd twist in his gut at how many of them looked only slightly older than his students. Their faces were a mix of determination and confusion as they looked at him and Jamie and the bland building behind them.

"I thought there'd be more," she said under her breath.

"So did I."

Pattern recognition kicked in as one of the Marines stepped forward. A man closer to Mike's age with captain's markings and the name Black on his patch. He glanced at Jamie and then Mike. "Are you Mr. Erikson?"

"That's me."

One of the younger men closer to the Humvees twitched. "Mr. Erikson?"

The ants carried out names, dates, and images. A grade of C+ on an Emily Dickinson quiz. Two overheard conversations in the halls and another one at graduation. He managed a small smile. "Hello, Jim. Or do I need to say Sergeant Duncan?"

The captain glanced back. "You know this man, staff sergeant?"

"Sir," said the Marine, "this is my old high school teacher, sir. I mean, one of them. One of the smartest guys I've ever known."

Jamie smiled.

The captain frowned. "A schoolteacher?"

"Not anymore," Mike told him.

"And what are you now?"

"Kind of in a hurry."

"Understood," Captain Black said with a curt nod. He gestured behind him, where two Marines stood with olive-green bags slung over their shoulders. One of them was a woman. Her patch said she was a lance corporal named Weaver. "We have your package," said Black. "Do you have ID?"

"Sorry, what?"

"ID, sir. My orders said to contact you and only you."

Mike pulled his battered wallet from his pocket, flipped it open, and tugged out his Maine driver's license. He spun the card in his hand and handed it to the captain.

The captain held it up and compared it to Mike's face. His eyes flitted back and forth. "Your hair looks different."

"It's a driver's license photo. It's six years old."

"Sorry, sir," he said. Another gesture summoned the Marines with the bags closer. "Your boss wasn't clear on what you were trying to do, so we've got five C4 charges. Should make a good-sized crater in just about anything for you. Just show us where to put 'em."

Mike gestured at the building. "Inside. Hopefully this can be quick."

Black glanced at the concrete structure and then at his men. "Is the building compromised, sir?"

"Not exactly."

"We were told there may be hostiles."

"That's correct."

The Marines looked around. "Are they somewhere on the grounds?"

"It's complicated."

Black took a slow breath through his nose and pressed his lips together. "Perhaps you can un-complicate it, sir."

Mike counted to three. "There's a machine inside. A highly classified, very dangerous machine. It's developed a fault and needs to be destroyed. There may be insurgents working against us."

"We'll set up a perimeter and—"

"No," said Mike. "We just need to guard the machine while your people set the explosives."

Black's lips became a thin line across his jaw. "Sir," he said, "I've been told to heed your advice, but tactically it's much better if we have an established perimeter to give us advance warning of any potential attacks."

"I understand that, captain. That's why you need to set up inside and guard the machine."

"It'll make more sense when we get inside," Jamie added.

Black gave a stiff nod and turned to the Marines. He gave three quick hand signals, and the group split into two teams. One hung back while the other moved toward the building. "Lead the way, sir, ma'am," he said.

They started toward the building, and the second group of Marines fell in behind them. "Insurgents?" she whispered to Mike.

"What was I supposed to say?"

ARTHUR WAS WAITING in the lobby with Olaf and Sasha. Arthur carried his briefcase. A canvas grocery bag packed with at least a dozen old books sat on the front desk. "I thought it might be good to pack up some of the rarer volumes," said Arthur.

The Marines spread out to each door and hallway, calling back "Clear," again and again.

"We shouldn't have any problem until we're in the lab itself," Mike said to Black.

The captain glanced at him, but made no move to call back the Marines.

"Where's Tramp?" asked Jamie.

"I took him down to your trailer," said Olaf. "I figured better he was out of the way, in case things went wrong."

"Don't worry, sir," said Black, "we'll take care of things."

Olaf shot a quick, worried look at Mike. "Do they know?"

"Not yet."

Black's lips got thin again. "Know what?"

"The equipment you're here to destroy," said Mike, "is a little unusual. Some of your people might find it a bit disturbing."

"It takes a lot to disturb us, sir," said Black. "We're Marines."

Olaf rolled his eyes. He made no attempt to hide it.

Black ignored him. "I'd like any unnecessary personnel to wait either here in the lobby or out in the parking lot," he said. "We're dealing with explosives, and there is a degree of danger."

"I think that would be me," said Arthur. He tapped his cane against the side of his foot. "I'd only slow you down."

"The rest of us all have technical knowledge about the equipment," said Mike.

"The equipment we're blowing up," said Black.

"Yes."

"And we would need your technical knowledge because . . . ?"

"It's unusual equipment, captain."

Black's lips became a thin line again. Frustration and anger flickered in his eyes. "Very well," he said, "but if I see anything I consider dangerous you're all gone. Even you, sir."

The last was aimed right at Mike. He nodded.

"I'll also be taking that Glock," added Black. He held out his hand. "I'd prefer it if we're the only ones armed in there."

"We're all on the same team," said Sasha.

"Yes, ma'am. And part of a good team is knowing who should be on first base and who should be in left field."

"I hate baseball," she muttered.

Black let out a short chuckle, but his eyes didn't leave Mike's, and his hand didn't move.

Mike reached back, pulled Arthur's pistol out, and handed it to the captain. Black handed it off to Jim Duncan without looking. Duncan inspected the weapon and it vanished into an oversized pocket on his thigh. He gave his former teacher a polite nod.

Mike gestured them down the hall.

Two Marines led the way, Duncan and a man named Chavez. Two more followed behind them, and then Black, Mike, and the rest of the Door team. Weaver and the other Marine carrying explosives, a sergeant named Dylan, were next.

They moved to the big door. Duncan tried the handle, glanced at the reader, and then back to Mike. "Locked."

Mike slid between the bulk of bodies and held his card out at arm's length by the reader. "Things in here might look a little odd," he told them. "Try not to be freaked out by any of it."

There were a few snickers and grim smiles.

"If there are any enemy combatants in here, please understand they are strong and fast. They may be wearing masks to hide their faces. They're also fond of sneak attacks, so watch everywhere."

A shift rippled through the hallway. The smiles faded and the Marines changed from a small crowd of young men and women to over a dozen hardened professionals. Weapons rose a few inches. Their breathing settled.

Mike swiped his card. The door thumped open, and the Marines poured through onto the main floor. Their boots were surprisingly soft on the concrete.

He went to follow them and a hand settled on his shoulder. "Give them a minute, sir," Black said.

Mike counted seconds. The team had been on the main floor for eleven of them when he heard a metallic bang, like a minor car crash. There was a flurry of activity, and he picked out four distinct voices. One of them was swearing in Spanish.

"Clear," yelled Duncan, but there was a note in his voice.

"Staff sergeant?" called Black. He'd heard it, too.

"We're clear, sir," said Duncan, "it's just . . . they were right."

Black looked at Mike.

They walked out onto the main floor.

Three identical tool chests stood a few yards from the door. The sides were swollen and pushed outward. One of the chests had strings of ones and zeroes on the labels instead of letters. A drawer in another had burst open, and small fuses poured out of it in a blue and green waterfall.

Duncan walked toward them and pointed at the chest with the binary labels. "This is gonna sound crazy," he told them, "but I'm pretty sure that one wasn't here when we walked in."

The color scheme was reversed on a fourth chest—black trim on brushed-silver metal. As they walked past it, the chest shuddered, and another dent appeared with a bang. The sound echoed in the big room. Olaf and Jamie yelped and stepped back.

"Did that a minute ago, too," said one of the Marines, a squat, muscle-bound man named Costello. He carried a larger rifle than the rest. Rather than the standard magazine, it had a camouflage bag fastened in front of the trigger.

"Fuck me," muttered Sasha, glaring at the tool chest.

"Just like Jiffy Pop," Mike said.

"Yeah, well, let's not be near it when it bursts."

Jamie's gaze ran down the side of the chest. "Do they still make that stuff?"

"What? Jiffy Pop?"

"Yeah?"

"I used to see it all the time back in Maine," said Staff Sgt. Duncan.
Sasha snorted.

They made their way around the cluster of tool chests. They all flinched when the silver chest dented outward again. This time the shape was long and wide, the blurred outline of a crescent wrench.

The rings stood tall in the middle of the room. The St. Elmo's fire spiraled along one ring, leaped to the other, and raced back. The air around them shimmered like hot pavement. They were a point of clarity in the middle of a huge double exposure.

The shimmer stretched out from wall to wall and up to the ceiling. The view of Site B spilled out beyond the rings, a crystal clear mirage hanging in the air, just like the view of the dead world had appeared on the security footage. Seven or eight feet out, the image blurred into a shimmering view of the main floor.

"Well," said Olaf, "this is new."

"Is this some kind of illusion?" asked Black.

"The instability's spreading out," Mike said. "The fold's getting bigger."

On the other side of the rings, Mike could see the safety light as it washed over Site B again and again. He watched four passes. On the third one, the light turned amber, then back to red for the fourth.

Hundreds of bright green roaches scurried back and forth across the floor. They traced paths around the workstations and chairs. They ran alongside the cables and hoses that were still stretched across the floor. They retreated from the booted feet, then rushed out onto the floor again.

One of the roaches raced up to them and stopped seven inches from Mike's toe. Its antennae swayed back and forth in the air. Then it raced past him and vanished beneath one of the black tool chests.

"I think he likes you," Jamie said.

They made their way toward the rings. The roaches cleared out of their way, dashing aside as each foot came down. The flatscreen Mike had broken on the creature's head was still on the floor in pieces. It was also on the workstation. One of the chairs lay on its side, while its twin stood next to it. Their bases were tangled together like grasping fingers.

Five of the Marines took up positions around the rings. They kept a healthy distance. Their eyes went back and forth across the glistening air.

"S'like one of those invisibility cloaks I was telling you about," Costello said to one of the other Marines.

"It's called optical camouflage," said Mike.

"And, no," Olaf added, "it isn't."

"Some kind of hologram thing," said Weaver. Her statement leaned toward a question. "Like a . . . a big projection screen or something."

"It's a doorway," said Duncan. "Like a wormhole."

Mike felt a quick swell of pride for his former student. "Don't step through the fold," he said out loud. "Stay on this side of it."

Weaver and Dylan slowed their movement up the ramp. "What happens if we go through?" asked one of the Marines near the nitrogen tanks. Her tag said her name was Sann.

"You could end up dead," Mike told her. "Or lost."

"Can't get lost walking a couple of yards," muttered Costello.

"It's a lot more than a couple of yards." Mike turned his gaze to Black. "Can you destroy it?"

Black glanced at Weaver and Dylan. The edges of their mouths twitched as they bit back confident smiles. They slid the bags from their shoulders. "Fast or quiet?" Dylan asked.

Mike looked at the bags. "There's a quiet option?"

Weaver shrugged. "Relatively speaking, sir."

"Fast," he said. "The sooner this is done the better."

She nodded once and looked around the main floor. "Do we care about anything else here?"

Mike glanced back at the others. Jamie looked over toward the room that held her homemade supercomputer. Olaf stared at the rings. His shoulders sagged, just a little.

Then he met Mike's eyes and shook his head.

"No," Mike told Weaver. "You can bring the whole place down if it means being sure."

"Shouldn't need that, sir." She looked over her shoulder and found Sasha. "You're the engineer? What's under this?" She rapped one of the plastic carapaces with her knuckles. "Can we take these off?"

FORTY-NINE

It took the Marines three minutes to accept the bolts holding the carapace sections couldn't be removed. A pile of over a dozen brass nuts sat on the pathway as a small monument to their efforts. Then Dylan had produced a small hatchet from his pack and removed several sections the direct way. It still took him four tries as he found another layer of carapace beneath each one he hacked away.

The charges were bundles of six dark green packets, bound together with loops of duct tape. They were long and rectangular and made Mike think of Jenga bricks, for some reason. The ants assembled a full label for him to read from the fragments he glimpsed. Each packet was a pound and a half, each full bundle was nine. There was a block of black plastic attached to each bundle. The detonator.

Sasha and Olaf had them place all the charges on the first ring. They used the locking points to direct the demolitions experts. Thirteen, fourteen, and fifteen had two charges each. The Marines were fast. They'd bent the charges around the carapace sections like clay and used duct tape to bind them in place, ripping off long straps of it and wrapping it around the ring. The first group had been placed in minutes.

Weaver produced a spare C4 packet and slit it open with a knife. She plucked out lumps of the white putty inside and packed it into the gaps around the charges. Dylan reached over and broke off a third of the stick and wadded it into a ball with one hand. Both of them made sure to keep their fingers clear of the threshold.

The other Marines circled the room. Two stood by the big door and two more watched the back door through the shimmering image of

Site B. Four of them stood near the workstations, keeping guard as the explosives were set. Black stood between them. His face was calm, but Mike watched his eyes scan back and forth across the rings.

The others did sweep after sweep, checking everywhere. Their expressions ran from bored to confused to nervous. Several of them shot looks at the rings. All of them now held their weapons ready.

The roaches scurried between their feet. Costello tried to stomp on a few, but most of them dodged his boots with lazy circles. Even the few he connected with skittered away, still alive.

Jamie stood at the workstation, making final checks. She pursed her lips and shook her head. All the readings were stubborn to the end.

"How are you detonating them?" Mike asked.

"Remote timer," said Dylan. "We cobbled it together to meet the specs your boss gave us."

"Cobbled," echoed Weaver with a smirk.

Dylan pulled something from his vest that looked like a pistol with no actual gun barrel. "Arm it, click it, and wave goodbye to it," he said.

"How long's the timer?"

"Five and a half minutes."

"Five and a half?" echoed Jamie, looking up from her monitor. "That's kind of random."

"We usually detonate manually, ma'am," Dylan said. "Like I said, we had to throw these together kind of quick with what we had."

Weaver shuffled to the other side of the pathway. She peeled off a length of tape and fastened another charge over point three. She tore a second strip free to secure it.

The light on her face changed. The room brightened. Her eyes shifted to the left. Toward the Door. Half the Marines paused to look.

"Ahhh, fuck me," said Sasha up on the pathway. "Do you guys see that?"

The other Site B, the other version of the other building, was gone. Through the rings was a vast expanse of gray sand, lit by a twilight sun. It stretched out for over two miles, dropped away into a canyon, and then continued on the other side. The dry scent of dust and sand drifted through the rings.

"I do," Mike said. He saw Olaf and Weaver nod in his peripheral vision.

"Mother of fucking God," said Black. The view spread out wall to wall, revealing the other world to the Marines. Whispers and mutters worked their way across the main floor.

Mike saw a few withered bushes and patches of brittle grass. Nothing moved. He could see for miles, and nothing moved anywhere.

He picked out rough lines across the landscape where the sand had piled up and covered things. The ants carried out the last view through this side of the door, and pattern recognition kicked in. The layout of Site B appeared in his mind, superimposed over the desert. He made out a few buildings in the distance as well. They'd all been crushed into concrete powder and dust.

As he stared, though, one bush shifted. Not an actual movement, but a change in perspective, even though he hadn't moved or even blinked. One moment the bush was a few hundred yards from the Door, the next it was twenty-eight feet, by his estimate. Then he blinked and it retreated.

His mind replayed Arthur folding a piece of paper.

On the other side of the Door, distance seemed to be a relative term.

Dylan slammed the next charge against the ring. The tape spun around it much faster this time. The sound of tape ripping off the roll was fast and steady.

Sasha walked down the ramp. She glanced behind her with every other step. "It's not going away," she said as she twisted off the end of the tape. She pushed it down onto the charge.

Jamie looked at her as they stepped across to the other side of the rings. "What?"

"The desert. Wasteland. Whatever you want to call it."

Mike studied her face. "You've seen it before?"

"This morning." She thrust her chin at the rings. "When we tried to take it apart."

"You didn't say anything about that."

"That's where I saw the bugman first. I thought I might've been seeing things. It was just for a second. And then it attacked us."

The duct tape let out a long raspberry as Weaver and Dylan wrapped the next charge in place between the rings.

Captain Black looked from Sasha to Mike. "Bugman?"

"I told you," said Mike, "they wear masks."

"That's not exactly ringing true anymore," the captain said. He used his chin to gesture at the wasteland. "Exactly what the hell is going on here?"

"Like Staff Sergeant Duncan said, it's a gateway. A fold in space."

"A gateway to where?" Black peered through the rings, and then he looked back at Mike and the others. "Is that Afghanistan? We're a few steps from Afghanistan?"

The tape roll hissed and turned to paper. Dylan growled and tossed the empty roll aside. Weaver dug in her pack for another roll.

And paused.

"What the hell is that?"

They all followed her eye line through the Door.

Miles away, something had appeared on the far side of the canyon. Several somethings. A cloud of dust went up behind them. They were short and lopsided, and this far out they made Mike think of men riding giant crabs. The limbs on the ground rose and came down, propelling the things forward.

They were moving fast.

FIFTY

Mike took three quick strides up the ramp with Black right next to him. Jamie, Olaf, and Sasha weren't far behind. They stood next to the two demolitions experts, still crouched to place their next charge but lost in the impossible view.

"Is that another one of those things?" Jamie asked. She tilted her head and tried to focus across the impossible distance.

The ants brought out pictures of the bugman they'd fought. Mike examined still images of it bent over on all fours, studied the way its spine had bent, watched it move forward on four limbs like some insectile centaur. The small shapes in the distance had the same profile. Their limbs moved the same way. He counted seven of them holding spears over their heads, but the dust cloud could be hiding more.

"I think it's a lot of them," said Mike. "At least fourteen, by my count. There could be more hidden in the dust cloud."

"Duncan," said Black. "Get a team out back and set up a line."

"Yes, sir."

"They're not out back," Olaf said. "They're right there."

"I can see them," Black snapped.

"You're seeing them but you don't get it," said Mike. "You're not looking out behind the building, captain. You're looking through a fold. They're coming through this." He gestured at the heat-haze field that stretched across the room.

"What the hell is this thing?"

"It's dangerous," Mike said, "and we need to destroy it before more of those things find their side of it."

Black made his decision in seconds. "Secure this room," he called out. "Dylan, Weaver, I want this done five minutes ago."

"Yes, sir," they both echoed.

"Lock and load, Marines," called out Duncan, all trace of the former student gone. "We've got incoming, probably fifteen minutes out. Let's get the welcome party ready."

The four around the Door dropped to their knees and brought up their rifles. The others dragged over tool chests for extra cover. One of them pointed a finger at the big tanks. "What are those?"

"Liquid nitrogen," said Olaf. "Try not to shoot them."

"Really cold?"

"Really explosive."

The Marine swore under his breath and shuffled a few more feet away. They crouched behind the workstations and tool chests. A line of rifles pointed at the Door. Costello swung his oversized rifle onto one of the tool chests and unfolded a bipod at the end of the barrel.

"I was really hoping they'd send more," Jamie murmured to Mike.

"Maybe you should get out of here," he said. "There's nothing more for you to do."

"It's our project," Olaf said.

"I think you all need to leave," said Black. "This is a combat situation now. Fall back to the door, at least." He looked at Mike, then down at the two Marines taping a charge against the ring.

The view through the rings drifted and blurred. Just for a moment it was Site B again. Then it was the empty lot behind the remains of Site B. And then it was the sprawling desert and the charging creatures again.

"Jesus," said Dylan. "What was that?"

"The fold's unstable," said Mike. "The other end of the tunnel is flailing around between different realities."

Weaver looked up at him. "What?"

Black shot a glance at them and the two Marines went back to their explosives.

"Fuck me," said Sasha. "They're on this side of the canyon. They all just kind of lunged forward half a mile or so when it flickered."

"Done," said Dylan. Weaver pressed one last small clump of putty into a gap behind the last charge. They stood up.

"Let's fall back," said Black with another look at the approaching figures. Over two dozen were visible now, and more shadows moved in the dust cloud. "Sir, I need all of you to evacuate the building now."

Sasha hopped off the pathway down to the floor. Mike opened his mouth to respond and something changed in his peripheral vision. On the other side of the rings, the middle charge had vanished. The loops of tape were gone. There weren't even any trails of sticky residue left on the carapace.

Jamie was about to hop down and saw his face. "What?"

"Problems."

She turned and followed his gaze. So did Black.

"Son of a bitch," said Weaver. "Where'd it go?"

"Fuck me," Sasha said.

Black glared at Mike, then at each of the others in turn.

Mike looked at Dylan and Weaver. "Will two charges be enough there?"

They traded a look between them. Weaver shrugged. "It should," she said. "Ten pounds'd take out that whole wall if you placed it right, and we've still got thirty-six on this thing."

He looked at Black. "Do it."

"When you're clear. We'll hold position until—"

"We've got time to get clear," snapped Olaf. "Blow the damned thing and let's go."

The sound of feet rumbled out of the Door. It was the noise of a herd. A stampede. They were less than a mile away.

"Five minutes, sir," shouted Duncan.

A healthy man could do a five-minute mile. Mike had no idea how fast a four-legged animal could cover the distance, but he was sure it was less.

"I've got another charge," said Weaver. "A spare."

Black looked at the approaching horde. "How fast?"

She didn't answer, just pulled the last bundle from her bag.

Black grabbed Mike by the shoulder and pushed him down the ramp. "All of you," he said, reaching for Sasha, "go now."

Mike stumbled on the ramp, and his eyes fell to the floor. He caught the movement on the concrete. He watched for three seconds to be sure. His pattern recognition skills were very good.

"The roaches," he said.

Black half-glanced over his shoulder. "What about them?"

"They're all moving away from the rings."

Dylan looked back. Black turned around. Jamie and Olaf took a few more steps down the ramp and looked out at the main floor.

The green cockroaches still scurried between tool chests and furniture, but they'd moved far back. The closest ones were almost ten feet from the base of the ramp. Even as Mike watched, their paths retreated a little more.

"Fuck me," Sasha said again.

One of them stopped between the workstations and bent its antennae toward the rings. The tips gleamed like tiny fiber-optic lines. They bent forward, back, forward, and then the cockroach turned and raced away.

"What's it mean?" said Black.

"It means we need to do this now," said Mike.

The captain took in a breath and nodded. "You heard the man, sergeant."

"Yes, sir," said Dylan. Behind him, Weaver swept her tools and leftovers back into her bag. She let out a sharp breath that fell somewhere between a whistle and a hiss. It was the sound of something moving fast through the air.

Dylan kicked himself away from the rings. He went off the edge and crashed to the floor in front of his fellow Marines. His body rolled to the side and the spear in his chest clattered against the concrete. His body armor bulged in the back where it kept the spear tip from bursting through.

Another blur of white shot through the rings. It hit the back wall with a crack and dropped to the floor. The next one tore through Olaf's sleeve before burying itself a foot into one of the tool chests.

Mike grabbed Jamie and pulled her down. Sasha threw herself on the floor. Olaf lunged off the platform and landed gracefully in a crouch. Weaver dropped flat on the pathway and rolled until she dropped off the platform and crashed on top of Sasha.

Black turned, and a spear went through the meat of his arm and into his ribs. Nine inches of the tip tore through his uniform on the other side of his body. It was barbed and bloody. His knees buckled and he fought to keep his balance with five feet of spear hanging off his arm. He coughed up a mouthful of blood and spat out the words "Blow it."

Then a second spear passed through his hip with a crack of bone. He roared once and then sagged on the pathway. The spears kept his body from falling flat, holding him up in a slouched position that almost looked like a yoga pose.

The sound of footsteps shook the huge room. Dozens of spears flew through the ring and the heat haze around it. They rained through the air.

Mike and Jamie huddled in the corner between the ramp and the walkway. He looked beneath the ramp and saw Sasha, Olaf, and Weaver in the corner opposite them. Olaf was staring at something out on the floor. The spears hissed above them.

Three more Marines were dead, skewered by spears. A fourth slumped behind a tool chest and grunted back screams while he held his shattered and bloody arm. Two others let off shots from their rifles. One of them was Costello with his big automatic weapon.

The sound reflected off the concrete walls. Duncan yelled something that was lost in the thunderous echo. Inside Mike's head, pattern recognition kicked out the word "sharp."

The rumble of footsteps turned into a clang of steel as the bugmen charged out of the Door and launched themselves off the pathway. Black's body slammed into the floor in front of Mike and Jamie, kicked aside by the invaders. The captain's chin and chest were dark with blood he'd coughed up in his final moments.

The bugmen hurled themselves at the remaining Marines. Their cloaks spread like wings, casting shadows across the room. Some had spears. Some had their claw-like hands stretched out. All three of their hands.

They were caught in midair by high-velocity rounds. Some were torn apart. Others landed with enough life to drive their spears into their killers. Across the main floor, the roar of weapons and the howl of monsters fought to be the loudest sound.

Costello cut down five of the leaping creatures before his weapon ran dry. The sixth punched its spear down through his throat. The jagged head tore out between his shoulder blades, and the bugman rode his body down to the floor. It wrenched the spear free and stalked away. Blood bubbled and spit out of Costello's mouth for a few moments while he died.

Dark blood sprayed across the floor. Spears and talons impaled the Marines. The few survivors fell back. Mike counted five of them. Jim Duncan was one.

Weaver rolled to her feet and brought her rifle up. She marched forward and shot three of the bugmen in the back. A fourth turned and she put a trio of rounds in its face.

Olaf leaped up behind her. Sasha grabbed at him, but he shook her off. He loped up behind Weaver, heading for Dylan's body.

Duncan and the other Marines got a cautious crossfire going. Two more bugmen dropped. Then one Marine's weapon *clacked* empty and a monster pounced on him. They went down in a swirl of cloak and screams. Another, Sann, tried to switch magazines. A spear went straight through her right eye and out the back of her skull, shattering her helmet as it did.

One of the bugmen pulled a spear from one of the corpses and hurled the weapon back at Weaver. It flew straight through her stomach and struck Olaf in the shoulder. She managed to kill the creature with two more bursts before she dropped her rifle and clutched at her gut.

Olaf bit back a scream. The spear hung from his shoulder like a rod on a puppet. He flailed at Dylan's body, stretching his fingers. Then another shaft hissed in the air and punched through his chest. He slumped. The spears held him up, forming a tripod with his spine.

Jamie shrieked into her hand.

Weaver tried to move. She took a few awkward steps to the side, clutching at the hole in her stomach. Blood gushed down from the matching hole in her back. It soaked through her uniform and splashed out onto the floor. She winced, her face paled, and she dropped to her knees in the puddle. Her shoulders slumped and her chin dipped down to her chest.

Mike saw it all. The ants carried out instant replays and freeze frames and assembled renderings for him to review. They tallied the dead and the living on both sides. Twenty-two dead monsters. Fourteen dead Marines. All committed to memory forever.

Four bugmen were still alive. Two of them were wounded. They were stalking the last two Marines.

Less than a minute had passed since the first spear impaled Dylan.

Black had a sidearm. It was in a holster on his hip. He'd never drawn it. It was twenty-three inches from Mike's left hand.

Why had Olaf been reaching for Dylan's body? What had he wanted? The Marine's rifle was still up on the pathway where he'd dropped it, right next to . . .

The ants showed him the image from three different angles. He'd seen it when the first spear hit and when he'd grabbed Jamie's forearm and when they were in mid-dive for cover.

Dylan's rifle sat right next to the remote for the charges. Mike looked up through the expanded steel and saw the two outlines a few feet behind Sasha.

Three fast shots rang out, another rifle burst, and one of the bugmen roared. Another one dropped. Its skull had been pulped.

Over by the tool chests, Jim Duncan screamed as a spear was driven through his shoulder and down into his chest. The creature twisted its weapon, shredding his insides, but Mike's former student managed to bring up his rifle. The bugman's cloak rippled, caught in nine small breezes. The two bodies slumped together.

Two bugmen left. One Marine. According to Mike's count, the last survivor was Banner, first initial J. According to her patch, she was a sergeant with type O positive blood.

Mike pointed out the remote to Jamie. He spread his fingers wide twice and mouthed "boom." She understood. He waved his hand to Sasha. The movement caught her eye, and he repeated his simple sign language to her. She nodded as well.

Somewhere out on the floor, Marine sergeant J. Banner fired off two bursts with her rifle and died screaming.

Two, possibly only one, bugmen left.

Mike used his fingers to mime running, pointed at himself, and then pointed to the far side of the main floor. He would run toward the tanks, away from the door. They could grab the remote and run.

He reached out and slid Black's pistol from its holster. It was heavier than he thought it would be. He twisted up onto his toes, kissed Jamie on the forehead, and lunged to his feet.

There were two creatures left. One had its hood up. The other one glared at him with three mismatched eyes.

Neither of them moved to follow him.

He heard the sound of feet in sand. Something pushed the smell of the desert at him through the air. And another scent came with it.

All the roaches were gone now. He couldn't see one anywhere. They'd all fled, following the primal instructions hardwired into their simple brains.

Mike turned.

Something else came out of the Door.

FIFTY-ONE

The ants leaped into overdrive. They counted and cataloged and quantified. They gave him more details than he wanted to know.

The thing's arm stretched out and lashed around the first ring. It had half a dozen cable-like fingers. Each of them had seven knuckles. They wrapped all the way around the broad ring like tentacles. The hand was on the end of a long, stitch-covered arm. Mike counted two elbows on the limb.

A second hand reached out and slapped itself down on the opposite side of the Door. And then a third hand reached out of the rings to grab alongside the first one.

Jamie skittered away from the ramp and almost crashed into Mike. Sasha did the same and ended up near Olaf's impaled body. She shifted away, but the thing on the pathway held her gaze. "What the fuck is that?!"

The slender figure dragged itself through the Door. It was tall, with too many joints in its legs and arms. Mike saw black, ragged armbands on each limb. It took a moment to identify the lines as stitches. He saw the coarse threads and his ants pulled up an image of the bugman's cloak.

Its limbs didn't bend. They coiled like snakes as they sought purchase in the world, dragging a bent torso after them.

The creature pulled itself through the Door and stretched up to full height on the pathway.

Each leg consisted of multiple limbs sewn together end to end to make a single long one. Each had three knees. Each arm had been rebuilt the same way, with two elbows leading back to a swollen, stitch-covered shoulder. A third arm was sewn into place under the figure's right armpit. The torso looked like two bodies stacked one on top of the other, with another line of coarse threads where hips met shoulders. There were five nipples and two navels. He couldn't be sure, but it looked like there were extra vertebrae in its neck. Its head looked tiny on such an overextended body.

The ants pulled up various anatomical images and jammed up as the conflicting facts told Mike how impossible the creature was. Such a thing couldn't move. Such a thing couldn't live.

It swayed on the pathway for a moment as it looked around the room. It took a few slow, wheezing breaths and clicked like the bugman had that morning. Then it turned its face to them.

It looked like it had been human once. Its upper lip had been cut into a dozen thin flaps, like a mustache of fleshy tendrils. Its hair had been pulled out, leaving scars and scabs across a bald head. One of its nostrils had been slit open to the bridge of the nose.

The right eye was gone. Two beady orbs glared out of the raw mess of the socket. Its lips pulled back into a smile that showed human teeth. Regular, normal teeth in a monster's face.

The remains of the croissant he'd had hours ago swirled around in Mike's stomach. The ants spun and thrashed and fought in his mind, searching for a point of reference. The only stable part, the only part not flailing to find something logical in the illogical monster, was focused on the detonator. He didn't look at it. He didn't want to draw attention to it.

The slender monster looked back over its shoulder and made a sound that fell somewhere between an angry laugh and a bark. Another cloaked, lopsided figure with a spear stepped through the Door. Then another one. And another.

The monster focused on Mike and leaned forward. Its two right hands let go of the ring. It balanced on the left arm as it dropped off the pathway. It landed on Black's corpse, and something crunched in the body.

As it stepped away, two more bugmen came through the Door to fill the space it had left.

The patchwork man loomed over them. Mike had seen that expression on kids in the cafeteria. And pets at feeding time. It plucked the pistol from Mike's hand, passed the weapon between its long-nailed fingers, and tossed it over onto the workstation.

The creature's gaze passed over Jamie and then Sasha. It sniffed the air around them twice, and what was left of its nose wrinkled as it did. It looked at Olaf's body, propped up by spears, and ran one of its spidery fingers across the dead man's scalp. It moved on to Weaver, touching and examining her slumped form before it placed a clawed digit against her temple and toppled her body into the surrounding moat of blood.

"Well, well, well," it said. The voice was wet and lispy as it filtered out between the slashed lips, although Mike wasn't sure if it was the lips or a certain . . . prissiness the voice had. An attempt to sound proper and important. The voice was uneven, as if it hadn't spoken—or maybe hadn't spoken English—in years. "This is looking to be a wonderful day."

It straightened up and wrapped its arms back and forth across its chest. Its head tilted back, and it glared down the ruined nose at them. It made a few clicking noises like the bugmen, as if settling back into a more comfortable language.

One of the creatures gnashed its teeth. Three of the ones on the platform turned to the rings. The sound of ripping tape filled the main floor again. The four charges were pulled free. One of them was torn in half, and the bugman sniffed at the exposed material. It poked at the white putty with a clawed finger.

The patchwork man made another noise, and the cloaked figures vanished back through the Door with the explosives.

The remote still sat on the pathway. It had been knocked aside, closer to the base of the rings, but it looked undamaged. Dylan's rifle had moved, too, and the stock was close enough to the device that, at a glance, they might pass for a single object.

But there were no more charges on the rings. One vanished, four taken away. Weaver hadn't had time to attach her spare. Mike wasn't sure where it had ended up. Or if it had a detonator in it. He'd seen a short video on C4 once. He knew it needed a detonator. Fire or gunshots wouldn't set it off. Maybe the patchwork man knew that, too.

His mind raced through possible scenarios and solutions. The ants listed obstacles and assets. Four bugmen left in the room, thought

Mike, and the tall thing. Against him, Jamie, and Sasha. Plus a pile of Marine equipment they didn't know how to use.

He came up with three options. He didn't have the resources for any of them.

Sasha shuffled over to join them. One of the bugmen had circled around to flank her. It was bleeding from its high shoulder. It took another step toward them, reached out, and wrenched the spear out of Olaf's shoulder. The body tipped and thudded to the floor. His eyes were half open.

The tall monster looked down at them and blinked its one human eye. It walked around them. It moved like an octopus, each limb curling up and then stretching back down.

Mike turned to watch it. So did Jamie and Sasha. They shuffled to keep their distance from the stitched-together thing, and something bumped Mike's heel. They'd backed up to Black's body.

Less than ten feet from the remote.

"So fortunate," the patchwork man lisped through his shredded lips. "First to feed our Great Lord." It moved to the ramp. They slid away again, backing toward the tanks. It let them move away. Its mouth pulled into a tight grimace. The remote slipped away in Mike's peripheral vision.

Then he blinked, and when he opened his eyes things were different.

Pattern recognition kicked in. As a child, he'd always been good at the game where there were two similar pictures with a collection of differences. He'd always been able to solve them in seconds, faster than he could write down the answers or say them aloud.

It took him four seconds to spot all the differences on the main floor. At the workstation, the cushions on one of the chairs had changed from dark green to dark blue. In his peripheral vision, there were now three black tool chests. On the far side of the room, a second warning light had appeared on the wall. And . . .

He counted off more seconds. One by one, the others noticed the changes. The patchwork man stared behind them. Mike glanced over his shoulder to see one of the bugmen studying a fourth nitrogen tank that had appeared. Sasha looked at the chairs. The bugman that had corralled her twisted its head to the tank to see what had caught her eye.

Jamie looked at the light, and then her eyes slid over to—

"Look at me," whispered Mike.

She turned and stared at his cheek, then at his left eye. She took three deep breaths through her nose and let them whistle out as she tried to get control.

"Look at the tool chests. How many are there?"

"Did you see the—"

"Don't. How many tool chests?"

Jamie swallowed. "Four. Three black ones and the silver one." She blinked. "No, wait. It's gold now. Gold with black trim, I think."

"Good. Don't look at it. Try to tell Sasha. She can't look at it."

She nodded and shifted her feet. Her hips swiveled and carried her over toward Sasha.

He made a point of staring up at the patchwork man. It noticed him after a moment and stared back. The two small eyes were just black dots, but the human eye looked down at him. Its lid blinked in a slow, deliberate manner.

In his peripheral vision he could see the rings. Not quite in the corner of his eye, but close to the ten o'clock position. The monsters hadn't been looking at the rings when the change happened. They still weren't looking. In their minds, the ring was the one place trouble couldn't come from.

Up at position fourteen, a loop of duct tape had reappeared. It was a three-inch strip of silver against the off-white of the plastic housings. Easy to overlook among all the supports and hoses and cables.

He could just see the C4 charge poking out between the two rings.

FIFTY-TWO

Mike summoned the ants. For his whole life he'd kept them locked away, letting them out in streams and clusters. He needed all of them now.

He needed to stop being Mycroft and become Sherlock.

The ants carried out swarms of images and sounds and raw facts for him. The scale model of the main floor grew, spun, zoomed in again and again to show him different details.

Other ants carried out the *U.S. Marshals* scene again, even though it wasn't entirely relevant. He looked at similar moments and images from movies and real life. He was pretty sure he had what he needed.

"Same plan as before," he whispered to Jamie.

"What?"

"You're not an alpha predator," Mike said to the patchwork man.

The tall creature turned from the Albuquerque Door and blinked twice. "I'm sorry," it said. Again, Mike was struck by the prissy aspect of the expression. Whoever the patchwork man had been before, he'd probably been very high maintenance. "Pardon me?"

Mike tried to stretch himself a little taller. He gestured at the bug-man over by the workstation. "You're not an alpha predator like them," he repeated. "So what are you?"

The patchwork man's human eye shifted. The hairless brow furrowed. The shredded lips moved, forming silent, unreadable words. It made Mike think of a fish.

And then the creature let out a few wet sounds. For a moment he thought it was choking. He saw the same hope in Jamie's eyes.

Then its chuckle became a full laugh.

"The seraphs are not alpha predators," it lisped. Its stitched-together chest puffed out. "They are the jackals waiting the return of the lion. The dust before the endless sandstorm. They are the tide going out before the wave comes in."

It recited the words with halts and accents. High maintenance and more than a bit smug, Mike thought. The cadence reminded him of overzealous people reading from the Bible, even though he didn't recognize any of the passages.

"So what's that make you?"

The slender creature uncoiled a long finger and touched the tip to its shredded lips. "I was a man," it said after a moment. "A family man who thought he understood the lessons of his congregation. Now I am like Enoch, ascended to become the voice of my Lord, and remade in the divine image with the flesh of Charles and Lucas and Howard and Timothy." The finger moved down the opposite arm, touching each section between the stitches.

The ants searched for a reference to the names, listed them in different orders, and found nothing. Mike nodded and counted to six. He didn't break eye contact with the creature. "One more question."

"Of course," said the creature. "Please make the most of your time as my Lord draws near."

He stared at its human eye. "Do you know what proprioception is?"

The patchwork man blinked at him. So did Jamie and Sasha.

"It's one of the few neurological terms I know," Mike admitted after a moment. "One of those extra senses you don't hear about often. It's how you know where your body parts are even when you can't see them. Like how you can reach into your back pocket without looking."

The creature loomed over him, and he retreated from it with a trio of nervous steps. But he didn't break eye contact. He could see Jamie tensing in the corner of his vision.

"In my case," he continued, still staring at the creature's eyes, "it's useful because I can remember where everything else is, too. So I can leave the lights off a lot of the time. I don't need to look at things around me to pick them up. And I can aim that way, too."

He reached back without looking, grabbed Black's pistol off the workstation, and fired at the target behind him.

Things slowed down as Mike took in every detail he could.

The recoil wrenched his wrist around, but the ants showed him diagrams and angles and he aimed again.

The patchwork man broke the stare after the first shot. It roared. Spittle rained on Mike's face as he fired a second shot. He heard one of the bugmen—the seraphs—hiss behind him.

The one by the nitrogen tanks.

Jamie flinched away from the gunshots and lunged forward. Sasha was a few steps behind her.

The tall creature shoved Mike aside on his third shot. It loped past him.

The lone bugman on the pathway had one of its arms up. The arm with the spear. It was already pulled back. Its eyes went between Mike and Jamie, picking a target. Mike heard a louder hiss behind him. A cold breeze hit his back. He braced himself and took a step away from the tanks. He swung the pistol around to aim at the seraph on the pathway.

The other seraph by the far workstation, the one with the wounded arm, growled at him. It reached for the spear that had impaled Sann, but its movements were slow.

Jamie's foot hit the ramp.

Mike took another step and squeezed the trigger two more times. His first shot punched through the cloak to hit the seraph in the thigh. The second round went straight through the rough leather and vanished through the rings as the seraph hurled its spear.

The nitrogen tanks exploded.

There was no heat, just a blast of freezing air. It slammed him into the far workstation and saved his life. The spear that was aimed at his chest wobbled and caught him in the side under his arm. The force and speed of the glancing blow shattered bone. His ribs blazed with heat and pain. The shaft sliced through cloth, flesh, and muscle.

A chunk of metal hit him hard in the back, and a second one slashed his calf.

Another second passed. His ribs felt like broken glass grinding under his skin. He could picture needles of bone breaking off as they rubbed against each other. He was wet with blood. The arm holding the pistol shook. He had no idea how he'd managed to hold on to the gun.

A chill ran through his body, like stepping into a cold pool. It could've been the cold air or blood loss. He wasn't sure which.

Jamie was sprawled on the ramp. Mike couldn't see any blood. He counted off another second and saw her take a breath. He didn't see Sasha anywhere and figured she'd been knocked down on the other side of the ramp.

The seraph on the pathway pushed itself up onto all fours. A gash in its side leaked dark blood onto the pathway. Its large eye was a wet socket. The two small ones glared at him, then down at Jamie. Its mouth opened to display the forest of narrow fangs.

His arm came up with the pistol and fired twice. The explosion still rang in his ears so the gunshots were muffled and flat. They both hit it in the torso, but nowhere near center. The creature let out another clicking growl and crouched lower. It reminded him of a dog getting ready to charge.

Then one of its arms collapsed under it and it slumped on the pathway. The cloak settled around it and grew still.

At least two seraphs dead. Maybe three.

Mike shifted his weight against the workstation and tried to balance. His knees were loose. It was as if they'd become ball and socket joints, and his body still needed time to figure out how they worked. His hips felt loose, too. His side was very wet, although it didn't hurt quite as much, and he was pretty sure he was going into shock.

His vision dimmed. The thought flitted through his mind that he was losing consciousness. Then he realized it was a shadow.

The patchwork man loomed over him and snarled something. Mike couldn't hear what, and it was impossible to read the shredded lips. The curved, Kindle-sized chunk of metal stuck in its shoulder had part of a green warning label on it. Six of the stitches along the shoulder were broken. Three fingers had vanished from its extra hand, and the whole limb sparkled with frost.

It reached out and grabbed his arm. The long fingers wrapped around his bicep twice. He could feel the knots on the stitches through his sleeve. The patchwork man yanked up, and the fire in Mike's side exploded. Shards of pain tumbled through his body. His fingers spasmed. The pistol dropped to the floor.

In the corner of his eye, Jamie lunged over the dead seraph on the pathway and grabbed the timer. She fiddled with the controls for a moment and squeezed it again and again. Mike's stomach twisted. She squeezed the remote again, and something clicked. A light on the half-hidden charge flashed on.

The patchwork man snarled again and let Mike drop. His side exploded with pain. The cut on his leg flared. The bandages on his wounded stomach felt hot and wet. He slumped against the workstation but forced himself to stay on his feet.

The tall creature stalked away, toward the rings.

One of the surviving seraphs crawled into view on the other side of the workstation. The hood of its cloak was shredded, and a piece of metal stuck out from the side of its skull. Dark blood ran across its face. The patchwork man growled and clicked at it, and it moved to follow him.

Jamie saw them coming. She tucked the remote under her arm and scooped up Dylan's rifle. She struggled with it for a moment.

The seraph raised its claws and snarled. Its feet clanged on the ramp. The patchwork man took another stride toward her.

Jamie looked at them, then at Mike.

Then she turned and ran through the Door.

THE DESERT
AT THE END OF
ALL THINGS

FIFTY-THREE

Jamie's feet landed on gritty sand and stumbled. She'd gone through the Door almost forty times, but it had always been the same experience— stepping from one room to another along the steel pathway. With no other reference points, it almost felt natural.

Now she was outside.

She was outside in what was left of Site B.

She ran for another minute. Her adrenaline was pumping. She didn't know if the stitched-together thing was coming after her. She just slogged across the sand until her heart rate slowed.

The wasteland stretched out before her, endless sand as far as she could see, spotted by a few rocks and withered patches of grass. A few feet away was some kind of bush that looked like it might've seen water a decade or so back.

Above her, the sun hung in the sky like an old ember. She knew *hung* was the right word. This sun was tired, almost exhausted, bled of all its strength and power. It was red and dull, not the harsh yellow she was used to.

She looked behind her and saw the fold, a hole in the air that blurred at the edges.

Just beyond the fold she could see the outline of a set of rings resting on the sand and concrete gravel. Jamie realized the pathway might still be there, too, a foot or two down under the strange desert.

She spent a moment trying to focus on the edge of the rift, unbound by the rings, but her eyes kept slipping. It was like trying to focus on part of an optical illusion. The part she was looking at would stabilize, but everything around it would blur and spin faster.

On the other side of the fold she could still see a wide swath of the main floor. The dead bugman lay sprawled on the pathway. Past it were the workstations and concrete floor and dead Marines and Olaf's skewered body and a collection of tool chests.

And the seraph crawling up the ramp.

And the patchwork man glaring at her.

Jamie took a few more steps away from the hole. The sand crunched under her feet. It didn't feel right. It was too coarse and too gray.

She turned and ran a few more yards.

In the distance, maybe two miles away, she could see the canyon. The canyon that was out behind Site B. She and Bob had hiked out there once to look down at the various office parks and storage units and one building Bob insisted belonged to some unnamed government group that was monitoring them.

There were four specks near the canyon. The bugmen with the C4 charges. It was hard to be sure at this distance, but she thought they were all facing the other way.

The air brushed against her face and hands. It struck her that it had been still until that moment, just as lifeless as the desert itself. No wind, no breezes, not even a slight difference in temperature.

She heard a grunt behind her and turned.

Sasha pushed herself up off the sand and scrambled away from the fold on all fours. She spat out a mouthful of grit, climbed to her feet, and took a few more unsteady steps across the desert. A Marine's rifle was clutched in her hands.

Then she looked up and stared at Jamie. "Oh, thank God," she said. She stumbled across the wasteland. They fell into each other's arms for a moment.

Then Jamie pushed her back to arm's length to look at her. "Are you okay?"

Sasha nodded and rubbed her jaw. "Didn't know he was going to blow up the tanks."

"Neither did I."

"I got hit by a nozzle. Lucky it didn't break my jaw."

"Why did you follow me?"

She glanced back over her shoulder at the fold. "There weren't many options. When you went away, the big skinny guy went after me." She glanced around at the barren wasteland. "Fuck me."

"Not now," said Jamie.

"Not here," Sasha agreed. She looked up at the dim sun. "Last days of Krypton. Where the fuck are we?"

Jamie looked around again. It was arid nothingness as far as she could see. There were hills and mountains near the horizon, but even they looked barren and lifeless. The only vibrant colors were the fold in space and Sasha's WALKING RED T-shirt.

"I think . . ." said Jamie, "I think this is the world without us."

"The world after people?"

"The world after everything. I think Mike was right. It's all been eaten." She pointed up at the sun. "Everything."

Sasha shook her head. "Did you get the charge set?"

"Yeah, I think so. We can't stay here. We don't have much time."

"Yeah, but what do we . . . crap." She looked past Jamie, toward the canyon. "Is that the bug people?"

"I think so."

"We need to get out of here before they—"

The air rippled again. They both turned.

The wounded bugman crawled toward them on all fours. It paused and took a deep breath. Then it pushed itself up onto two legs. Its head tilted back and forth, and they felt its focus shift between them.

It growled and bared its forest of fangs at them.

Jamie stumbled back, her feet dragging in the sand. Then she noticed the weight in her hand and glanced down. She still held the rifle.

She brought it up again. She wasn't sure why it hadn't fired before and wondered if it was out of bullets. Or maybe there was a safety switch. Did rifles have safeties?

She wondered if the creature would be intimidated by the weapon.

It didn't seem concerned. It kept marching across the sand toward them, flexing its claws. It chattered in the wet, clicking syllables of the other tongue, and something about the rhythm made it sound like a prayer or a psalm.

Jamie shook the rifle. "Stop right there," she shouted. "Stay back."

The bugman kicked up plumes of sand as it walked across the

wasteland toward them. Its cloak drifted around it. She could see the heavy stitches.

Jamie squeezed the trigger again. It didn't budge. It felt thick, as if it was caught on something. She took another step back. In the corner of her eye, Sasha stepped back with her.

She looked down and turned the rifle. In the dim light, she saw an oval of metal on the side. A line through it pointed at the word SAFE. She flicked at it with her thumb, and the line spun ninety degrees to SEMI.

She pulled the trigger, and the rifle barked. It twisted in her hands, and a bullet punched the sand in front of the bugman. It leaped back and glared at her.

The sing-song prayers stopped. It stalked toward her.

Jamie gripped the rifle, squeezed the trigger again, and another bullet hit the ground almost a foot away from the creature.

The bugman ignored it.

She knew there was a way to make it shoot more, but she didn't dare look away to study the rifle again.

A roar cut through the dead air. Sasha had her rifle up and fired off another three-round burst, and then another. The bullets tore up the sand, and then tore up the leathery cloak. The bugman twitched and stumbled. Its arms swiped through the air, flailing for the women even though it was still fifteen feet away.

Sasha pulled her trigger again and again until her rifle ran dry with a *clack*.

The creature staggered for a moment and fell over backward. There was almost no noise when it hit the sand. Its fingers twitched one more time. So did its tooth-filled jaw. And then it was still.

Sasha stared at the body for a moment. She kept the rifle pointed at it while she took in five deep, wheezing breaths. She blinked twice.

Jamie looked at the body and bit back the urge to scream.

Someone else screamed. It was a distant, alien sound, and the desert muffled it. The scream didn't roll across the sand as much as slide across it, sticking close to the ground.

The bugmen had turned from the canyon. Each dropped to all fours and raced across the desert. Each of them held an arm, the extra one, up in the air with a long spear ready to throw.

They looked like lopsided centaurs, but they moved like bugs. Like giant roaches.

Jamie glanced at Sasha. "Any more bullets?"

"I don't think so."

"Did that hurt?"

Sasha chuckled. "Yeah, I think I killed him."

"No," said Jamie, "did it hurt *you*? Your arm."

"What are you talking about?" They both looked down at Sasha's bare arms.

A chill danced down Jamie's back. "What happened to your stitches?"

"My what?"

She glanced back at the fold in space. "Where did you get the rifle?"

"What?"

"Where'd you get it?"

Sasha shrugged. "It was what's-his-name, the demolition guy's. It was sitting on the pathway, so I grabbed it before I dove through."

Jamie shook her head. "No," she said, "I grabbed the one on the pathway."

They stared at each other for a moment. Their eyes went to the identical rifles they each held.

"Fuck me," said Sasha. "Not again."

The bugmen in the distance howled. The sound made Jamie think of hungry people and starving animals. It wasn't a sound that meant they'd be taking prisoners.

If she was right, it had taken the bugmen almost five minutes to get to the canyon. They were moving much faster on the way back. Two of them used their extra arm to shake their spears in the air. The others carried the weapons up close to the shoulder.

"We *really* need to get out of here," she said.

"Where?"

"Back through," said Jamie. She pointed her empty rifle at the dead body and then at the approaching creatures. "It's safer there, and I think we've only got two or three minutes before that charge goes off."

She took a few steps toward the shimmering hole.

Sasha didn't.

"What?"

"I'm already there."

"What do you—" Jamie glanced through the fold. "Yeah, she's there, but you're here. And now we need to go there."

"What if I . . ." Sasha waved her machine pistol at the hole in space. "What if we cancel out or something?"

Jamie paused. "You won't."

"How do you know?"

"The apples," she said. "It'll be like the apples and the tool chests and the donuts. There'll just be more than one of you."

"Fuck that."

The bugmen roared again, but the tone was different this time. Upbeat. It almost sounded . . . happy.

The creatures had paused in their race halfway across the desert. Now it looked like they were dropping to the sand themselves. Bowing their heads. Kneeling. Their arms reached out toward Jamie and Sasha.

To something past them.

Jamie looked behind them to see if the patchwork man had come through the Door. But the coarse sand in front of the rings was empty, and so was the steel pathway on the other side.

Sasha glanced back at the bugmen, still sprawled on the ground, and then took a few steps to the right in the sand. A few more carried her over the line of crumbling cinder blocks that had been the wall of Site B, giving her a clear view of the wasteland that stretched out past the fold. Nothing but patches of dead grass and withered . . .

"Oh my God," she whispered.

Jamie trudged across the sand to see what the fold had hidden.

Something moved in the air. Her first thought was that it was a plane, but even in the strange distances of the desert she realized that couldn't be right. It was too far away. Too big.

And it was alive.

FIFTY-FOUR

At first glance it reminded Jamie of humpback-whale footage, the shots where the giant creatures glided toward the camera. Even seen from the front, they gave a sense of mass and size. And their faces always looked peaceful, like they were close to smiling.

Whatever was coming toward them through the air had that sense of mass, but it was hostile. Dangerous. Anger and rage came off it like heat. Instead of a whale's smile, the thing's face was covered with thick fur or some kind of mane that the distance blurred.

The huge thing pushed down on the air with its wings. They were huge sheets of flesh stretched over a bone framework, the limbs of a bat taken to a ridiculous scale. She'd seen wings like that on *Game of Thrones*, but even those were small compared to these.

As the monstrous wings beat down, the desert beneath the creature exploded into clouds of dust and sand. A skeletal tree was ripped up by the downblast and tossed away. It spun in the air and crashed to the ground behind the creature.

It gave her mind a way to judge scale. The thing in the air was four or five miles away. Whatever it was had to be bigger than a jumbo jet. It had to be *enormous*.

"Alpha predators," whispered Sasha. Her face paled.

It moved toward them. Toward the fold in space.

In the distance, the bugmen wailed and cried out.

"Come on," Jamie said. "Let's get out of here."

Sasha didn't move.

"Sasha?"

Sasha's lips went slack. The rifle dropped from her hand, and she staggered forward. Her eyelids stretched wider as she stared at the thing in the sky. One of the tiny veins across the white of her eye swelled up and burst. Red poured out across the white.

The dragon wings thrust down again. This time Jamie felt the air move. Sand and concrete grit pattered against her face and arms. The thing in the air had already cut the distance between them by a third.

"Sasha!" Jamie grabbed her limp arm and yanked. The two of them stumbled in the sand and fell. Sasha rolled a few feet down a small dune, and the thing in the sky vanished behind them.

She thrashed free of Jamie's grip. "Did you hear it?" she asked. "Could you hear it, too?"

"Hear what?"

Sasha looked over her shoulder at the thing in the sky, then looked away just as quickly. Her eye was bloodshot. "It's hungry," she said. "Oh, fuck me, it talked, and it's so hungry."

"It *talked*?"

Sasha pressed her hand over her bloodshot eye. "It's so hungry," she said again.

They could hear the sound of massive wings thrumming against the air like drumheads. The wind was steady now. Jamie had to squint against the dust and sand.

"We need to go," she said. She pulled on the strap and slung her rifle over her shoulder. She was pretty sure it still had bullets in it. "We need to go before the bomb goes off."

Sasha let herself be pulled to her feet. "Yeah," she said, squinting against the blasting grit. "Yeah, let's go."

They slogged across the wasteland, back toward the ruined cinder-block wall of Site B. Sand already covered half of the dead bugman, and the wind swept more onto it, even as she watched. Just past it, no more than a dozen yards away, she could see the shimmer of the fold around the rings.

Another blast of wind and sand brought them to a halt as the thing in the sky pounded at the air again. Small rocks and bits of concrete pattered against them. They covered their eyes and bent in to each other.

When they could look again, the alpha predator filled the sky in front of them. It was less than a mile away. Its wingspan had to be over a thousand feet. The wings drifted up, like someone stretching in the morning.

The front of the creature, what Jamie had thought was a face, was a cluster of tentacles. They reached out and twisted in a constant dance. Most of them looked about fifty feet long, but she could see half a dozen that looked three or four times longer. Two of the long ones stretched out to drag in the sand as it sailed forward.

Below each wing Jamie could see thin legs, or maybe arms. They were folded up against the body, the way a bird of prey would hold its legs while flying. Against the thing's sheer bulk, they reminded her of a T. rex, with its tiny front arms.

The wings reached their high point and slammed down again.

The blast of wind ripped at the desert around Jamie and Sasha. They grabbed each other and closed their eyes. The sand tore at their clothes and hair and skin. It forced Jamie back a step and she dragged Sasha with her. Then another step. And another.

The ground fell away from her feet. Her grip on Sasha's arm slipped. They were holding wrists, hands, fingers, and then they flew apart. Jamie risked opening her eyes and saw Sasha tumble away across the sand. The wind had thrown both of them into the air.

And in that half-second something blotted out the sun.

The alpha predator passed over them. It stretched on and on, like the freight trains that had rumbled past Jamie's after-college apartment at midnight. As her eyes flinched closed against the sandstorm, she glimpsed one of the dragging tentacles as it plowed through the sand. It was a tree trunk of flesh and muscle.

Then the sandstorm slammed her side-first into a sand dune and knocked the wind out of her. She gasped for air and filled her mouth with grit and dust. It turned to mud on her tongue, and she tried to spit it out between wheezing breaths.

Jamie covered her mouth and nose. She felt the sand piling up around her. The side of the dune slid down to bury her hips and feet. It trickled into her jeans and sneakers. She kicked sand off her legs, and it built up in her lap. Eyes closed, she tried to stand, but the weight of the sand and the wind pushed her back down.

Her heart raced. She shoved herself up again, and this time she stood. The wind slowed down. The battering sand turned to a patter against her clothes and skin.

She wiped sand from her lashes and risked opening her eyes.

The thing in the sky had roared past. Its long tail swung back and forth in the air. The wings came down again and kicked up another gust of sand, but it was already far enough away that only a few grains pelted her, like a windy day at the beach.

She looked around for Sasha. There was no sign of the other woman. Jamie took in a breath to yell and stopped herself. What if there were more bugmen around? She glanced over her shoulder. What if she attracted the alpha predator's attention?

The image of the dragging tentacle passed through her mind. She saw it finding Sasha half-buried in the sand, wrapping itself around her, lifting her up to the massive creature . . .

"Sasha!"

The shout rang flat in the wasteland. No echo came back through the air. Jamie looked around and shouted again.

Something bright red came out of the sand about thirty feet away. Sasha lifted herself onto all fours and coughed out a mouthful of damp grit. She rolled back and sat on her heels.

Jamie staggered across the sand. "Oh, Jesus," she said. "I thought it ate you."

"I thought it got you," said Sasha. "I think that big fucking tentacle went right between us."

Jamie pulled her to her feet. "You ready to get out of here?"

"Fuck, yes."

Jamie looked behind her and saw the rippling wasteland stretch out for miles. She turned and saw the alpha moving away. The clouds of sand and dust in its wake now hid the canyon. She traced the creature's path backward, but still couldn't see the remains of Site B. Or the dead bugman. Or the shimmer in the air.

Even free from the rings, it seemed the shimmer was only visible in one direction.

Sasha wiped the last bits of sand from her eyes. "Oh, fuck me," she said. "Where's the Door?"

FIFTY-FIVE

Even at his angle, Mike saw Jamie stumble in the sand on the other side of the Door and stagger away. He took a swaying step to the right, but she was already gone.

He counted five minutes, twenty-two seconds until the charge went off. He made a mental countdown timer and gave it the ants to hold for him.

The patchwork man glared through the rings after Jamie for a moment. Then he reached down and poked at the seraph. He shifted his fingers, looking for some sign of life. He sighed, and his crooked shoulders heaved.

Mike considered reaching for the pistol on the floor and rejected the idea. Crouching or bending over would not be advisable. He took a few moments to find his balance. The gash on his side was longer than his hand, but he didn't think there was any danger of anything falling out or getting worse. He could still move.

The seraph with the chunk of metal in its head took a few quick steps up the ramp and onto the pathway. It walked through the Door without hesitation. Mike saw it march off across the desert, following Jamie's footprints. He heard her yell in the distance.

The patchwork man still glared into the rings. On the far side of the ramp, hidden from the creature, Sasha lay in a heap. She'd been thrown down by the explosion. He saw a small cut below her ear, another on the side of her neck, and some seepage on her stitches, but not much blood. He counted to four and watched her chest expand with a slow, steady breath.

Mike took a few deep breaths of his own. The air tasted wrong.

He pushed himself away from the workstation, and fishhooks of pain tore at his side. The temperature in the room had dropped ten degrees already. The nitrogen was stealing all of the heat. Which also meant it was displacing all the oxygen in the room.

He forced himself to move. His attempt to run was more of a controlled stagger. Every time he swung his right leg the fishhooks pulled at his ribs and threw his balance off. He was pretty sure Arthur would've outrun him. He glanced back. Twisting his neck and shoulders didn't make his ribs feel any better.

The patchwork man came after him in long strides. It was like watching an old cartoon character move, rolling its legs forward one after the other. It flexed its half-frozen arm.

Where was the other seraph? Was there one? Was it just the patchwork man?

Mike hobbled toward the door, then cut back between the small forest of tool chests. The black one banged again as he moved past it. One of the rivets burst and the side panel pushed out a bit.

On the other side of the tool chest was Staff Sgt. Jim Duncan. His body was half covered by the seraph he'd killed as he died. The monster's corpse had forced the Marine's rifle away from him as it fell.

Mike dropped to his knees and pushed Duncan's cold finger off the trigger. He yanked at the rifle. A strap bound it to his arm in what was probably a very efficient way under other circumstances.

He heard sounds behind him. The slap of a bare foot on concrete. The tap of toenails that were too long. The wheels squeaking on a tool chest as it was pushed out of the way.

Mike pulled at the rifle again. The strap shifted, twisted, but didn't come loose. The ants diagrammed the strap, studied the body, traced lines of tension. His finger darted out to stab at a clasp, and the rifle was in his hands.

He rolled over, making his wounds shriek, and fired a burst of shots into the hand reaching for him. The patchwork man snarled. Two fingers spun away. Another swung on a trio of loose stitches.

Mike squeezed the trigger again and again and again. The rifle bucked in his arms as he tried to mimic the Marines' firing stance while laying on the ground. Half his shots went wild. Three more skimmed the creature's flesh. Two of those plucked at the stitches holding the thing together. The rest drove the creature back a few steps.

The rifle snapped empty after the sixth burst.

Blood leaked from half a dozen wounds across the patchwork man's body. It didn't seem to notice any of them. A single finger came up and bobbed side to side. The creature made a clucking noise, the sound of a disappointed teacher.

A roar of wind came from the rings. Behind the patchwork man, sand blew out of the Door. It pattered against the pathway and the floor and the bodies.

The patchwork man froze. Its expression softened and its eyes widened, even the tiny ones. The shredded lips quivered and flexed on either end.

"At last," it whispered. "My Lord has arrived."

Under the sound of wind, Mike could hear something else. A thrumming, rippling sound, like air pounding against a huge kite or flag. As it increased, the wind picked up.

The patchwork man turned to the rings and Sasha cracked it across the jaw with the rifle stock. The blow wrenched its head around. It straightened back, and she hit it again. This time a few teeth pinged against the toolbox.

Mike struggled to his feet.

Sasha tried to swing a third time, and the patchwork man grabbed her arm, squeezing the line of stitches and bandages. She screamed. The rifle clattered to the floor. The creature grabbed her by the throat, sinking its jagged fingernails into her flesh.

Mike grabbed his empty rifle by the barrel and swung it like a baseball bat. It cracked into the back of the patchwork man's skull. Mike ignored the pain in his side and swept the rifle back to hit it again.

The patchwork man staggered. Sasha dropped to the floor and slapped her hands over her throat. Her fingers were wet and red.

It turned to look down at Mike. Its human eye was dilated. "I will beg my Lord's forgiveness," it muttered, "for having no worthy food for his arrival. You are not worthy of joining with him."

Mike drove the rifle stock up into its face. The patchwork man stumbled back and crashed against the toolbox. Then it tumbled to the ground and tipped the steel case over on top of itself. A rain of fuses spilled over it.

It didn't move. It was still breathing, though.

Sasha wheezed. Mike dropped the empty rifle and kneeled by her. "Did it cut an artery? Your windpipe?"

"Can't breathe," she croaked.

"It's the nitrogen in the air. Try to be calm." He touched her fingers. "Let me see."

She shook her head and flinched back.

"Can you feel it pulsing against your hand? If it cut your carotid, it should feel like you're blocking a hose."

She shook her head again, a little slower.

"Trust me," he said. "Let me see."

Sasha closed her eyes. Her fingers pulled away from her throat. They were sticky with blood, and more of it ran down to stain the collar of her shirt.

It was a steady stream, though, not a pulse.

"You're going to be okay," he said. "It looks a lot worse than it is. Come on." He pulled her to her feet.

She pressed one hand against her throat and pointed at the patchwork man with the other. "What about Frankenstein?"

"Why didn't you just shoot it?"

"Because unlike some supposed fucking geniuses," she said, "I wasn't going to spray gunfire in the direction of one of my friends."

"Sorry."

"Forget it."

"So now we're friends?"

"Fuck off. What are we doing with him?"

"Nothing for now. We've got four minutes nine seconds until that charge blows." Mike hobbled toward the Door. The new wave of adrenaline and endorphins were helping to hide the pain.

She glanced at the patchwork man, scooped up her rifle, and followed Mike. "It's not enough. It won't destroy the Door."

"I know. But we need to get Jamie first."

"How?"

He crouched down and grabbed one of the nitrogen hoses. The blast had flung most of it to the far side of the room, but the heavy flange that had connected it to the rings was still near the ramp. He stood up and dragged more of it over. The far end was ragged from the explosion, but there was still over forty feet. "I'm going after her."

Sasha looked at the sand and dust whirling out of the wasteland. The winds on the other side of the Door weren't hurricane strength, but they didn't look much lower. She'd read stories about sandstorms cutting people apart and wondered how much truth there was to them.

And then the light shifted in the wasteland. She looked up through the shimmering haze around the rings and saw something dark stretch across the sky. It could've been a cloud, but it seemed too solid and too fast. Under the noise of the wind she thought she heard something, like a rumbling voice, and it was—

"Take this," Mike said. He shoved the end of the hose closest to the flange into her hands.

She blinked and looked at it. "What? Why?"

"I'm going to run the hose through the Door." He pointed at the whirling sand. It seemed to be dying down, but there was no way to be sure. "I'm hoping it'll act like a lifeline. Give me something to follow through all of that. Maybe it'll help keep the Door open, too. Keep it from switching to another reality."

"And if it does switch?"

"Then I guess we'll end up somewhere else."

There were five dead Marines near the ramp. None of them had a sidearm. Mike didn't trust himself with a rifle. The ants had enough reference pictures to switch out the magazine on Black's pistol, but the pistol was two yards to the right, Black's body was to the left, and Mike didn't have time to search for the magazines.

He took a deep breath. The air by the rings smelled dry and dead, but there was more oxygen in it. He took another breath and his head cleared. He hadn't realized it had been fuzzy.

"Three minutes, forty seconds," he said. "If I'm not back in two, you should run for the parking lot. Maybe keep running."

"I'll be here," she said with a firm nod. She wrapped one hand around the hose and held her rifle one-handed with the other. "Go."

Mike gathered a loose coil of hose under his arm. He took three quick steps up the ramp and took one more breath. Sand was pouring out of the rings and sifting down through the expanded steel of the pathway. He tasted dust and concrete on his tongue.

He stepped through the Door.

FIFTY-SIX

Mike stumbled in the sand. It was two feet higher on this side. The wind was burying the rings.

He marched forward. He didn't run. He didn't have the time or strength to fall and pick himself up again and again. When he had something to run to, then he'd run.

The hose stretched out behind him. It was eight feet, four inches from where Sasha stood to the threshold of the rings. He had just shy of thirty-four feet on the wasteland side, depending on if there was any stretch in the hose.

Pattern recognition kicked in fourteen feet from the rings. His eyes passed over a series of ridges and folds in the sand. The ants conjured up models and extrapolations based on wind direction and accumulation. There was a body buried there, just a few inches down.

It had three arms. He considered the possibility that it was the rifle Jamie had grabbed, but all three limbs were crooked. And the body was too long.

He moved through the sand. The wind was dying down, but visibility still sucked. The wasteland had been drained of all color. All life.

Thirty-four feet of hose ran out very fast. He looked back at the rings and then out at the desert. The sandstorm was rolling off toward the horizon, but it was still dense enough to hide the canyon.

Something moved in the sandstorm. A shadow up in the air. He tried to reconstruct the glimpse he'd seen, but the ants kept shredding the images. Nothing could have wings that big.

"Jamie!" He counted to three and yelled again. The wasteland swallowed it up without a single echo.

A pair of black ants held up the mental timer. Three minutes, thirteen seconds.

He let the ragged end of the hose drop and kept walking. When he last saw Jamie she'd headed off to the left, so he headed that way, too. The ants kept track of steps and angles and direction. The few landmarks were mapped and cataloged.

The sun was in the wrong place. It was too high in the sky for late afternoon. And too far south. He didn't trust it for figuring directions.

He trudged through the sand. Jamie had been wearing a white shirt and faded jeans. Not an ideal combination to pick out of the wasteland, but he was pretty sure the same mental skills that let him pick out camouflage would let him spot her.

In the distance, the sandstorm swirled into a series of dust devils the size of tornados. The ants focused on certain lines and shadows near the twists of wind and sand. He felt a twist, thinking he'd found her and she was too far to make it back to the rings in time. Then he realized there were too many figures.

Eleven seraphs stood off in the distance, all but hidden in the wasteland by their cloaks. Some stood, others seemed to be kneeling. Their arms were held up to the sky, toward the sandstorm that had just blown over them. They were all facing away from him. The winds died a little more and he realized there were another dozen of the creatures past the first line he'd seen.

The ants replayed moments of the seraphs running across the sand as they charged the Door.

"Jamie," he shouted again. He looked behind him and saw nothing.

He started forward again.

A full minute passed. One hundred-seventeen feet away from the end of the hose, one hundred-fifty-one feet from the threshold of the rings. He set his simple map of the wasteland against his memories of the area around the Door campus. He'd been heading north-northeast. He stood where an old east-west access road, not much more than a path, ran in his world.

Mike veered more to the north. Jamie hadn't passed back into his line of sight, so she had to have gone farther that way. He made his way over a dune and called out her name twice. He marched for another thirty seconds. One minute, forty-eight seconds left on the clock.

Barely enough time to get back to the Door.

"Jamie," he yelled again.

"Mike?"

He spun around. She lumbered over a dune through the loose sand with another woman. Someone tall with a bright red shirt and dark hair that had a white stripe.

The ants spent a few seconds figuring out hypothetical paths. Ways Sasha could have gotten into the desert and out to Jamie without his hearing or seeing her. Then she looked up and he saw the lack of stitches on her arm and her unmarked neck. Blood covered the white of her right eye.

Two identical chocolate croissants. *Quantum donuts.*

He brushed the ants aside and took long strides across the wasteland to join them. They were coming from farther behind the Door, as if they'd traveled in a wide circle.

"What are you doing here?" called Jamie.

"Looking for you."

"The bomb didn't go off?"

"We've got about a minute and a half."

"Did you reset it?"

"What?"

"We can't find the Door," the other Sasha said.

The ants pulled up their map and rendered it in three dimensions. He glanced over his shoulder. The rings were sixty-three yards away in the sand-covered remains of Site B. The off-white housings blended with the wasteland, and the shimmer in the air wasn't visible from this direction. He wouldn't have found it again if he didn't know just where to look. "This way," he said.

They turned around, and the ants in Mike's head went mad. The thing in the sky was turning, soaring out from behind the sandstorm in its wake. It was like watching a jumbo jet bank in the air, something that had to go miles out of its way just to turn around. Its wings thrust down again, and the far side of the canyon was swept clear.

He took in the size and the tentacles and the wings and the sheer impossibility of it. The ants scurried and flailed and came up with nothing to compare it to, nothing that could explain it.

More and more ants appeared and he forced them away. The ones that mattered were holding the timer. One minute, thirteen seconds. He'd wasted seven seconds staring at the thing in the sky as it swung itself around.

The seraphs on the ground seemed to shout and cheer at the thing even as the wind of its passing hurled them into the air or slammed them to the ground.

The dust before the endless sandstorm, the patchwork man had said. *They are the tide going out before the wave comes in.*

He traced the curve of the alpha predator's path. It led back to the Door. Straight to it.

"I think we should go," said Sasha.

He pointed the way again, and they ran for the Door. It was time to run. They stumbled and dragged one another across the sand.

Mike took a step, and the shimmer appeared in the air as if he'd walked around a corner and found it. Outside, without walls and a ceiling blocking the view, it was clear how big the rift had grown. The heat haze stretched almost fifty feet into the air and a hundred feet across.

Big enough for the thing in the sky to force its way through.

They found the hose, already slipping beneath the sand. Mike tripped over the buried cinder blocks, and his side flared hot and wet. They dragged him back to his feet and headed for the rings.

Twenty-eight seconds.

They slogged the few yards past the dead bugman to the fold in space. The air coming through it felt chilly. "Move fast," said Mike. "There's only one charge, but I think it's still enough to kill us if we're too close. Just run as far as you can."

They stepped through the Door.

The steel pathway clanged under their feet. A wave of cold hit them. They danced around the body of the bugman and staggered down the ramp.

Sasha—the Sasha at the bottom of the ramp with the bloody neck and bandaged arm—swung her rifle around. The Sasha with the bloodshot eye held up her hands. "Whoa."

"Fuck me," Sasha said over her rifle.

"No time," yelled Mike. "Go!"

"What? But you were barely gone a minute."

Mike stopped short and almost fell. Jamie caught his arm. "What?"

"A minute tops," said the Sasha with the rifle and bandages.

The ants spilled out. The relative distance. The bushes and the seraphs moving back and forth across the wasteland. He glanced up at the charge and looked at Jamie. "How long were you over there?"

Jamie shrugged. "Ten minutes, maybe."

Bloodshot Sasha nodded. "Sounds about right."

"Okay, then," he said. "Just over two minutes to save the world."

"Oh, fuck me," said bandaged Sasha. "It's gone."

They all looked up. The plastic carapace that Dylan had chopped away with a hatchet had reappeared. It was smooth and pristine. The C4 charge had vanished.

"I think it's inside the carapace," bloodshot Sasha said.

Mike closed his eyes. The side of his shirt was wet. The air was stale with nitrogen. The ants were seething. Red and black, carrying facts and snippets and ideas. What was setting off the bleed-through? Was it the items themselves? Certain actions or temperatures or . . .

Or what did Koturovic say would help break down the barriers?

"It's us," he said to Jamie. "The more of us here, closer to it, the more possible outcomes. The more potential. The more potential, the more bleed-through. We're making reality flip channels."

"What?"

"It's how we made the extra bolts appear, and how we brought one of the charges back when we all got too close. It's why more tool chests appeared when the Marines got here and why everything calmed down when they were killed." He stepped up onto the ramp. "Come on, get closer to it."

Bandaged Sasha raised her eyebrows. "Closer?"

Jamie looked past him. The alpha predator had finished its huge turn and was heading back to them. It was over the canyon, maybe two miles away.

But time went faster over there.

She stepped up onto the ramp. So did the Sashas.

Mike watched for a ripple or a change. He blinked, then blinked again. When he opened his eyes the second time, Dylan's rifle and the remote were back on the pathway.

"What are we doing?" asked bloodshot Sasha. She looked out across the wasteland. The alpha predator swelled in the sky.

"We're looking for quantum donuts," said Mike. The rings flickered. The carapace vanished again. One minute, twenty-one seconds. There'd been three of them by the rings when the first charge came back, and there were four now. The rate of change should be faster. Unless the Sashas counted as one mind. Or—

There'd been *four* people near the rings when the charge came back.

He looked across the room, then at the bandaged Sasha. "Did you kill him? Frankenstein?"

She shook her head. "I've just been stand—"

"Drag him over here. We need more minds. More potential."

The Sashas ran across the room. They dragged the patchwork man across the floor. The slender figure left trails of dark blood on the floor. Mike could see three good-sized lumps and bruises forming on its head from the rifle stocks.

"He used to be human," Mike explained. "I bet his brain still is. Enough to factor into Koturovic's equations, at least. The more minds, the stronger the rift, the more bleed-through."

They hauled the twisted body up onto the ramp. A few stitches broke open as they dragged it across the expanded steel. The fingers on one hand twitched and the lid over the human eye fluttered.

"I think it's waking up," said bloodshot Sasha.

Fifty-three seconds.

Mike turned his head and fishhooks of pain pulled at his ribs. The alpha predator filled the sky in the wasteland. It was less than a mile away.

Its tentacles splayed open like a green flower. Mike glimpsed huge amber eyes, each one twenty feet across.

Then the rings rippled in his peripheral vision. "Get back," he yelled at them. "Get back fast."

They leaped over the patchwork man and off the ramp. Mike's side and stomach were on fire, and they flared up as the shock of landing shook his body. Jamie grabbed him and tugged him away.

The first ring had turned silver and lumpy.

"What . . ." said Jamie.

It was tape. Duct tape. The entire ring was wrapped in it. The loops covered the whole thing, wrapped back and forth across almost every inch of surface.

The tape held down C4 charges. Dozens of them. They were doubled and tripled and quadrupled up at every point on the ring. All of them had jury-rigged detonators. On at least four-fifths of them, the detonator had a faint red glow.

Ten pounds'd take out that whole wall if you placed it right.

Mike made a conservative estimate that the front ring had eight hundred and fifty pounds of C4 attached to it.

FIFTY-SEVEN

"No fucking way," the Sasha next to Mike said.

Forty-two seconds.

"Go," he said. "Must go now." He tugged at the bandaged Sasha. She dropped her rifle, pulled his arm across her shoulders, and dragged him across the room. The fishhooks in his side tore down, their barbs scratching against his bones.

Jamie ran ahead, and he heard the magnetic locks *thump* open on the big door.

Other Sasha with the bloodshot eye gave a quick nod and pulled his other arm over her shoulder. He yelped as the bones stretched apart and the hooks sank in even deeper.

They ran across the room, and Mike glanced back at the patchwork man. It raised one clawlike hand and rolled over on the ramp. It glared across the room at him.

They ran down the hall toward the front entrance. "Where are we going?" yelled Jamie.

"Outside," he said. The air in the hall felt warm and humid, but it filled his lungs. "Bottom of the stairs."

She ran ahead again and pushed open one of the glass doors. The Sashas half carried Mike past Anne's desk, through the door, and down the concrete steps. They started across the parking lot.

"No," he shouted. He twisted around and pointed at the walkway down to the trailers. "There."

"We've got to get away," said bandaged Sasha. "There's too much—"

Mike shrugged loose, ignored the knives in his side and staggered a yard or so down the path. He stopped in front of the landing and dropped to his knees. "Here."

Jamie ran to join him. The Sashas did too. "Are you sure?" asked Jamie, crouching down.

He reached out and smacked his hand against the wall next to them. "Between this and the foundation, there's almost seventy feet of concrete between us and the—"

The ground rumbled.

The glass doors and windows were carried out on a wave of fire and hurricane winds. Something slammed into the railing above them and parts of the front desk were hurled out into the overgrowth. The air burned their eyes and lips and lungs and then the air was gone altogether and they were gasping for breath. Black clouds whirled around them and took away the world, and they screamed and the flames blasted over their heads and around the sides of the staircase.

A trio of cinder blocks crashed into the walkway near Jamie. A piece of rebar plunged into the ground next to Mike. What looked like an I beam flew out across the overgrowth and decapitated half a dozen trees before hitting the ground hard enough to shake it. Dust and gravel rained down on them. An oversized silver hex nut slapped into the ground next to one of the Sashas.

The overwhelming white noise became thunder and screaming and car alarms. A crack split the wall next to them. The railing tipped over and fell as one piece. It slid down the wall and landed across them.

The noise and clouds settled. Mike tried to shake his head and slammed it against one of the uprights on the railing.

"Oh, yeah," muttered the Sasha with the bloodshot eye, "you're a genius." She had dust and bits of grit in her hair. A sleeve had ripped free on her T-shirt and slipped down her arm. A wide scratch bled across the front of her shoulder.

"Everyone okay?" he asked, rubbing his temple.

"I think so," said Jamie. Her face was streaked with soot. Her hair was singed at the tips.

"My leg's pinned under the railing," said Sasha—the bandaged Sasha. "I think it might be sprained. It's throbbing."

Mike inched out from under the railing. The hooks and pins and blades in his torso wiggled and twisted as he did. They felt wet again. Jamie and bloodshot Sasha were already clear of the wreckage and helped him up.

They shifted the railing enough for bandaged Sasha to get her leg out. Her ankle had caught a lot of the weight. It was already swelling. Bloodshot Sasha stepped in to help herself up, but their eyes met and they both froze. She went to help Mike instead. Jamie moved in to give bandaged Sasha a shoulder to lean on. They hobbled away from the stairs, then turned to get a better look.

A blackened steel framework stood where there'd been concrete walls. The upper floor of the building was gone. It wasn't clear if it had collapsed onto the first floor or been blown clear off. A haze of dust and ash stretched out into the parking lot and past the guard shack. The guard shack, Mike noticed, had lost all its windows.

Almost every part of the complex that could burn was on fire. It hurt to look at it too long. It sent a pillar of black smoke into the air, letting every fire department within a few miles know they would be needed.

"Well," Mike said. "That was disturbing."

The Sasha with Jamie raised her eyebrows at him. "What part?"

He shrugged again. "Most of it."

"Most?" Jamie said.

"Fuck me," said both Sashas at once. They glanced at each other and smirked.

Then the one with Jamie straightened up. "Arthur!"

He was sprawled by a car with broken windows. Grit and dust had turned him into a monochrome ghost. He didn't move when they called his name again.

The Sasha with Mike—bloodshot Sasha—left him and ran. Jamie glanced at her Sasha who nodded, and then she sprinted across the parking lot, too. The wounded balanced against each other.

"He's breathing," the bloodshot Sasha called back to them. "He must've been on the edge of the blast."

"Try not to move him," said Mike. "If he's breathing and his pulse feels good, leave him alone for now."

"We need to call an ambulance," said Jamie.

He glanced at the burning building and the column of smoke. It was a good two hundred feet tall now, at least. "I think they're on the way," he said.

A smaller fire caught his eye. He led the bandaged and limping Sasha over to it. She balanced on one leg while he crouched. He winced and bit back a yell. His ribs felt like gravel under his arm, grinding nerves between them whenever he moved. He wasn't sure he'd be able to get back up.

It looked like the canvas grocery bag had smothered most of the flames. Three of the antique books had been knocked free by the blast, and they made a line of small fires leading back to the bag. Mike knocked the closest one away and pulled the bag close.

"What is it?" asked Jamie.

"His books." He lifted the top one out of the bag, watching for an ember that might make it burst into flame with more air. The canvas smoked a bit, but the other volumes seemed fine.

The third book down was leather-bound and odd-shaped. A little too tall and narrow compared to a modern book. The spine was wrapped in cloth. *A.K.* had been printed on it in black ink that had faded into the material.

Arthur coughed. Bloodshot Sasha knelt and whispered to him. He muttered something, coughed again, and went quiet. "He can talk," she said. "That's good, right?"

"I think so," said Mike. "What did he say?"

"Told me to watch out for debris."

"A little late," said the bandaged Sasha. "Shouldn't we cover him with a blanket or something?"

"I was just going to say that," bloodshot Sasha said.

Mike looked at the wrecked cars in the parking lot. "Does anyone have something in their car? Maybe a blanket or a towel? Even a spare coat?"

"I've got a beach blanket," said Jamie. "I haven't used it in ages, but it should be okay."

"There probably isn't a beach blanket in this Jamie's car," said Mike.

"Ahhh," she said. "Good point."

"I think I might have a sweatshirt," said both Sashas.

"This is going to get old fast," said Jamie.

"Fuck you," they echoed. They glanced at each other and smirked again. The one by Arthur walked into the lot and found a car with three windows smashed.

Mike tried to lift the bag, but his ribs were too far gone. "You need help?" asked Jamie.

He shook his head. "Stay with Arthur." He rewrapped Koturovic's treatise in the canvas, then pushed himself up off the stack of books with a wince. Sasha hopped over, and they counterbalanced each other enough for him to straighten up. "I hear sirens," he said.

Sasha lifted her head. "Yeah," she said. "Me, too."

A breeze swept across the lot and carried some of the smoke away with it. It smelled clean and alive. Mike watched the clouds around the building twist away. There were piles of rubble, but it was easy enough to reconstruct where the main floor had . . .

"Goddamn it," he said.

Bandaged Sasha hopped around. "Oh, fuck me hard."

"What?" Jamie craned to see from where she crouched with Arthur. Then the breeze took away the last of the smoke, and her eyes went wide.

Standing in the middle of the rubble, surrounded by flames and smoke, were the rings of the Albuquerque Door.

FIFTY-EIGHT

Bandaged Sasha let out a string of *fucks*.

"How?" said Jamie. "How can it still be in one piece?"

Bloodshot Sasha returned from the car with a dark blue hoodie. She spread it over Arthur's chest and arms. Then she saw what they were staring at and let out her own list of swears.

Mike stared at the rings. The breeze cleared the smoke, but the rings were deep enough into the rubble that there was always more. It took almost a full minute for him to see enough.

"They're dead," said Mike. "Shut off. It's done."

"What?" The bandaged Sasha hobbled around to look at him. "Are you sure?"

"Yeah," he said. He stretched out his arm—his left arm—and sketched the outline of the rings. "There are just two rings. Nothing on the other side. It's just like the one over on Site B. We did enough damage to shut it down."

"But they can't be standing," said bloodshot Sasha. "That explosion should've torn them to fucking pieces."

Mike pursed his lips. "Maybe," he said, "maybe because it was open, some of the blast went through to the desert. Enough that it didn't annihilate everything here."

"Including us," said Jamie. She glanced over her shoulder at the approaching sirens. "Fire department's here. Police, too."

"And ambulances," said Mike. He raised his good arm and pointed at Arthur on the ground.

———

THE PARAMEDIC HAD a shaved-bald head with five o'clock shadow across his scalp. Mike had been staring at it for ten minutes while the man taped up the gash in his side. He winced as the bandages tugged and made the gravel and fishhooks between his ribs shift.

The paramedic glanced up. "That hurt?"

"Still, yeah."

"A piece of rebar did this?"

"Pretty sure that was it, yeah."

"What about these gashes on your stomach?"

"They're nothing," said Mike. "Got in a fight with a dog this morning."

"You report it?"

"Nothing I couldn't handle," Mike gasped as the bandages rolled across his ribs again.

The paramedic shook his head. "You've had a shitty day."

"Tell me about it."

"You really need to go get this done right. You need stitches. X-rays to make sure you don't have a flail chest."

"A what?"

"It means you broke a rib in two places, so there's a spear of bone floating around in your chest waiting to puncture a lung or something."

"Great. Can you just tape the ribs for now?"

"Nobody does that anymore," said the man. "Too big a risk of pneumonia from restricted breathing."

"Really?"

"Yeah."

"Okay. I just need to make sure everything's safe here. Promise, I'll be in a hospital before the end of the day."

A few yards away, they closed the doors on Arthur's ambulance, and the sirens started up. He had a concussion, a broken arm, dozens of scrapes and cuts from flying debris, but the other paramedics seemed pretty sure he'd live. The ambulance rolled out of the gate and swerved between the police barricade.

Mike's paramedic patted him on the arm. "That's all I can do," he said. "Hold off on aspirin if you can—you've had some blood loss. Drink a lot of fluids. No alcohol. Take it easy until you get X-rayed."

Mike nodded, scooped up his shirt, and shuffled over to Jamie and bloodshot Sasha. They were watching the firemen hose down the building. Jamie had the canvas-wrapped bundle of books under her arm.

"Everyone still good?"

"Pretty good," said Jamie. She looked at his bandages. "How about you?"

"I'll live." He nodded at the building. "Anything?"

Jamie shook her head. "Nothing. Not a peep."

"Have they . . . they found anything?"

"Frankenstein?" Bloodshot Sasha smirked. Her torn sleeve was gone, and a piece of gauze was taped over her shoulder. "The body was right next to a few hundred pounds of C4."

"It was also right next to the rings," said Mike, "and they're still standing."

"There's not even a stain left," she said.

"No sign of Olaf or any of the Marines," said Jamie. "But one of the firemen told me it was still too hot to search properly. They'll have to look for . . . remains when the fires are out. It might take awhile."

Bandaged Sasha limped up with a flash of white around her ankle. "Light sprain," she said. "The medic said I was being a wuss for complaining about it."

Jamie looked back and forth between the Sashas, then made sure no one was nearby. "Did anyone ask about . . . you?"

"I told them we were twins," said bloodshot Sasha.

"So did I," the other Sasha said.

"Twins with the same name?" asked Mike.

The Sashas glanced at each other. "I thought you'd give a fake name," said bloodshot Sasha.

"Why would I? I thought you would."

Mike raised his hand. "We need to get it straight. Now. Before there are questions we're not ready to answer."

Jamie pointed at the Sasha with bloodshot eye. "You're Dasha now," she said. "D for being in the desert with me."

"Dasha?" echoed the Sashas.

"Just for now," said Mike.

"I sound like a porn star," said Dasha.

"I sound like twin porn stars," said Sasha.

"Why do I need to change my name?" Dasha asked.

"Seriously?" Mike gave them the Look. "Just for now. Deal with it. Pretend it's a *Star Trek* plot or something."

A faint smile flickered across both of their faces. "Oh, fuck me," said Dasha. "I'm Thomas Riker."

"You are," said Sasha. "You totally are."

"But before he went all Maquis."

"Maybe."

"No, not maybe."

"Speaking of awkward questions," said Jamie, "I think your boss is here."

They turned to the gate. Two people in dark suits, a man and a woman, stood by a gleaming black sports car that had slipped in through the same opening the ambulance had driven out. They ignored the police and firemen and spoke to each other.

The man was tall with broad shoulders. His hair was neat and slicked back, but on the long side. He had dark glasses more suited to the beach than a suit. His shoulders shifted twice, and he reached up to tug at his collar. Mike was pretty sure the man didn't even realize he was doing it. He looked more like a jeans and T-shirt kind of guy.

The woman was Arab, or maybe Indian. Her hair was short and black, and her hawkish nose was on par with Mike's own. She wore a sleek pair of silver-rimmed glasses that could've been a matched set with Arthur's. Even if the broad-shouldered man hadn't been next to her, she would've looked small. Her tie was knotted in a loose half-Windsor.

The man pulled a bright green phone from his pocket and took a few steps toward the building, relaying information to someone.

"Since when do the feds drive Teslas?" asked Sasha.

"Our tax dollars at work," Dasha smirked.

"I don't think they're with DARPA," said Mike.

"Who are they, then?"

He studied the two newcomers. "I'm not sure yet."

One of the policemen approached Jamie with a notebook. She gave Mike a nod, and they stepped apart. The woman in the suit straightened up and walked toward him. Two police officers inside the fence line glanced at the smoldering building, gave her a quick look, and one muttered something that Mike lip-read as *eff bee eye bitch.*

He took a few steps toward her. "Hello," he said as she stopped in front of him.

The woman pointed past him to the building. "Were you in there before it blew?"

He nodded.

"What was going on in there?"

"I don't think I'm allowed to say," he told her. "Not without checking some clearances. Are you part of the Department of Defense?"

The woman shook her head. Behind her, the man circled around the barricades to get closer to the building. He continued to talk into his phone.

Mike remembered Dr. Forrester, the medical examiner obsessed with people getting black-bagged. "Homeland Security?"

"No. We're with a group based out of Los Angeles. For the past few months we've been getting some low-level interference that's been affecting our equipment." She tipped her head toward the remains of the building. "It's been getting worse, and we finally traced it down here."

"That's not possible," Mike said. "We weren't putting out any signals that could register in Los Angeles."

"We've got some pretty specialized equipment," she said.

"It's almost a hundred and thirty miles," said Mike. "From that far out, San Diego can barely affect Palomar with light pollution."

She smiled.

Mike looked at her again. At the lines of their suits. The buttons. The stitching. The ants carried out a series of images. Both the man and the woman were wearing off-the-rack suits, not tailored at all. He'd seen the man's jacket before, two weeks ago at Target with Bob. They'd walked past menswear on the way to pick up a mini-fridge, and there'd been a rack of suit separates next to the aisle.

"Which agency did you say you were with?"

The woman crossed her arms and smiled. It wasn't an entirely friendly expression. "I never said we were with the government."·

"Nice job," said the man, walking up behind Mike. He held up a bright green phone for the woman to see. "Just heard. Everything's going back to zero."

"So what's that mean?" asked Mike. "'Everything's going back to zero'?"

The big man thumped him on the shoulder. It made his ribs throb. "Means you just saved the world, dude," he said. "Cool feeling, huh?" He gave the woman a nod and then walked back toward the building, snapping pictures with his phone.

Mike and the woman stared at each other for a moment.

"I'm sorry about all this," she said. "That all of you had to go through it and get hurt."

"People died," he said. "Nineteen people. Dead." The ants swarmed out of their faces. Sixteen Marines, including Black, Weaver, and his former student Duncan. Olaf. Neil. Bob.

"I'm sorry," she said again.

"So who are you?" he asked.

"I doubt you've heard of us," she said. "But we're government subsidized. Sort of. Did you see anything?"

"Sorry?"

"You were doing some kind of dimensional experiments here, right? Based off the work of a Victorian mad scientist?"

He furrowed his brow. "How'd you know that?"

"I've seen this a few times before. That's pretty much always how it goes."

"Is that supposed to be a joke?"

"I wish. What did you see before you blew the place up?"

He tried to read her expression. "I'm not sure you'd believe me."

"You'd be surprised." She looked over at the building. "Let me ask you this, then. Did you have a roach problem?"

His brows went up. "Yeah."

"Green roaches?" she added. "Kind of strange ones with an extra leg?"

"You've seen them before."

The woman nodded. "Them, and what comes after them." She looked past him to the building. "Again . . . I'm really sorry."

Another moment passed.

"Who are you?"

"I had a long drive to read personnel files," she said, ignoring him. She nodded her chin toward Sasha and Dasha. "I know all about you, Leland Erikson, prefers Mike, but I didn't know they had twins working here."

"Yeah," he said. "Yeah, they do."

The woman pressed her lips together and nodded. "That's new," she said after a minute. "You're sure she's not an evil twin or anything?"

"Pretty sure, yeah."

"I think I can help clear that up, then," she said. "That they're just twins. Who've always worked here."

"Thanks."

"Not a problem. At least we can help a little."

The spray of water from the fire hoses loosened a pair of cinder blocks. They plunged off what was left of their wall and shattered against the concrete floor. According to Mike's internal diagram, they hit right where the collection of tool chests had been.

"So," he said, "what was all this about?"

She nodded after the big man. "Like Roger said. Saving the world."

"You do this for a living? Stop alien invasions from other dimensions."

"Now and then. Most of the time, my job's more about historical research. And some hacking."

"Sounds interesting."

"You have no idea."

A fireman walked up and talked to Jamie and the twins for a moment. Sasha and Dasha relaxed. Jamie smiled. She glanced over at Mike, judged the conversation he was having with the Indian woman, and gestured at the path down to the trailers. He nodded. She nodded back and walked off with the two identical women.

"So," the Indian woman said as Jamie walked away. "You're not an English teacher anymore. They started advertising for a replacement a few days ago. Are you going to work for your friend at DARPA?"

"Doubtful."

"No job. Sounds like no place to live, either."

"Are you going somewhere with this?"

She tilted her head to one side and stared at him for a moment. Then she pulled a bright green phone from her pocket. Her fingers swooshed back and forth across the phone's screen. "We've got a vacancy. Two, if you want to bring your girlfriend. We can always use somebody else with computer skills, because I'm sick of doing everything."

"Vacancy?"

"Yeah."

"Which means . . . ?"

"I can't tell you that. Not yet. But you know what I can tell you?" She turned and headed back toward the Tesla.

He took a quick step to keep up with her and his ribs ached. "What?"

"This is going to keep you up at night," she said. "It's going to gnaw at you. Because that's what happened to me. And Roger. And some other people. We found clues. We saw things. And we wanted to know more. We *needed* to know more. Just like *you* need to know more."

"Says who?"

"Says me. Now that you've seen what's out there, your only two options are deep denial or finding the rest of the answers. It sucks, I know, but that's it."

He felt the corners of his mouth twitch. "I'm not really built for denial."

"Exactly." She held out the phone. "There's one number in it. Think about it and give us a call. You've got a week."

Mike took it from her. "And then what happens?"

"Then the number gets disconnected and the phone turns into a paperweight. You never get any more answers, and you lose a lot of sleep."

The man—Roger—walked back from the building and around the Tesla. He dropped his own phone in his coat pocket and pulled open the driver's door.

The woman opened her own door. "One week," she said. "Don't forget."

The Tesla made a tight turn inside the circle of emergency vehicles, slid between two barricades, and then headed off down the street.

FIFTY-NINE

The path to the trailers was clear, but clogged with smoke from the main building and the overgrowth. Mike walked the long way around. It was hard on his ribs, but he'd live.

He tried to slip the green phone into his back pocket while he walked, but reaching his arm back and up made his ribs flare again. He pushed it into his front pocket instead. It was a bit awkward there, but it would be in his hand again soon enough.

Mycroft wouldn't call the number on the phone. But Sherlock would. Really, if Mike was going to be Sherlock now, he'd call the number he'd seen when Roger held up his smartphone after talking to his boss. The ants carried out an image of the screen with CALL ENDED and the 323 number belonging to NATE. He expected it would be an interesting conversation.

The first trailer, Olaf's, was a burned out, soggy husk. Bob's wasn't much better. Puddles spread around them, soaking into the gravel.

His own trailer had lost its roof and part of one wall. That had opened it up enough for everything else to burn. No more futon. No more tablet from Reggie. He'd also lost his clothes and his duffel bag. And all the reports about the Door.

All the paper copies, anyway.

The Astroturf between the trailers had burned in some places, melted in others. Water from the fire hoses was pooled up on it. From lawn to swamp in one day.

Jamie's trailer had lost its windows in the pressure blast and had a few dark spots where heat had discolored the paint. Sasha's had black walls and broken glass, but looked overall intact. The trailer with the seraph skeleton, farthest from the main building, looked fine.

Jamie stepped out of her trailer, and something burst past her ankles. Tramp raced across the gravel, his tongue waving in the wind, and ran circles around Mike. "He okay?"

"Yeah," she said. "He got out but he was under my trailer. Soaking wet from the hoses. I just finished drying him off."

"Ahhh." Mike walked closer, and Tramp bounced around him.

"It's where he used to go, y'know, before anything happened to him."

Mike nodded. "I think I just got a job offer."

"From the Indian woman?"

"Yeah. You did, too."

"Cool. Doing what?"

"We can talk about it later, but I think you'll be interested."

"Oh, really?"

"Yeah. I'm taking it."

"Just like that?"

"Just like that." He nodded at the burned-out trailers. "Everything okay here?"

"It's great," she said. "Know why?"

"Why?"

She waved him inside.

He smiled. "I like where this is going."

"Please. I don't want to hear you crying about your ribs while I'm trying to use you for my own filthy needs."

He laughed and winced as his ribs stretched and contracted. She helped him up the steps into the trailer.

There was a lot of broken glass, but several clean spots. There was some water, but none of it seemed to be on computer components. "What am I looking at?"

She beamed and pointed behind him.

Mike didn't see it at first. There were so many differences that it took pattern recognition almost four seconds to isolate the ball of fur on top of the bookshelf. Glitch yawned, showing off a mouthful of white teeth, stretched out his paws, and then settled into a new position.

Mike grinned. "Holy crap," he said.

She laughed. "You're not a teacher anymore. You can swear."

"It's just who I am. Deal with it."

"So if the Door's shut down and they're both here," she said, "is this . . . permanent?"

"I think so."

"And Sasha? Sashas?"

He smirked. "Yeah. That's going to be a bit weird for them. Her."

"And us?"

"Us?"

She wrapped her arms around him, careful not to put pressure on his ribs. "Where does this leave us?"

"How do you mean?"

From his bookshelf perch, Glitch glared down at the canine intruder. Tramp bounced back and forth across the floor, eager for his new playmate to come down. The cat hissed at him.

"You're not the Mike I fell for," said Jamie. "I'm not the woman you fell for. Is it still going to work for us?"

"I hope so."

"How do I know you've got the same quirks I liked? The same laugh? The same annoying tendency to spout off information?"

"I'm annoying in every reality. Honest."

She laughed.

"The important clue, of course, is the chocolate croissant."

Jamie looked up at him. "Okay, I take it back. You lost me."

"They started bringing croissants for me the day after you crosswalked. But you ordered them the day before that."

"Yeah, so?"

"So she ordered them, too. The other you."

A slow smile spread across her face as her arms tightened around his waist. He winced. "Mr. Erikson, are you trying to imply that I fall for you in every possible reality?"

"I can only tell you, there are a lot of parallels."

Tramp barked again, and Glitch sent a paperback tumbling down at the small dog. He yipped at the acknowledgment and bounced some more.

"So now what?" asked Jamie.

He kissed her on the forehead. "We save what we can. We go check on Arthur. And then . . ."

"And then?"

"We keep getting to know each other."

Like some of them do, this book has been sitting in my head for years.

Back when I was in college, I wrote a short story called "The Albuquerque Door" for a junior year creative writing class. It dealt with several of the same ideas in this book, but with a much smaller cast of characters and on a much less talented level. Needless to say, it didn't go over well with the instructor's "literary" tastes, and while I didn't agree with him on a lot of his points, it left me feeling bad enough about the story that I just filed it away.

It was around 2006 when I came across that story again and realized, through more experienced eyes, that it could be expanded into a novel. I put some work into it and ended up with about 30,000 words of a book tentatively titled *Mouth*. It was at this point that a few different things lined up and *Mouth* was put aside so I could work on this idea I had of superheroes fighting a zombie apocalypse.

Jump ahead to December of 2012. My lovely lady and I were driving home from a small Christmas party, and I was bouncing ideas off her for a possible sequel to a semi-popular book I'd written called *14*. And it struck me that a bunch of elements from *Mouth* lined up with some things from that book, and they could go together quite well. Although, the more I thought about it, the more I thought it'd work better as a side-quel sort of story—more of a shared universe than a continuation of the same story.

And this took me to San Diego Comic-Con, where I had a drink with some folks from Crown and they asked what I was going to do next.

A lot of work went into this one, and—as always—there are a few people who deserve a lot of thanks for all their help. If you found a mistake somewhere, it was me twisting the facts and not them steering me wrong. In no particular order . . .

Mary answered countless questions about trauma, wounds, cancers, autopsies, cause of death, and more.

My dad, who used to work as a radiation protection consultant, explained some of the dangers of working with radioactive material and the various injuries and effects radiation can have on a human body. Say, if you were walking around after a nuclear war.

Tansey talked to me about the different types of testing that different technologies go through before being declared "market safe."

There was a whole subplot that revolved around endurance running. It's gone, for a couple of reasons, but SukGin helped a lot with it so she still deserves credit.

"Assignment: Earth" was always one of my favorite episodes of *Star Trek: The Original Series*. I felt exceptionally clever tying Gary Seven and company to the early life of Khan Noonien Singh, until I found out (around my third draft) that author Greg Cox had already done this in his two-part novel, *The Eugenics Wars*.

David, CD, and John all read an earlier version of this book and pointed out a few places I'd done things right and several more where I'd gone wrong. Craig let me ramble on about it for a few hours while he was visiting Los Angeles for his own book signing.

We struggled with a title for a while, so one day I bounced a bunch of options off the people on my Facebook fan page. So thanks to all of you who chimed in.

David, my agent, also gave me a bunch of valuable criticism and some good suggestions and let me bounce ideas off him during several long phone calls.

Julian, my editor, suffered through a much weaker version of this manuscript, then helped me break it apart and reshape it into the book you're holding now. He's incredibly insightful and patient.

Finally, many, many thanks as always to my lovely lady, Colleen, who listens while I talk for hours about things in vague terms, lets me whine for months about how things are going horribly, and doesn't mock me too much when I finally come around to thinking someone might want to read this.

P.C.

Los Angeles, November 2014